THE NIGHTINGALE
AND SPARROW CHRONICLES

TSARINA'S CROWN

JERENA TOBIASEN

TSARINA'S CROWN

Copyright © 2023 by Jerena Tobiasen

This is a work of fiction, inspired by historical events and people. The plot and the characters are a product of the author's imagination, and any similarity in names is a coincidence only. While real places and establishments have been used to create an illusion of authenticity, they are used fictitiously. Facts have been altered for the purpose of the story.

Cover Design: Ana Chabrand, Chabrand Design House
www.anachabrand.com

Author Photo: Robert M. Douglas, Copyright ©2019

Typesetting: Edge of Water Designs, www.edgeofwater.com
Ebook Conversion: Mariana Coello

ISBNs:
   978-0-9920503-1-3 (Print)
   978-0-9920503-2-0 (E-book)

DEDICATION

THIS BOOK IS FOR RMD, whose desire to record history accurately equals my own, and whose frustration is greater than mine, when the story requires it be adjusted.

ACKNOWLEDGEMENTS

I found the seed for this story in the Fabergé Museum in St. Petersburg, Russia, in 2018. Later, when I began researching Fabergé eggs, particularly the Rosebud Egg, inspiration bloomed. As historical fiction requires, I spent hours researching the history and circumstances of the early 1900s. Fortunately, I had been to Russia twice by the time I began writing, so I also had my own experiences from which to draw. Regardless, I could not have written the adventures of my characters without some help along the way. For their insight, guidance, and suggestions, I am truly grateful. Specifically, I'd like to thank:

- Captain Drezen Tijan and a Safety Officer of the MS *Nautica*, for allowing me to interview them during a voyage from Dublin, Ireland to Archangelsk, Russia in 2019. The knowledge they shared regarding ship operations, especially regarding the operation of ships in perilous situations and management of safety boats, was most insightful.
- Dr. Teresa Cordoni who helped me understand gunshot wounds.
- The kind folks of Hebburn and Jarrow Local History Society, who shared their knowledge of the town of Jarrow, South Tyneside, England, including Jarrow Hall, and for pointing me to Hylton Castle.
- Ben Coles who helped me turn my manuscript into

a novel. I'm also grateful for Ben's commitment and service to the Royal Canadian Navy. His experience ensures that my naval scenes are authentic. Any errs are mine alone.

- Michelle Balfour and the gang of talented individuals at Cascadia Author Services, who turn my manuscripts into marketable novels.
- Robert McKellar Douglas, an artist with vision. He not only encourages my writing but helps me with the research. He has travelled with me, listened to my ideas and concepts, and provided feedback.

PART ONE

CHAPTER 1

In early December 1914, RMS *Guardian* docked in Edinburgh to take on fuel and supplies. Sublieutenant Simon Nightingale-Temple took advantage of a rare shore day and hitched a ride into the ancient city. He wandered along the Royal Mile for a few hours, selecting Christmas gifts for his family, which he then posted to Newcastle.

Family obligations complete, Simon stopped for afternoon tea at a café midway up the Mile, where he ordered fresh scones with clotted cream and strawberry jam, along with a pot of hot tea. While he waited, he scanned the café, his mind flooding with delightful childhood memories.

But before he could surrender to them, he was distracted by the headline of a discarded daily newspaper: *Mighty Russian Army Dwindles*. The date on the paper suggested that it was already old news, but he was reminded of the precarious state of the battles along the Austro-Russian border just the same. Although Russia's army was massive so far as manpower was concerned, its military might seemed to flounder when pitted against the modern technology of its foes.

A matronly waitress shattered his thoughts when she

appeared at his small table and efficiently poured milk and tea into a fine china cup. She placed the pot on the table so he could add more later and scooted away to collect the remainder of his order.

Moments later, Simon's first bite summoned the recollections the daily headline had interrupted: of a family vacation when he was nine years old. His father had brought his mother, brother, and him to Scotland for two weeks. It was just prior to their departure to St. Petersburg in 1902, where his father had been posted as naval attaché to the British Foreign Office. As memories of visits to the Imperial Palace—days spent playing in the royal nursery, parks, and stables with the grand duchesses, and more snow than he thought he would see in a lifetime—mixed pleasantly with the silkiness of clotted cream and seedy strawberry jam, he felt himself relax. He allowed the temporary calm to negate the stresses and distractions of wartime service he experienced aboard a royal navy vessel.

Hmm, he thought, *I suppose I should get used to saying "Petrograd" instead of "St. Petersburg." Given the conflict with Germany, Russians are disinclined to have their beautiful city bear a German name.*

He popped the last bit of scone in his mouth and washed it down with a swallow of cold, milky tea. He then summoned the waitress and ordered additional pastries to take back to the ship. Once he had paid the proprietress, Simon stepped outside and hailed a motor cab, a box of tasty pastries in one hand and a sack of oranges, for which he had paid dearly, in the other.

———

A few days before Christmas, Simon surveyed the horizon from the bridge. At the end of the previous watch that morning, some of the officers had reported seeing a pod of whales. Hoping to spot them too, Simon peered through binoculars, adjusting the lenses.

"Sublieutenant Temple," the Officer of the Watch said, "a word please?"

Simon set the binoculars on a console and followed the Officer of the Watch, Commander Alexander Douglas, into the communications room. "How may I help, sir?" he said.

"Seaman Smythe has intercepted a coded message," Douglas replied, his Scottish burr sounding thicker as if to emphasize his concern. "It appears to be in German, and I'm wondering whether it makes any sense to you." He gestured, and Smythe handed a sheet of paper to Simon. "Captain Hartford mentioned a while back that you're a linguist."

Simon nodded and read the note. He toyed with his neatly trimmed, russet beard as he contemplated and reread the words for certainty, then returned the page to the signalman.

"It appears to be a communication between two friends," Simon said. "One on a submarine, the other on land." Simon considered the message further. "I suspect that, if either commanding officer were aware of the communiqué, the two men would be locked up for breach of protocol, possibly more."

He chuckled, then sobered in response to the commander's scowl.

"One is lamenting about enduring the holiday on a balmy beach with polar bears and a bunch of drunk submariners, while the other is dreaming of a *Tannenbaum*—a Christmas tree—and a pretty face, his sweetheart no doubt, even though he's locked in a sardine can. They close by wishing each other happy Christmas."

"Are you certain?" Douglas said.

"Yes, sir," Simon said. "However, while the exchange itself is harmless, doesn't our interception of it suggest that *Guardian* is in their vicinity? If so, we should be looking and listening for that submarine."

"Exactly my thoughts," Douglas said. "Smythe, continue to monitor transmission. If you intercept anything else from those two, pass the message to Sublieutenant Temple, in my absence. Temple, take the bridge and get eyes on the sea. I'll speak with Captain Hartford." He took two steps toward the doorway and stopped abruptly. "And try to identify any islands in the vicinity that might boast polar bears and beaches."

"Aye, sir," Simon said, turning on his heel.

As wintery weeks passed in the northern seas, ships passing near the location where the message had been intercepted watched the water for suspicious shadows. None were spied, nor were they able to identify the land site, although Norwegian allies had suggested possibilities.

CHAPTER 2

*S**pring must be well underway in Jarrow,* Simon thought, a sense of nostalgia catching him off-guard as he wiped the dregs of toothpowder from his face. A yearning for home clung to him as he completed his ministrations in preparation for bed.

"Good night, Jordy," he said to his bunkmate, switching the lamp off a few minutes later.

Simon's head had yet to touch his pillow when he thought he heard loud cheering coming from the deck below. The first watch bell had just rung. He scratched his head as he swung his feet back to the floor. "Did you hear that?" he said.

"Yes," Jordy Montrose said, rising on his elbows. "And I was just nodding off too."

"Are you coming?" Simon said.

In response to Montrose's affirmative reply, Simon switched the table lamp on again and began dressing. Moments later, they tied the last of their laces and shrugged into their pea jackets. Lamp off, they cracked open the cabin door and slid into the inky night.

The March sky was dark under roiling storm clouds, occasionally revealing an ominous sliver of moonlight.

Despite the movement overhead and the churning sea, the breeze was mild, speckled with a light rain that sprayed their cheeks.

"Looks like the storm's passing," Montrose said, his eyes roving the deck for movement as they listened for more hubbub. They strode toward it, tripping down the ladder to the lower deck.

"Look there!" Simon said, pointing toward a trawler bobbing off the port bow. "What's going on, petty officer?" he said, stuffing damp fingers into his jacket pockets.

"Cap'n's boarded that ship," the petty officer replied, leaning casually against a stanchion.

"The captain?" Simon said, incredulous to think that anyone would have boarded any vessel during the storm that raged a short while ago.

"Yes, sir," the petty officer replied, his chest seeming to inflate with admiration. He continued his comment, his words clipped by a Welsh accent. "Cap'n Hartford stepped right off this deck and into the sea boat, he did. He stood just where you are, an' when the small boat came up on a swell, even with this deck like, he jumped!" The crewman removed his cap and scratched his bald pate, appearing incredulous. "If anyone else had done it, I would nay believed it. But Cap'n Hartford"—the man gave a broad grin—"well, he does things like that, ya see. I seen it many a time."

"Indeed!" It was Jordy's turn to express amazement. "I wish I'd seen that."

The seaman gave the young men a side-long look and

scoffed a reply. "There's nay many who'd be out in heavy weather, but war changes things. E'en less 'ould step offa ship with nay a second thought to where he'd land." The petty officer appeared to immediately regret the retort. "I beg your pardon, sirs." He stiffened, as if remembering to whom he spoke, then promptly disappeared into the dark.

Simon glanced at Montrose with raised brows and shrugged. He returned his attention to the detained vessel. "The flag looks Swedish," he said, squinting into the dark at a limp ensign. As the trawler bobbed on the current, a *Guardian* searchlight caught the bow, illuminating its name. "SS *Sjöfågel*," he said aloud. "That translates to '*Seabird*' in English."

Seabird's captain appeared to be shouting at Captain Hartford. While his words could not carry over the distance, his annoyance was obvious. He shook his fist at the captain; in response, three *Guardian* marines raised their rifles threateningly and motioned the remainder of the crew to cluster near *Seabird's* captain.

"This could take a while, gentlemen," Lieutenant Commander Samuel Walters said as he paused next to Simon.

The two bunkmates stiffened, acknowledging the arrival of the senior officer. The slight taunt in the Commander's Scottish burr surprised Simon. When he glanced at Montrose and received a covert wink, his concern vanished.

"There's something amiss here, sir," Simon said, tearing his eyes from the trawler to greet the commander.

"You have that right enough," Walters replied. "We spied her at the end of the last watch. The current watch has been chasing her for an hour. I understand that as soon as she was signalled to heave-to she went dark, making her difficult to track in this mist. She's been outsmarted, though. Her course was successfully plotted and, when she approached the shoreline, the mist lifted briefly to reveal her precise location."

As they listened to the commander's explanation, one of *Seabird's* crewmen lunged toward the prize crew. A scuffle and shouting ensued. Suddenly, everyone on deck stepped back and watched in shock as a marine fell. His attacker stood motionless above him, knife in hand.

"Gosh!" Simon said. "So far, all the boardings have been straight forward. I never gave much thought to that kind of treachery."

"Most challenges *are* routine," Walters said. "*Nothing* has been routine about *Seabird*. That man's bleeding heavily." He lowered his spyglass. "Montrose, inform the doctor to expect another injured man, then report to me on the bridge."

"Aye, sir," Montrose replied, promptly departing for the sick berth.

As Simon stood alone at the railing, another marine dropped to his knees, applying pressure to the injured man's chest. While aid was administered, other marines secured the attacker in handcuffs and removed him from the deck. Although the fallen man appeared dead from Simon's vantage point, marines could be seen fastening bandages over his injury and lowering him carefully to the sea boat. Following a short discussion with the captain, the sea boat was released from *Seabird* and rowed hastily back to *Guardian*.

Simon pushed away from the railing, retrieving a handkerchief from his pocket to mop trickles of moisture pearling on his face. Continuing to focus on the errant vessel, he noticed the captain giving instructions to a signal man.

"Captain's asking for me?" Simon muttered aloud to himself. "And he wants me armed?"

Abruptly, he turned toward the nearest ladder and slid down to the next deck, where another sea boat was being readied for a drop.

"Ah! Sublieutenant Temple!" a marine said, his Newfoundland accent sounding almost Irish. "You must've seen the captain's signal."

"I did," Simon replied, swaying with the ship's movement. "I was watching from above and came directly here. I'm not armed."

"Very well," the marine replied. "Take me pistol." He withdrew his weapon and held it toward Simon just as the ship rolled. Simon staggered forward, grasping it firmly.

"Tuck it in the outer pocket of yer all-weathers so tis easily reached if needed. Mind ye button it." The marine pointed as the ship rolled again.

Simon staggered, turning around to see another marine holding out rain gear.

"Wind's died a bit, but water's still rough," the first

marine said as spray washed over the deck. "If the gun's in yer pocket, an' ye happen ta fall in, it may still be dry when yer fished out."

Simon shrugged into the gear, pocketing the sidearm and fastening the buttons.

"Ye'll find a rifle and ammo braced on the boat's inner wall," the first marine added as he handed Simon into the boat.

Simon scrambled onto a bench as the next wave caused the boat to swing out over the water. He clung to the bench, surprised at the gap between the two vessels, and how quickly it closed as the next roll sent the small boat swinging back toward *Guardian*.

"Do you know why Captain Hartford sent for me?" Simon raised his voice to be heard as crewmen reached to stop the safety boat from crashing into the rail.

"I suspect it has to do with Lieutenant Forniere's accident a bit ago and that scuffle," the first marine replied, jerking his head toward *Seabird*. "Lieutenant was boarding and the trawler lurched. He lost his balance and, whilst he grabbed fer something, the boat snapped back. He's in sick berth just now with broke ribs and a sprained wrist. That's why Cap'n's aboard."

"I witnessed the scuffle," Simon said. "I wonder what that was about."

"Can't say, sir," the first marine said. "I'll leave that for the cap'n to explain."

Can't imagine why Hartford needs me, Simon thought as he checked the fastenings on his floating vest.

"Ready, sir?"

Simon turned his attention toward the helmsman perched at the bow the boat and nodded dubiously. In the next moment, the davits suspending the lifeboat swung wide of *Guardian's* side and, engaging the synchronized pulleys and planetary gears, the crewmen lowered the boat to the churning sea below.

Simon adjusted his safety vest and tightened his grip on the bench, feeling his stomach lurch in response to the boat's rapid descent. With lips pressed together tightly, he offered a silent prayer for calm waters, doubting a favourable response.

Two of the eight marines accompanying him scrambled to release the remaining hooks, separating the two vessels. Then, together, all eight lowered their oars and began pulling hard. While the lifeboat approached the trawler, *Guardian* motored slowly around the smaller vessel, its guns and searchlights trained threateningly on the detained ship.

Ten minutes later, Simon and a rifle were safely handed aboard. Before he had time to steady himself and thank the marines, the sea boat pulled away. The next swell sent him staggering toward the wheelhouse, reaching for purchase.

"Sublieutenant Temple," Captain Hartford said, opening the door of the wheelhouse and acknowledging Simon's arrival.

"Sir?" Simon replied with a smart nod of respect. The smell of rotting fish, creaking rope, and clanging gear assailed his senses.

"Your linguistics would be very useful right now," the captain said, inviting him inside out of wind and spray. "Aside from German and French, remind me whether you speak Swedish, or Russian?"

"I'm fluent in all but Swedish," Simon replied. "But I'm sure I can manage if Swedish is required."

"I'm less concerned with Swedish than I am with the others," Hartford said, shrugging out of his rain jacket and hanging it near the door, indicating that Simon do the same. "The captain and crew of this trawler are being held below. The captain is a surly man. I often find Swedes uncooperative these days, and he has done nothing to change my opinion. I also have suspicions about some of his crew. Most say they're Swedes. Two say they're Dutch, but again … I have my suspicions."

Hartford withdrew a folded handkerchief from his pocket and mopped his face. "And the most curious of them is a fellow the marines found in a hold that should be filled with fish. While I don't think he's French, he speaks something similar. I'm hoping you might help sort everything out." The captain scrubbed his knuckles through a dense grey beard. "Mr. Forniere normally leads this prize crew. Aside from you, he's the only other linguist on board, but—

"He met with an injury earlier and is now in the sick berth," Simon said, finishing the captain's explanation. He grinned. "How may I help, sir?"

"I have a list of interrogation questions for the crew,"

Captain Hartford said, handing a sheet of paper to Simon. "I'd like you to assist with the administration."

"Yes, sir." Simon glanced at the paper and tried to memorize as many of the fourteen questions as possible. Most of them were practical questions, such as the vessel's port of departure and its route since then. Other questions were specific, including whether mine fields had been spotted, and whether any German ships, submarines, or other vessels had been sighted.

"This is quite the list, sir," Simon said, swaying with the rocking vessel.

"And I'm certain you'll agree that each question is essential."

"Of course, sir!" Simon said responding to the captain's piercing gaze.

"In addition to linguistics, I'll ask that you observe each of the individuals you address. Body language speaks volumes, particularly the eyes. If you have any doubt about the individual with whom you speak, watch the eyes."

"Yes, sir."

CHAPTER 3

As hours passed, Simon assisted Captain Hartford with the interrogation of first *Seabird*'s captain, then each member of her crew. Simon observed only two were reluctant to answer: the men who claimed to be Dutch.

Simon knew a little Dutch. When the first fellow claiming to be a Dutch citizen sat opposite him in the wheelhouse, he posed the initial question in English. The small, wiry man stared ahead without expression.

Next, Simon tried French, hoping to give the man a false sense of confidence. The man did not flinch. The third query was made in German, and, although the man's face remained unmoved, Simon noted a shift in his eyes.

Aha! Getting warmer. Without hesitation, Simon fired a different question … in Russian. The man's answer appeared in the sharpness of his eyes. Simon repeated the question more assertively. The man leaned back in his chair and crossed his arms over his chest. A hint of a grin twitched at the corner of his mouth.

"It is clear to me that you speak both Russian and German, sir." Simon snapped in fluent Russian. "If you do not answer the questions, you will be detained, and likely imprisoned for the duration of the war."

The man shifted his attention from Simon toward the captain, who stood near the door of the wheelhouse. His eyes narrowed into a defiant glare. Neither of the *Guardian* men flinched.

"I have nothing to say to you." The man spat his comment in English, the clarity of his words hindered only by a Russian accent. "I'm aboard this vessel as an observer. You cannot detain me. I am a Russian citizen, and I have not broken any laws."

"A Russian citizen, onboard a Swedish vessel, with a questionable travelling companion, both of whom claim to be Dutch?" the captain said, sounding incredulous. "That sounds very suspicious to me."

"I have papers," the Russian said, reaching into his jacket.

With a knee-jerk response, the captain pulled a revolver from his belt.

The Russian raised his hands in defence. "I merely reach for papers," the Russian said, lowering his hands to the table.

"Slowly then," the captain said, waving the nose of the revolver threateningly. "Keep one hand on the table."

The man withdrew the papers and spread them on the table, thrusting them toward Simon.

Simon scanned the pages slowly as he interpreted the contents. "I see nothing here that explains your right to leniency. Nor is there anything to suggest your innocence." He shoved the pages across the desk. "Feel free to show your papers to the officers in Lerwick."

"Lerwick!" the Russian said, spitting the word angrily. "You must return me to Russia. Britain and Russia, we have an agreement."

"Britain and Russia may have an agreement," Simon said authoritatively, "but your behaviour and presence on this vessel suggests that you are not part of that agreement."

The Russian jumped to his feet, knocking his chair backward.

"Enough!" the captain said, towering above him. He opened the door and instructed two marines to secure the imposter. One stepped into the wheelhouse and manhandled the man toward the door.

The Russian twisted free, knocking the revolver from Hartford's hand in his attempt to grab it. He shoved against his captor and pushed him through the doorway into the second marine. Both guards fell to the deck.

The Russian pulled the door closed and locked it. When he turned back to the captain and Simon, he raised the rifle he had snatched during the struggle and retrieved Hartford's revolver as it slid to a stop by his foot.

"You!" The Russian motioned to the captain. "Sit. And you tie him up." Using the barrel of the rifle, he drew Simon's attention to a slender cord hanging on the hook under Simon's rain jacket.

Noticing a tremor in the man's hand, Simon edged his way toward his gear. *He's either nervous or ill,* Simon thought. *Likely nervous. I can work with that.* Keeping an eye on his opponent and the rifle's wavering barrel, Simon permitted a quick glance to confirm that the captain was seated at the table. As he rummaged near his jacket for the cord, he managed to snag Hartford's eye long enough to convey a need for distraction.

"What do you expect to achieve?" Hartford's demanding voice drew the Russian's focus. "We're at sea! You've nowhere to run."

"You English are so blind," the Russian sneered, glowering at Hartford. "You have no idea what lies beneath the waves."

With the Russian distracted, Simon deftly unfastened the button of his jacket pocket and retrieved the marine's sidearm. He spun toward their captor, raising the pistol above his head. Without a sound, the man crumpled to the floor when the butt of the pistol cracked against bone behind his left ear.

Captain Hartford jumped to his feet and released the latch on the door, then stepped back to allow the marines entry. "Take him away. Stow him somewhere separate from the others and bring in the second one. Pay attention. He might try to resist like this arrogant cur."

———•—•———

The next fellow admitted to being German when Simon told him what had happened to his colleague. Then he declined to say more. The marines were ordered to arrest him, ensuring that he, too, was detained separately from the others.

"Thank you, Sublieutenant Temple," Hartford said. "I appreciate your assistance … and your heroics."

"Happy to be of service," Simon replied flatly. He stretched, enjoying the release of stiff muscles. "There is something you should know …"

With the left side of his mouth quirked in a half grin, Captain Hartford peered at Simon. "You saw something in those papers," he said. "Tell me."

"Right, sir," Simon said, straightening. "The papers are written in German. While the first fellow might *speak* German, I suspect he has little to no ability to *read* it. The papers suggest an introduction to a senior officer in charge of a base on Bear Island." Simon slid into the seat opposite the captain.

"The Russian was to examine the construction and performance of a new German-built submarine. From my quick scan, it seems the second fellow may be a German engineer or designer involved with the construction of the submarine. I can only speculate how that information might be beneficial to the Russian or his superiors."

Simon sighed, shaking his head in wonder as he chewed his lower lip. "Two concerns come to mind, however. First, why are the Russians interested in a German-designed submarine when Russia is supposed to be working with the British? This, I presume, will be followed up by Lieutenant Forniere in Lerwick."

The captain nodded and reached to steady himself as *Seabird* pitched unexpectedly.

"The second is, for me, more troubling. I'll share what I can, but you'll have to forgive me if I fall short …" Simon paused, giving careful thought to what he would say next.

"Go on." Hartford said.

"You'll recall that, when I was a boy, my father was posted as naval attaché to the Foreign Office in St. Petersburg," Simon said.

Hartford nodded.

"I was a boy," Simon said, "but not so young that I missed certain events. I remember the name Maksim Lebedev particularly. Lebedev and two others: Vasiliev and Yurovsky, I think, although I can't recall their first names. They were somehow involved in an attempt on the tsar's life. My father speaks of the event from time to time, when reminiscing, so the names remain in my mind."

In response to the captain's furrowed brow and hooded eyes, Simon elaborated. "In 1902, Lebedev was a junior Russian statesman with German connections. Those papers were co-signed by Lebedev a week ago. The other name is unknown to me, but appears to be German."

"Please ensure that Forniere receives this information in your report," Hartford said.

"Of course," Simon replied, stretching again. "Returning to the ship?"

"Shortly," the captain said. "The watch is about to change, and I can't very well accompany this trawler back to Lerwick." He fingered his bearded chin. "Perhaps if Forniere is up for it, I'll send him back so he can return to England for his convalescence." Hartford paced across the wheelhouse twice, deep in thought.

He stopped abruptly and peered through the sea-streaked window toward *Guardian*. "Hmm," he said as if speaking to himself, "that would work well. We'll be down two crewmen. I can arrange for replacements at the same time." He approached the table, stopping in front of Simon.

"We have one more crewman to interview," he said, "but this fellow is different. He doesn't seem to fit the character of the others, and he's black. As I mentioned earlier, we found him locked in a hold, apart from the others." Captain Hartford opened the door. "Bring the last fellow," he said.

"Aye, sir."

CHAPTER 4

The marines delivered the mysterious crewman into the wheelhouse a short while later. Simon smiled a welcome and directed him to the empty chair.

"Do you speak English?" Simon said.

Unlike the others, who tended to slouch in the chair as if closing themselves to his questions, the man sat tall, fastening his black eyes on Simon contemplatively. "*Non, monsieur, je parle français,*" he replied, folding his large hands on the table.

"*Merveilleux!*" Simon said, continuing the conversation in French. "I'm Sublieutenant Simon Temple, and this"— he turned toward the man behind him—"is Captain Archibald Hartford of RMS *Guardian*, a British-armed merchant cruiser."

"My name is Gerard Tremblay, formerly of Haiti and currently a resident of Montréal, Québec, in Canada," the crewman said, focussing on Simon. "You're British. You must rescue me!" He squirmed in his seat, sitting straighter and leaning toward Simon, his expression hopeful.

Simon heard the desperation in Tremblay's voice. He also noticed a lilt in the way that he spoke, and while it sounded French, it was not the language that Simon had studied, nor did it sound like the French spoken by a few of the crew who called Québec home. Simon considered the situation and decided that he understood well enough to continue.

"Before we talk about a rescue," Simon said firmly, "I have questions."

"Anything!" the man said, throwing his arms wide. His dark eyes appeared anxious. "I will answer anything, if it gets me out of here!"

"Very well," Simon said. "Have you been on this ship long?"

"What is the date?" Tremblay said.

"March 8th, 1915."

"I have been aboard this stinking trawler for seven months!" Tremblay said, spitting the words vehemently. "Last summer, I returned to Haiti for my grandmother's funeral. At the end of August, I purchased a ticket on a mail ship bound for Montréal—home. We were sailing north—near the American state of Georgia, I believe— when the ship was blown off course—north, yes, but also east—by a wicked hurricane." He wiped a ragged sleeve across his mouth, breathing heavily.

"After two days of bouncing around the Atlantic like a cork, the ship was struck broadside by a huge wave. It rolled onto its side, but never stood upright again. The captain ordered all to abandon ship. I happened to be on deck when the ship rolled; I fell into the sea. Some folks pulled me into a dingy. There were five of us in that small boat, clinging to whatever would keep us in it. We took turns using our hands to empty water from inside."

Tremblay braced his elbows on the table and rolled his head in his hands. "When the storm finally passed, we had no idea where we were. We had limited rations and no shelter—only oars. So, we rowed, not knowing where we were headed."

Simon filled a glass with water and handed it to Tremblay. The Frenchman accepted the glass and drank deeply, nodding his appreciation, then set it on the table and sighed.

"Eventually, the rations that had been stowed in the bow ran out and the weather grew colder. One man went crazy in the head; thirst drove him into the water. We tried to pull him back into the boat, but he just kept drinking and drinking the sea water."

Tremblay shook his head. "He was beyond our reach, and eventually he just sank out of view. Another man—he was older—his heart gave out the next day. We three remaining prayed for his soul and rolled him into the sea." Tremblay toyed with the glass, rolling its bottom on the table.

"The other two were women. A mother and daughter. The girl was probably twenty years. Both were pretty. Such a tragedy."

"What was a tragedy?" Simon said, leaning forward.

When Tremblay raised dark eyes to Simon, tears trickled down the man's ebony cheeks.

"Two days after the old man died, we saw this tub of a boat and summoned our last energy to flag her down.

That was a fatal mistake. Apparently, the currents had carried us north, to the fishing grounds off Newfoundland. The crew hauled us aboard, gave us food and warm clothes, and put us in the hold—where your men found me." He nodded toward the captain as he spoke.

"There are women on board?" Simon said, incredulous. "Captain, did you find two women?" he said in English. Stunned by the question, Captain Hartford pushed himself away from the ledge upon which he had been leaning.

"*Non!*" Tremblay interrupted. "No, they are gone." He dropped his head into his hands, fingering tightly curled hair , and sighed sorrowfully.

"Gone?" Simon repeated, holding up a hand to still the captain.

"Yes." Tremblay looked up, tears catching on his lashes. "The crew was uncomfortable having women onboard. It was bad luck, they said. The ship was not expected to be in port for many weeks. The captain finally agreed that they could use the women and dispose of them. Several of the crew took turns with them—*using them*—and sometime later, maybe days, they were thrown into the water and encouraged to swim to shore. It was too far for them. They were weak and broken; they drowned in minutes."

Simon interrupted Tremblay's monologue to provide the captain with a summary of what he had heard. Then, he returned to Tremblay. "That was months ago, you say. What's happened since?"

"They kept me on board to help with the heavy labour.

They promised to return me to my family at the next port, yet each time the ship docked, I was locked below."

Simon scrubbed his eyes, letting jumbled thoughts take order. "Captain," he said, "this man has been the trawler's prisoner since September."

"I see," Hartford said, pacing the wheelhouse, his features hardened with anger. "I'll need time to speak with the marines so charges can be drawn up. I also need to return to the ship to speak with Forniere." He closed the fastenings on his all-weather gear. "Sublieutenant, I'd like you to remain here with the marines while I return to the ship."

"Aye, sir."

Simon was startled by a large hand grasping his arm. "Please," Tremblay said, his eyes pleading as he squeezed Simon's arm firmly. "Please help me get a message to my wife. She will be wondering why I have abandoned her and the children."

"Of course," Simon replied. "Sir, will you wait long enough for Mr. Tremblay to write a message to his wife?"

"He has until the sea boat arrives." The captain jerked open the door, allowing a gust of wind entry, and went in search of the signal man.

"Your captain, he is angry," Tremblay said, indicating the change in the captain's demeanour.

"Of course he's angry," Simon said assuredly. "I've never heard of a Swede who'd treat people the way you and the women have been treated. Not these days, anyway. Here." Simon pushed pen and paper toward Tremblay.

"Write a note for your wife and the captain will send it when he returns to *Guardian*."

"Will the crewman be able to read French?"

"I'm not sure. Why don't you tell me, and I'll write it in English?" Simon said. "Will someone translate for your wife?"

"Ah!" Tremblay laughed a deep, throaty laugh, as if finally realizing he would soon be free. "Her English is very good. She was born in Canada, and reads and writes both English and French well."

"*Merveilleux!*" Simon replied, reaching for the pen and paper. "Once the captain is away, perhaps you can tell me more about the workings of this ship, and what would cause them to enslave you."

Tremblay agreed and quickly dictated a message for his wife.

CHAPTER 5

Whil e the captain returned to *Guardian* to collect Lieutenant Forniere, Tremblay relayed what he knew about the ship's responsibilities.

"The ship must keep up appearances, yes," Tremblay said, nodding for emphasis, "and so we drop the nets from time to time. That is what they were planning to do when your ship found us. Otherwise, they help the submarines of the Germans."

Simon retrieved another sheet of paper and began taking notes. "Go on," he said.

"There is a submarine base to the north, in a cove on an island named after an animal—*Ours Île!*"

"Bear Island?"

"*Oui!* Bear Island," Tremblay said. "In port, we load the ship with supplies for … Bear Island. Then, as the captain travels to the cove, he watches for German submarines and provides them with information regarding the location of various ships. The submarines tell him which areas to avoid because of the minefields. When supplies are unloaded at Bear Island, the captain takes the ship to the fishing grounds and returns to port with the catch. A great circuit, *non?* Very much business."

"Indeed," Simon replied, stroking his bearded jaw. "Very much business."

Simon hastily scribbled more notes and gazed out the wheelhouse window. "The sea boat is returning, Mr. Tremblay. Once *Guardian* crew is all aboard, they'll likely take this ship to Lerwick. It's a small town in the Shetland Islands, north of the coast of Scotland. There will be an investigation. *Seabird's* captain and crew will be detained, and the ship likely held or confiscated. When the investigation is complete, I expect arrangements will be made for your return to Canada." Simon rose from his chair and stretched. "What a night!"

"What freedom!" Tremblay said, grinning as he aped Simon's stretch. His tall frame filled the wheelhouse when he raised his arms in pleasure. "I have been cramped in that hold for so long …"

"I'm afraid that you'll be restricted a little longer," Simon replied, "while the prize crew takes this ship and crew into Lerwick, but you won't be cramped in the hold. I'll ensure that you're given a proper bunk."

"*Merci, Monsieur Temple*," Tremblay said, grabbing Simon's hands. "*Merci beaucoup!*"

The door to the wheelhouse flared open to reveal the return of Captain Hartford.

"Is Lieutenant Forniere with you?" Simon said, peering behind the captain.

"No," Hartford said, "we've had a change of plans. I've arranged for another prize crew to take over *Seabird*. The marines aboard will return to the ship. *Guardian* has been ordered to report to Lerwick as well. Forniere will remain aboard *Guardian* and will be transferred to the hospital ship *Berbice* when we arrive. We're to dock only long enough to take on fuel and fresh supplies. This trawler, its captain, and its crew will be detained and interrogated."

"Very good, sir," Simon said. "Uh, is it possible to have Mr. Tremblay transferred to *Guardian*?"

"Excellent suggestion, Temple," Hartford replied. "That will allow Forniere an opportunity to interview him in transit."

Simon quickly translated the news for Tremblay, who smiled broadly in response.

"Sir," Simon said, "while we've been waiting, Mr. Tremblay has advised us of some of the ship's unusual activities. I doubt they will coincide with the log entries." Simon handed his notes to the captain.

As the captain scanned the notes, Simon tapped a point near the centre of the page.

"Bear Island, sir!" Simon said excitedly. "I believe that's the elusive island we've been searching for."

"But we've passed Bear Island several times," Hartford said his voice amazed. "How have we missed it?"

"Apparently, there's a small opening into a cove on the north side. Deep enough to accommodate a submerged submarine entry without being seen."

"Forniere will need this information," Hartford said with urgency. "Please ask Mr. Tremblay to report everything to him so a full report can be prepared by the time this vessel reaches Lerwick. And I want your notes prepared for a full meeting with the officers at fourteen hundred hours. I know it's been a long night. Can you be ready?"

"Yes, sir."

"*Monsieur le Capitaine!*" Tremblay took a step toward Hartford, as if to halt his departure. He looked at Simon for help. "Please inform the captain that I believe he may find contraband, and perhaps even a radio and a record of this ship's unusual behaviour, in a hidden compartment in the stern. They don't think I know about it, but I've seen them put things there."

"Of course," Simon replied, then translated the information for the captain.

The captain left the wheelhouse in haste. Simon and Tremblay followed.

"Show me!" the captain barked his command.

Tremblay did not need a translation. He led the captain, two marines, and Simon to the stern and, in the predawn light, indicated a well-hidden compartment. The marines pried it open and handed the captain what appeared to be a shadow logbook. While they retrieved a variety of other items, including the radio presumably used to contact German vessels, Hartford opened the logbook and thumbed through the entries.

"Looks like Swedish," he said passing the book to Simon. "Can you read it?"

Simon studied the text briefly, flipping pages to dates more current.

"Enough to understand the locations of mines that may exist between here and Bear Island," Simon replied.

Tremblay looked on intently. "This will help?" he said in halting English.

"*Bien sûr,*" Simon replied. "We'll have to translate the information accurately, but I expect this will save many ships and even more lives. *Merci encore, Monsieur Tremblay.*"

"Forniere reads and speaks Swedish," Hartford said. "Let's see if he can provide enough information for us to reach Bear Island safely. Once we're sorted in Lerwick, we'll be on our way." Turning to Tremblay, he held out his hand. "Mr. Tremblay, thank you for your co-operation. A message has been sent to your wife. I took the liberty of explaining that you will be detained for a while and that you'll be in further communication with her once you've been debriefed."

Simon repeated a French version of the captain's remarks.

"Now, Sublieutenant Temple, it is time for me to instruct the marines so we can return to *Guardian.*"

As the sea boat bounced against the waves on its return to *Guardian,* Simon enquired about the condition of the marine who had been injured in the night. Hearing that the man had died, Simon reflected on the cruelty of some men toward others, regardless of the times. He also considered Forniere's successful translation of the shadow logbook, and what that would mean for the safety of the allied men and ships patrolling the northern seas.

———

Quiet blanketed *Guardian* as each man contemplated

the unexpected death and their own mortality. The following morning, when the ship entered quieter water, the ship's engines were ordered to a full stop. All aboard assembled amidships to witness the sea burial.

In the absence of the ship's chaplain, who had taken leave in Edinburgh, Captain Hartford oversaw the burial. The men waited patiently as an entourage, bearing a plank on which the shrouded body of the dead marine rested under weighted canvas, proceeded to the side of the deck. While the captain read from the Book of Common Prayer, the plank bearers tipped the board, and the body of the marine slid into the sea.

The wispy grey fog that had encased the ship since sunrise rolled away, allowing bright beams of sun to illuminate the sea. Voices of those present mingled and rose in an expression of awe. The bright light kept the descent of the marine's shrouded body visible until the ocean's depth would reveal no more. Captain Hartford concluded the service, and, as the ethereal fog had done moments before, the crew vanished.

Simon and Montrose stood at the railing, watching the empty sea. Waves chopped about the hull as the engine speed increased and the propeller advanced the ship on its course for Lerwick.

CHAPTER 6

Several days later, Simon stood near a port-side railing, peeling his last orange as he watched the port pilot oversee the docking of RMS *Guardian* into a Lerwick berth near Fort Charlotte. He made a mental note to look for more oranges. They were hard to come by, given the time of year and supply-chain interruptions since various embargos began.

As the false dawn broke, two pilot tugs appeared alongside *Guardian*, guiding her from Bressay Sound into Lerwick Harbour. They led her through a forest of not only naval ships, but armed drifters, trawlers, barques, merchant cruise ships, and an assortment of other vessels armed for sea battle.

When a pilot from the first tug boarded *Guardian* to better advise the captain, the second tug slipped away. A third pilot tug escorted the Swedish captive *Seabird* toward a guard ship, where all neutral vessels were required to report for examination.

When the pilot boat returned for its officer, Simon crossed the deck to watch as *Guardian's* ropes were tied to cleats and the brow readied. He surveyed the dock, then sauntered to the bow where he could better observe the activities in the harbour. He identified the location of *Berbice*, not only by the large red crosses painted on her hull, but by one of their sea boats being lowered with Lieutenant Forniere propped between two marines. The marines rowed with purpose toward *Berbice*.

The previous evening, Montrose had reminded Simon that the most efficient manner by which to convey Forniere to the hospital ship would be by safety boat. Land travel in Lerwick was slow, and would be uncomfortable, if not painful, for the injured officer.

Simon checked his watch and turned abruptly to the ladder leading to the bridge. His shift would begin in ten minutes.

Mid-morning, Simon received a message from Captain Hartford with details of their debriefing regarding *Seabird's* detention.

"It's just a formality," Hartford said as the sea boat cut through murky water. "Our written reports are thorough, but we may have overlooked something that to us seemed obvious or inconsequential."

He scanned the harbour as marines rowed toward the guard ship, neatly avoiding collision with a small fishing boat. "Prepare to wait," he said to the marine lieutenant standing at the helm. "The sooner our interviews are concluded, the sooner we'll be underway."

"Aye, sir," the man replied.

When the meeting ended, Simon and Hartford clambered back into the sea boat.

"So much for a hasty departure," Hartford said,

grumbling sotto voce. "Since we're expected to remain in port for several days, the crew may as well take shore leave." He glanced sidelong at Simon. "Some of the examiners seem quite interested in that submarine and your story. Be prepared to be grilled on that topic."

"I'd better speak with Father first," Simon replied. "I was comfortable sharing details with you, but I need to know what I can disclose to others." He leaned toward the captain so as not to be overheard. "Will the authorities truly release a BBC announcement?"

"Of course," Hartford replied. "Someone is expecting that trawler's arrival, and they need to know that she's not coming."

Eight hours later, BBC radio released a brief report stating that, during an attempt to overtake a Swedish trawler in the North Sea, the vessel had exploded. *Sjöfågel*, suspected of carrying contraband, and all crew were lost.

Simon grinned at Montrose knowingly as he snapped the radio off. "That was simple," he said. "Now no one will be looking for the missing vessel, it's cargo, or crew."

"Nice and tidy," Montrose said in agreement. "Makes you question the reliability of other reports we've heard."

— · —

The ship remained in port for almost a week. During that time, her hull was filled with fuel and supplies, and the crew took advantage of shore leave. In the meantime, Hartford, Simon, and the others involved in *Seabird's* seizure were interviewed while the vessel was subjected to a thorough search to ensure nothing was missed. At the conclusion of the investigation, all documents and records concerning Bear Island and submarines were sent to the Admiralty in London for additional consideration.

In the meantime, Gerard Tremblay had been lodged at a hotel not far from the naval yard. With the captain's blessing, Simon spent much of his free time keeping the man company until *Guardian* was released for her next assignment.

"Unfortunately," Simon said during their last meal together, "you're to be detained for another two weeks. An interpreter is expected to arrive tomorrow and will appear with you when you give your testimony. After that, arrangements will be made to return you to Canada."

"*Dieu merci!*" Tremblay said, fingering his beard. "I'll have to remove this before I greet my wife." He grinned. "It is the idea of her that has kept me going these many months. Always, my mind plotted an escape. Never in my greatest dreams did I imagine who would be my saviour." His expression softened. "I am grateful that it was you."

"I may have helped," Simon said humbly, "but it has been a group effort, and we all wish you well." Simon gulped the dregs of his wine and rose to his feet. "Time to go."

Tremblay rose and together they walked through the doors of the hotel and onto the street.

"Goodbye, my friend," Simon said, extending his hand.

Tremblay accepted the offered hand, then pulled Simon into a great hug that left his new companion breathless.

"I can't thank you enough—for listening to my story and believing its truth,"Tremblay said. "If ever you travel to Canada, you must visit us, and confirm my tale." A broad, gleaming smile lit his face, and he embraced Simon again. "*Merci*, my friend, Simon Temple."

Simon touched the beak of his cap and turned smartly, striding toward the pier.

On departure from Lerwick in late March, the captain ordered the charting of the location of mines and submarine tendencies that were recorded in *Seabird's* hidden logbook. Once the work was complete, it was shared with other Allied ships. When on deck, all eyes were naturally trained to the sea, watching for mines and submarine shadows.

At the same time, *Guardian* maintained a steady course for Spitsbergen, where the ship was scheduled to make a supply drop. Daily routines continued, including zigzagging, sounding, dropping and retrieving the log, target practice, shooting drills, physical drills, and hailing vessels sighted en route, all of which hindered a direct route to the Svalbard archipelago.

The number of unregistered vessels dwindled once *Guardian* crossed the Arctic Circle. Sightings tended to include other armed merchant cruisers, including sister ships RMS *Virginian* and RMS *Victorian,* SS *India,* and RMS *Columbella.* In each instance, those ships were hailed and, upon receiving the correct response, allowed to proceed.

CHAPTER 7

During the ensuing weeks, Operation Bear Island began to take shape, building to a night attack with Allied support, including two naval ships and a submarine. In June, with the caution required of a summer night invasion—commonly referred to in the north as "white nights" because skies only reached twilight from April to August—the four vessels closed on their target.

In the early hours of the assigned date, prize crews and combat-ready junior officers from each ship were rowed ashore on the shadowed side of the island. Passing through water-worn rock cathedrals hollowed beneath sheer rock faces, half of the sea boats rowed toward a beach littered with the remains of an ancient whaling village. From the beach they skirted the island, heading for the cove and the German encampment. Their orders were to disable enemy operations and take prisoners.

The remaining sea boats bobbed in coastal shadows just beyond the cove, waiting for landing orders. Presuming their landing went undetected, the beached crews proceeded with confidence and intent until they arrived at a rendezvous point above the German encampment. Three flicks of a torch, three seconds apart, alerted the ships and bobbing sea boats that the landed group was in position.

When *Guardian's* bridge sighted the flickering light, gunners from all three ships fired six-inch guns. Warning shells exploded mere metres beyond the occupied area. The delayed timing of return fire from a pillbox perched above the cove suggested that the attackers had avoided being sighted until the firing of the big guns.

Although heavy fire followed from the cliff as well as the cove, it was less than expected. Beach crews endeavoured to draw fire, allowing the sea crews entry to the cove and time to reach piers where three submarines were tied. The surprise attack caught most of the unsuspecting submariners ashore. The few who remained aboard provided little resistance to the Allied attack and soon surrendered.

As the fight for control of the cove progressed further inland, the marine crew to which Simon and Montrose had been assigned diverted uphill, in the direction of the pillbox. In single file, ten men dressed in dull clothing scrambled along the rocky cliff, swinging wide to avoid detection.

Reaching the crest of the ridge, they realized that the pillbox sat roughly fifty metres below them, at the foot of a gently sloping hill. Between them and the pillbox sat one very large boulder. The marine lieutenant pointed at loose stones scattered across the decent.

"One careless step could send a man over that edge," Simon said sotto voce to Montrose as they lay flat on the hilltop waiting for each of their colleagues to reach the boulder. "It's at least a three-storey drop to the rocks below."

"Take care, then," Montrose replied. "I don't want to be collecting your remains with a sieve!"

When the signal came for the two sublieutenants to follow the last marine, they pushed off the knoll, crouching as they scooted toward the large rock. In the next moment, the marine ahead of them cried out. His foot slid forward on loose pebbles, twisting his knee awkwardly and catapulting him toward the ledge.

Without hesitation, Simon and Montrose dove after him, each snagging a worn boot, halting the marine's probable demise.

Dragging the marine by the feet, Simon and Montrose belly-crawled backward until they were certain the three of them were safe. So focussed were they on the dilemma, none of the trio noticed two German soldiers scrambling from the pillbox, rifles aimed at them.

The Germans spied only the three men sprawled on the gravel and marched up the hill with purpose. As they rounded the boulder, half the marines rounded the opposite side, circling from behind. Caught unawares because of their carelessness, the gunners surrendered with minimal struggle.

Leaving Simon, Montrose, and the recently rescued marine to detain the two prisoners, the marines then advanced into the pillbox. From their vantage point near the boulder, captors and prisoners heard shouting and gunfire, then silence. A few minutes later, four more

German soldiers marched out of the blockhouse ahead of the armed marines.

When they reached the boulder, sublieutenants, marines, and prisoners fell in step, heading toward the knoll. Unstable ground made the downward decent on the far side treacherous. Even the prisoners understood the need for care.

Near the base of the ridge, however, one of the prisoners broke free, racing toward a well-worn path leading to the shoreline. Loose stones rolled ahead of him. He slid, ran, stumbled, and recovered repeatedly.

From his vantage point, Simon realized that the path curved back on itself, leading the escapee toward the foot of an old rock wall merely metres from his location. He scurried toward the edge, half sliding, half running over loose pebbles as the fleeing man had done. He paused atop the wall to assess his next move, then leapt, landing on the man's shoulders.

The two men slid several metres down the path's slope, gravel digging into cloth and skin indiscriminately. They came to an abrupt halt, crashing into another section of the rock wall.

As Simon struggled to his feet, he heard a high-pitched whistle and immediately felt a burning in his left leg, just above his knee. The impact sent him into the wall again, headfirst.

When the marines and their prisoners caught up with him, they found Simon as he had fallen: sprawled on top of the escapee. Two marines heaved Simon to a sitting position, exposing his injury for a medic to examine. As rifle fire whizzed overhead, Simon responded to the ministrations with grunts and gasps of agony.

"You two," the marine lieutenant said, pointing to his men, "take out that shooter before he hits someone else."

The soldier who had fled was dead, his neck fractured when he collided with the wall. By the time the medic had assessed and triaged Simon's condition, the gun tower had been located and the shooter terminated.

Two of the prisoners were ordered to aid Simon during the remaining decent while the marines maintained an active watch.

"What about our comrade?" one of the soldiers said, resisting orders to move. "You can't just leave him here!"

Simon pressed the heel of his hand against the gauze that covered a deep gash on his forehead, praying for quiet. "Someone will collect him," he replied flatly in German. "He won't be left."

"*Danke*," the soldier said, turning to follow the others.

"*Bitte*," Simon replied, casting his eyes toward a marine. "Please ensure this man's body is retrieved and buried."

"Aye, sir," the marine replied.

By the time they arrived at the shoreline, the fighting was over. Prisoners had been detained and assembled in a crude courtyard, and senior officers were subjected to preliminary enquiries.

The entire operation took less than twelve hours. Prisoners were divided amongst the three ships, which then promptly set course for Lerwick. Crew of the British submarine scoured the three captive vessels and awaited back-up, which was scheduled to arrive within eight hours. Only five German soldiers had been killed. Aside from Simon, injured Allied soldiers received only superficial wounds.

When a handful of senior *Guardian* officers, including the captain, came ashore, Montrose commandeered the sea boat. At Hartford's suggestion, Montrose stayed behind to report on the securing of the pillbox, and the marines returned Simon to *Guardian*, ensuring his immediate delivery to the sick berth.

The doctor repaired the hole in Simon's leg. The bullet had passed through the muscle, missing the femur by a millimetre. He also set two bones in Simon's left wrist and stitched a deep gash near his hairline.

Sedatives kept Simon dozing for several hours. As effects of the last injection began to ebb, he awoke slowly to a dull ache that throbbed down the left side of his body. He moaned, slitting his eyes against a dim light shining from across the room. He rolled his head to the right. Finding it too dark to see anything, he turned his face slowly toward the light again.

"How are you feeling, son?" Hartford said, sounding concerned.

Simon squinted, trying to locate the captain. A silhouette blocked the lamp light temporarily as the man lowered himself into a chair near the bed. He seemed weary.

"Alright, I guess," Simon said, his voice dry and croaky. "I presume I'll live." His eyes fluttered as he tried to make sense of what had happened. He raised his right hand toward the gash. "What time is it?"

"The first watch bell just rang," Hartford said. "Doc says you'll live. He'll keep you comfortable until we reach Lerwick. Then you'll be transferred to *Berbice*, and once you're stable, they'll send you home for a while."

"Home?" Simon said, closing his eyes to the aches. "Am I that bad off?"

"A broken wrist, a hole in your leg, multiple abrasions, and a head injury," the doctor said, coming to a standstill next to the bed. "They'll need time to mend." He reached for Simon's right hand and checked his pulse, then investigated the injury sites. "You're of no use to the ship just now. You should be mobile in a few weeks, but you'll need a few months of recuperation before you can return to full duties."

"Months!" Simon tried to rise on his elbows, feeling the cumbersome plaster hampering his left arm. "But—"

"No buts, son," Hartford said, pressing Simon into the cot. "You need to mend. As the doctor says, I suggest you do it well. You have further work to do."

"Sir?"

"I'll be back later," the doctor said, patting Simon's shoulder.

The captain followed the doctor to the door, paused to accept a message from a crewman, then closed the door and returned to the vacant chair. He scrubbed his face and peered at Simon.

"The papers that we secured from *Seabird*," Hartford said quietly, leaning toward the bed. "Thanks to you, we had vital information going in and knew what to look for. Turns out, Bear Island isn't simply a submarine base: it's a testing site. In addition to securing the vessel in which the Russian was interested, the other two vessels were prototypes as well. We haven't had time to conduct thorough interviews yet, but we do know that the submariners have been testing the vessels. In addition to test crews, we've also nabbed engineers and scientists. *Seabird* was one of several vessels used to secret supplies and personnel into the cove. We haven't discovered the Russian's role in all this, but we will."

While the captain read the message and tapped his nose in thought, Simon shifted, seeking a more comfortable position.

"Every man will undergo a thorough questioning." The captain placed a firm hand on Simon's shoulder, his eyes gleaming. "If anyone else had seen those papers, the significance might have been missed. I'm convinced that your knowledge—be it limited, as you say—of that Russian fellow and your having spotted the reference to a new submarine were critical to the success of the operation. A team is underway to take control of the island operations and intercept any communications. The longer they can delay intelligence reaching the Germans, the better it is for us. By the way, I cabled the Admiralty. This is the response." He waved the message given to him earlier by the crewman. "Instead of Lerwick, all ships involved in this mission are to report to Portsmouth directly."

"That's great news, sir," Simon said, trying to rise to an elbow as he realized the enormity of the operation. Fatigue washed over him, and he collapsed into the cot.

"I'll leave you to rest," Hartford said. "There's much to organize. The other two ships will arrive in Portsmouth before *Guardian*, though. We'll have to make haste to drop a special cargo in Newcastle first." He winked at Simon as he rose from the chair. "I'll check in later."

Moments later, Simon realized he was alone. In the quiet of the medical berth, he closed his eyes, intending to contemplate the news Hartford had shared. Sleep overwhelmed him, leaving one word to echo in his troubled dreams: *home.*

CHAPTER 8

Simon arrived home toward the end of July, courtesy of the Newcastle diversion.

During the month of August, he found himself subjected to the over-indulgent ministrations of his mother, a member of the Voluntary Aid Detachment. Three days a week, she worked at Walkergate Hospital as a volunteer nurse. On her days off Simon benefitted from her attentions, much to his chagrin.

He loved his mother dearly but, having lived on campus as a student, he had come to enjoy his independence. And, having been at sea for almost a year, he also missed the camaraderie of his shipmates. He chafed to be aboard *Guardian* again.

Lounging in the sunroom with an open book on his lap and a cooling cup of tea and a plate of orange peels nearby, his mind wandered. "How long must I be land-bound?" he grumbled aloud.

"Excuse me, sir," the butler said, appearing near the chaise lounge, "a telephone call for you."

"Who is it?" Simon said, curious yet reluctant to leave the peace of the atrium and its rare plants.

"Your father, sir," Tompkins replied. "Lord Charles

is calling from London."

"Then I suppose I'd better speak with him," Simon said, hoisting himself awkwardly from the chair as he reached for the cane that had been his companion since his return.

"I believe my office has the nearest telephone, sir," Tompkins said, eyeing Simon's unsteady gait.

Simon thanked him and hobbled after him toward the kitchen. Several minutes later, he limped quickly through the kitchen and ascended the servants' stairs to the main floor of Jarrow Hall with renewed vigour.

"Mother," he said, panting slightly from his exertion as he stopped at the entrance to his father's study.

Lady Ann sat behind his father's desk reviewing the weekly menu with the housekeeper. She lifted her eyes and focussed on her son. "Simon," she said, rising from her chair, "are you alright? You look flushed."

"Yes, Mother," he said enthusiastically. "Father just telephoned. During lunch with the king yesterday, he happened to mention that this bloody plaster—pardon me ladies." He felt heat rush to his cheeks. "He mentioned my appointment this afternoon to have the plaster removed, and that I won't be returning to duty until I'm stronger. It appears that the king has an assignment for me while I recuperate." Leaning against the door frame, he grinned under raised eyebrows. "Father asked that I travel to London tomorrow for a meeting with King George."

"That sounds intriguing," Ann said, eyeing her son. "Do you think you're up to it?"

"Absolutely!" Simon replied. "Despite everyone's kindness, I'm starting to go stir crazy. I'm looking forward to a distraction."

"Whatever could Georgie be up to," Ann mused. "Did Father say anything about the assignment?"

"No," Simon replied. "I'll hear soon enough." He straightened, smiling at the housekeeper. "I should dress for my medical appointment and think about packing for London. Mrs. Wright, do you suppose Crocker could give me a hand?"

"Certainly, sir," she replied. "If you'll excuse me, my lady, I'll look for Crocker and return shortly."

"I'll meet him in my chamber," Simon said, pushing away from the door frame. "Mother, if you'll excuse me …" He nodded and turned toward the staircase that led up to the second floor.

———•••———

"An interview with the king!" Crocker said, repeating Simon's news.

"Yes," Simon replied. "I thought I'd mention it now, so you have time to sort things while I visit the clinic." He shook himself out of his green silk lounging coat. "I'm going to need some help. Do you suppose you might be spared? Come with me to London?"

"London!" Crocker seemed keen at the idea. "I'll speak to Mr. Tompkins while you're out."

He held up a tweed jacket, inviting Simon to insert an arm. Then he settled the coat over Simon's shoulder and sling.

"If you'll excuse me, sir," he said, "I'll arrange for the motor car to be brought 'round for you."

———

The following morning, Simon and Crocker boarded the early train for London. During a subsequent telephone conversation with his father the evening before, Charles had advised that an appointment with the king had been set for late that afternoon.

"I'll meet you at Grosvenor House," Charles had said. "We can have a late lunch, then take a motor car to the palace. I can't imagine that you're up to a walk across St. James' Park just yet."

"No not yet," Simon had replied.

———

Simon and Crocker arrived at Grosvenor House just before noon.

"It's been a long while since I was here," Simon said, setting his hat on the hall table. He gazed about the black and white marbled foyer, crowned by a sparkling candelabra, a faint smile marking his recollection of old memories.

He inhaled deeply, appreciating aromas that wafted from the back of the house. "This house has a personality far different from Jarrow Hall," he said aloud. "It even smells different."

"As you say, sir," Crocker replied. "I'll take our cases up, sir, and unpack while you find your way at your own pace."

"Thanks, Crocker," Simon said. "I'll be up as quick as I can. I need to freshen up and change before lunch." He glanced at his pocket watch. "Father said he'd be home at one o'clock. I dare not dally!"

———

Simon followed his father into the private quarters of King George V.

"Your Majesty," Simon said, greeting the king with a nod of his head as he stepped forward.

"Young Simon!" George replied warmly. "How good of you to come." He gestured toward a grouping of chairs, inviting the two men to sit while coffee was poured.

When they were finally alone, the king spoke candidly. "Your father tells me that you are a talented linguist, as well as an accomplished athlete. How did you find studying at Cambridge? Do you feel it was worthwhile?"

"Yes, sir," Simon said. "I learnt a great deal and, as you know, took some of the same classes as the princes."

"Indeed," George replied. "I'm quite familiar with their studies. At the moment, however, I'm more interested in your experience."

Simon happily obliged the monarch, concluding with a modicum of regret that he was unable to seek employment after graduation. "I felt it prudent to enlist first," he said.

"Any regrets?" George said.

"No, sir," Simon replied, adding a hasty afterthought.

"It's been a rewarding experience for me."

"Indeed," George said, glancing at Simon's cane. "Your choice was admirable, Simon, and I'm grateful for your loyalty. It's most unfortunate, however, that you were injured. At the same time, it is most convenient for me." He smiled genuinely. "Your father explained my concerns, I presume?"

"He gave me some background, yes," Simon said, "but I'm not clear what you require of me."

"Let me deflect, first by enquiring about your injuries," George said. "You're still limping and using a cane. And your arm?"

"Our physician advised that my injuries have healed and that it will simply take time to recover my strength. As soon as my leg can take my full weight, the cane will disappear. As for my wrist…" Simon flexed the joint. "It's mended well enough. I just need to put it to work."

"That's good news, indeed," the king said contemplatively. "I've always worried about our children being injured. On those rare occasions when bleeding occurred, we held our breath waiting for it to stop. Injuries in our family have always been a worry." A frown darkened his countenance momentarily.

"Now, let me explain what we'd like you to do," George said, seeming to brighten with the change of topic. "If you agree to do it, of course. And excuse my repetition of anything Charles has already told you."

"Yes, sir." Simon said, straightening in his seat and leaning toward the monarch with keen interest.

"My wife and I are concerned about the current situation in Russia," George said. "In particular, we're concerned about my cousin, Nicholas, and his family. The queen and I would like to place someone in Petrograd, without going through diplomatic or military channels. We'd also prefer to avoid the Foreign Office, if possible. We'd be grateful if you would consent to act as our liaison in Petrograd; be someone in whom we can place our confidential and personal trust. Someone who will have the trust of the tsar and tsarina, as well." He rose from his chair and paced along a heavily-curtained window that rose from chair rail to high ceiling.

"We're worried for their safety," George said in conclusion, "but we have our doubts whether our current administration or the British populace would support any sort of safe harbour for them. Not that they've asked for it, mind you. If we—personally, that is—are to lend support, it will have to be discreet. We can't have others knowing about it, and we don't have time to waste. Plus, we can't keep you from your duties once you've recovered. As a result, you'll need to leave soon."

George resumed his seat, pressing his back into the chair, sighing heavily. "While we'd like to give you time to contemplate this task, we ask that you be sensitive to the urgency."

"I am honoured to have your trust," Simon said, rising from the settee. His clammy hands trembled with excitement. He placed his empty cup on the serving cart, trying not to rattle the china, and gazed at his father, who, to that point, had been remarkably quiet.

When his father blinked overlong—a motion Simon perceived as encouragement—he turned toward his host. "I will accept the challenge that you've set for me, sir." He stood at attention and nodded his head sharply, an affirmation of his promise.

"Thank you, Simon," the king said rising as well. "My wife and I are in your debt. Charles, may I impose on you to ensure that our young man is prepared for his journey?"

"You may," Charles said, rising to his feet.

"By the way," George said, "when in Russia, please present yourself as a young aristocrat, not a naval officer. You don't want to draw attention. You might also consider taking a valet along."

"Excellent idea," Charles said in agreement. "Simon still needs help. The assistance of a valet won't go amiss."

"Crocker's been most helpful," Simon said. "He's reliable and discreet. I'll speak to Tompkins when I return to Jarrow."

CHAPTER 9

The following morning, Simon received a letter from the king's equerry. The letter advised that arrangements had been made for RMS *Guardian* to meet him and Henry in Newcastle the following week, with orders to deliver them to Arkhangelsk posthaste.

The letter also suggested that, while aboard, Simon should resume limited duties and Henry might take on duties of a midshipman. As soon as a list of Henry's measurements could be provided, uniforms would be delivered, along with pamphlets and other material that the valet might find useful in understanding his duties. In closing, the equerry advised that Simon and Henry would each receive royal insignia badges to be worn on the shoulders of their uniforms.

Simon found the subsequent discussion with Henry amusing. The valet, who had been denied enlistment with the army, was quick to realize that he would soon be a midshipman, albeit temporarily and without formal training.

Later conversations reminded Simon that Henry's mother was born and raised in Paris. He was pleasantly surprised to learn that Mrs. Crocker had insisted that her children learn to read and write French from an early age.

"Why, that's marvellous!" Simon said. "French is the language of the Russian court. Your training could come in handy."

———•———

Simon's departure dinner included several of his favourite dishes.

"Cook spoils you," Charles said, rubbing his belly contentedly. "Not that I mind. Roast beef and pudding is my favourite dish too." He pushed away from the table, inviting Simon to join him in the study for a whiskey.

While Henry poured two fingers of peaty liquor into crystal glasses, Charles retrieved an item from behind his chair.

"I know your leg is healing well, and that you may not have need of a cane much longer," he said, holding the stylish cane toward Simon, "but—for the next while—you will be travelling on unsteady conveyances, and it may come in handy."

"Grandfather's cane!" Simon said. "But, Father, he willed it to you. I can't take it with me. Suppose I were to—"

Charles raised his hand to halt his son's protest. "Yes, it was my father's cane, and his father's before him, and it's a treasure, indeed." He peered at Simon as if deep in thought. "But I would like you to take it with you. It has more than one use, you see."

He raised the cane and demonstrated several defensive strokes that could be made against an assailant. Then, he held the cane parallel to the Persian carpet and released a switch on its neck. Simon heard a snick and gasped as a short blade shot out of the end of the cane.

Both men looked in Henry's direction in response to the rattling of glasses on the silver tray he held.

"Pardon, my lord," Henry said sheepishly. "The blade surprised me!" He set a whiskey glass on the table near Charles' chair and lowered the tray for Simon to retrieve the other glass. "Will that be all, sir?"

"No, Crocker," Charles said. "There's more, and you'll want to see it, if you're to be travelling with my son."

"Yes, sir." Henry stepped out of range of the cane and waited.

Simon rose and accepted the cane from his father. On examining it further, he realized that a reverse of the switch retracted the blade.

"Very clever," Simon said, grinning at Henry. "Look here …" He held up the cane to allow Henry to see the switch, engaging it to reveal the concealed blade.

"There's one more feature," Charles said, reaching for the cane. "Its structure is intricate." He turned it parallel to the rug again. "Grasp the handle here and tug the shaft just behind this band." His finger tapped an ornately-carved band near the cane's handle. "Be firm with the tug." He then returned the cane to Simon.

Simon followed his father's instructions. In response the shaft gave way, leaving a modified palm pistol in his opposite hand.

"How marvellous!" Simon said. "Here, Crocker, give it a go."

Henry stepped forward and accepted the cane. He worked the switch and the blade, then tugged the shaft to reveal the pistol. He turned the gun in his hand for a closer examination, then froze. Slowly, he raised his widened eyes to his employer.

"What is it?" Charles said, sounding concerned as he observed Henry's response.

"I just realized," Henry replied, his voice almost a whisper, "how dangerous this journey could be."

Simon laughed as he accepted return of the cane. "This from the mouth of a man who tried to enlist in the army!" he said, teasing. "Did you forget that guns are part of a military man's kit?"

"It's easy to say, sir," Henry replied, running his finger along the inside of his shirt collar and swallowing audibly, "but we don't really think about it until it comes down to the actual doing, do we?"

"That's true, Crocker," Charles said reassuringly. "It's time to keep danger in mind." He collected the parts of the cane, reassembled it, and handed it to Henry. "Now, Crocker, I'd like a few minutes alone with my son."

"Of course, my lord."

Once they were alone, Charles spoke again. "Now, let's talk about the second part of your assignment," Charles said, lowering himself into an armchair. "As you learnt at Whitehall a few days ago, finding Lebedev and unearthing his plans is not without risk. Keep any notes and correspondence secure, away from prying eyes." He reached into the pocket of his dinner jacket and retrieved a folded piece of paper. He unfolded it, scanned it, then handed it to Simon.

"I understand," Simon responded, accepting the folded paper. "What's this?"

"You'll notice two lists," Charles said, "The first is a list of names and titles of individuals who may be helpful to you. The other is a list of certain individuals of whom you should be wary. As you prepare for your journey, study it."

Charles rose and paced across the room; his hands were clasped behind his back. "Memorize it and destroy it before you leave. The individuals on those lists are highly placed or dangerous, or both." He stopped pacing and stood before Simon. "Don't presume familiarity with anyone. If you need the confidence of a contact, begin by using the code word 'tea rose' in an unassuming way."

He sighed deeply, an expression of concern masking his face. "Beware of those named on the second list." Charles' hooded eyes glared at his son. "Understood?"

"Yes, Father." Simon scanned the lists, recognizing some names, including Lebedev, Vasiliev, and Yurovsky on the wary list. The importance of his assignment radiated through his solar plexus. "Will that be all?"

"Go with God, son." Charles extended his hand again. When Simon accepted the handshake, his father drew him into a tight embrace that left the young man fighting for breath.

CHAPTER 10

"This way!" Simon said, shouting over the din. "She's at the end."

Henry pushed the luggage cart in step with Simon's hobbled gait, not taking his eyes off the surrounding activity.

"It's a challenge to push this ungainly cart around the obstacles," Henry said. "I'm worried I'll run someone over or lose your box of oranges off the top."

"Here," Simon said, grabbing a rail on the front end and bracing the orange box with his free hand. "I'll try to steer." A few minutes later, he glanced over his shoulder at the valet. "How about a breather?"

Henry nodded, and together they brought the cart to a halt out of the way of traffic.

"Phew!" Henry said panting. He removed his cap and wiped his brow with a starched white handkerchief. "Which one is RMS *Guardian*?"

"Just there," Simon replied, pointing to the camouflaged vessel towering over the end of the dock.

"Cor, she's a big one!" Henry said, whistling.

"Yes, she is," Simon said, beaming with a sense of pride.

"May I help you, sir?" a young crewman said, hurrying

toward them. A *Guardian* crest was stitched to his shirt.

"Yes," Simon said, responding to the man's salute. "Midshipman Crocker is finding it difficult to traverse the dock with this unwieldy cart."

The crewman eyed the cart dubiously, then joined Henry, and together the two men pushed the cart into motion again. Simon limped behind the cart, taking advantage of its wake. Moments later, the three men stood on the pier at the foot of the brow.

"Lieutenant Temple, sir," the crewman said, "I've been ordered to help Midshipman Crocker to his quarters. The captain is waiting for you. If you'd like to go ahead, we'll be along shortly."

Simon nodded and hobbled ahead of them, presuming he would find the captain standing on the far side of the prow, where he had first met his superior.

"Lieutenant Temple!"

Hartford's voice reached Simon across the brow. Simon's delight coursed through his veins. He saluted the captain crisply as he stopped to face him. "Captain Hartford," Simon said formally.

"Good to see you, again, son," Hartford said, "although I wasn't expecting to see you so soon." He eyed the royal insignia badge on Simon's shoulder. "Join me for dinner, second dog watch. I suspect we have a great deal to discuss."

"Thank you, sir," Simon said, blushing. "I believe we do."

"And congratulations on your promotion, by the way!" Hartford said, turning toward the stairwell. "Well earned, I'd say."

"Thank you, sir," Simon said, hesitating at the foot of the ladder. "This is where I become a hindrance. I won't hold you up." He stiffened smartly and waited while Hartford darted up the stairwell ahead of him.

Henry was already in the cabin setting the last of Simon's small things in an empty drawer. Beyond the valet, Simon noticed a door slightly ajar.

"Is that an adjoining door?" Simon said.

"Yes," Henry replied. "It's fortunate that *Guardian* once served as an ocean liner; we're able to take advantage of it. On the other hand, the door to the inside passage has been locked shut. Our only way in and out is by the deck."

"Those doors are locked in every cabin, except for the captain's," Simon said. "We'll manage fine. Normally, we'd each be sharing a bunk with a fellow officer. Captain Hartford seems to be accommodating my assignment." He glanced about the cabin.

"This arrangement is far better than I expected," Henry said. "The beds are a decent size—long enough to accommodate two tall blokes too! Plus, a bureau, a coat closet, bedside table and lamp, writing desk and chair, and a lavatory—and a small bathing tub!" With flair, he pushed a closed door ajar, revealing the bathroom.

"The cabin I shared with Montrose was similar to this," Simon said matter-of-factly, "which wasn't bad either. Lots of space, but no adjoining door. I'll make a note to thank the captain for the special allowance. Yours is the same, I presume."

"Mirror image, sir."

In that moment, the ship seemed to shudder, her sudden movement causing both men to take a sidestep and reach for something stable.

"I believe we're under way, sir," Henry said, his eyes gleaming.

"We are," Simon replied. "Shall we step outside and watch the ship pull away from the dock?"

"I'll just scoot through to my cabin and grab my cap and jacket," Henry said, disappearing through the shared door.

Simon opened the outer door and stepped into the brisk breeze that whipped the early mist across the deck in delicate swirls. Feeling it tug at the peak of his cap, he sighed with the pleasure of being on board *Guardian* again. He was ready for another adventure, even if it proved a simple, short-lived, royal assignment.

He and Henry stood at the rail, watching a pilot vessel manoeuvre *Guardian* away from the pier and into the harbour, guiding the cruiser toward open sea. A mixture of sea spray and mist ran in rivulets down their faces. They each chuckled and reached for a handkerchief.

"Well, Crocker," Simon said, his expression serious. "We're on our way. Too late to turn back now."

"I'm looking forward to it!" Henry replied, his eyes glinting with excitement.

They leaned against the rail, watching land pass by,

until the ship was well clear of land.

"Shall we go back inside?" Simon said when only sea was visible. "We have some things to discuss."

Henry nodded and disappeared through his cabin door, while Simon re-entered his own. Before he could shrug out of his coat, Henry was at his side, all signs of wind and weather tidied from his appearance. The valet took Simon's coat and hat, shook them out, and hung them on a rack near the door.

"Were you given a tour of the ship?" Simon said, lowering himself into an armchair.

"Yes, sir. I have a good idea of where everything is, and I've arranged to eat with the junior officers during the first dog watch." He grinned at his employer.

"The first dog watch?" Simon said, incredulous. "You've mastered the bells already?"

"That was the first thing my guide drilled into me," Henry said with a chuckle. "I don't mind saying to you that the lads think I'm a bit of a simpleton, because I don't know all the proper nautical terms. They seem to sense that I'm an imposter, and I don't correct them. Although … they backed off a bit when one of them pointed out the royal badge." He grinned sheepishly, the tip of his nose and cheeks reddening.

"I was given the choice of eating during the first dog watch or the second. I thought I should take the early watch so I can help you dress for dinner."

"This vessel is now classified as an armed merchant cruise ship, Henry, not an ocean liner," Simon said, chuckling. "Normally, we don't 'dress for dinner.' However, given that it's our first day at sea, and I'll be dining in the Captain's quarters, mess kit is appropriate."

Simon pointed toward an armchair. "Have a seat," he said. "Certain things about my assignment need to be discussed; things that I haven't been at liberty to say before now."

Simon explained the nature of his assignment and his expectations for Henry's role, and answered questions as best he could.

"I'll provide more details as the project unfolds," Simon said, "but that should do for now." In response to Henry's nod, he glanced at the travel clock. "It's just past noon. Hungry?"

Simon led Henry into the wardroom and indicated an as-yet unoccupied table near a window.

"Why are most of the windows covered?" Henry said.

"During foul weather and dark nights," Simon replied, "they block visibility. When it's dark on the sea, a light can be seen for miles, and the last thing we want is for the ship to be sighted by a submarine. Right now, the light remains well into the evening, so it's not much of an issue. When it's dark, however, especially later in the fall and through the winter, it's a different story."

Henry's eyes widened below a puckered brow. "I've been so focussed on everything else," he said, "that I never gave thought to submarines and the danger involved."

CHAPTER 11

Several hours later, Simon rapped on the captain's cabin door. When beckoned, he entered, saluted, and hung his cap on a hook near the door. He scanned the familiar cabin, recalling the first time that he had been invited to dine with the captain. He had remarked on the spaciousness of it, noting that it had not been converted to standard naval specifications.

Hartford had replied that the owner—Allan Line of Montréal—had insisted that the captain of any company vessel retain and occupy a luxury stateroom in its original state, as part of the ship's secondment by the British fleet.

"Whiskey?" the tall, swarthy captain said, pouring the amber liquid into two crystal glasses. "Neat, if I recall correctly."

"Thank you, sir," Simon replied, "yes."

Hartford handed Simon a glass and invited him to sit in one of the armchairs. "Dinner will be along in a few minutes," Hartford said. "Shall we talk about your assignment in the meantime?"

Simon nodded, inviting the captain to continue.

"I understand that our mission is on a need-to-know basis." Hartford took a sip of the whiskey, seeming to contemplate his next thought. "Is there anything you can tell me aside from the fact that we are to deliver you to Arkhangelsk posthaste?" His salt-and-pepper brows rose questioningly.

"You'll be pleased to hear—if you don't already know—that the detained personnel recovered from Bear Island were released to authorities in Portsmouth, and have all been questioned," Simon said. "Although the German officers were less forthcoming, the civilians proved quite agreeable. Overall, Operation Bear Island is considered a success."

"I've heard that, yes," Hartford replied.

"My task in Petrograd will be to find Lebedev, determine his interest in the submarine, and any other information that may be a threat—whether to England, Russia or elsewhere," Simon said. "The hope is that I will uncover sufficient information by the end of the year to thwart Lebedev's plan. If I can't, then I am to remain in Petrograd for as long as it takes. Crocker, on the other hand, will meet you in Arkhangelsk for return to England at the designated time, regardless."

Simon sipped his whiskey, contemplating whether any other information was relevant. "I'm expected in Petrograd by the end of September," he said. "While we're aboard, I'd like to carry out any duties for which you think I'm suitable. I also intend to participate in fitness drills; I need to build up my strength. So, if you have duties that don't involve manual labour, two sturdy legs, or a strong left wrist, I'm your man."

He rolled his glass, watching the whiskey trickle down the sides. "Crocker, on the other hand, is ready, willing, and able, but has no training. He is employed at Jarrow Hall as my valet, and he will continue to be so once we disembark. However, if his skills can be of use … he is meant to blend in as much as possible, and he knows to be discreet."

"Very well," Hartford said, "then he should feel free to participate in any drills that interest him, and I will consider some easier duties for him—to help him blend in."

A rap sounded at the inside door, announcing the arrival of an undercook pushing a dinner trolley.

In the hour that followed, Simon reported on the time he spent with his family during his recovery and enquired after Montrose. He expressed delight at the news that his friend had recently been promoted to lieutenant as well, and that he was currently in Kirkwall with a prize crew.

"He should be with us by year end," Hartford said. "I expect you'll catch up then." Hartford straightened as Simon swallowed the last of his wine. "Eight bells!" He dabbed at the corner of his mouth with a napkin. "Time to go."

"Of course," Simon said rising slowly to his feet. He fastened the buttons of his coat and collected his cap from a nearby hook.

"By the way," Hartford said as he removed his dress jacket and hung it in his closet. "Have you ever examined a tea rose?"

Simon's head snapped toward the captain, his eyes

wide.

"Sir?" Simon said. "I've heard about the tea rose, but I've yet to examine one."

"You have my ear and my support, should you require either," Captain Hartford said, smiling kindly.

"Thank you, sir," Simon replied, settling his cap on his head, "and you mine."

Before opening the exterior door, he saluted and thanked the captain for his hospitality.

"Mind how you go, Lieutenant."

When Simon entered his cabin, Henry was waiting for him, reaching for his jacket. "Good evening, my lord," Henry said. "Was the meal to your liking?"

"It was, indeed, Crocker," Simon replied.

Simon's bed had been turned back and his nightclothes rested at its end.

"I think I'll retire, Crocker," he said. "By the way, I spoke with Captain Hartford. He advised that you are welcome to participate in any drills, and he will request some light duties to keep you occupied."

"I look forward to it, my lord!"

"And Crocker," Simon said, "I think you should drop 'my lord,' at least until we're off the ship. 'Sir' will do."

"Yes, my l- er, sir," Henry replied, appearing flustered.

CHAPTER 12

Before the morning watch, Simon and Henry reviewed the list of drills scheduled for the week, then made their way to an outer deck. Leaning against a taffrail, they each peeled their way through one of Simon's coveted oranges and discussed possibilities.

"Since you're new to this," Simon said, "I recommend the man-overboard drill. The physical drill is worthwhile too." He gazed toward the horizon, contemplating. "Have you ever handled a firearm?"

"I have," Henry replied.

"Then you might consider participating in the rifle drill and the small arms drill. You would probably benefit from the marines-to-infantry drill as well. There's a big gun drill later in the week. You'll have no need for that training, but I highly recommend observing it; the process is impressive."

Simon knuckle-scrubbed the new growth on his right cheek. "I'll be on the bridge for each of the morning watches," he said. "Aside from that, I plan to attend as many firearm, marine-to-infantry, and physical drills that I can in the short time that we're aboard. I need to strengthen my wrist and leg."

"I've been assigned to light duties during the morning watch as well," Henry replied. "I'll make a point of attending physical drills with you, if you don't mind."

"Excellent idea!" Simon replied. "By the way, you said that you've handled a firearm. I had no idea. Tell me about it."

"I used to help my da lay rabbit snares and shoot grouse and small game when I was a boy. When he retired and my oldest brother became gamekeeper of the Hall, I entered service. I haven't had reason to fire a gun since."

"Well, you might give some thought to picking one up again," Simon said encouragingly. "Given the current political climate, you might find the training to be an asset in the future. I hope you don't have a need, but ..." Simon shrugged. "One never knows. There's a rifle drill an hour before the physical drill."

"I'll give it some thought," Henry replied, seeming hesitant. "I don't fancy the thought of shooting anyone."

"Regardless," Simon said, pushing himself away from the rail, "if I don't see you before, I'll see you at the physical drill this afternoon."

"Yes, sir," Henry said, standing to attention and saluting.

Simon grinned and returned the salute. "By the way, Crocker," Simon said, "what do you say to honing your French and learning some basic Russian? If you're interested, we could set aside some time each day and work on that too."

"I'd be very grateful for that, sir," Henry replied.

"How about I review our interests and create a schedule for us?"

"Great idea, Crocker!" Simon said.

That afternoon, Henry surprised Simon, appearing at his side just in time to receive a rifle. A marine officer guided the men through various exercises, including target practice, affixing bayonets, and how to use them. Simon expressed surprise at the accuracy of Henry's marksmanship and acknowledged the valet's complaint that fixing bayonets exceeded his expectations.

"I don't like the idea either," Simon said, "but conditioning is important."

"I suppose," Henry said. "It just goes against my conscience to kill anyone."

"War is a nasty business," Simon said, jabbing an amicable punch to his valet's arm, "and I'm happy knowing that you'll have my back should the need arise. Come on. We'd better get changed for the physical drill."

Unlike his earlier training, Simon found the physical drill difficult. Although invigorating, he was acutely aware of the limitations his recent injuries presented. He gasped when a sharp pain shot through his leg, forcing him to step away and massage it before continuing.

"Crocker, I had no idea you were so fit!" Simon said as the deck cleared of participants. "I was surprised to see how well you kept up with the others."

"Well, there's plenty of exercise to be had in service," Henry replied matter-of-factly. "Running up and down the stairs several times a day, fetching and carrying."

He blushed. "I'm sorry, sir, I'm sure you are well aware of my duties."

"I am," Simon acknowledged, "but I've never given serious thought to the effort they entail. These drills will be good for both of us!"

"Yes, sir."

Simon mopped his face with a towel, sensing a slowing of the ship. He leaned over the rail, then pointed for Henry to observe the lowering of a sea boat.

"They're off to investigate that barque: SS *Delft*. The flag suggests she's Dutch."

Simon and Henry watched as *Guardian* circled the detained vessel while marines boarded it. Some time later, the crew signalled the all-clear and returned.

"You read the flagman's all-clear, didn't you?" Henry said.

Simon nodded.

"I can see how it would be beneficial to understand the signals too," Henry said. "If we have time, I should like to learn."

"Perhaps one day, Crocker," Simon said, "you will."

When *Guardian's* speed increased, the two men pushed away from the railing and headed for their cabins.

"This has been an interesting day, sir," Henry said as he hung an ironed shirt in the closet. "I enjoyed watching the prize crew board that ship. I wonder how many vessels are actually boarded in a day."

"It depends more on what vessels cross *Guardian's* path than meeting any quota," Simon replied. "Have you changed your mind about the shooting?"

"Yes and no," Henry said, putting laundered items into drawers. "I still can't imagine killing another human being; but, as you say, better to be prepared. I'll continue with the training. Who knows what the future might bring?"

He placed clean nightclothes at the foot of Simon's bed. "Sir, might there be an opportunity for me to observe on the bridge?"

"I don't see why not," Simon replied. "Let me speak with an officer of the watch.

"Thank you, sir," Henry said with earnest. "I'd appreciate that."

———————

Eight days later, Hartford appeared on the bridge during the morning watch. "Lieutenant Temple," he said, approaching Simon and Henry.

The two young men snapped to attention.

"We're nearing the White Sea and your destination. We'll continue to patrol the coastal area tonight. Tomorrow morning, we'll dock in Arkhangelsk."

"Thank you, sir," Simon said. "It was great to be back on board, even if my duties are short-lived. I'm looking forward to fulfilling my assignments in Petrograd; yet I'm disheartened to be leaving the ship so soon."

"If all goes well," Hartford said, "we'll be back to retrieve you in a few months."

Simon nodded.

"And you, Midshipman," Hartford said. "Have you

enjoyed our hospitality?"

"I have, indeed, sir," Henry said, his eyes alight. "I'm very grateful that you've permitted me the opportunity, even it if was a ruse."

"Perhaps you'll give the navy a try, when your duties in Russia are fulfilled."

"Sir?" Henry's eyebrows almost engaged with his hairline. "Me? In the navy? But I—"

"I'm aware of your … impediment," Hartford said, rocking on his heels. "But, if you're interested, and available"—he glanced toward Simon—"I'd be happy to put in a good word. The navy is always looking for good men with potential."

"Yes, sir! I'd be honoured, sir!" Henry glanced shyly at Simon.

"Follow your dream, Crocker," Simon said encouragingly.

Simon and Henry worked together to ensure their belongings were packed in a timely manner and that both were able to attend a last meal aboard the ship before disembarking.

When Henry returned at the end of the first dog watch, he reported to Simon that the officers had been kind to toast his accomplishments while onboard and wished him well.

"I should have our last things packed and ready to go when you return, sir," he said. He snatched the clothes brush and whisked the shoulders of Simon's jacket. "The captain's suggestion of full mess kit for this evening is a nice send-off, don't you think?" He stood back and admired Simon's dress uniform. "Very handsome, sir, if I do say so!"

Simon preened as he considered his full mess kit in the large mirror that hung on the outside of the clothes closet. "It is a smart uniform," he said, pressing the front of his tunic. "These days, there's not much opportunity to wear it though."

By the time the lines of RMS *Guardian* were secured to cleats, Simon was at the rail standing next to Captain Hartford. "Thank you, again, Captain," he said.

"You're most welcome, *Lord* Temple," Hartford said, smiling as he regarded the young earl, now clean-shaven and attired as a young aristocrat. "Mind how you go."

"I will, sir." Simon saluted the captain. "I wish you a safe journey as well, and hope to see RMS *Guardian*, her captain, and her crew hale and hearty before the end of the year." With one last nod to the captain, Simon crossed the brow and headed for the ferry terminal.

PART TWO

CHAPTER 13

Simon scanned the archaic port of Arkhangelsk as he limped across the tarmac. He was grateful for his grandfather's cane, yet felt renewed strength in his leg and wrist. His superficial wounds had healed, and the seaboard drills had been helpful.

Realizing that the dock had few modern conveniences, he was struck with the thought that the trains may be just as archaic. *It's busy and industrious, though*, he argued with himself. *One can only hope.*

Relieved of naval duties, Simon mentally mulled over the notes he had written in preparation for the next leg of his journey: by train, the imperial capital of Petrograd was about 1,173 kilometres, or 730 miles. He and Henry would have to change trains in Vologda. However, before they could reach Vologda, he needed two ferry tickets to transport them and their luggage across the Northern Dvina River to the train station on the left bank.

While Simon set off to purchase their tickets, Henry oversaw the delivery of their luggage to the ferry terminal. Two crewmen assisted him to the terminal, then abandoned him for *Guardian*.

As Simon tucked the tickets into an inside pocket,

he spied Henry near the terminal entrance trying to convince a dock worker to help him with their luggage. Puzzled, the man scrubbed his hatless head and shrugged.

Simon quickly intervened, apologizing for Henry's limited Russian and asking for aid. He held a fisted hand toward the man, who seemed to understand Simon's intention. The man extended his own hand, accepting the concealed currency.

The dock worker whistled shrilly to attract the attention of his co-workers. Together, they loaded the luggage onto a small wagon and hauled it onto the ferry. Henry followed closely, keeping an alert eye on their belongings.

"Meet me on the main deck," Simon hollered before Henry disappeared into the ferry's hold.

———

Simon was leaning against a railing on the stern of the ferry when Henry found him.

"Look at this!" Simon remarked. "Isn't it amazing!" He panned the river and city in the distance. "We're so close to the Arctic Circle. The average person wouldn't dream of industry so far north but … there it is!"

He pointed out some of the highlights, including a market, a small herd of reindeer, and hut-like buildings with thatched roofs.

"I wish we had more time to poke around," Simon said. "I think we'd learn so much here about the history of Russia."

When the ferry began to distance itself from the dock, Simon shoved away from the rail, heading toward the opposite side of the ship.

"Things here are about to change," Simon said as the left bank neared. "Naval activity will increase as the war continues. See there"—he pointed toward the approaching dock—"a good percentage of the people heading for the train are military."

"Speaking of trains," Henry said, "were you able to find suitable passage?"

"Yes," Simon replied. "When I purchased the ferry tickets, I was able to purchase train tickets as well. Now we can board the train directly. And … you're in for a treat."

Simon glanced at Henry mischievously. "We have three days on the first train—which is small, not what we're used to in England—then we transfer to a larger one in Vologda for a few more days. I didn't care for the look of the second-class passenger cars on either train."

He raised his hand to shield his eyes and gazed at the dock as the ferry slid into its berth. "The seats are wooden benches. I couldn't imagine you rocking on a wooden bench for three days, after the comforts of *Guardian*?" He shook his head and glanced sideways at Henry. "I've booked you a first-class berth next to mine, all the way."

Henry's eyes widened. "Truly, sir?"

"Yes, Crocker, truly," Simon said, laughing. "You'll have a bit of a jaunt to the luggage car, but I think your bones will be grateful at the end of each day."

"Very grateful, I'd say, sir," Henry replied. "Thank you!"

"Is it just me, Crocker," Simon said, a few hours later, "or does this train seem to be moving remarkably slow?" Simon made a face, looking up from an assortment of rye bread, biscuits, and strong-smelling cheese. "I bet any horse in Jarrow Hall's stable could easily outrun this rattle trap!"

"It does feel slow," Henry replied, "compared to busy sea days on the ship." Spying his employer's inspection of an empty cup, he sprang to his feet and collected an urn from a nearby counter. "Let me, sir!" When the cup was full of steaming tea, he resumed his seat.

"It doesn't help that we stop at every village," Simon lamented. "Maybe it's time to break out the playing cards. There's not much else to do … unless someone decides to commit a crime." He wiggled his dark brows for emphasis.

"I expect that's highly unlikely, sir," Henry replied, chuckling at Simon's animated response. "Once we're finished with breakfast, I'll dig out the cards."

True to the observation, the train ride over barren and sparsely-populated landscape proved dull and uneventful. The young earl and his valet passed the time with card games and reading, but were certain to step off for fresh air at any stop where time permitted.

After three days of rocking on the small train, Simon and Henry were happy to abandon it and board the larger transport headed for Petrograd. Knowing that they were mere days from the imperial city, their anticipation increased, and they found themselves restless.

CHAPTER 14

On the last evening of their journey from Vologda to Petrograd, Simon and Henry attempted to pass the time with a card game. However, thoughts of their pending arrival in Petrograd rendered their dinner bland and the game uninteresting. Half-way through the second hand, they agreed to abandon it. Instead, they opted for the lounge, hoping a drink might help.

Cigar smoke hung heavy in the car, as if snagged by the thick, velvet draperies that swung gently in rhythm with the train's rocking. Several of the plush, red chairs and sofas held occupants who chatted companionably. A bar situated against the forward wall and soft lighting created a welcoming ambiance.

"This car offers comfort to those who can afford it," Henry said quietly. "I feel for the poor sods in the lower-class cars."

"I'm sorry to say," Simon said, "that most of them won't ever know the difference, unless they have an opportunity to peer through a window." He handed Henry a glass of port and sat opposite him.

For a while, neither spoke, enjoying the atmosphere of the coach and the antics of its other occupants.

"Crocker, you're not drinking," Simon said, noting that his own glass was nearly empty.

"I've never been much of a drinker," Henry replied, "but being served a tot of watered-down rum every day while on the ship weakened my resolve to never drink. My grandfather, you'll recall, drank too much, and made our home life miserable. I don't want to be like him."

"Your father never touched alcohol, did he?" Simon said.

"No, never. He had the same worry," Crocker replied. "I won't have much opportunity for drink when I return to England, so I'd best wean myself now. I'll just sip. Besides, I don't feel particularly comfortable in the current company."

"Do you find two statesmen and a handful of Russian officers intimidating?" Simon said.

"That, and the way the older officer seems to be treating his daughter," Henry replied, sipping his port. "She is beautiful, isn't she? A chap like me would never have a chance with someone like her."

"She is attractive," Simon said, regarding the young woman, "but I'm not convinced that she's his daughter; I think she's sitting too close."

Henry choked and sputtered a mouthful of port. He quickly snatched a handkerchief from his pocket and mopped his face. "You seem to be enjoying the conversation," Henry replied, croaking on his words. "Are you able to follow it?"

"I am," Simon said. "They're discussing current politics. It never hurts to know the opinion of the locals."

He glanced sideways toward the heated discussion between the elder statesman and the senior officer.

"If you'll excuse me, sir," Henry said, whispering as he leaned toward Simon. "I think I'll turn in for the night."

"Of course," Simon replied wearily. "I won't be long. I know we've an early start, and the smoke in here is overwhelming."

"As you say, sir. Good night." Henry rose from his chair and staggered slightly against the rhythm of the train.

"Easy, Crocker!" Simon said, raising a hand as if to block the valet's fall.

"I'm fine, sir. Good night, again."

As Henry made his way toward the door, Simon noticed the young woman begin to rise.

"Where are you going?" the older officer said harshly, grabbing her wrist.

Simon tensed, preparing to intervene if necessary. A quick look toward Henry suggested that he had the same idea.

The officer's action seemed to startle the young woman. She braced herself against another lurch of the train, placing her free hand on a chair back.

"I'm tired," she said shakily, blushing at the attention. "If you'll excuse me, I'd like to retire." She gazed down at the hand that pinned her wrist to the table.

"Very well," the officer said, releasing her wrist with a casual snap. "But don't expect me to join you anytime soon. I'm enjoying this conversation." He glared at her from under knitted brows. The smile below them appeared far from pleasant. "You! Egorov! See that Mrs. Voronov reaches her berth safely."

"With pleasure, sir!" a young officer said, jumping to his feet and saluting his commander. As he approached the young woman, he offered his elbow.

She placed her small, gloved hand within the crook of it and turned to the others. "Good night," she said softly, allowing Egorov to lead her toward the door.

Simon's tension eased, but he did not relax. While he was unable to isolate the source of his discomfort, he sensed that the elder officer was likely involved. *Her eyes don't reflect the pleasantness of her voice.*

As the two neared him, Simon noticed Mrs. Voronov tighten her grip on Egorov's arm. *Looks like she's afraid of that old fellow. Curious.*

Henry held the smoking car door open and let them pass ahead of him, his brow wrinkled in a frown.

Henry's departure left Simon sitting alone. He raised the refreshed glass of port and sipped, noting the senior officer summon a private and speak quietly in the man's ear.

"Excuse me, sir," the private said, startling Simon from his thoughts. "Major Vasiliev asks that you join the table for a game of cards. You will have noticed the empty chair."

Vasiliev! Simon stiffened at the name and glanced toward the table, where the major raised a hand in beckoning. *How fortuitous,* he thought, nodding to acknowledge the invitation.

Before Simon accepted the chair offered, he extended

his hand toward the major. "Simon Temple," he said, glancing around the table in time to catch the slight widening of the elder statesman's eyes.

"My comrades," Vasiliev said, waving his arm around the table. "Let me introduce my brother-in-law, Statesman Maksim Lebedev and his aide Aleksandr Volkov, and …"

While Vasiliev's introductions continued, Simon's mind struggled to put faces to each name, distracted to realize that he sat at the same table as Lebedev and Vasiliev, the two individuals he had been assigned to locate and, if necessary, intervene against. Slowly, his thoughts cleared into order.

Although the card game and banter resumed, Simon felt as if he were an insect under a microscope, catching odd glances between Vasiliev and Lebedev. *I wonder what's going through their minds*, Simon thought, adding another card to his hand. He grinned at the others as the next round began.

CHAPTER 15

As the train rolled toward the Petrograd station, Simon and Henry stood in the hallway outside their berth, peering through the carriage windows to watch the Imperial City revealed before them.

"Sir," Henry said, "I observed something last evening. I think you should know."

Simon glanced at Henry and returned his attention to the scenes flicking past the window. "Go on," he said.

"You'll recall that, when I returned to my berth last evening, the young woman and the soldier were ahead of me."

"The young woman is Mrs. Voronov, and the soldier is Lieutenant Egorov," Simon said, nodding.

"Yes, sir," Henry replied. "They stopped at the berth we've known to be occupied by the older officer and the young woman. As I unlocked my door, I noticed that E-egorov had Mrs. V-voronov in a light embrace." He spoke the names hesitantly, unfamiliar with the pronunciation. "I suspected he was consoling her, until I saw a look of surprise when she noticed me. That made me wonder whether there's more to their relationship. Especially since the young officers are supposed to be billeted in the next car."

Simon tore his gaze from the window and peered at Henry quizzically. "That could indeed suggest a curious situation," Simon said. "I don't know that it will have any bearing on our business, but consider it noted, Crocker. Thank you."

A whistle and a slowing in the train's movement interrupted the conversation.

"Let's watch from the smoking car," Simon said, leading the way along the corridor. "We'll have a better view, and someone might point out some highlights."

———

"Good morning, Mr. Temple," Maksim Lebedev said, his English seemingly stilted from lack of use. "We didn't have time for a proper conversation last evening. Too much frivolity." He eyed Simon overtly. "Tell me, how do you plan to pass your time in Petrograd?"

"My colleague and I have been engaged by the British government to review plans concerning the Murman coast development. While we're here, we hope to enjoy some of the beauty and history of Petrograd as well," Simon replied, sensing the same scrutiny he had experienced the evening before. "This is my companion, Henry Crocker, by the way. Mr. Crocker abandoned us before you had an opportunity to meet him last evening. Henry, Mr. Lebedev is one of the Russian statesmen I mentioned earlier."

Simon saw Henry's eyes flicker in response to the statesman's name. He admired the valet's ability to conceal his reaction and readily adapt to the circumstance. *I'm glad I brought him along. He will be an asset, indeed.*

"Then I must point out a few highlights before we enter the station," Lebedev said, appearing dubious as he drew them further into the smoking car and asking for tea service.

The train rumbled slow and heavy through the city, their guide pointing out obvious sights, including the dome of St. Isaac's Cathedral, the walls of the Peter and Paul Fortress, and the spires of the Church of Our Saviour on Spilled Blood.

"You must make time to visit the cathedrals and the Fortress. You will find much amazing history and beauty there. And, of course, there are the palaces. Surely, you will be invited Mr. Temple?" He let the inference dangle, as if hoping Simon might elaborate his intentions in Petrograd.

"I don't suppose the palaces are open for public tours when the royals are absent? I recall reading somewhere that they're not usually in residence at this time of year," Simon said, countering Lebedev's taunt.

"Perhaps. I suggest you enquire at your hotel," Lebedev replied evasively. "There is one palace you must visit for certain, however. You'll find it on Yelagin Island, a small island right in the centre of the city! They say"—he raised his hand as if to share a secret—"that, some years ago, the tsar—he was only *tsesarevich* at the time—had an affair with a Polish ballerina, and he *kept* her there." He winked, then turned toward the car's door as officers entered.

"Major Voronov, is it?" Simon said, nodding discreetly

toward the officer entering the car. "Am I recalling his name correctly?"

The statesman snorted at Simon's presumption. "Don't let him hear you say that!"

As if in response to Simon's startled expression, he elaborated. "Major *Vasiliev*. Mrs. Voronov is his—ahem—mistress. If Mrs. Vasiliev knew of the arrangement … well, I'd hate to be within earshot, to put it simply." He smirked, seemingly pleased at his understatement. "She's the one with the deep purse. If she knew what he was up to …" He drew a finger knife-like across his throat. "That would be the end of *everything* for him."

"Good morning, Major Vasiliev," Simon said, greeting the elder officer as he neared. "I was hoping to see you before we reached the station to thank you for the enjoyable evening."

The major's eyes seemed cold and disinterested when he greeted Simon with an insincere smile and reached for a cup of tea.

"Will Mrs. Voronov be joining you?" Simon said, minding the major's eyes.

Vasiliev seemed to contemplate the tall, young man before replying. He inhaled deeply, standing taller and peering down his nose at Simon. His actions had no effect on Simon, since the officer stood six inches short of Simon's chin, his height dwarfed by his robust belly.

The officer stepped back as if to lessen the tilt of his head. "Mrs. Vasiliev will be greeting me at the station," he said curtly, glaring at Simon. "The woman to whom you refer has made other travel arrangements."

Terminating the opportunity for ongoing conversation, the major turned on his heel and joined his subordinates. Lebedev excused himself and trailed behind.

CHAPTER 16

Simon noticed that the young officer, Egorov, was also absent from the military party.

"Where's his daughter?" Henry said quietly, leaning toward Simon. "I thought I heard reference to Mrs. Voronov."

"Ah, well that's an interesting story," Simon replied, his voice low. A mischievous grin threatened at the edges of his lips. "It seems that she is not his daughter, nor is she his wife—which is what I thought. The young lady who accompanied the major last evening may well be his little something-on-the-side. Apparently, his wife is to meet him at the station. Furthermore, given the absence of Lieutenant Egorov, I'd say that he's been tasked with the job of discreetly whisking the poor woman away."

"That explains part of what I saw last evening," Henry said, sotto voce. "Presuming she was his daughter, I wondered whether they were secretly carrying on behind her father's back."

"Well, that may yet be," Simon replied. "She could have the two of them on the hook." He shrugged, glancing covertly toward Vasiliev. "I've heard of stranger arrangements."

"Aye, so have I," Henry said, "but I feel like something's amiss."

Henry gazed out a window, watching the cityscape transform into a train station, then straightened as if a reflection in the window roused a thought. "Sir, those two men"—he tipped his head toward the military party—"Vasiliev and Lebedev … you mentioned them on the ship."

"Later," Simon replied, curtailing Henry's line of questioning.

When the screech of the train's wheels ended further conversation, Simon motioned for he and Henry to return to their berth. Several minutes later, Simon stepped down from the car onto the platform, his fedora planted firmly on his head. Spying a porter, he used his grandfather's cane to catch the man's attention.

Henry followed Simon off the train, carrying their small valises. As Simon provided instructions to the porter, he noticed Lieutenant Egorov descend the steps, scanning the platform as he did so. At the foot of the steps, the officer stopped, turned, and reached upward.

Mrs. Voronov gathered her dove-grey skirt and stepped down. As she did so, her free hand reached for the one extended by Lieutenant Egorov. While Simon appreciated the brief view of her daintily-booted ankles, his attention was drawn particularly to her broad-brimmed hat, from which a heavy veil fell. Had he not known her silhouette from the evening before, and her escort, he would have been unable to recognize her. He glanced at

Henry, noting from the valet's expression that he likely had similar thoughts.

In the next moment, the train's shrill whistle pierced the station and echoed off the tile walls. Mrs. Voronov raised her hands to protect her ears, the motion freeing the veil to flutter in an unexpected current caused by a discharge of steam.

"Mrs. Voronov," Simon said, calling out as he strode forward.

Simon's crisp greeting startled the woman and her escort. They each looked toward Simon with blank stares.

"I'm sorry to disturb you," Simon said as he approached them. "We missed you earlier when the train was winding through the city. We had hoped to say goodbye. Major Vasiliev informed us that you have made other travel arrangements."

Catching Simon's eye, Henry nodded toward the porter who waited for him.

"Of course, Crocker. You tend to the luggage while I say goodbye. I'll catch up with you shortly."

Leaning cavalierly on his grandfather's cane, Simon attempted to engage Mrs. Voronov in conversation for a few more minutes. He was curious to note whether her behaviour revealed anything more. He encouraged her and her escort to step further into the platform, away from the car, but before they could do so, the engine discharged more billows of steam, setting Mrs. Voronov's heavy veil aflutter once again. She snatched it and held it fast.

"This is the final stop," the lieutenant said. "The

engineer must take the train into the maintenance yard." He stood beside the young lady, tall and straight, if not a little anxious.

"Hopefully, Crocker and the porter can discharge our luggage quickly then," Simon replied, quirking one side of his mouth into a half grin.

"Have you made arrangements for transportation?" the lieutenant said, sounding disinterested.

"No, not yet," Simon replied. "I'm not confident that we have accommodation." Simon twisted toward the back of the train. Spying Henry and the porter headed toward him with a luggage cart, he realized that he had little time to enquire further. Any attempt to engage Mrs. Voronov in conversation so far had failed. She hung back, either distracted or unresponsive. Instead, the lieutenant provided directions to the passenger stand.

"I don't suppose you might recommend accommodations?" Simon said. "This is our first time in Petrograd. We have suggestions from friends, but a recommendation from residents would be most welcome."

Mrs. Voronov fidgeted, clearly anxious to be away. She turned toward the train abruptly, the whine of rolling wheels seeming to alarm her. In that moment, her veil fluttered again, the breeze lifting it away from her face. She reached to pull it down, but her response was too late; Simon saw what she appeared determined to conceal. Her left cheek was swollen and red, her eye beginning to show signs of deep bruising.

"I say, Madame," Simon was quick to respond. "Are you

alright? I mean …" He turned a questioning gaze toward the lieutenant, noting Henry's approach as he did so.

"Come, my dear," Egorov said. A small scar near the corner of his left eye twitched as he seemed to ignore Simon's question. "We should be going." He placed a white-gloved hand on Mrs. Voronov's back and began to lead her away.

"I'm sure you will find suitable accommodation anywhere," Egorov said, speaking over his shoulder. "Please excuse us."

Mrs. Voronov held the veil securely and dipped her head, using the brim of her hat to hide her face. With her other hand tucked firmly in Egorov's elbow, the two briskly departed.

"She's so lovely, is she not? Henry said, his eyes seeming to soften as he watched the man and woman disappear around a corner.

"She is," Simon replied. "Pity about her face, though."

"That's of little consequence," Henry said, his brown eyes puppy-round. "I glimpsed the bruising when her veil lifted. It will only mar her beauty temporarily, not replace it."

Simon gave Henry a quizzical glance. Noting the valet's rapture, he bit back a retort. "Well, Crocker," Simon said, stepping out of the path of the luggage cart, "I think you're correct. Something's afoot, and I intend to discover what that might be." Turning to the porter, Simon asked to be taken to the area designated for passenger pick-up.

As they neared the pick-up area, a dark, horse-drawn

coach rounded the corner of the train station, the emblem of the British Embassy clearly marked on its doors.

"Good morning, Lord Simon," the driver said. "The ambassador received your telegram from Vologda. Everything is ready for you."

CHAPTER 17

Twenty minutes later, the conveyance stopped at the entrance of the British Embassy.

"Sir," the driver said, "please use that door. You'll be directed to the ambassador's office."

The large door to which he pointed opened slowly to reveal a uniformed guard. "Arrangements have been made for you to stay at the Trezzini Palace Hotel, until other accommodation can be arranged."

"Thank you," Simon replied. "Crocker, I'd appreciate it if you'd go with the driver to the hotel."

"Of course, my lord."

"And look into whether any oranges can be had in this city, will you?"

Before the carriage pulled away from the embassy, Simon stepped through a great oak door and into a marbled hallway.

"The ambassador is expecting you, my lord," the guard said, his British accent evident. "If you'll follow me …" He swept his arm, indicating the way, and led Simon up a semi-circular staircase to the balconied floor above. At the second door opposite the balcony, he rapped briskly, opened it, and announced Simon's arrival.

"Lord Simon," Sir George Buchanan said, rising from a chair behind an ornamental desk strewn with official-looking papers, "welcome!"

Sir George extended his hand as he approached and shook Simon's heartily. "We've been waiting for you! Please, do sit down." He led Simon toward a sofa and two wing-backed chairs. "It's a tad early for lunch. Perhaps some tea?"

"That would be appreciated," Simon replied. "I was up early this morning, and have had little time for a meal."

"Excuse me a moment," he said. "Let me speak with my secretary. She'll make arrangements." Sir George turned on his heel and disappeared out the door.

Minutes later, he was seated across from Simon, lounging comfortably in the second wing-backed chair. "Now, I know that I am obliged to bring you up to speed regarding the tsar and his family, and the state of politics in Russia, but, if I may, I'd certainly enjoy hearing of your adventures at sea while we await our tea." He rubbed his palms together as if to warm them, and grinned widely at Simon, an invitation for him to begin.

"I presume you are aware of my service as a naval officer. A few months ago, I was involved in a skirmish, during which I received injuries that required home rest." Simon massaged his leg as he spoke. "They still pain me from time to time, but each day is better than the last. I'm confident that I'll be able to return to duty when my tasks here are complete."

"Ah! That explains the matter of your availability

quite clearly," Sir George replied.

Simon nodded and described life at sea enthusiastically, providing details that he thought might interest Sir George. When the tea arrived, he embraced the interruption long enough to prepare a scone with clotted cream and raspberry jam. He took a few bites and washed it down with a sip of hot tea. Then he dusted his hands and sat back into the chair, appreciating the comfort and the space in which to stretch his legs. He told the ambassador of the train journey from Arkhangelsk to Vologda and the subsequent transfer to the high-speed train.

"The journey to Vologda was fairly uneventful," Simon continued. "However, we met some very interesting individuals when we changed trains, including two statesmen: a Major Vasiliev, some junior officers, and a Mrs. Voronov."

"You met Major Vasiliev and Mrs. Voronov?" Sir George said with awe. "Do tell. I am very interested to know more about their relationship. Not as a gossip, mind; that is for old women. No, in our business it is helpful to have knowledge of assorted intrigues. Allows us to at least keep pace with, if not have a leg up on, some of the folks with whom we must engage." He winked at Simon.

Simon glanced at the remainder of his scone. Before he could decide whether to eat it, he had the plate in his hand and was chewing. He smiled at the diplomat as he set the plate on the table and reached for his cup and saucer.

"Oh, surely that has gone cold," Sir George said, fussing over his guest. "Leave that and take a fresh one."

In an instant, he retrieved an empty cup and poured hot tea for the young lord.

The distraction allowed Simon time to collect his thoughts and decide what might be of interest to the ambassador. In the end, he shared the entire series of events involving the major and Mrs. Voronov, including his suspicion that the young lady may have been beaten. He chose to withhold his knowledge of Lebedev and Vasiliev, and their possible involvement in the Bear Island incident.

"Your story, sir, does not surprise me. I've heard that Major Vasiliev can be, shall we say, assertive. One does not want to be out of step with him. He has been known to wield some power in the military quarter, despite his demotion."

Sir George sipped his own tea, frowning. "Drat! Now mine's gone cold." He reached for the tea carafe and warmed the remains in his cup. "You mentioned other travelling companions—statesmen?"

Simon sat forward in his chair, setting his cup and saucer on the table. "I was introduced to both, but I only conversed with Maksim Lebedev. I think the other may be his aide. I'm sorry, I don't recall his name."

"Would that have been Aleksandr Volkov?" the ambassador said.

"Yes! Do you know him?" Simon replied.

"Let's just say that I've been introduced to him," Buchanan said. "He didn't strike me as someone I needed to know."

"He seemed to hang on Lebedev's every word," Simon said. "I'm interested to know more about Lebedev, if you're of a mind to enlighten me. I'd also like to hear more about Vasiliev's demotion."

"Perhaps you'd join me for lunch a few days hence," Buchanan said. "A discussion of Lebedev and company will take more time than we have today. It will also give me time to gather more intelligence."

"I'll look forward to it," Simon replied.

CHAPTER 18

Simon rose from the chair and strode toward large windows that overlooked a garden and a manicured lawn. The ambassador walked to the window and stood, hands on hips, for several minutes. He opened French doors that led onto a balcony and inhaled deeply.

"Ah! The sun is warming the roses," he said. "The scent always reminds me of home." He turned away from the doors, his countenance appearing to cling to a memory that offered him sanctuary from his daily responsibilities.

I wonder whether that garden is the root of the code word "tea rose," Simon mused, recalling that the ambassador's name was at the top of the list of allies given him by his father. "Does the garden include a variety of tea rose, by chance?"

"It does indeed," Buchanan said with a knowing smile. "Now, shall we talk about the reason you're here?"

"Of course," Simon replied.

"I received a brief communiqué from the king ... as well as your father," Buchanan said. "I understand that you are to renew your acquaintance with the royal family on the king's business." In response to Simon's nod, he continued. "I believe you were in Petrograd some ten years ago. Is that not so?"

"Yes," Simon said, marvelling at his father's reach once again. "At the suggestion of King Edward, my father was posted here in 1902, as a naval attaché to the Foreign Office. My brother and I passed time with the princesses during social events."

"That was well before my time," Buchanan said thoughtfully. "Do you know why your father was posted here?"

"No, sir," Simon replied. "I was only eight at the time, and totally ensconced in the experience. I found the culture fascinating, the language a challenge, and the young princesses charming."

He smiled, reflecting on his boyhood experience. "They were like little sisters to me. If I recall, they would have been seven, five, three, and a few months when I first met them. My brother, Richard, and I entertained Olga and Tatiana at functions as well. Maria and Anastasia were too young to be without a nanny."

"Maria and Anastasia are still quite young," Buchanan said, pacing across the window, his hands clasped behind his back, "in my opinion, that is. Olga and Tatiana are out in society and turn the heads of many young men."

In contemplation, he tapped a finger on his lower lip. "You've painted a fine picture of Petrograd as it was thirteen years ago, Lord Simon, but, as with the city's old name of St. Petersburg, it's all in the past. Things have changed noticeably in Russia since I arrived in 1910. At the moment, I see the Russian court as conflicted. Some have pro-German sympathies, which makes a British relationship prickly."

He shook his head, as if in deep thought. "Plus, I feel that Tsarina Alexandra Feodorovna may yet be influenced by her German connections. She seems to turn the tsar's mind away from the Allies, making it difficult for him to see the current political situation clearly."

"Is Tsar Nicholas averse to your reports?" Simon said, piqued with interest.

"No, not at all," Sir George replied. "As a matter of fact, when we meet, he is quite engaging." He selected a cigar from a humidor sitting on a side table and snipped the end. "Cigar?" he said, offering one to Simon. Simon shook his head.

The ambassador lit the cigar and drew several short puffs. "Don't get me wrong," Buchanan said, exhaling. "I'm fond of the tsar. I think he and I get along famously. We have a bond of sorts."

He drew on the cigar, turned it as if to inspect the lit end, then released a swirl of smoke from his lungs. "We've often discussed the unrest in this country, and whether he should assume control of the military. Regarding the first, I've suggested that a little constitutional reform might inhibit a revolution. If he'd only support the Duma and allow some alteration to the state administration, I think the Duma would have more faith in his abilities. Unfortunately, the tsarina's influence seems to stymy any possibility. She insists that he has royal privilege—and control—that should not be relinquished. Plus, there's the suspected German interference."

Simon listened intently as Sir George's words drew a picture of the Russian political climate, which expanded the details that he had heard on the train.

Sir George continued. "I do worry about the tsar's military leadership, however. I don't think he has what it takes to lead such a powerful machine, and I can't imagine anyone who'd disagree with me. More opinionated individuals speak out against him: at their peril, of course. If you find yourself in company with anyone who shares those opinions, I suggest you watch your back."

"Thank you, sir, for the advice, and for the catch-up." Simon gazed at the ornate gold mantle-clock sitting over the fireplace. "I'm afraid I've taken a great deal of your time, Sir George. I should be going."

"Nonsense, young man," Sir George refuted as he butted out the cigar stub, "I've enjoyed your company, and look forward to your next visit."

Sir George strode across the hall and asked his secretary to arrange Simon's conveyance to the hotel. The two men watched from the balcony as the shapely secretary disappeared down a service stairwell. Once she was out of sight, Sir George pointed out a few of the finer details of the Embassy's foyer, including statues and paintings.

As they descended the grand staircase, Sir George stopped for a moment, contemplating. "I say, the royal family is expected to return to Petrograd shortly, and I've heard that a grand dinner is in the works. You must accompany us. Georgiana, my wife, and Meriel, our daughter, would welcome the addition of another man to our party."

"I'd like that very much!" Simon said. "I'll look forward to it."

"By the way," Buchanan said, "I think you'll find your interim accommodation quite suitable. I asked for rooms overlooking the Neva River, with a view of the Fortress. I expect your man will have everything organized by now."

"I'm certain he will," Simon replied, accepting his hat and gloves from the guard who had welcomed him earlier. "Thank you, Sir George."

The guard led Simon outside to the awaiting coach and gave instructions to the driver.

CHAPTER 19

When Simon arrived at the Trezzini Palace Hotel, he was shown to a luxurious suite on the second floor. Henry appeared as soon as he entered, relieving him of his hat and gloves.

While Simon met with the ambassador, Henry had industriously unpacked their luggage and sent the travel trunks to the hotel's storage.

As Simon wandered from room to room inspecting their latest accommodation, Henry pointed out the views that had not so long ago been described by Buchanan. He also reported that the suite came with two bedrooms, the smaller of which he had claimed rather than incurring the additional expense of another room, and went on to boast that the suite contained a bathroom and a water closet as well.

"So, we're self-contained," Henry said in conclusion. "We won't be expected to share any facilities with the other guests."

"Crocker, remember to hold your tongue when you get back home," Simon said, teasing. "You're going to find it hard to live with the simplicities of Newcastle when you do."

"Quite right!" Henry replied. "It will certainly be a step down."

"Plus, you'll be returning to the hierarchy of the staff below stairs …"

"I'm well aware of that, my lord," the valet said cheerily. "At least I'll have had an adventure that will take me into my old age." He grinned impishly. "I'll run a bath, sir, and lay out some fresh clothes. Do you plan to dine in or out this evening?"

"Oh, let's just dine downstairs, shall we?" Simon replied. "I'd like to be still for a while."

"Yes, my lord," Henry said, disappearing into the bathroom.

———

An hour later, Simon and Henry were shown to a table in the hotel's small dining room under a vaulted red-brick ceiling, surrounded by complementing brocade-covered walls of cream and crimson. Candlelight resting on ledges of ecru wainscoting illuminated the cozy room. Simon indicated a preference for a table in the back corner.

"Hope you don't mind sitting with your back to the room, Crocker," Simon said, "but I'd like to check out the other guests."

"I have no expectation of choice, sir," Henry said, shrugging. "I'm simply honoured that you've asked me to accompany you."

"Perhaps a stroll along the river after dinner?" Simon said. "We've been cooped up on a ship and trains for weeks.

It might be nice to walk on land for a while."

As they chatted, the waiter served a meal of traditional Russian dishes: beginning with a small bowl of borscht, an entrée of steamed vegetables and chicken cutlets stuffed with garlic butter, and concluding with an assortment of pastries and tea.

"I've never had Russian food before," Henry said, popping the last pastry into his mouth. He rubbed his belly contentedly. "I think I'd rather curl up in bed right now, but a stroll along the river will serve me better."

"Let's go, then," Simon said, rising from the table.

Opposite the hotel, the Troitsky Bridge crossed the Neva River. Near the centre of the bridge, Simon and Henry stopped to enjoy the area of Petrograd that surrounded them.

"We have a great view of the Fortress and the far side of the river from our rooms," Simon said, "but from here we can see the hotel-side and the colourful buildings that line it. My mind is flooded by so many memories of the time my family was stationed here."

"I've heard so much about Russia, especially Petrograd," Henry replied, looking awestruck. "It's always been a far-off place for me. Standing here, in the pale of a summer's night and seeing the lights twinkling, feels magical."

"Easy, Crocker, you're starting to sound like a poet."

Henry dipped his head, embarrassed. "I do enjoy

a good book of poetry, but I wouldn't admit that to anyone else."

"A bit of a romantic?" Simon said. "Just when I thought I knew everything about you!"

The two men continued across the bridge and followed the roadway that skirted the Fortress. Eventually, they completed a circuit by crossing the Birzhevoy Bridge and the Palace Bridge. As they walked past the Winter Palace along the Palace Embankment toward their hotel, they could hear loud voices that seemed to indicate a festive occasion nearby.

"What do you suppose that noise is about?" Henry said.

"I don't know," Simon replied, "but it has me curious. Shall we investigate?"

They increased their pace in pursuit of the noise, passing behind their hotel to the corner and turning right. The din grew louder as they neared the Field of Mars. Soon the shouting was audible, full of laughter and a sense of celebration. They paused outside an imposing structure which, according to the city map that they had been referencing, was the barracks of the Russian Imperial Guard.

"So," Henry said, "some sort of military function. They certainly know how to throw a party."

"Well," Simon replied, "at least we've satisfied our curiosity."

As they turned back the way they had come, Simon thought he heard his name called.

"Wait!" he said, placing a hand on Henry's arm. "Did you hear someone call me?" He turned, tugging at his ear in wonder. *Who knows I'm here? Who would call my name?*

"I didn't hear anything," Henry replied, "Given the fracas, I'm surprised you did."

They stood where they had stopped, waiting to hear the voice again. They were not disappointed. The next time Simon heard his name, it was accompanied by rapid footsteps clacking on the cobblestones under an archway.

"Lord Simon!" Lieutenant Egorov said, sounding breathless and somewhat inebriated. He waved his arm in greeting as he approached. "I was hoping I'd run into you again soon." He snapped his heels and delivered a sloppy salute. "Mr. Crocker, good evening."

Simon extended a hand toward the young officer, who grabbed it and shook it heartily. *Quite the change in humour from the train platform*, Simon observed.

"Are you celebrating something this evening?" Simon said politely.

Lieutenant Egorov half-turned toward the archway. "Yes." He swayed slowly, leaving Simon to wonder how much alcohol the officer might have consumed. "One of our colleagues has been promoted. We have been feasting and drinking. We were about to begin the dancing."

As if awaiting an introduction, distant notes of a balalaika floated toward them.

"I saw you from the window," he said, his whisper sober and urgent. He swayed again, pointing toward some open windows on the second floor where Simon observed boisterous movement. Music and song filled the evening. Simon extended a hand to steady the soldier.

Abruptly, the smile on Egorov's face disappeared. "I must speak with you in private … tomorrow." He cast a furtive glance toward the windows, and he seemed to force a toothy grin as he waved to his companions.

"I must return now," he said, his gaze sombre. "I'm being watched."

"Fine," Simon said, surprised by the officer's suggestion and his sobriety. "We are staying at the Trezzini Palace Hotel. Do you know it?"

Egorov nodded curtly.

"Leave a message at the front desk, and I will find you," Simon said.

Egorov swayed slightly, snapped his heels together, and delivered another sloppy salute. Then, he turned on his heel and staggered toward the archway.

"What was all that about, sir?" Henry said. "The bits that I understood made no sense to me."

"Come on," Simon said, "I'll tell you on the way back to the hotel."

CHAPTER 20

The following day, Simon and Henry decided to be tourists. While Simon shared recollections of an earlier time, he memorized locations that he thought might be relevant to his current visit. Henry embraced the day as any tourist might, enjoying the sights, sounds, and tastes.

Late in the afternoon, they hired a conveyance to return them to the hotel, with a diversion to the British Embassy.

"Wait here," Simon said. "I'll be right back."

He hopped from the carriage and dashed into the Embassy, leaving Henry and the driver waiting at the curb. Inside, he asked the guard whom he had met the previous day for directions to the administrative office, which turned out to be on the main floor near the rear of the building. He easily found the oak door marked with a small brass plaque that read *Administration*, opened it quietly, and peered inside.

He did not expect to find the hubbub of a very busy office. Three young women sat at desks transcribing documents on noisy typewriters, one fellow behind a glass wall shouted into a telephone, and two telegraph machines clacked industriously in a corner, each monitored by a young man.

"Excuse me," Simon said, interrupting the work of one young woman. "My name is Simon Temple. The ambassador said there would be an envelope for me to pick up—"

"Mr. Nightingale-Temple?" the young woman replied, her voice officious. British with a slight Russian accent. "Yes, we have an envelope for you." She rose from her chair and selected an envelope from a pile on a nearby cabinet top.

Simon accepted the envelope and thanked the young woman who seemed, by this time, to be ogling him as if she had never seen a man before. Uncomfortable with her perusal, he backed out of the office and hastened down the hall to the awaiting conveyance.

"Crocker, how about some tea?" Simon said as he climbed back into the carriage. "This envelope should contain information about suites to rent and the staff I'll need to employ. We can review its contents together."

"I'll make the arrangements as soon as we return," Henry replied heartily.

<hr>

By the time a tea tray arrived, Simon was examining pages of information spread across the desk in his sitting room.

"This is interesting," Simon said, stacking one sheet on top of the others before sitting in one of the winged chairs. "According to this list, we should find several furnished rooms nearby. The ambassador has recommended we look at the Rosenshtein House, the Nikolayev House, and the Lidval House. The Rosenshtein House and the Nikolayev House are located over the bridge and several blocks beyond the Fortress, but Lidval House is closer to the hotel. I like the sounds of all three, but, while Rosenshtein House is probably the farthest, it sounds most suitable. Before I decide on anything, I'd like to see all of them."

He reached for a sweet from the tray that Henry had placed on the low table in front of him. "I'll give the agent a call in a few min—"

A brisk rap at the door interrupted Simon's comment. Henry was quick to answer it, accepting a small envelope and a rather large bowl of fruit from the hotel clerk in exchange for a few coins for the service. He returned to the sitting area, sat the fruit bowl on a credenza, and handed the envelope to Simon.

Simon slit the seal and tugged out a note, nodding toward the fruit with one raised eyebrow. "No oranges?"

"Yes, sir," Henry replied. "It's a mix. The desk clerk sent what the hotel had and promised one with your breakfast every morning. Apparently, oranges are still hard to find, so he sent a selection of other fruit too."

"Very good," Simon said, muttering as he examined the envelope. That it was written in French told Simon that it had been sent by someone of a higher social standing. The common language in the city was Russian, which was spoken primarily by trade workers and those in service. Members of aristocratic families tended to speak French amongst themselves, but most spoke Russian when required.

Henry began to tidy away the tea things while Simon considered the correspondence.

"Well, Crocker," Simon finally said, "you will find this most interesting! This message is from Lieutenant Egorov."

"He did say that he would contact you today."

"Indeed." Simon tugged his watch from his pocket and checked the time. "He is suggesting that I meet him in the lounge … in fifteen minutes!" Simon snapped the watch cover closed and jumped to his feet. "Which is more likely five or ten minutes now," he said tugging at his vest. "I should go straight down, but I think I'll change for dinner first."

"Will you need me, my lord?" Henry said, his voice sounding hopeful.

"Not immediately," Simon replied, unbuttoning his shirt as he strode to his room. "Come down when you're ready. Afterward, we'll eat in the dining room again." He stepped out of his trousers, tossing them on the bed. "If I look trapped, you might find an excuse to extract me."

"Very well, my lord," Henry replied. "I'll make a reservation while I'm at it. Same table as last evening, back to the wall?"

"That would be perfect!" Simon said. "Good of you to remember."

Refreshed and attired in an evening suit, Simon hastened down the stairs to the main floor, and found Lieutenant Egorov pacing at the entrance to the lounge.

"Ah, Lord Simon!" Egorov said in greeting.

Simon noted that he spoke Russian, rather than French as written in the note.

"I was afraid you might not be in to receive my message." Egorov's eyes seemed to search the lobby for threats before he led the way into the lounge.

"Are you off-duty this evening?" Simon said casually. "You're not in uniform."

Egorov glanced down at his evening suit. "Oh! I'd forgotten. I'm off-duty, yes." His voice was low, quiet. "I have a dinner engagement later."

Egorov led Simon to the far corner of the room. It sat in shadow away from the light. It was not until the soldier stepped back, pulling out a chair for Simon, that he realized they were not alone.

Simon stood next to the chair, trying to conceal his surprise. "Mrs. Voronov!" he said, glancing toward Egorov. "I wasn't expecting to see you again so soon. Rather, I wasn't expecting to see either of you so soon."

Egorov motioned for Simon to take a seat, then sat himself on the far side of the circular table, his back against the wall.

That's the chair I'd have preferred, Simon thought, hitching his chair to give himself a better view of the doorway.

A waiter appeared and Egorov ordered three teas.

"Er, would you mind making that four teas?" Simon said. "Mr. Crocker will likely join us shortly." Out the corner of his eye, Simon noticed Mrs. Voronov straighten in her chair.

"By all means!" Egorov said.

Simon declined Egorov's suggestion of sweets, admitting to having already indulged. While the waiter retreated to the kitchen, he contemplated the young couple, noting that she, too, was dressed for an evening out.

"Your message was a little cloak-and-dagger," Simon said when the door to the kitchen swung shut. His use of French elicited a smile from Egorov. "Would you prefer that we speak French?"

"That might be safer," Egorov said, glancing around the otherwise empty room.

"How may I help you, Lieutenant Egorov?" Simon said, leaning forward.

"Artyom, please. My name is Artyom." Egorov turned toward the woman sitting next to him, her features accented by a pale blue ostrich feather. "And this is my sister, Varvara Voronov."

"Sister!" Simon said, hissing in surprise just as the waiter returned with their tea. The three sat in silence, waiting for the man to leave, before Simon repeated his question. "How may I help you?"

Egorov glanced at his sister. She reached across the table, resting a gloved hand on his, and nodded encouragement.

"First, I must apologize for our cool reception at the train station," Egorov said, the small scar twitching. "We were anxious to be away quickly. I feared that even a moment's delay might compromise my sister."

"No need to apologize," Simon said. "Please continue."

"I gathered from conversations on the train," Egorov said, "that you are in Petrograd for a visit, and that you will be returning to London in a few months. Is that correct?"

"Not exactly," Simon replied, allowing several heartbeats to pass. "I could be here for a while longer. I've been engaged to review plans concerning a new railway line to the Murman coast, as well as the port that's to be built there."

Simon noted a discreet shift in their posture. *They're disappointed. Whatever they want of me, that reply wasn't it!*

CHAPTER 21

"Ah, Crocker!" Simon said, rising, "we've just ordered tea. You must join us." He swept his hand to a vacant chair.

"Good afternoon, Mr. Crocker," Egorov said, jumping to his feet. "You will remember my sister, Varvara Voronov."

"Varvara, please—you must both call me Varvara," she said, resting her gloved hand in Henry's.

Henry bowed respectfully before sitting between her and Simon. From his vantage point, Simon recognized the surprise in Henry's eyes, and admired once again the valet's composure—that is, until he accepted a cup of tea from the woman and his slight tremor rattled the cup. He also noticed a pink tinge to Varvara's cheeks and her demure glance toward Henry.

Simon bit his lip, trying to hold back a grin. In the next moment, he was forced to cough as he struggled for composure. Taking a deep breath, he picked up the thread of their conversation. "Clearly, you need something from me," Simon said kindly. "You wouldn't have gone to the effort of seeking me out and trying to conceal your identity if it wasn't important to you."

Varvara peered at her brother; her eyes were wide

with pleading.

"My sister is in trouble," he said abruptly. "She needs to leave Petrograd as soon as possible."

"Trouble?" Henry said, concern furrowing his brow and darkening his brown eyes as they fell on the young woman's face.

In response, Varvara blushed again, her eyes locking momentarily with Henry's.

"Yes," Egorov replied, breaking the silent exchange. "Let me explain—knowing the full story will help you understand the urgency. My sister's husband, Evgeni, was an officer in the Imperial Guard as well. He was a lieutenant, you see, and he loved being part of the Imperial Guard. In fact, the only thing he loved more was my sister. He is the one who encouraged me to enlist."

Varvara leaned toward the table. Lifting the tea pot, she refilled the four cups. As steam wafted above the tea, Egorov continued.

"Last fall, Lieutenant Colonel—as he was then—Ivan Vasiliev was installed as temporary commander of our unit. On behalf of the tsar, the Imperial Guard hosted a grand ball to welcome him. Varvara caught his attention when they were introduced during the reception line. We all noticed that he drank heavily, and by the end of the dinner, his true nature became obvious. He is a ruffian, a foul-mouthed bully, and he does not hesitate to take what he wants. He presumes that he has the willingness of every woman and takes advantage of their gentle nature."

He added a small spoonful of sugar to his tea, stirred

once, then sipped it. "During the dancing, Varvara excused herself. Before she could return to the ballroom and her husband, the Lieutenant Colonel trapped her in a hallway and forced her into a vacant room, where he assaulted her." Egorov coughed, glancing toward his sister as he did so. She nodded, as if encouraging him to continue.

"My brother-in-law became concerned when she didn't return in a timely manner. Together, we went in search of her. I found her in that room: crumpled, ruined, distressed. She begged me not to tell her husband, so I helped her straighten her clothing and found a small mirror so she could tend to her hair. Then, we went in search of Evgeni. When we found him, she told him that she was unwell. We left shortly thereafter."

Simon drank down his tea, wishing he had accepted the offer of sweets: something on which to gnash his teeth.

"But what—" Henry said.

"There's more," Egorov said, interrupting the question with a raised hand. He twisted the spoon he had used to stir his tea. Simon noticed yet again the twitching of the small scar beneath Egorov's left eye and made a mental note that it only seemed apparent when Egorov appeared anxious for his sister's safety.

Egorov continued his story. "A few days later, I received a note from Varvara asking to meet me. During that meeting, she told me that the Lieutenant Colonel had sent a note. He wrote that, if she did not attend the address that he provided, something dreadful would happen to her husband. Of course she went, fearing what

Vasiliev might do to her husband. And, of course, he was waiting for her. Not only did he assault her again, but he beat her too, telling her that the next time would be worse if she betrayed him."

Simon regarded Varvara's discomfiture, noticing Henry tensing beside her. When the young woman sniffled, Henry promptly produced his handkerchief.

"Fortunately, Vasiliev didn't mar her face. She claimed ill health again and Evgeni let her be. The next time a note arrived, she summoned the courage to meet the man, and told him that she would never see him again unless in the company of her husband or me. They struggled, but, before he could assault her again, she managed to escape. Instead of returning home, she went to my apartment and hid there until it was time for Evgeni to return home.

"In the meantime, Evgeni and I had no idea. We were conducting drills in the Field of Mars." He placed a hand on his sister's arm, hesitating.

"Continue," she said flatly.

"Looking back, I recall the Lieutenant Colonel's arrival. He yelled at everyone and insisted that we needed to apply ourselves: we weren't working hard enough. He snatched a horse's reins from one of the riders and mounted. He then drew his sword and demanded an opponent. No one responded, so he ordered Evgeni to mount up. His eyes were wild. It was as though he were possessed! Evgeni did as he was ordered. He was no sooner mounted than the Lieutenant Colonel charged his horse toward my brother-in-law. Evgeni raised his sword in defence and blocked Vasiliev's first blow. Everyone moved back, stunned. Evgeni turned his mount and prepared to receive another attack." Egorov paused again and regarded his sister. When she nodded, he continued.

"Lieutenant Colonel Vasiliev attacked several more times, as if he were jousting. Each time he passed, he screamed at Evgeni to man-up. Evgeni refused to respond to the attack, begging Vasiliev to withdraw. Finally, armed guards arrived and demanded that Vasiliev stand down." Egorov dashed tears from his cheeks and swigged the last of his tea.

"It happened so fast. That momentary distraction by the guards. Vasiliev's determination to cause harm. Evgeni wasn't expecting another attack. The Lieutenant Colonel raised his sword and viciously sliced Evgeni's arm. He cut clear through the shoulder joint and into his chest."

Mrs. Voronov slumped in her chair, sobbing quietly into Henry's handkerchief. Egorov retrieved his own handkerchief, wiped his eyes, and blew his nose.

Simon straightened, disgust churning in his belly. He retrieved his own handkerchief and offered it to the young woman.

"Sir," Henry said in English, "I've been trying to follow the French. Did I hear correctly?" He summarized his understanding and Simon confirmed the accuracy.

"My brother-in-law died later that day. Vasiliev was reprimanded, demoted to major, but allowed to continue his temporary posting. He claimed that it was Evgeni's fault for not being alert during a drill. A week later, my sister received another note from Vasiliev telling her that if she did not meet with him as and when requested, I could encounter a similar misfortune. I didn't know about the demand at first, nor that she was complying. I only discovered the arrangement when she showed up at the train station two weeks ago; Vasiliev had insisted that she travel with us to Moscow. His wife was ill, he claimed. When he returned to their berth on the last night, he beat her again."

"That night," Varvara said in a whisper, "Mr. Crocker—H-henry—saw Artyom consoling me in the hallway." She sighed deeply before raising her eyes to meet Henry's.

"Yes, he told me," Simon replied, running his knuckles along his cheek as he contemplated the matter. "That is quite the accounting. Troubling, to say the least. You have my deepest condolences, Mrs. Voronov. I can only presume that you have imparted your story because you think I can help in some way. I can't see how. I have no status or leverage here. What would you have me do?"

"We had hoped that …" Varvara said, "that I might travel with you to London. We have money. I will not be an expense and hopefully not an inconvenience. I simply cannot travel alone. I have no one except Artyom, and I must escape that horrid man. So long as I am here, Artyom will remain in danger."

"If I were to leave now, to try to take her away," Egorov said, his voice sounding urgent, "I would be accused of abandoning my post. And my absence would put both of us in danger." Egorov sighed deeply. "But now you tell us that you are uncertain of your travel plans. That is very disappointing."

"Not necessarily," Simon replied, tugging his watch from his pocket. "We have a dinner reservation shortly. Would you care to join us?" He stuffed the watch into his pocket. "I want to help, but I must give your request thought. Can you give me some time to sort things through?"

Brother and sister looked at each other, as if amazed to think they had been thrown a lifeline.

"We have dinner reservations elsewhere," Egorov said. "But we are happy to afford you time to consider our dilemma. Anything you can do to help will be greatly appreciated."

Simon rose from the table and offered his hand toward Egorov. "Where can I reach you?"

Egorov rose to accept Simon's hand, then withdrew a calling card from the inside of his coat pocket. "Thank you, Lord Simon, for your time, and for any assistance you might be able to offer."

Varvara stood next to her brother, casting a sidelong glance toward Henry, and extended a lace-covered hand in farewell. Her other hand snaked through her brother's elbow and clung firmly to his sleeve.

Simon considered the brother and sister for a moment, wondering how he could possibly help. "Please, call me Simon," he said. He peered into the ice blue eyes of first Varvara, then Artyom, and resolved that he would help them regardless of his other commitments.

CHAPTER 22

"Well, that was interesting," Simon said, slapping Henry on the back as they watched the departure of Egorov and his sister. "Dinner?"

Henry seemed to decipher Simon's two-pronged remark—the Egorov story and the scene between him and Varvara—his ears reddening as thoughts of the young woman swirled in his mind.

"Are you up to another stroll after dinner?" Simon said, scanning the room as they approached the reserved table.

"Hmm, sounds intriguing," Henry replied. "Perhaps we should begin with dessert so we can be on our way quickly."

"I'm afraid not," Simon said, countering. "After that conversation, I need something substantial to gnaw on!"

A moment later, the waiter appeared. As he shook out linen napkins and placed them across the laps of his customers, he described the daily special. Simon ordered for the two of them, agreeing with the waiter's suggestion of vodka to start.

"Did you have a look at the information regarding the room rentals?" Simon said, changing the topic.

"I looked through the photographs," Henry replied,

"and read the few notes that were written in English. The three suggested by the ambassador seem suitable." He sipped the vodka and sighed.

"Careful, Crocker. At this rate, you'll be an aficionado of spirits before you get home!"

"I expect I'll be dry before I do, sir," Henry said, toying with the glass. "I enjoy the tipples I have in your company, but, as you know, I have no intention of making it a habit. With regard to the rooms, sir, I took the liberty of making an appointment for a tour tomorrow morning. The agent will meet us in the hotel lobby at ten. I hope that's agreeable ..."

"That's quite fine, Crocker!" Simon's reply expressed surprise that Henry was able to make the appointment. "How did you—"

"I found a brochure at the bottom of the pile of papers you left. The agent's name sounded British, so I took a chance that he might speak English and called the number. Turns out, he's from Bristol, but his parents were born in Russia. Emigrated to England thirty years ago."

"Very resourceful, Crocker! Well done!"

———

During their after-dinner stroll, Simon and Henry reviewed the curious encounter with Egorov and his sister.

"I can't believe that she's his sister!" Henry said. "But that explains a lot."

"It certainly does," Simon agreed, "and reveals a lot. It's quite the tragedy."

"Is there anything to be done?" Henry said.

"I'm thinking it through," Simon said. "I'm determined to help them. I just have to figure the best way to go about it."

"You can count on me, my lord, if there's any part for me in it."

"Thanks, Crocker. I appreciate that, and I'm sure they will too."

—————

The following morning, Simon and Henry took the stairs to the lobby, arriving five minutes ahead of their appointment with the real estate agent.

"Mr. Temple?" a short, balding man said as he came through the entrance and introduced himself.

"Simon Nightingale-Temple." Simon shook the offered hand. "My associate, Henry Crocker." Simon motioned toward Henry. "I understand Mr. Crocker spoke with you yesterday."

"Indeed," the man said. "I took the liberty of reviewing the properties submitted for your consideration, and your preferences as suggested by Mr. Crocker. I agree the three locations are worth a look. I have a carriage waiting outside. Shall we go?" He turned toward the entrance. "We can discuss these properties further while we travel."

"Excuse me, sir," a desk clerk said, addressing Simon. "A message has just arrived for you."

Simon flipped him a tip and, noting the embassy seal, excused himself to read the note. Before the clerk reached his station, Simon detained him, requesting a carriage to take him to the embassy.

"I've been summoned," he said, waving the envelope. "Crocker—you go and have a look. We can discuss everything later."

———

"Lord Simon!" Ambassador Buchanan said. "I wasn't expecting you so soon."

"Crocker and I were on our way out to visit the flats that you recommended," Simon said. "Another five minutes, and we would have been gone."

"Fortuitous, I must say," Buchanan replied. "I have some news on Vasiliev and Lebedev. Tea?"

"Thank you," Simon said, accepting Buchanan's invitation to a chair. "Tea would be welcome."

Buchanan arranged a service of tea, then selected the armchair opposite Simon. "Where to begin," the ambassador said, rubbing his hands together as if readying to share the latest gossip.

"How about we start with Vasiliev?" Simon said. "I may have some news on that front too."

"Very well," Buchanan said, reaching for his cigar box.

Simon shook his head, declining a cigar, and waited while the ambassador prepared his.

"You asked about the demotion of Vasiliev," he said, puffing to light the tightly-rolled leaves.

"Actually," Simon said, "since I posed the question, I've learnt that he was involved in a nasty incident that caused the death of Varvara Voronov's husband, and, as a result, he was demoted to major."

"Indeed!" Buchanan replied, sounding disappointed. "I'm wondering now whether you might know more than me?" He raised an eyebrow, accenting the question.

"Crocker and I recently met with Mrs. Voronov and her brother," Simon said. "Lieutenant Egorov provided a detailed description of the incident. It wasn't pretty. He then went on—with her encouragement—to tell us how she became involved with Vasiliev. Since her husband's death, Vasiliev has been imposing on her time … at will, shall we say?"

"Do tell?" Buchanan replied, waving forward a clerk carrying a tray of tea.

Buchanan leaned toward Simon, listening to a description of the attack while steaming tea was poured into china cups. Once the door closed and they were alone again, Simon reported Vasiliev's ill abuse of Mrs. Voronov.

"Why ever should they come to you with such disclosure?" Buchanan said, awed by the story.

"They were hoping I could help her escape to England," Simon replied. "I told them that I would have to give the matter some thought. In the moment, I find it difficult to imagine what I might do, but I'm determined to come up with a plan."

He tapped his lower lip, remembering the desperation in the young woman's eyes. "I couldn't in good conscience ignore her plight. Crocker has even expressed a desire to help."

"I may be able to offer some assistance," Buchanan said. "Periodically, we assist embassy staff and dignitaries with travel arrangements. Perhaps she might be included in one of the departing groups." He rested his smouldering cigar in a marble ashtray and sipped his tea. "Ah, the very best of Darjeeling!"

"Thank you, sir," Simon said. "I look forward to hearing more, when available. In the meantime … you mentioned news of Lebedev?"

"Lebedev, indeed!" Buchanan said snidely. "The man is a wonder! He seems to have his finger in several devious plots."

The ambassador poured more tea in his cup and offered a top-up for Simon, then continued. "I received a report last evening from a major in our internal intelligence office," Buchanan said, glancing at the mantle clock. "Unfortunately, he's out for the morning; otherwise, I would've asked him to brief you. Regardless, I'm quite capable." He grinned mischievously. "Are you aware that Lebedev is married to Vasiliev's sister?"

"No!" Simon shook his head, eyes round with surprise.

"Then you'll enjoy my story," he said with a smirk, eyes alight. "Although Vasiliev and his sister were born in Germany, their parents are Russian-born. Herr and Frau Vasiliev work with German foreign intelligence. Ever since the foiled assassination attempt in 1902, they have been contriving—on behalf of the German government—to bring about the demise of the tsar. Now, they're hoping to try again under the guise of the tsar's absence in Moghilev and the tsarina's inability to manage the country."

The ambassador steepled his fingers, tapping his two index fingers while he thought. "With all eyes on royal debacles, Lebedev will be at liberty to covertly manoeuvre matters to his own advantage. Spurred on by his wife, he wants ruling power of Russia for himself, and is slowly amassing a gang of thugs to form an army. Vasiliev is responsible for assembling and organizing that army. Although you know him as a disreputable major in the Imperial Guard, in actuality he is an Okhrana plant. A little at a time, and with the Vasiliev family's assistance, Lebedev has acquired military equipment and supplies, which he stashes in the community of Russko-Vysotskoye about twenty-five miles from here."

"But how?" Simon said, incredulous. "That would cost money. Where's the funding coming from?"

"Germany, of course, via the father-in-law, Herr Vasiliev," Buchanan replied. "The German administration is using Lebedev to undermine Russia's vulnerability. With the tsar distracted in Moghilev, focussed on the Austria-Hungarian troops, and the tsarina offending every government official introduced by the Duma, they are completely unaware of the subterfuge surrounding them. All Lebedev needs to do is sit back and wait for a situation in his favour, and—presto—surprise take-over!"

Sir George snapped up his cigar and focussed on lighting it again as quiet settled between them. Simon rested his chin in his palm and slowly stroked his cheek, trying to make order of the intelligence.

"Mark my words, Lord Simon," Buchanan said, breaking the silence and sending smoke circles into the space between them, "if Tsar Nicholas doesn't start paying attention, he will lose everything! I've said as much to him on a few occasions, when he was open to hearing the warning, but he's yet to heed it."

CHAPTER 23

Simon looked up from his paperwork when Henry returned later that afternoon. He set his fountain pen on the writing desk and regarded the valet as he hung his coat. "Tea?" he said.

"That wouldn't go amiss, sir," Henry replied. "The agent ploughed through all three viewings, with no rest in between, other than brief carriage rides." He rubbed his hands together. "I'm starving!"

"Perfect," Simon said. "I just ordered a tray; it should be here shortly."

As if in response, a brisk rap sounded at the door. When Henry opened the door, a server entered and placed a tray on one of the tables. "A message has arrived for Mr. Temple," he said, presenting to Henry a small silver tray that bore a white envelope.

Henry snatched the envelope, leaving a coin in its place, and closed the door when the server left. "British Embassy," Henry said, turning the envelope back and forth before handing it to Simon.

"Another one!" Simon said, straightening in his chair as he read the letter.

"It seems, Crocker," Simon said, "that the royal

family will be returning to Petrograd soon. The Polish war is not going well for Russia. Tsar Nicholas needs to be in Petrograd to focus his attention on current events, and he wants his family nearby." He paraphrased the ambassador's message for Henry, eliminating the finer details. "They intend to host a dinner upon their return, and an invitation will be extended to me." He grinned, recalling past occasions in the company of the Romanovs.

"I'll ensure that your tails are fresh and ready, sir," Henry said. "Or would you prefer that I set out your uniform?"

"Tails, please, Crocker," Simon replied, sitting at his secretary and withdrawing a crisp sheet of paper. "You'll recall that our orders include no uniforms while in Russia."

He picked up his fountain pen and twirled it between his fingers before dipping the nib in the ink well. Then he wrote with enthusiasm:

> *Sir George,*
> *I am delighted to be included amongst the British*
> *party to attend the royal dinner. I, too, agree that*
> *we should meet again before then.*
> *Your servant,*
> *Simon Nightingale-Temple*

"Crocker, once we've had tea, please ask the front desk to send this," Simon said, folding the note and sliding it into the already-addressed envelope. "You might also see about a dinner reservation. Perhaps tomorrow evening we can dine elsewhere."

"Wonderful!" Henry said. "I noticed some interesting restaurants during the tour today."

"Now," Simon said with enthusiasm, "tell me about the accommodations."

"I liked all three flats," Henry said. "Each building comes with its own interesting points. If I were going to rent one for myself, however, I'd take the last—the Rosenshtein House. The building is new and modern, centrally located, and furnished. It's a short way from here, but still close to the Winter Palace—which I presume will be important for you, my lord." His raised brows seemed to emphasize his assumption.

"Excellent point," Simon replied. "Close to the palace, but not so close as to be intrusive. What else?"

"All aspects of the flat are interesting," Henry said. "It even has a gas stove and a large, sunken tub—long enough to stretch out in! Oh … and three large bedrooms."

"I couldn't imagine my parents living in such a small space," Simon said, chuckling, "but, aside from servants, I'll be alone once you're gone, and I doubt I'll be in all that often."

"Is that a decision then, my lord?" Henry said. "Shall I arrange for a viewing?"

"No need, Crocker," Simon said. "I trust your judgment. Why don't you contact the agent tomorrow and make arrangements?" He strolled toward the window that overlooked the Neva. "I'll miss this view."

He turned abruptly and faced Henry. "Our next

challenge will be staffing. Perhaps you could make a list of qualities that we'll need for a valet, a maid, and a cook. Sir George's office provided me with the name of a personnel agency. I'll telephone tomorrow to make an appointment."

"Certainly, sir," Henry said, his voice flat.

"What's wrong, Crocker?" Simon said. "You seem a little down in the mouth."

"Nothing serious, my lord," Henry replied, shaking his head. "I'm just disappointed that I can't be of further service."

"I'm grateful that you agreed to come along," Simon said, "but you know you're needed back home."

"Have you given any thought to Mrs. Voronov?" Henry said, his ears reddening at mention of the woman's name.

"I'm still considering a few options," Simon replied. "Ambassador Buchanan mentioned the possibility of travelling with a group of returning Britons. He's looking into it."

Simon dropped into an armchair. "Which reminds me, the summons from the ambassador this morning regarded intelligence involving Lebedev and Vasiliev."

For the next several minutes, he recounted his conversation with Sir George. "You should know what was said, if for no other reason than for your own safety. I doubt you're in harm's way, but you could find yourself in a compromising position, simply because of your association with me."

While Henry delivered the letter to the front desk,

Simon recorded the events of the day in his journal. A sense of elation crept up his spine as he anticipated an evening social with the royals. *A perfect and timely opportunity to rekindle old acquaintances and size up the lay of the land.*

While Simon awaited the possession date of his new home at Rosenshtein House, he contemplated references received from several candidates and pared the list down to those whom he thought might be suitable, choosing to conduct the final interviews in the rented flat.

The last two candidates arrived together, a man and a woman. Simon's curiosity piqued when they reluctantly informed him that they were married.

"You will not be wanting a married couple, we think," the gentleman replied. "We shouldn't have come." They turned toward the door.

Simon scratched his head. "Well, since you're here," he said, "why don't we see the interview through?" He raised an eyebrow, inviting them to follow.

"Both of us?" the man said.

"Together?" the woman said.

"Yes," Simon replied, "both of you . . . together."

Sokol Zima and his wife Alina had met while in the service of a Romanov family who claimed to be third cousins to the tsar. The duchess for whom they worked was adamant that her staff should never be involved with one another. The couple had hid their relationship for several years, but, when the duchess learnt that her lady's maid was pregnant and married to her husband's valet, the elderly woman was infuriated and released them both immediately.

Zima easily found employment in another house, but his wife was shunned. His income was insufficient to pay for a flat, so Mrs. Zima was forced to seek accommodation with her family until the child was born. The village in which her family lived could not support a doctor; when the woman's travail started, she had only a midwife to assist with the delivery. The child died of complications, and the woman was told that she would never carry another.

"That was long ago," Mrs. Zima said. "Now we are too old for children. We have lived apart ever since then, my husband in his job, and me finding work as a maid or a cook, but always somewhere else and never for long. As soon as an employer hears of my history, I am shown the door."

"We would like to be together," Mr. Zima said. "When we heard of your requirements, we—"

"We had to ask," Mrs. Zima said, interrupting her husband with eagerness.

Simon contemplated the middle-aged couple sitting before him. Although younger than his parents, each wore a crown of silver hair. They peered at him earnestly. He chewed his upper lip, contemplating the advantage of having a married couple living with him versus younger or single individuals. He found them charming, easy to be with. They seemed sincere, not pretentious like the other candidates.

"There is one thing," Simon said, his face sombre. "I need to be absolutely certain of loyalty and confidentiality." He looked each of them in the eye. "Whatever you might see or hear spoken within these walls must never be repeated beyond them."

The applicants regarded each other and nodded. "You have our word, sir, that nothing seen or spoken within these rooms will be repeated beyond them," Mr. Zima said, his hand over his heart. His wife quickly aped the gesture.

"Marvellous!" Simon said, clapping his hands with finality. "How soon can you start? Mr. Crocker, my current valet, must return to England."

The couple looked at each other agog.

"We have the jobs?" Mr. Zima said, seeming incredulous. He reached for his wife's hand, whose face beamed with joy.

"Both of us?" Mrs. Zima said, squeezing his hand in return, seeming equally amazed.

"Yes, both of you," Simon said smiling.

"I-I can start tomorrow," Mrs. Zima said, sitting straighter in her chair. "I work only part-time now. When someone has a dinner or a party, I help."

"Good!" Simon replied. "You may continue to do so, so long as I don't need your services. Your pay will be constant; no deductions if you choose to take on small jobs from time to time. Mr. Zima?"

"I will give my notice today. I can begin here in one week."

"I've taken possession of these rooms, and my valet"—he indicated to Henry, who sat in one corner of the parlour—"has been organizing the space, but I prefer not to live here until I have staffing arrangements settled."

Simon switched to English for Henry's benefit. "Crocker, will you show Mr. and Mrs. Zima the suite?" He returned to Russian. "Mrs. Zima, if you'd like to move your things in tomorrow, you are welcome to do so."

"Mr. Zima too?" she said. "He can live here, too? We will be together?"

"Certainly!" Simon replied. "I apologize. I presumed that was understood."

The couple followed Henry through the flat, appreciating the large room that was to be their private chamber. Mrs. Zima's face lit up with pleasure when she saw the kitchen and took time to open the cupboards, the ice box, and the cooking range. She stood with her hands on her hips and turned around full circle, speaking rapidly in Russian.

After they had gone, Henry asked Simon to explain the results of the interview. "I understood some," Henry said, "but they spoke so fast. I found most of it difficult to follow."

"They are married," Simon said, "but have been forced to live apart for years. I couldn't bear the thought of them being separated any longer. She will act as cook and maid. He will be my valet and fill in wherever else he's needed.

They are happy for a chance to finally live together and are willing to do whatever is necessary so that they can. I just hope I don't disappoint them.'

"You've a soft heart, my lord," Henry said matter-of-factly, "just like Lady Ann. By the way, why was Mrs. Zima twirling in the kitchen?"

"She couldn't believe that she will be mistress of such a modern kitchen, and was listing off all of the dishes she plans to cook for me," Simon said, chuckling. "I didn't have the heart to tell her that I won't be here often. I'm sure her husband won't mind; if I'm not here, he alone will benefit from her attention."

"I feel good about this arrangement, sir. I think I'll be leaving you in good hands. They seem to be a personable, competent couple."

"I think so too," Simon said. "Shall we return to the hotel?" He tugged his watch out of his pocket. "We have just enough time to dress for dinner and get to the restaurant."

They grabbed their coats and hats and tripped down the stairs to the street.

"By the way, Crocker," Simon said as the valet waved his arm toward an available carriage, "did I mention that I encountered Lieutenant Egorov the other day?" Not waiting for Henry's response, he added hastily, "I invited him and his sister to have dinner with us this evening." He laughed at Henry's startled expression.

Henry, mouth gaping, opened the carriage door and waited for Simon to enter. The pink of his cheeks had yet to dissipate when they arrived at the hotel.

CHAPTER 24

"Crocker," Simon said the following morning, "have you ever attended a ballet?"

"No, my lord," Henry replied, appearing at the doorway of the adjoining room. "I've never heard of a ballet performance in Newcastle, and I could never afford to see one in London."

Simon shook out the morning newspaper and folded it to reveal an advertisement. "This ad says that tickets are available for a performance this evening," he said. "Would you like to go?"

"Me?" Crocker said, surprised at the invitation, then immediately hung his head. "I still don't think I could afford it, my lord."

"Crocker, you dolt!" Simon stared at the valet, shaking his head. "I'm inviting you to come as my guest."

Henry straightened, his face beaming. "Cor, sir! I'd be honoured!"

"Good. Would you mind making arrangements with the front desk? See if you can book us a box. Otherwise, something near the centre, lower floor, not too far forward."

"Yes, sir!" Crocker said with enthusiasm. "I'll just hang this in the cupboard and run straight down."

Simon and Henry arrived shortly before the first gong, checked their outerwear, and hastened up the red-carpeted steps to the balcony boxes located on the second level.

"You were lucky to get the box seats," Simon said, "given how many patrons are here this evening."

As they shuffled into their seats, Simon glanced toward the adjacent box, his face breaking into a broad grin. He paused before he sat and bowed smartly to the couple who seemed to be as surprised to see him as Simon was to see them.

"Well done, Crocker," he said, leaning toward Henry to be heard.

Henry turned to follow Simon's gaze, hesitating briefly before he sat down.

"Drinks at intermission?" Simon said over the diminishing din.

Artyom Egorov nodded, then glanced at his sister, whose eyes glinted with delight.

"That was a bit of luck," Simon said, noting a blush on Henry's cheeks that seemed to fade with the light of the theatre.

"We had no idea you were coming this evening," Egorov said during the intermission. "If you'd said something, I would have arranged a box for four."

"We didn't decide until this morning," Simon replied, accepting a glass of wine from a server. "Crocker made the arrangements." He leaned toward the lieutenant, speaking quietly. "Perhaps we should switch seats?" He turned his amused gaze toward Henry and Varvara, who carried on an animated conversation as if they were alone.

"Indeed," Egorov said, contemplating the same scene. "It's most fortunate that he speaks French." He shrugged his shoulder as if dismissing the couple. "Have you located a permanent residence yet?"

The conversations continued for several more minutes until a gong rang again, beckoning patrons to return to their seats for the second half of the performance. When offered the opportunity to switch seats, Henry and Varvara welcomed the idea, subject to Egorov's one condition. They were to sit in his line of vision, so he could ensure no impropriety ensued. The couple laughed and promised to behave.

As the house lights rose at the end of the performance, Simon noticed a familiar face in the crowd trudging up the middle aisle of the lower floor. Major Vasiliev's angry glare seemed focussed on Henry and full of fury. He followed a matronly woman animatedly chatting a step ahead of him. The glare broke when the woman jabbed Vasiliev with her elbow, as if demanding his attention.

———

The foursome stepped out of the Mariinsky Theatre into a quiet evening. Snow still lay upon the ground, muffling the sounds of gaiety. Henry hastily advanced, offering his hand for support as Varvara stepped into an awaiting carriage. He and Simon tarried long enough to bid farewell to their friends.

"I can't remember the last time I enjoyed such a lovely evening," Varvara said, stilling clasping Henry's hand. "Good night." Her ice blue eyes fastened on Henry's light brown ones, effecting pink stains on their cheeks. Suddenly, she froze. Her smile was replaced with an expression of fear.

The three men followed her gaze. At the sight of Vasiliev, their smiles became scowls, and each bristled with defiance. Vasiliev stood next to the matronly woman, his arm raised to flag a taxi. He fixed his attention on the foursome as the carriage halted, then opened the door and roughly handed the woman inside. Tearing his eyes away from the small party, he stomped behind the sleigh, barked instructions to the driver, and climbed in the opposite side.

Egorov urged his sister further into the carriage and climbed in next to her. He slammed the door shut and knocked rapidly on the ceiling, indicating that the driver move on. Although he could not have seen it in the evening darkness, Simon imagined the tell-tale twitching under Egorov's left eye.

When Egorov's carriage disappeared around a corner, Simon suggested they meander back to the hotel, along the Ulitsa Glinki toward the Moyka River.

"Gladly," Henry said. "I need to work off some of my anger."

Before they spoke again, they had reached the end

of the next block.

"So … what did you think of the ballet, Crocker?" Simon said, his voice calmer as he tucked his father's cane under his arm and donned his white evening gloves.

"I can't say how grateful I am, sir," Henry replied, reaching for the cane. "I've never seen anything so lovely."

"To whom are you referring?" Simon said, "Varvara … or the ballerinas?"

"What do you mean?" Henry said, sounding defensive as he returned the cane.

"Well," Simon said. "Given the puppy-eyed gazing that was going on between the two of you, I'm inclined to think your description of 'lovely' is intended for Mrs. Voronov, not the dancers."

Even under the streetlamps, Simon found it easy to discern Henry's blush. Henry coughed several times, as if trying to compose himself.

"Well," he said at length, "If I'm to be caught out, I'll agree with your assessment. However, I did find the dancers quite graceful. But … I have to wonder … about the men who like to prance about in tights, almost exposing themselves."

"Crocker," Simon said, choking on his mirth, "they're artists. What you have to understand about artists is that they will do whatever it takes to perfect their work."

"But … who was the pervert who dictated male ballet dancers sh-should dress like that!" Henry shook his head, his round eyes expressing his amazement.

"I truly don't know, Cr—" Simon's reply stalled when

they heard a man scream ahead of them. "Hurry, Crocker. Someone's in trouble!"

Simon broke into a run, listening carefully for the sound of ongoing conflict as his dress shoes slid over icy patches on the walkway. Near the naval barracks, he hesitated long enough to find his bearings, then continued to an alley where the sounds of a scuffle could be heard clearly.

Simon pressed his back into the wall of the corner building and peered into the alley. A bright moon and cloudless sky offered sufficient light for him to see that two men dressed in dark clothing were beating on a sailor.

"What do you see, sir?" Henry said sotto voce, his back pressed into the wall next to Simon.

"Enough to say that a petty officer is in need of assistance," Simon said. "Let's go!"

Simon marched into the alley, exhibiting more confidence than he felt. Memories of Bear Island flooded his thoughts as adrenaline surged through him. "Good evening, gentlemen," he said, his voice commanding. "Is there a problem here?"

One of the assailants completed his blow to the sailor's head, appearing to knock the man senseless. No sooner had his victim fallen motionless to the cobblestones than he spun around and charged at Simon. His companion rushed with impetus toward Crocker.

Simon raised his cane in defence, while Crocker was forced into hand-to-hand combat. The two young men were fit and ready. They met their assailants with strength, form, and determination. Within minutes, they had the two attackers pinned to the ground, groggy from the unexpected counterattack. As Simon stood and backed away, he released the catch on the cane to reveal its pistol.

"Crocker, see if you can find something to restrain these two thugs," Simon said, aiming the pistol threateningly.

While Henry scouted the alley, the sailor rose from the cobbles, staggering like a drunkard.

"Thank you, gentlemen," he said in Russian, swaying next to Simon. He pressed a hand to the side of his face, where blood flowed freely. "I hope you didn't spoil your evening clothes."

He rubbed his head where the first assailant had struck him and glared at the thieves. "If you thought to steal my purse, you idiots," he growled at his attackers with a raised fist, "you picked the wrong man. You probably have more rubles in your pocket than I do in mine!"

"Sir," Henry said, "I can't find anything to tie them with."

"I don't think that's necessary now," Simon replied. "I think that, between the three of us, we can take them to the naval lock-up." He looked over at the petty officer. "Do you think you can guide us?"

"Yes, sir," the petty officer replied, reaching to grab one of the thieves.

In that moment, the two culprits exchanged a brief glance and twisted away from their captors, running further into the shadows of the alley.

"After them!" Henry said loudly, racing a few steps ahead.

"No! Wait!" The petty officer's voice was devoid of emotion. "Let them go."

"Are you certain you want to do that?" Simon said, incredulous.

"Yes," the sailor said, bending over with his hands on his knees. "Did you see how poorly they're dressed? They're probably just hungry."

"Are you injured?" Henry said. "Should we take you to the infirmary?"

"No. No need. I'll be fine in a day or two," the sailor said, wincing as he gingerly fingered the crimson gash on his forehead. "Takes a lot more than a couple of thugs to beat me down." He limped toward the street, guiding his rescuers out of the alley.

"I'm sorry to report," the sailor said, "that these sorts of attacks happen often enough that we're sort of prepared for it. We don't carry anything of much value when we're out and about, and we usually have enough time to turn out our pockets."

He shook his head, looking back down the alley. "Those men were quick though, stronger too. If they weren't so poorly dressed, I'd have thought they were Okhrana. But what would the Okhrana want with the likes of me?" He shrugged.

"Okhrana?" Simon said, surprised to hear reference to the Russian police outside of his own circumstance.

"It's not above them to rough us up if they're looking

for information," the sailor replied. "Always wanting to know more than they should. It's about power and who holds it." He spoke as if to himself.

Realizing Simon and Henry were waiting for him to continue, he frowned, wiped drying blood from his hand, and thrust it forward. "I never forget a kindness or a face," the sailor said with enthusiasm. "If all goes well, I'll repay you one day." He tapped his forehead as if to fasten the memory, wished them a good evening, and marched briskly toward the barracks.

"How was that for an emotional release?" Simon said as they resumed their trek.

"In the moment," Henry replied, "much better, but come tomorrow, I expect I'll have found a few cuts and bruises of my own to show for it." He laughed heartily. "Mind you, each time I beat on that poor fellow, I imagined him to be the major." He shook his head as if in disbelief. "I expect he'll be feeling it tomorrow too!"

CHAPTER 25

"Lord Simon!" Sir George greeted Simon a few days later. He stepped from behind his desk and invited Simon to sit in a winged chair while a tray of tea and pastries was placed on the low table between them. Sitting opposite Simon, he accepted the cup of fragrant tea from a clerk.

Over the next hour, Sir George provided Simon with highlights and expectations of the upcoming dinner with the royals.

"I spoke with the tsar yesterday," Sir George said. "He and his wife remember you fondly, and I understand that the young princesses are looking forwarding to seeing you again."

"I'm pleased to hear," Simon replied, "that the expectation is mutual."

"From your note," Sir George said, "I had a sense that you have other matters on your mind."

"Yes, sir," Simon replied. "That's actually why I wanted to speak with you. I've pulled together a plan regarding Mrs. Voronov's dilemma, part of which involves your offer of help with her travel arrangements."

Twenty minutes later, Sir George walked Simon to the

door of his office. "Leave this with me," he said, shaking Simon's hand. "I'll see what arrangements can be made."

———

That evening, Henry announced that the rented flat had been organized to Mrs. Zima's preferences and that Mr. Zima's employment would begin in one day.

"It's time for us to move to Rosenshtein House," Henry said with a heavy sigh. He gazed around the hotel room as if to memorize its every detail. "While this accommodation has been lovely and convenient, it hasn't felt like home. I think you'll enjoy the flat, sir. Mrs. Zima is most pleasant and agreeable, and she's done everything possible to make it feel welcoming."

"That's a good thing, Crocker," Simon said, "especially if I'm to be here for a while. He scrubbed the day's whisker growth with his knuckles. "I still haven't met with the royals, and my investigation into Lebedev's pursuits is proving difficult too. I'll leave it to you to ensure Mr. and Mrs. Zima have everything they need. Sir George is helping me with your travel arrangements, by the way. You can expect to be home by year end, if not before Christmas."

Henry's head snapped toward Simon, his face expressing a combination of surprise and disappointment. "Very good, sir," he replied, his voice sounding devoid of his usual enthusiasm.

"Say," Simon said, seeing Henry's sad expression, "why don't we mark our last night in the hotel with a nice meal tomorrow evening … and invite our new friends to dine with us?"

"You mean Mrs. Voronov and Lieutenant Egorov?" Henry replied, raising his head up. Seeing Simon's grin, his face brightened. "Yes sir … thank you, sir!"

———

Had it not been for an obvious interest between Henry and Varvara during dinner, the meal may have been uneventful. As it was, Simon struggled to contain his mirth. Between the constant blushing, stuttering, and gestures of over-politeness, the attraction was clear. Even Egorov, on occasion, raised an eyebrow toward Simon.

"I say, Artyom," Simon said when the meal was cleared, and dessert had yet to be served. "I don't suppose you'd care for some fresh air?"

"I'd welcome it," Egorov said, rising to his feet. "What about you, my dear: would you like to step outside?"

"N-no, thank you," Varvara replied. "I'm feeling a slight chill." She lifted her wrap over her shoulders as if to cocoon herself in warmth. "I'll wait here."

"A-and I'll keep you company," Henry said, gazing hopefully at the young woman. "If you don't mind."

"Thank you," she said, lowering her eyes demurely, "your company would be welcome."

Outside the hotel, the two men crossed the road to stand next to a stone wall that ran along the river.

"My sister is quite taken with Henry Crocker," Egorov said as he lit a cigarette.

"The attraction appears mutual," Simon said, leaning against the wall.

"Varvara loved her husband dearly," Egorov said, releasing a stream of smoke to dissipate over the Neva, "but I never saw her as flustered with him as she is with Henry Crocker."

"I always thought Crocker reflected the epitome of bachelorhood!" Simon said, chuckling. "I never thought I'd see him brought to his knees by a woman."

He shifted against the railing and regarded Egorov. "I feel duty-bound to tell you, though, that while I consider Crocker to be a loyal friend, he is also engaged by my family as a valet. Tell me now if that concerns you, and I'll put an end to it."

"I will mention your offer to my sister," Egorov said, "but I doubt she'll care. She is both determined and wealthy. If she wants Henry Crocker, she'll have him!"

"Very well," Simon said, planting a backslap on Egorov. "I'll leave it in your capable hands. Shall we return?"

———

Several days later, while Simon finished his coffee, a firm rap at the door interrupted the quiet of the flat. Zima rushed from Simon's chamber to answer it.

"Thank you," he said, reaching for a coin from the hall table and handing it to the delivery person. "An envelope for you, sir." Zima placed the envelope on a small tray and carried it to his employer.

Simon set his fountain pen on the secretary and

cracked his knuckles before taking the snowy white envelope from the tray. The coat of arms of the Russian tsar had been pressed into the corner of its face. Henry looked up from a map he had been studying, his brow raised enquiringly.

Simon noticed and chuckled. "Crocker, you are going to have to curb your curiosity when you get home. Anyone else might accuse you of being too nosey for your own good."

"Sorry, my lord." Henry blushed as he folded the map.

"I'm not concerned, Crocker," Simon said, grinning. "Ours is a different relationship. There are those at home, however, who might take exception to our degree of familiarity, and that could cause you trouble."

"Understood, my lord."

"Why are you studying the map so intently?" Simon said.

"Varvara suggested that we meet for lunch soon, and take in some sights," Henry replied. "I thought I'd study the city layout so I understand better where we might be going."

"I see," Simon said with one quirked brow and a lopsided grin.

"I know, sir," Henry said with a heavy sigh. "She's above my class, and I could never afford to support her, but I'm not here for long, and I may never share her company again ... at least not as her equal. Can you blame me for basking in her presence while I'm able?"

"There you go again," Simon replied, "waxing poetic.

Listen Crocker, she's a lovely young woman and, if she's happy to share your company without complaint, then … by all means … enjoy the moment."

Simon regarded the royal seal on the envelope, slit it with a letter opener, and tugged the card from inside.

"This is a formal invitation to the royal dinner at the end of the month." He held the card for Henry to see. "Is everything in order?"

"Yes, sir," Henry said. "I've explained everything to Zima. He doesn't really need me to tell him how to do things; he's very capable. I've only provided insights into your personal preferences."

Simon made note of the dinner date in his calendar and returned the card to the envelope, propping it against a lamp.

"When are we expecting Artyom and Varvara?" Henry said.

"They should be here within the hour," Simon replied. "Lunch is organized?"

"Yes, my lord."

"And you're certain you don't mind playing a part in all this?"

"I am certain, sir," Henry said emphatically. "I'll help in any way I can."

CHAPTER 26

"Crocker has arranged lunch for one o'clock," Simon said. "I hope the timing is convenient for you."

"It is, thank you," Egorov said, handing his coat to Zima while Henry helped Varvara with hers.

Brother and sister had arrived minutes before. Once again, he was not dressed in his usual uniform, and she wore a large-brimmed hat with a veil that covered her face. When Zima excused himself to check on lunch, Simon invited his guests into the salon, pointing toward a sofa and armchairs.

"My sister begs that you excuse her appearance," Egorov said, spitting words angrily, the twitch evident. "She was forced to spend another evening in the company of Major Vasiliev, and he has rewarded her for it. Apparently, he didn't enjoy the ballet as much as he expected he should." His fists clenched as if to restrain his ire. "Varvara doesn't wish to lift the veil without first warning you."

Simon heard contempt in the soldier's voice, and saw hatred flare in his darkened eyes.

Varvara slowly lifted the veil over the hat brim and lowered her head, as if to delay the exposure of her injuries. Then, she inhaled deeply and raised her head. Defiance and pain reflected in tear-filled eyes.

Despite the room's shadowed lighting, Simon easily saw the purple bruise of a large handprint that covered her left cheek, and the fingerprint bruising that wrapped around her slender neck. Henry gasped.

"My dear Varvara," Simon said, reaching for her hand. "I'm truly sorry for the suffering you have had to endure. Your injuries make me even more determined to find a way to help you."

A pale blush traced up the young woman's neck and covered her cheeks. It was a startling contrast to the bruising.

"One of the reasons I've invited you here today is to suggest a plan that might resolve your predicament," Simon said.

"Please," Varvara said, "continue."

Simon glanced at Henry, seated on his right. Henry nodded, as if keen for him to continue as well.

"Alright," Simon said. "As you know, I have no plans to return to England soon. However, Crocker is expected to meet a ship in Arkhangelsk in early December, travelling by train from here to Vologda, then north. He has commitments in Newcastle beginning in January."

Egorov and Varvara nodded their understanding.

"Then, you will be leaving in a few weeks?" Egorov said, looking toward Henry, whose nod confirmed the timing.

"Further," Simon said, "I met with the British ambassador recently to ask his advice, and, if possible, his assistance. Yesterday, I received his reply. Simply put, Varvara, if you are comfortable travelling with Crocker, he will escort you to England. I will send a letter of introduction to my father, asking him to assist you. Crocker and others will be travelling with diplomatic immunity under the auspice of the British Embassy. The ambassador is prepared to include you in the party posing as Crocker's wife."

Simon leaned back into his chair, allowing his guests an opportunity to digest the news he had imparted. "If you need some time to talk this over, Henry and I can step out or—"

"No!" Varvara said, boldly interrupting Simon's comment. "No," she said again, quietly. "I apologize for my rudeness." A pale blush appeared again. "No discussion is necessary. I must escape this madman who thinks he owns me!"

Her brother placed his hand over hers as if offering comfort. "We have discussed the matter at great length, Simon," Egorov said. "Your suggestion is by far the best option." He turned his attention to Henry. "My sister will be your wife. I give my blessing happily."

"Sir?" Henry blurted in English, looking from the siblings to Simon and back again.

Simon raised his hand to stay Henry's question. "I apologize for the misunderstanding once again, Artyom," Simon said, hoping to offer clarity. "The suggestion is that they travel together as man and wife. The embassy will create papers necessary to confirm the relationship. However, Varvara is not expected to actually marry Crocker. It will simply be a ruse."

"Not marry my sister!" Egorov sat erect in his chair, sounding incredulous. "But they will be expected to share quarters, will they not?"

"No," Simon said. "One of the party is a single woman, and she is willing to share accommodation with Varvara."

"Ah!" Egorov said, relaxing into the chair.

"Will that not raise suspicion amongst the other travellers?" Varvara said, squirming in her seat.

"The ambassador has assured me that the members of the party are all reliable British subjects, and none will question the relationship or your travel arrangements," Simon said. "Once aboard the ship, the ruse can be dropped."

"Sir, may I speak with you privately?" Henry said in English.

Excusing themselves, Simon rose with Henry and followed him into the valet's room.

"Sir," Henry said, lowering his voice, "I'd like to propose marriage to Varvara. If she doesn't share my feelings, then we can carry through with the ruse."

"Marry!" Simon was incredulous.

"Sir, please listen to me," Henry pleaded. "You know full well that I have feelings for Varvara. Strong feelings." He blushed as his words quickened. He cleared his throat and continued. "I actually love her and would gladly m-marry her."

"But you hardly know her!" Simon said, stunned.

"I know enough," Henry said, defending his interest.

"I've had feelings for her since the train from Vologda. I can't bear to see her used and beaten. I want to marry her … if she'll have me."

Simon thought for a moment. "Very well," he said. "I may have to ask the ambassador for another favour though. I don't know what the Russian marriage requirements are, but I'm sure we'll find out."

Simon preceded Henry into the parlour.

"It seems we have one more option for you to consider," Simon said, addressing the siblings. "Crocker, it's your idea. Would you like to put it forward?"

"I have given the matter a great deal of thought over the past weeks," Henry stammered, frustrated that his French was not as fluent as Simon's. He inhaled deeply, as if to steady himself. "Varvara, I would like to accept Artyom's blessing of our marriage."

He stepped closer to the widow, dropped on his knee, and took her hand gently from her lap. "You know little of me, as I do of you, but I would consider myself most fortunate, Madame, if you would consent to be my wife. We will have a lifetime to learn about each other, and … I sincerely hope … time enough to love each other well. Varvara Voronov, will you marry me?"

Varvara looked upon Henry's sincere face and smiled gracefully. "Henry Crocker, you are a most kind man. I came here today prepared to comply with whatever my brother might arrange. I am desperate to escape the manipulations of Major Vasiliev. I never dreamt to receive a proposal of marriage from such an honourable man as you."

Henry took a deep breath, preparing to argue the benefits of marriage.

She held up her hand. "Please," she said, "you must let me finish. When we prepared to come today …" She glanced at her brother. "Artyom suggested that marriage might have to be considered."

Simon's eyes widened in astonishment, but before he could speak, she raised a hand to him as well.

"I told my brother this morning that if a proposal of marriage was to be made, it had to be with you, Henry Crocker. And not just because I must evade Major Vasiliev. I felt drawn to you the night you saw my brother consoling me on the train." She squeezed the hand that still held hers. "Henry Crocker, if you would like to marry me, then I would certainly like to marry you!" The smile that followed disguised her bruised countenance, revealing the true beauty of her face.

A tiny tear traced along Henry's nose and rested in the divot of his upper lip.

***

During the following weeks, while Simon continued his sleuthing of Lebedev and friends with the aid of the internal intelligence office at the British Embassy, Henry and Varvara prepared for their pending nuptials and travel arrangements. Varvara's luggage was delivered discreetly to Simon's flat to avoid any prying eyes as the departure date neared. Simon's naval uniforms were carefully packed into Henry's trunk as well, reducing the risk of anyone discovering his military connection.

Under overcast skies and feathery snowflakes, on the last Sunday in November, Simon, Egorov, the ambassador, and his wife bore witness to the marriage of Varvara Voronov and Henry Crocker. As a wedding gift, Simon had made arrangements with the Trezzini Hotel for a private suite in which Mr. and Mrs. Crocker could celebrate their nuptials while they awaited their departure.

When the long-awaited morning arrived, Simon and Egorov accompanied the newlyweds to the train station, where they were introduced to the other British travellers.

Once the train was out of sight, Simon and Egorov walked along the promenade and stopped at a pastry wagon. They reviewed the events of the previous weeks and marvelled that everything had been accomplished efficiently.

"Has Varvara heard from Vasiliev recently?" Simon said.

"She has, yes," Egorov said, smirking, "but she wrote back to say that she was ill with a seasonal malady. He let her know that he was not impressed and demanded that she recover quickly if she hoped to protect me from unforeseen circumstances.

"For the first time since Evgeni Voronov's death," Egorov said, "my sister is truly happy. Simon, I can never thank you enough for your help. And, of course, I owe Henry Crocker much more."

"I had little to do with that." Simon chuckled.

"Crocker is the man of the hour! Their life may not be as opulent as hers has been here, but I can guarantee you that he will take care of her, and my father will ensure that they're looked after."

Simon tugged his watch from his pocket and popped the cover. "Speaking of Father," he said, "you must excuse me. I need to send a telegram to let him know that Henry is on his way home. Then, I must dress for dinner at the palace. Are you attending this evening?"

"I will be there as Major Vasiliev's junior officer, yes," Lieutenant Egorov replied, grimacing. "I can't wait for the time when he can be informed that my sister is well away from him, but I won't do that until you tell me that she is safely beyond his reach."

"What about you?" Simon said, "Do you not worry for your own safety?"

"No," Egorov replied, as if contemplating his own future. "The Imperial Guard has too much on him, and he won't be here much longer. His replacement should arrive by next month." His gaze seemed far off. "One day, when this damned war is over, I will join my sister and her new husband in Newcastle!" He raised his cup of hot tea in a toast. "To the future!"

CHAPTER 27

Simon contemplated the light snow that had begun to fall while he dressed for dinner. He stood on the curb waiting for his transportation to the palace, grateful that he would not have to walk. He raised his cane and flagged the attention of a sleigh headed toward him.

"Lord Simon!" Sir George said, calling out as it slid to a stop. "I hope you haven't been waiting long."

In a flurry, the carriage door opened, and Simon climbed in. "I only arrived on the curb five minutes ago, Sir George," he said, smiling at the two women seated opposite. "Thank you for offering to collect me. I know it's out of your way."

"Not at all. Not at all!" Sir George replied.

As Simon straightened his cape and rested his tall hat on his lap, Sir George introduced his wife, Lady Georgiana, and their daughter, Meriel.

"Lord Simon," Mrs. Buchanan said, "how nice to see you again. And thank you for inviting us to Mr. Crocker's wedding."

"My father has told us of your intriguing adventures," Meriel said, eyeing Simon thoughtfully.

Once again, Simon felt like an insect being scrutinized

under a magnifying glass, as both she and her mother fixed their eyes on him.

"Perhaps you might regale Meriel with some of your stories." Lady Georgiana turned her gaze upon her daughter and raised an eyebrow, as if to encourage the conversation.

"I would be delighted to share the less colourful stories," Simon said kindly.

"No need to censor anything for me," Meriel said, her tone waspish. "I lead an unsheltered life, Lord Simon. I volunteer with the tsarina and the grand duchesses at the hospital. We tend to the wounded. *Nothing* escapes my sharp eyes."

"Then, perhaps it is I who should be regaled with tales," Simon said smoothly, hoping to beguile her with his best smile.

The carriage came to a halt and the door opened once again. Simon stepped out first and turned to offer a steadying hand to Lady Georgiana and her daughter. A red carpet led them away from the curb, up a short, marble staircase, and through ornate, gilt-covered doors. They followed a parade of dignitaries and many men in dress uniforms accompanied by women wearing elaborate gowns and tiaras.

"Here you have it," Sir George said, sotto voce, "the promenade of the Romanovs!"

The red carpet led them along a brilliantly-lit corridor lined with members of the royal guard dressed in their finery. At the end of the corridor, the carpet made a sharp turn and led the guests down another lengthy hallway, this time lined with senior staff and footmen.

"At this rate, we may reach Moscow in time for breakfast," Sir George said, as if amused at the distance they had walked.

"George!" Lady Georgiana said. Her hissing voice suggesting annoyance at his inappropriate remarks.

At the hallway's end were two grand doors that opened into a ballroom. Each door was guarded by a tall, black-skinned man.

"Are they not imposing," Meriel whispered in Simon's ear, as if awed by the sight.

Simon gave her a questioning look.

"The guards." She nodded toward the sentries. "They came to the palace with the tsarina for her wedding, and they've remained with her since. I've heard that they're twins, from Abyssinia. Her father hired them to keep her safe, and so ... here they are. Their mere presence tells us that she is nearby."

Before they reached the entrance to the ballroom, footmen stepped forward and relieved the gentlemen of their outerwear and hats, and the ladies of their capes. As an afterthought, Simon handed his cane to the footman, not wanting to be encumbered with it during dinner.

The footman's expression changed to surprise when he accepted it. Anticipating the man's reaction, Simon shrugged. "It belonged to my great-grandfather," he said, muttering in Russian. "Lovely to look at, but a bit on the heavy side."

"It's a handsome piece, sir. We'll take good care of it," the footman replied quietly.

The foursome wandered into the ballroom, where they were eagerly greeted by servers who offered wine and aperitifs in delicate crystal glasses.

"Come with me, Lord Simon," Sir George said, "and I'll introduce you to a few individuals whose acquaintance you may find beneficial in the future." He turned to his wife and daughter as if to apologize.

"Go!" Lady Georgiana said firmly. "I see—"

Before she could finish her comment, the two men had disappeared into the milling guests.

"Lord Simon!"

Simon and Sir George both stopped abruptly when they heard the younger man's name. Simon turned his head toward the voice and smiled warily.

"Maksim! Aleksandr!" Sir George greeted the two statesmen, chuckling as he shook their hands heartily. "I never see one of you without the other."

"This is very true, Mr. Ambassador," Lebedev said. "Lord Simon, what a pleasure it is to meet you again. I enjoyed our journey from Vologda, and when I received the invitation to this evening's event, I took the liberty of wondering whether we might see you here." He gestured toward his companion. "Is it not delightful to meet up with these gentlemen, Aleksandr?"

"Indeed, it is, Maksim." Aleksandr Volkov bowed

stiffly from the waist. "How have you found Petrograd thus far?" he said, directing his query toward Simon.

Simon marvelled that the two statesmen spoke English as well as they did. He regaled them with stories of his first evenings in the city, the challenges of finding accommodation less temporary than the hotel, and the task of hiring staff.

"And your companion, Mr. Henry Crocker?" Lebedev said, peering over his shoulder. "Is he with you this evening?"

"No, sir," Simon replied. "He's on his way to England."

"We did hear something to that effect," Lebedev said, glancing covertly at Volkov. "Was it not a little hasty, his departure?"

"No, not at all," Simon replied, wary of the line of questioning. "Crocker's intention was only to stay in Petrograd briefly. He has responsibilities in England, and was expected to return by the new year."

"But not you?" Volkov said.

"No, not me." Simon forced a smile, hoping to allay their suspicions. "I expect my work with the Murman projects will keep me in Petrograd for a while yet."

"That, I think," Sir George said, "could be quite a while. Do you not agree, gentlemen? I expect you are quite aware of the port development and the new railway, are you not?"

"Yes, yes," the two statesmen said in unison, looking like a pair of curious birds bobbing on a tree branch.

"I thought perhaps it was a temporary consultation,"

Lebedev said. "However, it sounds more involved than I initially understood. I hope you'll find time to enjoy the city … as we discussed on the train."

"I intend to!" Simon said heartily.

"Maksim, Aleksandr," Sir George said, "if you will excuse us, I'd like to introduce Lord Simon to some of the others." He looked about the room. "One never knows with whom one will be seated during dinner, and it helps to have a tad of familiarity."

Each man made a small bow, and the foursome splintered.

"Allow me to introduce you to the French Ambassador," Sir George said, guiding Simon deeper into the room. "He's been around awhile—was the Embassy Secretary for France in Tangiers, then Beijing, and later Italy. At the turn of the century, he was appointed Minister of Plenipotentiary, and represented France in Bulgaria for five years. He arrived on our doorstep last year. He's a cultivated man, and fancies himself a writer, of all things."

Simon observed the fair-haired, middle-aged man sporting bifocals on the bridge of his nose. As they approached, he spoke with great animation to a group of gentlemen, who burst into sudden laughter.

Beyond them, Simon caught a glimpse of someone familiar, then realized Major Vasiliev was scowling directly at him. Simon shuddered and promptly returned his attention to Sir George.

"Monsieur Ambassador," Sir George said, "may I introduce my acquaintance, Lord Simon Nightingale-

Temple. Lord Simon has recently arrived from Britain, and is planning to live amongst us for a while."

Taking their cue from Sir George's interruption, the French ambassador's audience departed.

"Indeed," the ambassador said, extending a hand in greeting. "But you are so young, monsieur; I am surprised that you are not in the services, fighting in some battle."

"I'm pleased to meet you, sir," Simon replied. "I've been engaged as an engineering consultant, to help move along the paperwork for the new railroad and port in the north. If I have free time, I hope to do a little sightseeing as well."

"That is a good idea, no?" the ambassador said. "One must find pleasure where one can. Employment is merely a necessity of life. You must enjoy the riches of this beautiful city. She has many stories to share."

"That is very true, Monsieur Ambassador." A threatening voice spoke from behind Simon. "Petrograd has many riches indeed."

Shifting from English to Russian, the speaker intended his next comment for Simon alone. "But be warned, Lord Simon, that you do not secret away her treasures. Anyone caught with their hand on Russian property will be penalized severely."

"Ah! Major Vasiliev, good evening," Simon said, turning sharply to face the portly officer. He felt a shiver wash over him as he realized the depth of evil he saw in the officer's pale, beady eyes.

"I have never been one to take things that are not

mine," he said, returning the conversation to English, "but ownership is not meant for all things. Do you not agree?"

Simon repositioned himself to include Vasiliev in the small group. "Gentlemen, I do apologize," he said. "Have you met Major Vasiliev?"

Vasiliev's eyes narrowed again as if to intimidate Simon, then he greeted the others amicably, speaking in broken English.

"Are you alone this evening, Major?" Simon said, searching the room. "I have yet to meet your wife. If she's with you, I'd welcome an introduction." Simon smiled insincerely.

"I am here alone," the major said curtly. "Excuse me." He made a stiff bow and tromped away.

"Whatever was that about?" the French ambassador said.

Before Simon could reply, a hush fell over the room, and the tsar and his wife entered, her white-gloved hand perched on his.

CHAPTER 28

The royal couple stood together at the top of the staircase, as if waiting for all eyes to focus on them alone. They stood regally, side by side, equal in height, waiting for the din to settle.

Formally adorned in red and white, the tsar's military uniform complemented the tsarina's gossamer white gown trimmed with diamonds and rubies. The double strand of pearls that she customarily wore rested on her bosom. Pearl drops dangled from her ears, and a diamond-and-ruby tiara trimmed with seed pearls nested in her elaborately-coiffed, light brown hair.

As one, the gathering bowed. In return the tsar nodded, then accepted a glass of sparkling wine, which he raised in a toast.

"Welcome!" he said in the language of the court. "As many of you know, I have been in Moghilev this past while with the troops."

Heads nodded as a murmur spread through the hall.

"It is most fortunate that my urgent return to Petrograd has coincided with this evening's event. My loyal supporters, I salute you!" He sipped his wine, then he and his wife descended the stairs and mingled amongst the guests.

The French Ambassador abruptly excused himself and waded through the milieu, trying to catch the tsar's eye.

Sometime later, a footman stood at Sir George's elbow and whispered into his ear.

"Lord Simon, you must excuse me," he said. "I've been summoned."

Simon watched the British ambassador wend his way toward the staircase and follow the footman through the same door used by the tsar thirty minutes prior.

"Lord Simon."

Simon turned in the direction of the unfamiliar British voice.

"We have yet to be introduced," the slender man said. "Bertie Stopford, at your service."

"Mr. Stopford," Simon said in greeting. "What is it that brings you to Petrograd?"

"I deal in antiquities and artwork," Stopford replied, handing Simon a card. "Please call me Bertie."

"Bertie," Simon said, repeating the name as he glanced at the calling card, noting the contact information.

"I travel between Petrograd and London," Stopford said. "I seem to have found favour amongst the nobility here. On occasion, I'm asked to liquidate certain jewels or old pieces of art."

He glanced hastily around him, retrieved a stylish, silver cigarette case and lighter from his jacket pocket, then lowered his voice while he tapped a cigarette on its case. "On very rare occasions, I may even be asked to carry correspondence for someone wishing to avoid the usual channels."

He placed the end of the cigarette between his lips and lit it, then drew upon it deeply. "If ever I can be of service …" He twisted his lips sideways and released the smoke.

"I'm afraid I don't have anything—"

Stopford raised his hand, halting Simon's remark. "Of course, you don't," he replied. "Not now, at least. But, if ever …" He winked at Simon, smirking as he spoke. Then he bowed slightly and disappeared into the crowd.

Simon tucked the card into the inside pocket of his coat, frowning. *I wonder what that was about.*

"Excuse me, sir," the voice of a nearby footman said. "Please follow me." Realizing that the servant was addressing him, Simon turned on his heel and followed up the stairs and through a familiar door.

The footman rapped lightly on a gilt door, opened it, and ushered Simon through.

"Ah! Lord Simon," Sir George said, stepping aside to reveal the monarch.

"Your Imperial Majesty." Simon's voice was calm as he bowed low before the emperor.

"Young Simon!" Tsar Nicholas said enthusiastically, the rows of medals on his jacket gleaming. "We're pleased to hear that you've settled comfortably in Petrograd." The monarch eyed the young man standing before him.

"You've grown. I reckon you're as tall as, if not taller, than your father. How fare our cousins, Charles and Ann?"

"They are both well, sir," Simon replied, "and send their greetings to you and your family."

"And we are most pleased that you have accepted our invitation," Tsarina Alexandra Feodorovna said as she entered the room. She smiled warmly at her husband, then at Simon. "This evening's dinner is merely a marking of our family's return to the city. Usually, we would have a grand ball, but given the political circumstances, we thought it more appropriate to host an intimate dinner—especially since my dear husband must return to the front almost immediately."

Jewelled bracelets on her wrist reflected light from the candelabra suspended above them as she selected a glass of champagne from a footman's tray. "As a result, we have excused our children from attending this evening. Tomorrow, you must return to the palace and allow us a proper visit. Our daughters will be delighted to see you again, and you have not yet met our son!"

"Your Imperial Majesty," Simon said, bowing deeply, "I look forward to the opportunity."

"Ahem," a footman said, interrupting the conversation. "The meal is ready for service."

"Of course!" Tsarina Alexandra replied. "Please come along." She gracefully beckoned the men to follow her.

Tsar Nicholas stepped to her side and offered his hand as they made their way to the grand dining room.

The dinner seemed to last for days. During the multi-course meal, Simon sat opposite Bruce Lockhart, British Consul General in Moscow. Lockhart had taken the train from Moscow the previous day to ensure that he was in Petrograd for the royal event. He was a young man, not much older than Simon.

During the meal, Lockhart entertained his table companions with tales of his life in Malaya where, at the age of twenty-one, he had joined his uncles, who were rubber planters. He was to open a new rubber estate near Pantai. Since the presence of white men was rare in that area, he said, he was openly admired by many of the local women, one of whom eventually turned his head. However, three years later he was forced to leave.

"The doctors determined that I had malaria," Lockhart said with a facetious shrug, "but I've never had a recurring bout. Frankly, I suspect it was poisoning. Prince Dato' Klana, the guardian of my beautiful Amai, was less than thrilled when I arrived in his country and objected soundly when she moved into my quarters. Before I knew what was happening, my uncles were packing me up and sending me home via Japan and America! Soon after, I joined the British Foreign Service. The next thing I know … I'm posted to Moscow as Vice-Consul."

He leaned back in his chair and lit a cigarette, releasing a stream of smoke before continuing. "People in Moscow had heard that I was a footballer from Cambridge," he said, shrugging modestly. "I was invited to play with the

Morozov team—Morozov being a textile factory—and I played for most of 1912. We won the football championship of the Russian Empire for Moscow that year!"

He paused while his audience marvelled at his accomplishments. "Of course, I'm the black sheep of my family. Everyone else is a scholar!"

Simon found Lockhart charming and entertaining, and he could readily relate to the man's interest in football at Cambridge. At the end of the evening, they walked out to the street together, Simon lamenting that he had not encountered Lockhart during their brief overlap at Cambridge.

"I hear you are fascinated by the tea rose," Lockhart said when talk of Cambridge and football evaporated. "I find it to be an interesting flower myself."

Simon halted mid-step and turned to his companion as the last comment penetrated his tired brain. Lockhart's toothy grin assailed him.

Simon laughed, shaking his head to clear his thoughts, and extended his hand. "Well, I'm just beginning to learn about its finer points, but I suspect it has more merit than I can possibly imagine in the moment!"

"Until next time, then," Lockhart said, plopping his top hat cavalierly on his crown.

"Indeed!" Simon replied, watching the man disappear around a corner.

———·———

Simon sat on the edge of the plush red sofa in the

salon, his elbows braced on his knees. He turned a glass of Scotch whiskey slowly, watching the light snag the prisms cut into its side to throw miniature rainbows on the opposite wall.

He sighed and leaned back. Henry was gone, and he was alone—except for the Zimas, of course—for the first time in months. His thoughts wandered in contemplation of the evening's events and, more particularly, his anticipated reunion with the royal family in a matter of hours.

Remembering Lockhart's departure, Simon swirled his whiskey and raised the glass to his lips. Gulping the last of it, he rose from the sofa, intending to refill the glass. When the room listed, the sensation startled him. He steadied himself on a chair's back and determined that he had consumed enough alcohol for one evening.

"I'd better turn in now," he muttered as he staggered into the bathroom, "if I'm going to be ready for luncheon at the palace tomorrow."

CHAPTER 29

The morning was overcast with moody clouds. The fall of snow had ceased in the early morning, leaving behind ruts that made street travel cumbersome.

Simon turned from the window edged in frost and sat before a plate of aromatic breakfast prepared by Mrs. Zima. He absently massaged a dull ache throbbing in his leg. Enjoying a cup of tea, he scoured the morning paper.

"Good morning, Lord Simon," Zima said. "Shall I order a sleigh?"

Simon glanced at the window again to see fat snowflakes swirling lazily on a slight breeze. He dabbed a crumb from his chin, contemplating whether a walk to the palace would clear another slight throb behind his eyes, a remnant of the previous evening's merriment.

"Perhaps that would be wise," he replied. "It wouldn't do to arrive for an imperial audience covered in snow."

"I'll make arrangements," Zima said, beginning to clear the table.

"Say," Simon said, folding the newspaper, "have you ever had an encounter with the Okhrana?"

Zima paused, looking aghast. "I do my best to avoid such situations, sir," he replied, his voice suggesting slight indignation.

"My apologies, Zima," Simon said, "I didn't mean to offend …" When Zima paused to contemplate his employer, Simon continued. "I haven't either, and I am curious to know more about them."

"Of course, sir," Zima replied. "I've never encountered the scoundrels who call themselves Russia's secret police, but am happy to relay stories, if you like."

"Please," Simon said, inviting the valet to sit with him.

Zima topped up Simon's tea, poured a cup for himself, and began reciting what he had heard. Sometime later, Zima concluded the last anecdote and, realizing the time, began collecting the dishes hastily.

"If you are to lunch at the palace, sir, I must arrange the sleigh," he said.

"Quite right," Simon said, "and I should dress."

A while later, Simon stood in the doorway, fastening the buttons of his overcoat.

"Lord Simon," Mrs. Zima said, approaching him. "You have asked for a light meal this evening, yes?"

"Yes, please," Simon said. "I expect I'll be well fed at the palace."

"Very well," she replied, sounding disappointed. "I hope that soon I will be able to prepare a proper Russian meal for you."

"We have plenty of time for that," Simon said, smiling kindly. "I'm not in a hurry to be away from Petrograd. I'm quite enjoying my stay."

"You are making many friends?" Zima said, joining

his wife to see Simon off.

"I'm not so certain about friends," Simon replied, "but I met a number of interesting people last evening, and I intend to follow up their acquaintance." He rested his hand on the doorknob, then hesitated. "In the pocket of the coat that I wore last evening, you'll find a stack of contact cards, Zima. I'd appreciate it if you'd set them on my secretary. I'll sort through them tomorrow."

As the horse-drawn sleigh glided through the slushy streets, Simon wondered why he felt so chipper. *Perhaps it's because I'm about to meet Olga, Tatiana, and Maria. They were charming little girls. What must they be like now?*

The evening before, Tsarina Alexandra had suggested that Simon bypass the main entrance and go directly to the Hermitage gate off Palace Square. The sleigh slid to a stop near the gate and waited for a guard to notice.

Over his shoulder, Simon scanned the empty square, catching a glimpse of movement near the Alexander Column. He stared hard, not certain that he had seen anything. A second later, he was rewarded for his persistence. A man clad in grey apparel and a worn, cloth cap stepped from behind the Column, eyeing the sleigh. As if realizing the sleigh had not moved on, he stepped back abruptly.

A guard's greeting distracted Simon. When he announced his purpose, the guard opened the door of the sleigh and directed him inside. Simon glanced one last time toward the Column, noting that the man in grey walked casually in the opposite direction, his hands cupped around a cigarette as he lit it.

Simon frowned. He followed a footman into the palace, contemplating the man in grey. *I must pay more attention. If I'm being followed, I need to find out why, and fast!*

Visions of Lebedev and Vasiliev came to mind, sending a shiver down his spine. *Vasiliev is overtly threatening. Superficially, Lebedev seems nondescript, but there's something about him that's unsettling, and I mean to get to the bottom of it. Of course, it doesn't help that the two are related by marriage, and likely in cahoots. But what does any of it have to do with me? Do they somehow know that I'm here to investigate them? None of the detainees could have sent word. They couldn't possibly know of my intentions.*

The footman halted outside the morning room, where two Abyssinian guards stood on either side of the door and knocked.

Tsarina Alexandra welcomed Simon with evident pleasure and introduced each of her daughters in turn.

Olga and Tatiana, the two older grand duchesses, were born two years apart. From his research, Simon knew them to be twenty and eighteen years old, respectively. They carried themselves as confident young women: attractive with light brown hair and blue eyes.

Anastasia, a rambunctious fourteen-year-old, looked to be a younger, plumper version of her elder sisters, while sixteen-year-old Maria stood out amongst the four. She was by far the comeliest of the tsarina's daughters, with dark blue, saucer-like eyes and hair much lighter than the others. *As if it's been kissed by the sun,* Simon mused to himself.

As if she heard his thought, Maria gazed at Simon with her large, dark eyes. When his steel blue ones met hers, she smiled, warm and beguiling. He was surprised to feel a shift somewhere deep inside and swallowed hard to stifle any outward reaction. The moment left him feeling confused and unsettled, wondering what separated her from the others that he should have such a reaction.

"My son, Alexei, will be along shortly," the tsarina said, her words slicing into Simon's thoughts. "He is with his French tutor at the moment. And my husband had a meeting with members of the Duma this morning to hear their concerns about political issues that have arisen in his absence. Nikki promised that he'd be back in time for luncheon." She invited Simon to sit in a chair next to the unlit fireplace.

"Perhaps a little music, girls," she said. "It will give Simon an opportunity to familiarize himself again; except for Anastasia, of course, who was but a baby the last time he was here."

"Mama!" Anastasia protested, defiance darkening her eyes.

Olga and Tatiana sang a duet, while Olga accompanied them on a white piano sitting next to the window.

Simon sank into an embroidery-covered chair and relaxed, feeling as comfortable in that moment as he had when he was a boy of eight who played with three young girls in that very room. Tranquility cocooned him while he enjoyed their entertainment and the view of the gardens. Snow-laden clouds parted, as if inviting an illuminating ray of sunshine. Melting snowflakes glistened on the plants and bushes that formed the garden's skeletal shrubs.

An hour after Simon's arrival, Alexei appeared. He was tall like his father, although only twelve years old. Immediately behind him, a footman arrived to announce the return of the tsar, and that luncheon would be served shortly.

By the end of the mid-day meal, Simon felt welcomed again into the fold of the tsar and his family. *Nothing seems to have changed*, he thought, *other than the fact that we've all aged a bit.*

"Young Simon," the tsar said as the meal ended, "perhaps you might join me in my office for a while before you are once again released to the pleasant company of my daughters? And you, Alix, you will join us too?"

"Of course," Simon and the empress replied in unison.

"Simon, my wife and I sincerely thank you for assuming the role of liaison with our cousins," Tsar Nicholas said, motioning for Simon to sit in a guest chair next to his wife.

"I'm happy to be of service, sir," Simon replied. "I have a letter here from King George." He reached inside his jacket and retrieved an envelope bearing the royal seal.

"It was written several months ago, before I left England, but the king assured me that it was a timeless message of well wishes."

"If it is not time sensitive, then we'll read it later," the emperor said, taking the envelope and sliding it under the lip of a blotter. "Now tell me, what is your sense of politics, both here and in Britain? Did you glean anything noteworthy during your travels? Please be candid. After all, that is the point of your visit, is it not?"

"My travels only confirm the extent of the war," Simon said, and elaborated further by describing his many months at sea with Britain's Royal Navy. He concluded with an accurate telling of the Bear Island incident that had resulted in his injuries, as well as his suspicions regarding Maksim Lebedev, possibly others.

"What adventures you've had!" the empress said.

"I've certainly felt my adrenaline pumping a few times," Simon said, grinning sheepishly. "My valet and I also had an interesting encounter on the train from Vologda to Petrograd. We were introduced to two statesmen: Maksim Lebedev—whom I've already mentioned—and his colleague, Aleksandr Volkov. Both attended the dinner party last evening as well."

"Yes, yes," the emperor grumbled, a frown darkening his countenance. "I know of them, and would pay little heed, but for two things: Lebedev's involvement in the 1902 assassination attempt, and now this submarine business. Lebedev's been a thorn in my side for more than fifteen years. If he could, I'm sure he'd see me dead tomorrow!" Spying his wife's glare, Nicholas ceased his rant. "Excuse me. Please continue."

"We also encountered a few officers from the Imperial Guard on the train," Simon said, "including a particular major. I believe he's temporarily standing in for the garrison commander. His name is Ivan Vasiliev. Do you know him? He attended the dinner party as well."

The monarchs shook their heads.

"He seems an unsavoury sort from all I've heard, and based on recent observations, he appears to be collaborating with Lebedev. I intend to investigate further—with your blessing, I hope. I'm worried that they may be conspiring another assassination attempt."

"Another!" The tsar jumped to his feet, shock replacing his earlier frown. "I'm bedevilled as it is, with the contrariness of the Duma and the military madness in Moghilev. Now my life is in danger ... again?" He threw his arms in the air, as if overwhelmed by his predicament. "You have arrived just in time, I'd say, Simon. I must return to Moghilev. In my absence, Alix will represent the Crown. I ask that you support her any way you can."

He paced across the room, mumbling through his agitation. "Am I never to trust anyone again? Present company excepted, of course."

Simon felt a familiar chill run down his spine.

CHAPTER 30

Simon and Tsarina Alexandra found Olga and Tatiana with Pierre Gilliard, a Swiss academic hired as a French tutor. Anastasia and Alexei, they learnt, were with Sydney Gibbes, a British academic hired as an English tutor. Maria was with neither instructor. Instead, she had returned to the morning room, where she sat in the company of Anastasia's governess, embroidering.

"Maria," the tsarina said as they entered the morning room, "your sisters and brother are occupied with their tutors. Will you give Lord Simon a tour of the Hermitage and the Winter Palace?"

"Of course, Mama," Maria replied, ceasing her fancy work. She gazed coquettishly toward Simon. "I'd be delighted." She carefully folded the fine cotton stitched with assorted flowers and butterflies and handed it to the governess.

"Where would you like to start, Lord Simon?" she said, her hands clasped demurely behind her back. Large eyes gazed back at him.

"I am at your mercy, Grand Duchess Maria," Simon said, catching a light scent of lilac as he made a courtly bow.

They strolled out of the room and along the corridor.

As they walked, Maria described the merits of each room. "The upper floors are mostly for storage, with some sleeping quarters for servants and staff who might reside here. Let's go downstairs. I'll show you the grand rooms, then we can wander through the palace proper. After that, I'll show you the gardens."

"Sounds wonderful," Simon replied, finding himself admiring the fall and bounce of her glistening hair as he followed in her wake.

"Before we leave the Hermitage," Maria said a while later, "there's one last item that I'd like to show you. Perhaps you'll find it a pleasing memory if you've seen it before." She rounded a corner and entered a great white hall trimmed in gold. Along the windows, opposite an aisle of paired marble pillars, stood a gilt aviary that seemed to fill the height of the vaulted ceilings.

"This is known as the Peacock Clock," Maria said, pride and awe tingeing her voice. "Do you know it?"

When Simon shook his head, she elaborated. "The clockworks were made in the late 1700s by a British jeweller renowned for making automata. He hoped it would endear him to Empress Catherine II. He arranged for the pieces to be shipped to Petrograd, and then had them assembled here." She paused in her narrative and glanced at Simon. "What time is it?"

Simon tugged his watch chain and flipped open the watch cover. "It's almost three o'clock," he replied.

"Wait," she said excitedly, "and see what happens!" Delight danced in her dark blue eyes. "I can never see this too many times. You're certain you've never seen it before?" She looked directly at him and held his gaze as he returned the watch to his pocket.

"Not that I recall," he said. As he spoke, his ears picked up odd sounds: ticking, chiming, and whirring sounds that seemed to bring the golden clock to life.

Creatures around the clock began moving, drawing Simon's interest. The large peacock upon which the assembly focussed spread its tail feathers. An owl twisted within a small cage, and a rooster crowed the hour.

"What an amazing work of art!" Simon said excitedly. "Every creature seems to have a task!"

"It's enchanting, is it not?" Maria replied proudly.

"It truly is," Simon said, finding her enthusiasm effervescent. "I can tell you honestly that I have never seen this clock."

"Come," Maria said, "there's more to see, but I doubt nothing as marvellous."

As they explored the corridors, Maria provided Simon additional insight.

"The Winter Palace used to be the home of the tsar and the tsar's relatives. As you will have noticed, we've passed through several very grand rooms and some lesser chambers, all of which have been modified on numerous occasions to suit the needs of the day. Eventually, Alexander the Great built the Hermitage, and it became the residence of subsequent tsars. Now, we keep only temporary apartments in a corner of the Hermitage," Maria said, "when we need to be in Petrograd overnight or for several days. However, our proper home is Alexander Palace, in a town south of Petrograd called Tsarskoye Selo. We're going back tomorrow, after Papa leaves."

Her enthusiasm seemed to wane, her expression becoming sad. "I'd rather stay here," she said peering straight into his eyes. A shy grin tugged on her lips.

"Peacock Clock and other sights aside," Simon said, the flutter in his belly convincing him of the need to stay on topic, "I find the craftsmanship and structures most interesting. I suppose that's my engineering studies poking through. The Hermitage is an elegant home. Given the choice, I too would live there over the Winter Palace."

"But the palace is useful for state affairs and dinners, like last evening," Maria said, matter-of-factly.

"Do you like oranges?" Maria said, grinning mischievously as she fastened the buttons on her coat.

"In fact, I do!" Simon replied, taken aback by the question. "Why do you ask?"

"You smell like oranges," Maria said with a giggle, her cheeks reddening.

"I think you're right!" Simon replied, sniffing his fingers. "I prefer to eat an orange every morning when they're available. The war embargos have made them difficult to find though."

"Do you ride?" Maria said, mercurially changing topics, her words frosting ahead of her as they walked through the gardens.

"I do," Simon replied, blowing warm air onto his chilled fingers. "Do you?"

"Yes, but not well," Maria said, her blush of admittance casting a pale hue on her cheeks. As she fastened the top button of her coat, her fur collar tightened, framing her delicate features. "I'm not confident around horses."

"I've been invited to visit you at Tsarskoye Selo," Simon said, feeling giddy. "Perhaps we could ride together then?"

"Oh, yes!" Maria said with enthusiasm. "And you can help me improve my skills?"

"I'd welcome the opportunity," Simon said with equal enthusiasm, his features brightening with the thought of spending more time with her.

"You attended university?" she said, her voice rising with interest.

"I did," Simon replied enthusiastically.

"What did you enjoy most about it?"

"Ha!" Simon felt a surge of passion rush through his veins, remembering his days at Cambridge. "So many things. The academic studies were mind-opening. They left me with a sense of wonder and a need to know more."

The two young people stopped outside the stable, enjoying the warmth of the pale winter sun.

"I also enjoyed the athletics: football, track and field, wrestling, boxing—"

"Wrestling! Boxing! Why, it all sounds marvellous! I should like to learn wrestling and boxing so I can defend myself," Maria said. "Papa says it's not necessary. Security guards are with us wherever we go … to keep us safe. Still, I should like to be able to defend myself, if necessary. After all, Russia is at war!" Her voice rose in defiance.

Maria stopped abruptly and turned to face Simon. Mere steps behind her, he was unable to avoid the imminent collision. His hands clamped firmly on her waist as he attempted to maintain a respectable distance between them. A moment passed between them, their eyes locked.

"Pardon me," Simon said, feeling embarrassment burn his cheeks. He promptly dropped his hands and stepped backward. "I—"

"Will you teach me?" Maria said, ignoring the accident.

"Teach you?"

"Boxing, wrestling, and other defensive moves." Her grin could not have been wider, and her expectation could not have seemed greater.

"I could," Simon said, quickly recovering from the near-breach of protocol. "You might raise the matter with your parents first, though. They're not genteel activities."

"I know, but don't you think war makes extenuating circumstances?"

"You have a point," Simon replied.

"Then I shall speak with Papa. I want to learn! I want to be prepared!"

CHAPTER 31

During the first quarter of 1916, Simon became a regular visitor to Alexander Palace. He enjoyed the ninety-minute train ride from Petrograd to Tsarskoye Selo along the rail line that the tsar had built to allow his family safe and efficient travel between the town and the Hermitage. His ulterior motive, Simon had learnt, was to ensure that in the event his son required immediate medical attention, he would have access to it.

After the first visit, Simon carried an overnight valise with him and often stayed at Alexander Palace for two or three nights. He never disclosed to Mr. and Mrs. Zima where he went, suggesting only that he took small business trips on his father's behalf.

He was plagued, however, by the man in grey, who continued to tail him. Recalling that Vasiliev had been transferred to the frontline in late December, he wondered who might have so keen an interest in his activities as to warrant having him followed. He took great care to evade his follower each time he set off for Alexander Palace, often catching the train at different times and from different stations.

In a letter to his father, Simon wrote that he felt

caught up in a cloak-and-dagger mystery, and that he endeavoured to determine the reason for it, but so far he had had no success and too many suspicions.

Simon employed a coded message system that his father had taught him before he had left for boarding school. At the time, he thought it a fun and interesting way to write letters. Lately, however, he had begun to fully appreciate the benefits of the code. Employing those techniques, he had only recently asked his father to investigate whether British records might reveal any historical concerns involving Maksim Lebedev, Aleksandr Volkov, and Major Ivan Vasiliev.

By return mail, his father's coded message advised that Henry and his new wife had arrived safely with the diplomatic entourage. He also advised that Henry and Varvara had provided details of events leading up to their departure. While the newlyweds had little to offer regarding the two statesmen, Varvara did share her own experiences at the hands of Major Vasiliev.

Because of the covert nature of Simon's presence in Petrograd, Charles cautioned his son to take care when making enquiries. He took it upon himself to contact Ambassador Buchanan directly and was pleasantly surprised to hear that Simon had already discussed his concerns with the ambassador.

Those men seem careful not to betray their intentions. However, Buchanan wrote to Charles, *I sincerely believe they are involved with revolutionaries, though I have yet to see any evidence. I've discussed the matter with Lord Simon and suggested he be wary. I've introduced him to individuals here who may be of assistance, and have encouraged a particular connection with Mr. Bruce Lockhart, British Consul General in Moscow.*

Regarding Major Vasiliev, I'm afraid that I have limited personal knowledge, but can report that he is an aggressive, impatient, vengeful, and often cruel man. He will let nothing stand in the way of his military advancement, which suffered as a result of recent hot-headed actions, of which I am confident you have been informed. I also understand that you have had prior experience with the man's capacity for dastardly deeds.

"Lovely," Simon said aloud, "he's simply confirmed my own suspicions and offered me no remedy. Except, perhaps, with regard to Mr. Lockhart. I'll send the chap a note right now!" He snatched a crisp sheet of paper and his fountain pen and wrote with haste.

In February, Bruce Lockhart notified Simon that he expected to be in Petrograd on business at the end of the month and would like to accept the invitation to visit. Simon wrote back suggesting he stay at the flat for a few days, and Lockhart accepted.

Lockhart stayed four days, spending much of his time with Simon. Together, they explored a different side of Petrograd as Lockhart introduced Simon to the art of espionage, an interest to which he had been drawn soon after his posting to Moscow in 1912.

"I have learnt from a few acquaintances that the art of espionage requires five things: a knack for languages and dialects, a capacity for disguise, a strong awareness of surroundings, the ability to think quick on your feet, and at least some defensive training. How do you fare with that list?"

"Not bad," Simon said. "I know several languages and, since coming to Russia, have learnt to switch from one to another quite effortlessly. I could stand to improve my use of dialects though. My spontaneity is improving. I like to think that I have a keen awareness of my surroundings, and I'm trained in a variety of defence tactics. I'm quick on my feet and athletic. The talent I lack is disguise or deception."

"That's not so difficult," Lockhart said. "A disguise need not be complicated unless you want it to be. You just need a few tools that will ensure that you're overlooked."

They were reclining in Simon's sitting room, enjoying a brandy after feasting on one of Mrs. Zima's fine meals. Lockhart excused himself and disappeared into the guest room.

A few minutes later, Simon saw movement out the corner of his eye, but paid it no heed, presuming Zima was tending a task.

"Well? What do you think?"

Simon started at the unexpected voice and turned in his chair to regard the man who spoke. On guard, he rose to his feet, identifying the voice as Russian, likely from the north, but the timbre of the voice stumped him. He frowned as he sidled toward the fireplace, intent on snatching a poker for a weapon. Before he could demand the man identify himself and his purpose, the intruder burst into laughter.

"You should see your face," Lockhart said in his own voice.

"Why!" Simon said, surprised. "It's you!"

At the revelation, Simon examined the diplomat further. His typically neat, wavy hair was mussed forward over his brow and around his ears, held in place by a woollen cap. His cheeks were flushed, as if he had been working outside, and he sported a small moustache and goatee. He also wore rough, woollen trousers and an overlarge coat made of leather. On his feet he wore the curious leather boots Simon had seen worn by men in northern Russia.

"My gosh! I didn't recognize you," Simon said. "But, on close examination, I can't see how I could miss the fact that it truly is you."

"That's the point, Temple!" Lockhart emphasized. "Don't draw attention to yourself. When you finally noticed me, all you saw was a Russian peasant; that's all anyone sees. I can slip in an out of all sorts of places without being noticed, and I needed only a few items to fool you."

Simon marvelled at Lockhart's easy deception.

"Teach me!" he said. "I'm sure I'm being tailed, and I need to stop whoever is doing it."

"Tailed? Now, that's a concern."

"Indeed," Simon replied.

"Alright," Lockhart said, laughing. "Let's get some sleep, and we'll start first thing in the morning. I've had a lot to drink tonight, and I'm exhausted."

"Done!" Simon said. "I'll see you in the morning."

During the next forty-eight hours, Simon focussed intently on Lockhart's instructions.

"I can't imagine why you think you've a need for advanced deception," Lockhart said, amused at Simon's interest, "but I'm quite happy to share what I know when I return."

Simon stood on the platform and waved as Lockhart's train to Moscow pulled away from the Petrograd station. Then he strode off to await his own train, departing from a nearby terminal.

Simon closed his eyes and leaned back into the seat, marvelling at the tips he had learnt from Lockhart and the fun that they had had roaming freely through the city streets disguised as peasants. He sighed deeply and relaxed into a semi-state of sleep. They had shared a long night creeping through alleys, hiding in shadows, and following folks without being noticed.

That morning, as Lockhart had prepared for his

departure, Simon had shared information imparted by Buchanan several weeks earlier, including the stash of military equipment and supplies maintained by Lebedev in Russko-Vysotskoye. As he hoped, Lockhart had found the idea intriguing and suggested that, when he returned, they make a point of investigating further.

Simon sighed, welcoming the brief respite that the train ride offered. He would need energy when he reached the palace; the grand duchesses had planned a small dinner for him in their private quarters.

CHAPTER 32

"I have great news!" Maria said, rising from the table at which she and Anastasia had been playing a card game. She was the first to greet Simon, kissing him on each cheek, awakening in Simon a familiar sense of discomfiture that had come to haunt him when in her presence.

Simon said nothing while her sisters and brother greeted him. When they all stepped back, their faces seemed to show their pleasure at Simon's arrival.

More than usual, he thought. *Almost mischievous.* "What's this 'great news,' Maria?" he said dubiously.

"Please come and sit with us," Olga said, beckoning him with her hand.

Maria quickly plopped into a chair near the one Olga had recommended for Simon. "I spoke with Papa about learning methods of defence," Maria said enthusiastically, "and he thought it was a smart idea—so long as we are careful not to injure ourselves!" She dropped her chin and lowered her voice, as if to imitate her father.

"Monsieur Gilliard and Monsieur Gibbes have taught us simple defence techniques," Tatiana said defensively.

"Yes, but not sufficient!" Maria said with certainty.

"Of course," Olga said. "And I agree that we could all learn more."

"Alexei has more training than us," Anastasia said. "He trains with the guards."

"Well," Simon said, speaking over the discussion with raised hands as if to diminish the din, "I am glad to hear this. Defence techniques are important."

"And you will teach us!" Maria said with satisfaction, sitting on the edge of her chair.

"Me?" Simon said, surprised.

"Yes," Olga said. "Messieurs Gilliard and Gibbes are already occupied with our education, and they agreed that they could use the time to prepare advanced studies, instead of having to interrupt our lessons to oversee our physical fitness. That responsibility will now fall to you." She crossed her arms over her chest, as if to finalize the edict.

"Mama plans to ask you to live here at Alexander Palace," Tsesarevich Alexei said. "I do hope you will. We need more men around here!" His hooded eyes met those of each of his sisters.

"Messieurs Gilliard and Gibbes are also pleased," Olga said, "that you speak several languages. They hope that you'll engage us in general conversation so we can improve in that regard too."

"My word!" Simon said, surprised again. "Maria, it seems my small agreement to teach you some defensive techniques has come alive in ways I never imagined!"

"Isn't it wonderful!" she said, glowing in response.

"Mama asked that you visit with her after our meal, so she can discuss the details."

"I look forward to it," Simon said. "Speaking of food …"

"Of course," Olga said, jumping to her feet, "you've been travelling all day. You must be famished."

"I'll check," Anastasia said and quickly disappeared down the hallway, calling for a footman.

"So, what news have you since I was here last?" Simon said, trying to divert the attention from himself.

———

A few hours later, Simon excused himself and went in search of the tsarina.

"You were asking for me, ma'am," Simon said, entering the sitting room indicated by her footman. "Oh, pardon me, ma'am," he said stopping mid-step. "I'll come back later."

"No, Simon," Tsarina Alexandra said, waving him into the room. "Come and meet our dear friend, Grigori Rasputin."

"Mr. Rasputin," Simon said, advancing warily, "it's a pleasure to meet you. I've heard your name mentioned on several occasions. It's always nice to put a face to a name."

"You've heard my name," Rasputin said, his brooding eyes seeming to pierce Simon's soul, "but it very likely was not mentioned kindly."

"I can assure you, sir," Simon replied, "that your name is always mentioned in high regard within this house."

Simon smiled reassuringly. He did not want to admit that he had discussed the man's reputation with others, although the name was always on the tongues of gossip mongers and concerned individuals.

"Thank you for your kind words," Rasputin said, rising from the chair where he had been sitting. "I was just leaving." He bowed respectfully to the empress and left quietly.

"Simon," Tsarina Alexandra said. "Please, sit with me for a while. I'm sure my children have been pestering you about the tasks I'm hoping you'll accept."

"What exactly would you like me to do, ma'am?" Simon leaned forward, elbows on knees.

"Tea?" she said, turning her gaze toward the footman who stood near the doorway.

"Thank you," Simon replied, watching the footman pour.

"We—my husband and I—would be grateful if you would teach all our children advanced defence techniques. It's a little unorthodox for young ladies to learn sword fighting, but I think you should teach them everything. Don't hold back. We want them able to defend themselves. You will find Alexei is more skilful than the girls, but you must be careful with him. His sailor nurse will guide you." She thought for a moment as if on reflection. "Actually, please keep the nurse's suggestions in mind for all of them."

Simon sipped his tea, listening intently to her instructions.

"I also understand that Maria has asked for equestrian

instruction. That too is a good idea."

"My pleasure, ma'am."

"As Alexander Palace is our winter home," the tsarina continued, "we'll dwell here until March. You are most welcome to reside in the Palace too. It would save you the frequent commute. And we will, of course, compensate you for your time and effort."

"Thank you," Simon replied. "I'm grateful for the employment, and I'll give the offer of residency some thought. I do have reasons for keeping my flat in Petrograd. In particular, it's easier for me to communicate with …" Simon glanced covertly at the footman. "With my family."

"Understood," the tsarina said, with a brief nod. "I will leave it to you to make your own arrangements, so long as you know that you are welcome at the palace any time." She looked toward the footman. "Leave us, please."

As soon as the footman closed the door, Alexandra spoke again, with urgency. "Take this," she said, tugging a wooden box from beneath an over-large satin pillow and handing it to Simon. "Open it."

Simon set his cup and saucer on the table. Lifting the rosewood box into his lap, he raised the lid carefully, commenting on the beauty of the carving. "Ma'am?" Simon peered in the box, then gazed at the tsarina.

"In the box is an assortment of jewellery, Fabergé ornaments, and an egg." She listed the items, watching Simon finger through them. "Please find a way to liquidate them. I don't know what the future will bring, but I suspect we'll need money."

She dropped her eyes to her lap, where her thumbs tumbled in circles in her folded hands. "Please don't mention this to Nikki," she said, raising her gaze to Simon. "He doesn't understand my need to be prepared. He would consider it a betrayal. Plus, he'd be very upset to think that I sold any of his gifts."

She squared her shoulders and spoke with determination. "However, one of us must be proactive. I hear what lies the gossipers say about me. The Russians are blaming me for their misfortunes. They believe I've sold my country to the Germans."

Simon closed the lid and listened, seeing defiance in her eyes.

"Will you do this for me?" she beseeched him, eyes glistening.

Simon sighed deeply, feeling weighted by responsibility.

"I know someone who might be able to help," he said. "You may have heard—"

"No," Alexandra said, holding her hand up, palm forward. "I don't want to know. The less I know, the less need I'll have to lie to my husband."

"Yes, ma'am. As you wish."

"Before you remove the box, may I see it one last time?"

Simon returned the box to her grasp and watched her set it reverently on her lap. Raising the lid, she lifted the items lovingly. "Nikki gave these to me," she said softly. "They're all tokens of his love. I should cherish them, but they are the only things that are truly mine. The only things that I can sell."

She lifted the egg from the box and caressed it. "He gave me this—the Rosebud Egg, Mr. Fabergé called it—to mark my coronation." She held the red-enamelled shell and pressed it apart at the centre, causing it to open on a hinge.

"This," she said, removing a yellow-enamelled rosebud trimmed in gold, "represents my favourite rose. It grows in the gardens of my childhood home. The gardeners here have tried to grow them in the greenhouse, but even in the summer it's too cold for them."

She pried the rosebud open and tipped out two more items. "This"—she held up a dainty gold chain from which dangled a cabochon ruby—"represents his heart, and this …" She opened her palm. "This is a miniature of the crown I wore on my coronation day. It was made with tiny diamonds, seed pearls, and a red spinel." Her voice was forlorn. "I will treasure them always, in here," she said, patting her breast. She placed the re-assembled egg in the box, closed the lid, and lifted the box for Simon to take.

"I will keep your request in confidence," he said, "and I will ensure I'm paid the best price for everything."

"Simon," she said, "perhaps you might not sell the egg until absolutely necessary? If something happens to threaten my family, use it to pay the cost of taking my children to safety."

"Yes, ma'am." Simon pushed himself from the chair and arched his back. "If I may be excused, I'd like to turn in. I've had a rather long day, and I'm quite exhausted."

"You may, of course," the tsarina replied. "And …
thank you, Simon."

Simon made his way to an assigned chamber with
the rosewood box tucked securely under his arm. In his
room, he contemplated the offer of employment, and the
task of selling the contents of the wooden box.

He had not expected a formal offer of employment,
and quite liked the idea. *I've felt like an aimless rudder
since I arrived here. This will give me purpose. Before I make
plans, though, I should like to speak with Messieurs Gilliard
and Gibbes. They have been with the royals for a while. I'm
sure they'll have plenty of insight that will help me prepare
a program suitable for each of the girls. I especially want to
understand Alexei's limitations, and whether the girls might
be affected similarly.*

*As for the jewels, I certainly didn't expect that task either!
I'll have to return to the city and look up Bertie Stopford. I
hope he's in town.*

CHAPTER 33

Simon visited the palace often, enjoying the company of the royal family and spending time with their tutors, who were happy to learn of his formal engagement.

Following an unusual storm in early March, deep snowdrifts around the estate made it too difficult for riding. Instead, the girls treated Simon to a sleigh ride, introducing him to the town and showing him the countryside. A drop in temperature kept the snow from melting for several more weeks.

On better days, they stomped along a path to the lake and spent time ice skating. Simon was pleased to see that they were comfortable on the ice, and encouraged them when they illustrated the figure skating techniques that they had learnt in earlier years. As the snow melted and cold weather gave way to the chill of spring, Simon devised other games and exercises to burn excess energy.

On his days off Simon returned to his flat in Petrograd, where he spent several days at his desk recording events in his diary, writing letters to his parents and the British royals, and planning the next escapade with Lockhart.

During the last week of March, Lockhart returned to Petrograd for several days. On the first day, the two sleuths planned an expedition to Lebedev's encampment and tended to preparations, including borrowing a Berliet limousine from the British Embassy. On the second day, they set off on their adventure.

Near midday, Simon stopped the motor at the side of the road so they could stretch their legs and dive into the basket of sandwiches and beer provided by Mrs. Zima. Guzzling the last of his beer, Simon noticed an open motored vehicle round the previous bend in the road and stop abruptly. A moment later, gears grinding, it reversed direction.

"That's curious," he said, packing up the basket and securing the empty bottles. "Did you notice that motor come around the last bend and reverse instantaneously?"

"I did," Lockhart said, chuckling. "Maybe your tail's found a new mode of transportation too."

Oh, I hope not," Simon replied flatly. "If they have, the fools must be bloody freezing! At least our motor is closed against the wind." He set the basket and bottles on the floor in the back. "More to the point, if they truly are tailing us, our plans could be compromised.

"Let's get going, then," Lockhart said, climbing behind the steering wheel. "I'll drive. You keep watch."

A few minutes later, as they approached the end of a straight stretch of road and entered the next curve, Simon saw the motor creep forward.

"No, no, no," he muttered to himself. "Not now!

You'll ruin everything!"

"Let's see if I can reach the next bend before they catch up," Lockhart said, grinding gears as he accelerated with purpose.

At the next bend, he turned sharply to the right, skidding to an abrupt stop and sliding into a cluster of bushes. He let the Berliet roll forward, sheltering it behind a stand of fir trees. The two men exited the motor and ran back toward the road, crouching behind the brushes.

A short time later, the Russo Balt careened around the bend and sailed passed them. Two men bound in tightly wound mufflers bobbed in time with the bouncing motor.

"Quick! Get in!" Simon hopped in behind the steering wheel, reversed the Berliet onto the road, shifted gears, and accelerated. As they neared the next curve, he slowed to a crawl, as if tiptoeing into the bend, and stopped unseen on the side of the road.

The Russo Balt rested at the edge of the road about a half mile ahead of them. Its two passengers stood behind it, angrily gesticulating.

"Looks like we've outsmarted them," Lockhart said, happily.

"Maybe," Simon said, "but we still don't know who they are. Come on." Simon jumped out of the Berliet and disappeared into pungent-smelling fir trees that lined the road. Lockhart followed. They raced along a well-worn animal path until they were within earshot of the two strangers.

"So, what should we do now?" a tall, thin man said

to a shorter version of himself, who happened to be dressed in grey. He twisted from side to side as if looking for direction.

"Vasiliev said we're to keep eyes on him all the time," the man in grey said sullenly. "Temple's a slippery devil, though. At this rate, we'll never get paid."

"Why d'you suppose he's headed this way?" the tall man said, flapping his arms against the cold.

"I guess we'll never know," the man in grey said forlornly. "Now that we've lost him again."

"How about you tell me why it's so important that you follow us?" Simon said, his voice deep and demanding, the pistol in his hand authoritative.

Startled, the two strangers jumped and turned smartly toward the voice, their faces puckered with confusion.

"We're just carrying out Major Vasiliev's orders," the man in grey said, whining defiantly. "We're only s'pose to watch you. See where you go."

"Hmm," Simon said, waving the pistol toward some large boulders. "Why don't you sit over there and tell us what you know." He wiggled the tip of his pistol again, encouraging them to move.

As the men backed toward the boulders with their hands in the air, Lockhart raced back to the Berliet.

Keeping the pistol trained on the two men, Simon walked around the Russo Balt, contemplating the best way to detain the strangers.

"We don't know anything more," the tall man stammered. "We're just supposed to follow you and report back."

"But you don't make it easy," the man in grey said grumpily. "We're always losing sight of you."

"Well, I don't think you'll be following us any more today," Simon said, ripping the crank shaft from its storage case and tossing it far into the bush.

"No!" the two strangers said as one.

"How will we get back to Petrograd?" the tall man said.

"If I were you," Simon said condescendingly. "I'd start looking for the crank shaft. If not, I suspect you'll make it back to the city before dark. Perhaps someone might stop and offer you a ride. Otherwise, the walk will keep you warm."

Simon hopped into the Berliet as Lockhart slowed alongside. Lockhart shifted gears and accelerated.

"That's rid of them for a while," Lockhart said, chuckling.

Simon looked over his shoulder to see the two men standing in the middle of the road, shaking their fists in protest.

"Yeah, but now I have more questions than answers," Simon replied. "They said that Vasiliev set the tail, but we don't know why. And how is it that they found us despite our disguises? Something's amiss. I wonder whether Lebedev's aware of the tailing."

"We'll have to puzzle that out later," Lockhart said shrugging. "How much further to the encampment?"

"Not far," Simon said. "I'm hoping we'll find an inn in the village. We can have a warm meal and catch some shuteye before we head out again."

Three hours before midnight, Simon and his companion both dressed in black and armed themselves with a haversack containing sundry necessities, including filament torches, pistols, a vest pocket Kodak camera, and a map. They then set out on foot in search of Lebedev's encampment. During the evening meal, they had made subtle enquiries that confirmed its existence and precise location. They had listened as others discussed the nature of their employment and the security surrounding it. To their relief, the camp was a mere ten-minute walk further along the road.

As Simon and Lockhart made their way toward the stairwell leading up to the guest chambers, they overheard one of the employees mention that their boss had arrived late in the afternoon, intending to inspect the warehouses. Simon grinned in response to Lockhart's wink.

Simon and Lockhart skulked close to a chain-link fence. For a long while, they simply watched and waited. Twenty minutes later, the entrance gates opened and an entourage of three black vehicles rolled up to the security hut. Each was inspected by a guard before being waved forward. As the rear car passed under a bright search light, Simon spied Lebedev.

"That's convenient," he said hastily focussing the camera lens, hoping the search light was sufficient to provide detailed photographs. "There's Lebedev in the last vehicle."

"So, we know he's connected to this place," Lockhart said. "That's a start. Now we just need access. I don't suppose you have wire cutters in your haversack, do you?"

"I certainly do!" Simon said.

They circuited the fenced encampment until they found a secluded spot obscured in shadows. Once Simon had snipped enough links to allow them passage, they skulked along the back of the buildings, peering into windows, making notes, and taking photographs of all they saw. Their hope, of course, was for sufficient lighting; otherwise, the photographs would be useless.

In one tall building, they counted six transport trucks and two armoured vehicles, each shiny with newness and clearly marked with Russian military logos. Three lower buildings appeared to be full of boxed supplies. A fourth, similar building appeared partially constructed. On the far side of the fourth structure stood a building that resembled a railway roundhouse.

"We need to get into one of these buildings," Simon said, crouching at the corner of the third building, which was situated furthest from the guard house. "Then, I want a look inside the roundhouse."

"Shhh," Lockhart said beside him. "I hear footsteps."

A dog barked nearby.

"Shit!" Simon hissed the word quietly.

"What is it, Boris?" a man's voice said. "Another rabbit?"

Boris yipped twice in response. The dim, overhead light cast a silhouette of Boris and his handler on the newly-constructed wall of the fourth building. Boris yipped again when his handler scrubbed his head. Then they turned and walked in the opposite direction, their shadows fading as they passed beyond the light.

"That was close," Lockhart said, releasing his breath.

"Yeah, come on," Simon said, crouching in the shadows as he scooted toward a doorway. "We don't have much time."

Once inside, Simon switched on the light of his torch, aiming it low until they were far enough inside not to be seen from windows. He swept the torchlight up and down and across the vast aisles of boxes, calling out the labelled contents for Lockhart to record in his small notebook.

"There's enough supplies in these three buildings—presuming the other two are similarly stocked," Lockhart said, running his finger down a page of scrawl, "to support a war for weeks. I doubt six trucks is enough to move men and supplies, though."

"It's not for a war," Simon said, whistling softly through his teeth. "He's amassing this to take control of the country. He'll use the railway to move everything."

"What—"

"Come on," Simon said. "If I'm right, and that is a roundhouse …

They quickly exited the supply building and headed toward the curious building. Simon opened the door quietly and slid through a crack. Lockhart followed.

"My suspicions are correct," Simon said, inhaling the

familiar smells of a railway yard. He scanned the building with his torch and stopped abruptly when something shiny caught his eye. He beckoned Lockhart to follow, holding the torchlight on the shiny machine as its size increased with their approach.

"Whew!" Lockhart said, releasing a long breath. "So, he's managed to skim a few of the old engines."

"Yeah, and I bet if we look through that window, we'll see a yard full of abandoned cars, and a rail line for bringing them into the encampment."

Lockhart whistled his amazement as they approached the window and the shadows of large machines came into view.

"Look," Simon said, pointing beyond them. "New tracks. Too bad we couldn't get a closer look during the day. This site must be huge."

"It explains a lot about the new housing that we saw as we entered the town, and the inn's clientele," Lockhart said, sounding impressed.

In the distance, Boris began to bark again.

"Let's get out of here," Simon said. "Our observations will all be for naught if we're caught."

———•———

On their return to the city, Simon and Lockhart reported their findings to senior military staff at the embassy. Although the discovery and accounting of Lebedev's trove was a significant line item in their report, they had yet to confirm how or when Lebedev intended to use it. Speculation that Lebedev intended to take control of Russia remained to be proven. The report and accompanying photos provided concrete evidence of the possibility.

Thanks to Lockhart, Simon had discovered ways in which to hide delicate correspondence in a variety of Russian souvenirs, which he then sent to England marked to the attention of his mother. His next correspondence included an outline of his findings and confirmation that a detailed report would be sent with the embassy's courier.

In late April, Simon returned to the palace and requested an audience with the tsarina, who, in turn, invited him for coffee the following morning.

"Tell me, Simon," she said as she poured coffee for them, "have you any news for me?"

"I do indeed, ma'am." He lowered his voice. "While I have many things upon which I can report from Petrograd, I think the greatest news concerns your little box."

Alexandra set the coffee urn on its warmer and gazed at him with a hopeful look. "Were you able to sell anything?" she said in a whisper.

"I was, ma'am." He patted his breast pocket, reaching inside his coat to withdraw a leather billfold.

The empress hesitated before accepting it from his outstretched hand. With trembling fingers, she opened the cover and gasped.

"You'll find an assortment of currencies, including

rubles, pound sterling, and American dollars," he said. "I also have coins." He withdrew a pouch from another pocket and handed it to her.

"I presume," she said, opening the pouch to find smaller ones inside, "that each small pouch contains coins in the respective currencies?"

"Yes."

"Thank you, Simon." She sat the billfold on her lap and the pouch on top of it. "Now, I have another request, if you don't mind."

"Ma'am?" Simon replied, sitting forward on his chair.

"I'd be grateful if you would take this away and conceal it," she said, handing the two items back to him, "for safekeeping. No one must know about it. Once you've found a safe place, you may tell me, but only me. Understood?"

"Understood," Simon assured her. "I have just such a place in mind." He rose, preparing to leave. "If you'll excuse me, I have a lesson with Grand Duchess Maria."

"Of course," she replied, watching him turn toward the door. "Simon—"

"Ma'am?" Simon twisted toward her.

"Is everything gone?" she said quietly, stressing 'everything.'

"Everything?" Simon said, not readily grasping her meaning, before recalling her earlier instructions. "Ah! No, I took the liberty of setting the egg and its contents aside; except for the necklace, which I included with the other items. It's all stowed safely in my flat with other important items. I have written a message as to ownership and placed it inside the box as well. In the event anything happens to me, it will be returned to you or sold as you have instructed. For now, however, I will store the money in the rosewood box, too."

"Thank you, Simon," she said with a sigh of relief. "I am truly indebted to you for your kindness and loyalty."

"Ma'am," he said, paying her a courtly bow.

"You'd best be off," the empress said brightly. "Maria will be waiting—impatiently, no doubt!"

CHAPTER 34

The tsar remained in Moghilev for most of 1916. As a result, the family rarely visited Petrograd. Instead, Nicholas preferred to travel directly to Tsarskoye Selo, where he knew his family to be safe.

Simon noticed that, in addition to the constant and varied visits of other members of the royal family, Rasputin was often in attendance, providing him many opportunities to overhear conversations between the monk and the tsarina.

Staff who saw to the personal needs of the royals were particularly concerned that Rasputin never hesitated to enter the private chambers of the grand duchesses and often stayed well beyond a respectable length of time. This too Simon had witnessed, much to his consternation.

Simon observed that, although Rasputin was deferential to the Romanovs, he did nothing to endear himself to staff and guests, including Simon. During the first months that their paths crossed, Simon wondered why the family tolerated him.

On one occasion, however, the palace erupted in chaos, resulting in an urgent message being dispatched by the tsarina to the guest house, where the monk often resided with his mistress. Several minutes later, the monk rushed up the palace stairs, his unfastened cassock billowing with each stride, and barged into Alexei's chamber without knocking. He remained there for several hours, keeping company with the tsarina and her son.

While Rasputin saw to the tsesarevich, the grand duchesses kept Simon occupied, explaining how Rasputin was the only person who truly understood Alexei's hemophilia. Only he could calm the condition and restore the boy to good health. Without the Divine intervention of Rasputin, Alexei would not have lived beyond his fifth year.

Although Simon found the explanation confusing, and contrary to any medical cases he had occasion to read, he admitted to himself that the tsesarevich's ill health seemed to improve whenever Rasputin tended his ailments. He was careful not to vocalize any doubts, however, not even to Maria—with whom he had become uncomfortably close—or the royal doctor.

On those occasions when Tsar Nicholas returned to Alexander Palace, he never stayed for more than a few days. His attention was almost always diverted to unrest caused by rebellious strikers, conscripted soldiers, and the protests of hungry peasants.

On one occasion, Simon happened to be present when Ambassador Buchanan warned the tsar that if he failed to support constitutional reforms, he would find himself in the midst of a revolution, not unlike those brought on by other monarchs who failed to react soon enough.

"With respect, sir," the ambassador said firmly, "your people are hungry. They have no food, fuel, or other living essentials. Your soldiers are even worse off. Many of them don't even have shelter, and, I understand, they haven't been paid for months."

"That's ridiculous!" the tsar said, his response sounding contrary to Buchanan's comments. "The royal advisors tell me otherwise; they say that alcohol is the source of their difficulties. I shall simply ban all alcohol. We merely need to boost patriotism and productivity! In sobriety, the Russian people will see why we must hold our position: why the war is important, and why they must tighten their belts."

Buchanan tried to reason with him, but the monarch refused to listen. Instead, he issued the proclamation, which resulted in a disastrous backlash. Too late, the tsar realized that by prohibiting the sale of alcohol, the treasury—which was supplemented by a tax on all alcohol—began to deplete at a rapid rate.

"I'm grateful that we live in the country," Tsarina Alexandra lamented one afternoon in early summer.

She had invited Simon to have lunch with her and her sister-in-law, Grand Duchess Olga Alexandrovna.

"Here, we live sparsely. If we lived in the city, we would be expected to live in grandeur."

"Indeed," Olga said. "If you'd remained in the city, you'd have had to sell your jewels by now!"

Stunned by the all-too-real comment, Simon recognized Tsarina Alexandra's expression for what it was.

Her surprise quickly dissolved, and she glared at her sister-in-law. "Still, no matter how thrifty we might be, we are plagued by the same shortfalls as the peasants," she said in lament. "We can't eat what we don't have! And we've had to limit the number of rooms that we heat. Even in the middle of a forest, we don't have sufficient fuel to burn. Perhaps it's a good thing that they are oblivious to our suffering. What would they think of us if they knew? No doubt, they'd blame me!"

"Indeed!" Olga said, her expression seeming slightly less than compassionate. "I suppose it's a good thing that summer is coming. Perhaps you can stockpile some wood for next winter."

Simon listened to the conversation as the tsarina plopped a spoonful of sugar in her teacup and stirred aggressively. "When will this evil war end?" She clasped her trembling hands in her lap as if to still them.

Simon relaxed casually against the back of his chair, hoping the women had forgotten his presence to spare them from the embarrassment of the outburst.

"Do you suppose the British are forced to endure such hardships?" Olga said, turning her attention toward Simon.

"Pardon me?" Simon said.

"Do you think our cousins are scrimping?" she said again.

"I presume they must be," Simon replied, "considering the embargo and blockades imposed by opposing parties." As he spoke, he recalled the palace opulence he had observed when last he met the British monarchs.

The question left him wondering, more so about his parents. He made a note to ask when next he wrote. Since they lived primarily in the country, where food sources were easily accessible, he had not thought to ask. Regardless, Mrs. Zima's grumbling was a constant reminder that even his little world was forced to do without many things.

By the summer of 1916, Simon had fallen into a somewhat predictable routine travelling between Tsarskoye Selo and Petrograd. In the city, he tended to his usual correspondence and reports, and admitted, if only to himself, his relief that Maria was not near at hand. He was finding her presence increasingly distracting, which in turn raised the concern that he do nothing to offend his hosts, or compromise the young woman's reputation or international protocol.

From time to time, Simon met with Egorov for an evening at the ballet or opera and a meal out. He enjoyed the easy-going companionship with no responsibilities or obligations attached. He also looked forward to irregular visits from Lockhart, who continued to mentor his covert training while they delved deeper into unearthing Lebedev's plans.

When not focussed on Lebedev, he and Lockhart

mingled with the masses and reported civil concerns back to England. Any recommendations received from Britain and intended for the tsar were delivered discreetly as soon as an opportunity arose.

The tsar's insistence that the Russian people would eventually come to their senses and support his ideals frustrated Simon. While residents of Tsarskoye Selo tended to support the royal family, Simon realized that overall public approval was negligible. He realized too that those remaining in Tsarskoye Selo were true loyalists only because they benefitted from the flow of royal coin that paid for their services. Residents of differing opinion had long since departed for one of the bigger cities.

During his wanderings with Lockhart, Simon heard for himself the rumble of suffering citizens growing louder. Newspaper articles ranted that the Duma's demands were increasingly insistent.

To his surprise, Simon found Mr. and Mrs. Zima to be excellent sources of information. While he had never divulged to them his true purpose for being in Russia, they seemed to sense it was important. Zima, after all, was the one to post and collect Simon's messages, and was certain to recognize the seals of the British crown and Simon's own family.

Simon embraced the prudence of wearing a disguise each time he took the train to Tsarskoye Selo, in addition to selecting a variety of stations from which to depart, hoping his actions would be unpredictable. Since the road trip to Russko-Vysotskoye, he had not noticed the man in grey again. Although he had no solid proof, he continued to sense that he was being watched.

On one occasion in early July, Simon passed the evening with Mr. and Mrs. Zima. As they enjoyed their meal together, Mr. Zima noted that the flat appeared to be under surveillance by two men, dressed like Okhrana, who regularly hung around the end of the street and glanced often toward the flat's windows.

———

"Say, do you have plans for a week Saturday?" Egorov said, as he and Simon strolled along the Neva River late one evening.

"No," Simon replied with a grin, "not yet. What do you have in mind?"

"My uncle is hosting a summer soirée," Egorov said. "Would you like to come as my guest?"

"Evening suit or ballgown?" Simon said, teasing his friend.

"Evening suit will do," Egorov said. "My uncle stopped expecting me to attend his functions with a woman on my arm long ago. You'll like him. He reminds me a lot of Father, and he could be a good contact to have in your pocket if you find yourself in trouble—as I am certain that one day you will!" He smirked, seeming delighted to have delivered his own jab.

"And your uncle is?" Simon said.

"General Count Fyodor Arturovich Keller," Egorov said, "Imperial Guard."

"Indeed!" Simon replied. "You've certainly kept him under your hat!"

"Need to know, brother," Egorov said. "At the rate you and Lockhart are going—poking at the Lebedev wasp nest—you may need rescuing."

"I will ensure that I am back in the city by Friday night," Simon replied, "and I look forward to meeting General Count Fyodor Arturovich Keller!"

A week later, Simon, dressed once again in formal evening attire, accompanied Egorov to his uncle's soirée. Since his aunt had died some five years earlier, much of the colourful attire consisted of military officers in formal uniforms, unintentionally competing with the ornately-designed gowns worn by the few women present. Expecting to fade into the background, Simon realized that he and the few other men dressed in white tie and tails were the ones to stand out.

Simon accepted a glass of champagne and followed Egorov from group to group, warmly greeting those to whom he was introduced.

Not fifteen minutes later, the general exited a study at the end of a long hallway, with an entourage of senior officers strolling behind. He snatched a glass of bubbling wine from a tray and stepped onto a dais, where a band was playing ambient music. When he raised his glass in salute, the band silenced.

General Count Keller kept his welcome short, encouraging his guests to enjoy themselves, then hopped off the dais and strode directly to his nephew. The two men embraced affectionately.

Before Egorov could introduce his friend, the general asked after his niece, and Egorov provided the obligatory update. Then, he turned toward Simon and introduced his uncle. "Uncle, you will recall that I've mentioned Lord Simon Nightingale-Temple before," Egorov said, "in connection with Varvara's rescue."

"Of course!" the general said. "While I miss my dear niece sorely, I'm truly grateful for your aid, Lord Simon." The general clasped Simon's hand and shook it heartily. "If ever I can do anything to assist you, please don't hesitate to speak up."

"Thank you, sir," Simon replied, "I won't."

As Simon faced the general and shook his hand, he noticed a familiar leer beyond the soldier's shoulder, and pleasantly nodded an acknowledgement.

A moment later, the general excused himself to greet his other guests.

"Impressive," Egorov said, "isn't he."

"He is, indeed," Simon said, scanning the room. "You resemble him in several ways."

"I've often heard that said," Egorov replied. "Are you looking for someone?"

"Is he also friends with Lebedev?" Simon said.

"Definitely not," Egorov said. "He has little time for politicians, but my aunt was a firm believer in keeping your friends close and enemies closer. Although she passed years ago, he still adheres to her suggestion."

"Good evening, gentlemen," Lebedev said, stopping

next to Simon. "I had hoped to see you this evening, Lord Temple. Lieutenant Egorov, nice to see you."

"Mr. Lebedev," Simon said. "Here alone?"

"I am, yes," Lebedev said. "My wife is under the weather, as you English say, and my brother-in-law has yet to return from the frontlines. I would have stayed home, but my wife insisted I attend." He shrugged and accepted a flute of champagne from the silver tray extended before him.

"Excuse me," Egorov said, "I see someone I must greet." He made a shallow bow and departed briskly.

"I've learnt that you have found occasion to tour the countryside," Lebedev said, drawing Simon's attention.

"Oh?" Simon replied. "I can't imagine why you would be interested in how I pass my time."

"I'm not," Lebedev replied, his voice no longer pleasant, "unless it intrudes on my interests." Lebedev reached into a pocket and extracted small, black-and-white photographs. "These were delivered to me this morning."

Simon accepted the photographs and flipped through them.

"The first photos were taken from a guard tower," Lebedev said, eyeing Simon. "and the other was taken the following day."

Simon examined several photographs of two men dressed in black—photographs he knew were of him and Lockhart taken outside the gate to Lebedev's encampment—and one of the hole cut in the chain-link fence.

"What are you suggesting?" Simon said nonchalantly, scanning the room for a reason to escape his current encounter.

"Merely that, the last sighting of you and your companion was mere miles from that location," Lebedev said, "only hours after the two of you rented rooms at the only inn in Russko-Vysotskoye."

A corner of Simon's lips tugged to form a grin. He kept his eyes still, focussed on the photographs, and pressed his thumb into his twitching lip.

"I suggest, Mr. Temple," Lebedev said, his voice threatening, "that you curb your travels to only those between Petrograd and Tsarskoye Selo. Further travel south of the city could result in grave injury." He snatched the photographs from Simon's hand and slid them casually into his pocket before disappearing into the animated gathering.

Simon selected another glass of champagne from a passing tray and wandered through the crowd in search of his friend.

CHAPTER 35

Two days later, Simon welcomed an unexpected visit from Lockhart and shared his encounter with Lebedev. Realizing there was nothing more to be done about the encampment—at least until further instructions arrived—the conversation shifted to encoded messages and how Simon's father had taught him.

"You know," Lockhart said, expelling cigarette smoke, "I bet you'd make a great spy."

"Spy!" Simon said, sputtering. "Why do you say that?"

"Think about it," Lockhart said. "From what I've heard about espionage, your talents would be an asset." He drew on his cigarette and exhaled again, then began reciting Simon's talents. "Athletic, observant, multilingual, classless, deceptive, and now … a master of disguises." Lockhart grinned, his eyes twinkling with mirth. "How's it going with the hidden messages, by the way?"

Simon laughed, then sipped from a brandy glass. "I've been giving my father a merry chase. I've sent a few souvenirs to my mother; Father always suspects there's a message hidden in them. His challenge is finding it."

"And … does he find them?"

"Right enough, then he grumbles in his next

communiqué that the task is never easy."

"That's a good thing, is it not?" Lockhart said.

"I suppose," Simon replied. "My father expects a hidden message and looks for it, but not everyone would expect me to hide a message. Why would I? This all feels like a game to me. If it weren't for the fellow in grey always following me, I never would have pursued this curious path."

"Are you still being followed?"

"I don't think so," Simon said thoughtfully. "But Zima believes the flat is being watched." He sipped the brandy. "I wish I knew who was doing it, and why. My guess is either Vasiliev or Lebedev. Until we investigated the encampment, I'd done nothing to warrant their scrutiny, unless they're painting me with the same brush as my father."

"That's very likely," Lockhart said, eyeing his friend. "But think about this: you appear out of nowhere with upper-class British connections. You are welcomed into the royal household without question. You spend, what …?" He glanced at Simon as if expecting an answer. "Maybe three days a week at your flat, during which time you keep company with a variety of curious individuals, including the Buchanans and me, and then you disappear. Except Lebedev just revealed that he knows you frequent Tsarskoye Selo. On your arrival, you announced that you were engaged by the British government as an engineer, here to inspect construction of the Murman sea port and the new railway. Yet, you're engaged by the Romanovs as a tutor. I'd be suspicious."

"You're right, of course," Simon replied, shaking his head. "Unless I'm travelling about the city, I wear a disguise, but I see what you mean. If someone wanted to suspect me of mischief, they could certainly read deception into my behaviour, and they only need one ally in the palace who can report on what goes on." He scrubbed the bristles that shadowed his jaw. "Should I stop using disguises and tricks, and just let the rascals follow me?"

"Why?" Lockhart said. "They'll still come to the same conclusions, and you'll no longer have fun making them work for their money."

"Ha! Right you are!" Simon said, laughing. "Why do you do it? Are you a spy?"

"Excuse me?" Lockhart replied, choking as he inhaled cigarette smoke. "What would make you ask that?"

"Well," Simon replied, "you seem to be doing the same sorts of things that I'm doing ..."

"Fun, man! It's all about the fun!" Lockhart said enthusiastically, as if trying to divert Simon's question. "Think about it ... I'm attached to the British Consul. I sit in an office all day and listen to people complain that they've lost their identification papers, or they're ill and need to get home to England, or they can't find suitable accommodation."

He jumped out of his chair and paced across the room, jabbing his fingers through his dark hair. "I tell you ... sometimes I feel like a bloody receptionist or, worse yet, a nursemaid! I need a challenge, and these arts of deception are just that."

"I understand," Simon said. "I quite enjoy the challenge too. Besides, given the current political climate in this country, I wouldn't be surprised to see our skills come in handy."

Lockhart set his brandy glass on a nearby table. "Well … I'm off to bed. I have an early train to catch tomorrow." He stretched appreciatively. "Next time," Lockhart said, his voice quiet, "let's talk about weapons."

"That remark will keep me waiting with anticipation," Simon said, a sinister grin forming. "I look forward to next time! Good night."

Simon was glad of his escape to the country during the heat of late July and August and the light summer nights. The forests provided shade and cooler temperatures, and he enjoyed instructing the daily exercise programs.

Early on, the grand duchesses had begun dressing in trousers, the empress being concerned about discretion, especially when they were wrestling. As their skills advanced, however, they returned to their skirts and dresses. Simon soon overcame the discomfort of exposed petticoats and stockings by maintaining a focus on the skills he taught.

"Mama means well," Maria said at the end of a lesson, "but she doesn't think about the occasion of an attack. If we're accosted, we'll most likely be wearing a skirt of some sort. We need to be able to react despite fabric clawing at our legs." She yanked a ribbon that had held back her hair and shook it loose. Scrubbing her fingertips through the roots, she sighed.

"Regardless," Simon said, his breath catching as he cautioned his pupil, "I think trousers are still the best choice for wrestling. Should the moment arise requiring you to use wrestling techniques, you won't be stopping to think about skirts, but you will have mastered the techniques undeterred in the meantime."

"I see your point," Olga replied.

"I prefer to wear trousers for riding too," Maria said defiantly. "I don't like riding side-saddle." She smiled sweetly at Simon before turning to her sisters. "Simon has been teaching me to ride astride."

"What!" Tatiana said, shock rattling her voice. "Mama won't—"

"Mama knows," Maria said calmly, interrupting her sister's protest. She raised her head in rebellion. "We're experimenting! Besides, Mama agreed that, if my riding improves, then you three will be allowed to wear trousers, too."

"I'd like to try riding astride," Anastasia said, declaring her opposition to her oldest sister, who glared disapproval.

"Speaking of riding astride," Simon said, his voice raised to be heard over the animated discussion, "Maria, it's time for your lesson. The rest of you," he said, flicking his hands to encourage their departure, "have other lessons to attend."

"I'll meet you at the stables," Maria said, shouting over her shoulder as she raced toward the palace, skirts billowing. "I have to change!"

Simon sauntered toward the stables, shaking his head at the recent exchange. He would never understand the insistence of women to ride side-saddle, but respected them for their accomplishments.

I couldn't do it! Alexei is another matter. I know he needs to hone his riding skills, but I worry every time he approaches the stables. One fall. One kick. Anything and nothing can start the bleeding. I don't even want to think about it! Thank goodness his sailor nurse is always with him and knows what to do.

CHAPTER 36

"You seem to have the tsarina's ear," Gibbes said during a lesson break near the end of summer. "Not in the way that Rasputin does, mind you, but you seem to have a connection of sorts."

"Of course, we find no fault with you," Gilliard said, quickly interjecting. "We appreciate your deference, ensuring that our lessons are given priority."

"That's kind of you to say," Simon replied, abashed at the compliments. "I'm not here to make more work for you, and I hope that whatever I do enhances the children's education."

"It does, indeed!" Gilliard said. "I've already noticed an improvement in their focus and their grasp of the other languages." He gazed out a window that looked upon the gardens, lost in momentary thought. "If you don't mind me asking, how is it that you have a familiarity with them? They seem to adore you."

"Well, there I have two advantages, I'm afraid," Simon said with a sheepish grin. "First, I passed more than a year with all but the tsesarevich when my father was posted here in 1902. Plus, you are their teachers—you must maintain a professional distance. Regrettably, they see me more as a friend who can teach them things than a teacher."

"Ah!" Gibbes said. "That makes everything clear!"

"Thanks for not making it an issue," Simon replied.

"Listen," Gibbes said, his voice serious, "we'd rather be working with you than that Rasputin character. He seems a sinister sort of chap, and we don't trust him."

"And frankly," Gilliard said, huffing "you're a far better influence on the royals than he ever could be. Him and his hocus-pocus cures that don't help the tsesarevich one bit."

"One day," Gibbes said, "someone will do him harm. Mark my words."

By autumn, Simon's comfortable routine included three days a week at the palace overseeing self-defence lessons, supervising riding lessons, and encouraging academic discussions in various languages. He also responded when the empress summoned him.

The remaining days were consumed with travel to and from Petrograd, meeting with Buchanan, Lockhart and Egorov, investigating any leads that would substantiate Lebedev's perceived intentions, attending to correspondence, and an occasional meeting with the tsar. Considering the list of concerns on his agenda, he was relieved to know that at least Vasiliev required little thought. According to Egorov, the major's return from the front was not imminent.

In mid-November, Simon returned to the flat to find an invitation from Prince Felix Yusupov amongst his usual pile of cards and letters. When he mentioned to Egorov later that evening that he had received an unexpected invitation from a prince of whom he knew nothing, Egorov admitted to having received the same invitation.

"You'll enjoy the gathering," Egorov said. "Prince Felix's family history is older than the tsar's and richer. Plus, he's married to Princess Irina, the tsar's niece. Her father contributed a handsome dowry to the marriage coffers as well. To say they don't lack for funds is an understatement." He drew on a cigarette and exhaled. "Presuming you plan to attend, you'll find the company quite fun. You are going, aren't you?"

"I was thinking I should," Simon said. "One never knows what connections can be made. It sounds as though you know him well."

"I do, yes," Egorov replied. "Our families belong to the same social circles. I can assure you that any event hosted by the prince is worth attending. His colourful parties are renowned. Lots of food, drink, hashish, whatever! You name it. He'll try anything at least once!"

"Have you attended many parties?" Simon replied.

"A few," Egorov said, "before the war." He exhaled cigarette smoke, trying to create circles, then laughed. "The last party I attended, he flounced down the staircase in one of his wife's gowns."

"Let me guess," Simon said. "Was his wife wearing

an evening suit?"

"Precisely!" Egorov said. "She's as much a character as he is!"

"Then, I have no choice," Simon said decidedly. "I will attend."

In early December, a year after Henry Crocker and his new wife had departed for London, Simon and Egorov attended the annual December gala hosted by Prince Felix Yusupov and his wife. Simon had never attended an event like it, and said as much to Egorov.

"The entire intent," a familiar voice said from behind Simon, "is to break the winter monotony, is it not Lieutenant Egorov?"

Surprised at the familiarity of the voice, Simon spun around, pleased to see one of his newer acquaintances. "Bertie Stopford!" he said. "I didn't expect to see you here."

"Mr. Stopford can be found at any social event hosted by an aristocrat," Egorov said, chuckling. "You must be popular in British and French circles as well, sir?"

"Right you are, Lieutenant," Stopford said. "That is where I find my best clients—a painting here, a tiara there." He grinned, making light of his profession. While Egorov's gaze fell elsewhere, he winked knowingly at Simon. "Good to see you this evening, gentlemen. Please keep me in mind if you find yourself with something to liquidate." He flagged a server and exchanged an empty wine glass for a full one. "Must mingle!" A moment later, he disappeared into the throng of gaiety.

"Ah!" Egorov said enthusiastically. "Here comes the

prince and his wife. You must meet them, Simon."

The two men worked their way through a disorganized receiving line. When Egorov introduced Simon, the prince eyed him for an overlong moment.

"We must speak privately," the prince said sotto voce. "Lieutenant Egorov, bring Lord Temple to my study in …" He glanced at a crystal clock over the fireplace. "An hour? I have a proposal of sorts, and would appreciate your thoughts."

An hour later, Simon and Egorov entered the study to discover a small gathering of men known to Egorov, none of whom Simon had met. Prince Felix had everyone served with a beverage, then asked his staff to leave them and ensure that no one else entered the room.

"Well gentlemen," he said, raising his glass. "This is it. We are about to participate in a decidedly underhanded event that will save us all from evil. Tonight, we'll review our plans. Soon, a few of us will carry them out."

Simon sat quietly, wondering what the man was not saying. He glanced at the faces of eight other men, including Egorov, all of whom seemed to hang on his every word.

"Those of us who will carry out the execution of Grigori Rasputin know the time and place," Felix said. "The rest of you will be spared the details. With the exception of Lord Simon, my thanks go out to all of you for your encouragement, recommendations, and opinions. In a few weeks, that devil will no longer control my cousins … and our country will be free of his influence."

He raised his glass. "To us!"

"To us," the others said as one.

"Now, gentlemen," Felix said, turning toward Simon. "Lord Simon is wondering what we're about. Are you not, sir?"

"I am," Simon said, sitting forward in his chair, feeling awkward when all eyes turned on him. "Since I'm not party to your treachery, I'm left wondering why I'm here."

"Of course, you are," Felix said, his voice sober and serious, devoid of his earlier gaiety. "The answer is simple. We"—he circled his hand around the room—"we are all concerned, as I said, about the influence that Grigori Rasputin holds over the royal family, and by virtue of that influence, Mother Russia. He will bring us all down if we don't stop him."

Felix glanced at his nodding guests. "Amongst us we have discussed several options, but the assassination of Rasputin is the only conclusion upon which we could agree. We need an outsider to witness that we have conducted ourselves with great repute. Artyom put your name forward as one who is honourable and trustworthy, and most importantly … British, not Russian."

Felix paused in his explanation and regarded his audience. "In short, we need you to vouch for us should the need arise. Plus, I'm certain that the British will be particularly interested to know what happened. We'd like you to be the one to deliver the news."

Simon glared at Egorov as he set his empty glass on a marble table. "I'm—"

Egorov abruptly jumped to his feet, cutting off Simon's comment with a raised hand. "Simon," he said, "I apologize for not informing you ahead of time. I wasn't at liberty to say anything earlier; we've all taken an oath of secrecy."

He turned to the others, who muttered their assurances to Simon. "You need do nothing but bear witness that no man here intends to bring harm to the royal family. We are all loyalists who have concerns about Rasputin. I know that you've met him, seen how he influences the tsarina and her children. We believe that, if the monk is not removed from the royal court, he will destroy the family if by no other means than by reputation. You know as well as I what people are saying about him and his liberties."

Simon sighed, scanning the faces of the other men, recognizing what they stood to lose if anything went wrong.

Finally, he rose to stand near the warmth of the burning fire. "I'm not comfortable knowing that someone is about to be murdered," he said, feeling his belly twist. "In good conscience, I should intervene, but it's not my place to do so. Clearly, you have all determined that Rasputin is a threat to the royal family and Russian society. As Artyom has said, I'm an outsider, and as such am not one to judge. I don't care for the task you've set me, but no harm will come to me if I do act as your witness."

"Thank you, Lord Simon," Felix said. "Let's have one more drink to seal the bargain; then, we must return to the party."

CHAPTER 37

On the morning of December 18th, Simon sat at his desk overlooking the palace herb garden while he reviewed Maria's afternoon riding lesson. As he turned on a desk lamp, a light rap on the doorframe announced a footman carrying an envelope on a silver tray. Simon beckoned him forward. He recognized Ambassador Buchanan's handwriting and slit the seal.

Lord Simon, Buchanan wrote, *I've received word of a very curious nature. Rumour is circulating amongst Russian nobility that Grigori Rasputin has been assassinated. Since no body has been discovered, there is no certainty. British intelligence is investigating. Details to follow. In the meantime, I'm wondering whether it might be a kindness for the tsarina to hear the news from you, if you've a mind to inform her.*

Simon marvelled as he recalled Gibbes' recent prophecy and the clandestine meeting during Prince Felix's gala. His stomach knotted as he wondered how to deliver the news to the tsarina. He tucked the message in his jacket pocket and hastened to find her.

Two Abyssinian guards stood outside the morning room, marking her presence. He tugged the hem of his jacket and rapped tentatively on the door.

Alexandra's face lit up when he entered. "Simon," she said, "please come and join me for tea!"

Simon waited while a servant poured and served the tea. Once they were alone, he steeled himself and delivered the news.

"Dead!" she said. "But how!" She retrieved a lace handkerchief from her pocket and dabbed her eyes. "He was just here." She swung her feet to the floor, wringing her hands around the handkerchief. "I can't believe it! Are you certain?"

"I have a note from Ambassador Buchanan," Simon said, tugging it from his pocket. "He thought it prudent to dispatch a message straight away, so you'd learn of the matter from me rather than other, less scrupulous sources. Apparently, several dubious rumours are circulating. Ambassador Buchanan didn't want to worry you, and writes that British intelligence is investigating, with details to follow. In the meantime, I think it prudent to believe the news as Ambassador Buchanan has reported it." He eyed the tsarina directly. "As the most reliable rumour, ma'am."

Two days later, Simon received a second message from Ambassador Buchanan, enclosing a copy of an article from the *Stock Exchange Gazette.* The article reported that

Rasputin's death occurred after a party hosted in the home of a Petrograd aristocrat. The monk's body was discovered the following day under the ice of the Neva River.

Immediately following Simon's delivery of the news, Tsarina Alexandra Feodorovna dispatched a palace representative to claim the body of her dear friend. Twenty-four hours later, a private service was held in a small Tsarskoye Selo chapel. Only immediate members of the tsar's family attended the service.

Those concerned about the royal reputation and the political circumstances in Russia breathed a collective sigh of relief, hoping that rumours of Rasputin and the royal family would soon end.

CHAPTER 38

I n a correspondence sent to his father in late December
1916, Simon expressed an ongoing frustration with the
tsarina's attitude.

> *She often complains that, in the tsar's absence, she is
> forced to make important decisions of state. Because
> she is in the seat of power, albeit temporarily, the
> Duma distrusts her, and she distrusts its members.
> In the many months that she's held control, Russia
> has had four prime ministers and a plethora of lesser
> ministers. Competent men have been removed from
> power and, because no one is able to hold a position
> long enough, disorganization reigns.*

> *Initially, the blame was placed at the feet of Grigori
> Rasputin, but since his recent murder—a very
> nasty affair by all counts—the finger-pointing
> has turned to the empress. Contrary to the hopes of
> Rasputin's executioners, Mikhail Rodzianko, the
> Duma president, reportedly said that the tsarina
> 'exerts an adverse influence on all appointments,
> including even those in the army.' Now she is*

being blamed for taking guidance from German connections.

Recently, Rodzianko, Grand Duchess Marie Pavlovna, as well as Ambassador Buchanan, joined a collaboration insisting that the tsar remove her authority. He declined, of course, and promptly returned to Moghilev.

———

Late in January 1917, Lockhart met Simon at the Petrograd flat. On one particular evening, Egorov joined them, and they took to the streets in disguise.

On a corner, near the rail yards, they encountered a group of men gathered around a bonfire for warmth. The rhetoric spewed from a few vocal men who raved on about lack of food and fuel for their families, and encouraged those present to unite in a general strike.

"Why should I listen to you?" one man said, shouting to be heard over the protesters. "My family is starving! How will a strike help them? If I walk out, we will have nothing to buy food, not even a bone for broth. Where are the promised trains full of supplies?"

"The government is corrupt, my friend," the first speaker said with assurance, hoping to still the group's rising anxiety. "If we strike, the politicians must listen. If they don't, it won't just be the people who will starve. Even those with jewels and rubles must eat. They will pay us to move the trains. You'll see."

"We can't move trains in this snow!" another man said, raising a fist at the speaker. "Why bother with a strike? The weather will do the work for us, and we don't need to freeze our backsides!"

"Down with the German woman!" strike supporters said, chanting in chorus. "Down with the war! Down with the tsar!"

"Come on," Lockhart said, "there's nothing for us to do here. They've said it all."

The three friends wandered further until they encountered several small gatherings beginning to assemble in the streets. As more joined a mob formed, advancing on the palace.

"The tsar will feed his people," a woman said, her voice hopeful as she encouraged others onward. "He will hear us."

"The tsar isn't here," a guard said firmly when they entered the square outside the Hermitage. "Go home to your beds. He's not here!"

"Then tell him to come," another woman said angrily. "Tell him we're hungry."

The crowd began to disperse.

"We'll be back," a man said, shaking his fist. "Tell the tsar we'll be back."

"That soldier won't be here much longer either," Egorov said quietly. "We haven't been paid in weeks. I have a home where I can go for food and warmth, if needed. But most of the young fellows who've signed up to fill the void of older ones sent to the front have nowhere to go.

They signed up hoping for food and shelter. If the trains don't come, the garrisons will be in the same situation. I see a mutiny coming soon."

A moment later, the last man threw a fist-sized stone, striking the guard on a cheek. The guard fell backward, bashing his head on the pavement. A crimson puddle seeped from under his head.

The crowd quickly dissipated, abandoning the injured man where he fell.

"He needs help," Egorov said, running toward the soldier.

"He's dead," Lockhart said, pressing a finger into his neck. He closed the soldier's unseeing eyes and stood up.

Simon glanced around the square. It was empty but for him, his friends, and the dead soldier.

"We can't leave him here," Egorov said. "Help me get him inside the garrison."

———

Early the following morning, while everyone still slept, Simon flicked on a desk lamp and scribbled a letter to his father, detailing his recent observations. In closing, he wrote:

Tsar Nicholas is expected home tomorrow. I've been informed by a reliable source that, if he fails to co-operate with the Duma, he will be presented with a manifesto to establish 'dual control.' Frankly, Father, I don't believe the tsar has the capacity to turn this dire situation around by himself. He needs help. Sadly, I believe he's too set in his beliefs to compromise.

CHAPTER 39

In February, Simon summarized journalists' reports regarding the continuing collapse of Russian infrastructure. In his diary, he wrote:

> *Twenty thousand locomotives on rails when war began. Now less than eight thousand functioning. Sixty thousand railcars standing still. Fuel and supplies scarce. Delivery transport nonexistent. Citizens stealing last food from store shelves. Riots. Police shootings. Cabinet begging tsar to return to Petrograd.*

On a snowy evening in early March, Simon, Lockhart, and Egorov wandered the streets yet again. As they neared a group of men loitering on a street corner, soldiers approached, rifles at the ready.

"Return to your homes," one of the soldiers said, shoving an elderly man.

Younger men shoved back in the old man's defence. Five soldiers cocked their rifles, preparing to shoot.

"Stop!" Egorov said, shouting to be heard over the encounter.

He approached the soldier who appeared to be in charge. "These men are hungry, officer," Egorov said quietly. "Just like you and your men. Leave them be."

He held the eyes of the officer, who narrowed his eyes in return.

"I know you," the officer said.

"You do," Egorov said, leaning toward the man's ear, "and I'd be grateful if you'd keep that to yourself." He placed a hand on the man's arm, as if to cease a motion. "Don't! Don't salute. I'm undercover."

The officer's nod was negligible. "At ease," he said sharply to his men, then signalled them to follow him.

The loitering men moved closer together when Egorov approached. They eyed him with suspicion, seeming surprised by his successful effort to diffuse the soldiers' aggression.

When the soldiers rounded a corner, the elderly man stepped forward to thank him for his actions.

Egorov dismissed their praise and encouraged their return home. A moment later, the gathering dispersed, the hollows left by their snowy footsteps swiftly obscured by falling flakes.

Simon, Egorov, and Lockhart sauntered down another street in the opposite direction, their frozen breath forming ice crystals on their beards.

———

The following morning, Simon began to record the evening's events in his diary, but rested his pen when he heard familiar noises in the kitchen. *I wonder what Mrs. Zima will use as a coffee substitute today,* he thought.

His diary remained untouched for several days. When he took up his pen again, it was to write a brief message:

Father, on March 11th Tsar Nicholas suffered a mild heart attack; he was forced to return to Petrograd for treatment. As I happened to be in Petrograd, I was able to meet his train when it arrived from Moghilev. He was weak and disoriented. I stayed with him until his family arrived from Tsarskoye Selo.

The incident shook him deeply. The doctors informed him that his heart will not withstand continued stress. He conceded to me privately that he no longer feels capable of commanding the military or controlling the country.

The following day, riots broke out in the streets of Petrograd. One of the generals tried to regain control, and although orders were given to fire over the heads of a mob, bullets struck civilians. Hundreds were killed.

The next day, most of the imperial regiments had mutinied, the arsenal had been pillaged, and administrative buildings had been set afire, including military and police headquarters and law courts.

Soldiers have since joined the rebellion. A provisional government has been struck, and is now seeking to restore order.

On March 15th, the tsar surprised the country by signing abdication papers presented to him by representatives of the provisional government. He acknowledged that he had no other option, but he in turn shocked the representatives when he removed the tsesarevich's name as his successor. He told me later that he could not burden his son with such responsibility, especially given the boy's poor health. Instead, he insisted that his brother, Grand Duke Michael, be named.

What news from our friends? Accommodation required. Urgent.

Soon after, he handed Zima a parcel addressed to his mother containing a miniature Fabergé dog and a hidden message for his father. He asked the valet to deliver it to the embassy for inclusion in the next diplomatic pouch for London. Before Zima returned, Simon had reconsidered the time involved for his parcel's delivery and opted for a second message.

"Ah, Zima," Simon said, briskly approaching the valet when he stepped into the flat and deposited his wet umbrella into a nearby stand. "I'm afraid I have another task for you."

He handed Zima a small, white envelope. "Please have this telegram sent straight away." He smiled apologetically. "I'll ask Mrs. Zima to have a hot drink waiting for you when you return. I understand that she may still have a box of cocoa."

"Then I shall not be long, my lord," Zima replied, taking the envelope and retrieving his soggy umbrella. "It is raining like—how do you English say—cats and dogs?"

"That is exactly what we say," Simon said, chuckling.

"The temperature is dropping," Zima said. "I will hurry. I don't want to be outdoors in wet snow." He shuddered as he shut the door behind him.

Simon paced to the window and watched Zima scurry down the street.

"I hope Father understands my message," he said, muttering as he recalled the brief message he had given to Zima:

Urgent accommodation required. Family of seven. Good references. Must include servants' quarters.

The following day, Simon sat at the dining table munching through a meagre breakfast of dark bread and cheese. Before him sat a copy of every morning newspaper Zima had been able to find.

Simon wiped his fingers, took a sip of tea, then turned to the edition by his plate. He scanned each page, searching for more information regarding the abdication.

Down the hall, he heard a brisk rap on the outer door, and moments later Zima arrived with a small silver tray, on which sat a telegram.

Simon snatched the correspondence from the tray and tore open the envelope.

Considering. Need time.

He folded the message neatly and set it above his plate. "Zima, I'll need my bag, please," Simon said, contemplating his father's reply. "I'll be away for a few days."

"Yes, sir."

Twenty minutes later, Simon was heading for the train station via the British Embassy.

CHAPTER 40

"Lord Simon!" Sir George said, rising from his desk. "This is a surprise. Is there something with which we can help?"

"I'm curious, Sir George," Simon replied, declining the chair suggested by the ambassador. "Have you heard anything from London regarding sanctuary for the Romanovs? I read in the paper this morning that the tsar has asked to be sent to the United Kingdom if he's exiled."

"I haven't heard anything, other than consideration is being given," Sir George replied. "I believe King George wants to help, but he continues to meet government resistance. The recommendation is that the Romanovs seek asylum with a neutral country. I doubt we'll hear anything more until later this month."

"That's what I thought," Simon said, his voice full of resignation as he walked toward the door. "Thank you, sir. I won't take up more of your time."

"Not at all," Sir George said, seeing him off.

Simon tripped down the stairs and headed toward the lavatory. In a cubicle, he quickly changed into a disguise and slipped unseen out a side door onto the street.

At the train station, he purchased a ticket ensuring

that he would arrive at Alexander Palace within the hour. As was his norm, he changed out of his disguise before the train arrived in Tsarskoye Selo.

———·+·——

"Come in, Simon," Lady Alexandra said when Simon was shown into her sitting room. "Will you advise my husband that Lord Simon has arrived," she said to the footman, "and arrange a hot beverage for the three of us?"

"Simon," Nicholas said, hastening into the room. "Have you any word? Will they take us?"

"As I understand it, sir," Simon replied, "your request is being considered. It may be a few days before any further word is received. I'm sure I'll hear from Sir George or my father as soon as a response is available."

Nicholas paced across the room, then stopped abruptly before the fireplace. He leaned both arms on the mantelpiece and dropped his head to his hands. The room was quiet but for the crackling fire and the former tsar's deep sigh.

"I've made a mess of this, haven't I," he said, turning to face his wife and Simon. "I thought I was doing the right thing for my people, but clearly I have been wrong. Now, I can't even find a home for my family."

"Nikki," Alexandra said, "surely they won't turn us out of our home. You have given them what they want! What more do they need?"

"Alix, the people are angry ... and hungry," Nicholas said, his voice heavy with regret and surrender. "And this is not *our* home. It belongs to the state. We must leave."

"Sir, ma'am," Simon said, "I should like to return to Petrograd this evening. May I have your leave to be excused until I hear further from England?"

"Of course," Nicholas replied. "We'll hope for your speedy return."

"And Simon," Alexandra said, raising her hand to halt his departure, "please be careful. I couldn't bear it if you came to harm as our dear Rasputin has. His miserable death at the hands of an assassin was quite alarming!"

She turned her dewy eyes toward her husband, then swung her gaze back to Simon. "You will be careful, won't you?"

"Thank you, ma'am, for your concern," Simon replied. "I will indeed take care." He bowed deeply from the waist and headed for the door. "I'll just stop in to say hello to the children and let them know that they're to fill any spare time with practice." He grinned impishly at his last statement, eyes twinkling.

"A good idea, Simon," Nicholas replied, his voice flat, as if distracted.

Simon strode along the corridor and took the stairs toward the classrooms. He rapped lightly on a door and opened it to find his students reading. When they spied him, they jumped to their feet.

"Oh, Simon," Maria said breathlessly. Her hand landed feather-light on his arm, sending tingling sensations up and down. "We have been so worried. We thought we might never see you again."

"Nonsense," Olga said, "Don't be so dramatic! When we're all settled in the United Kingdom, we'll see Simon often." She looked toward the other two instructors. "And Gibbes and Gilliard," she said, as if to assure herself that life would alter little once they were relocated, "you'll come with us too. Won't you?"

"Of course, we will," Gibbes said confidently. "We will be with you until you no longer have need of us!"

"Alright, back to work," Gilliard said. "You'll be tested tomorrow. If you are to do well, you must focus now."

The three men stepped out into the hallway, leaving their students to their work.

"Have you any word?" Gibbes said. "Is King George going to help?"

"I only know what the papers say at the moment," Simon replied, shaking his head. "I just wanted to let you know that I am returning to Petrograd for a while. I intend to tell them"— he cocked his head toward the classroom—"to practise, so you need not assume my responsibilities. I don't think I'll be away long; perhaps a week or two."

Simon said goodbye to his students and returned to Petrograd to await his father's reply.

———

On March 19th, 1917, an invitation was extended to the Romanovs, inviting them to take asylum in the United

Kingdom. There was one caveat: they should seriously consider relocating to a neutral country, like Canada.

"Finally!" Nicholas said. "God bless England!"

"God bless George and Mary," Alexandra said. "I shall begin organizing our departure immediately."

In early April, Simon received a message from Ambassador Buchanan requesting that he report to the embassy posthaste.

"I've been instructed to deliver the most dreadful news to the Romanovs," Sir George said. "I'm told that the British Labour Party has been in an uproar ever since the offer of asylum was made. Even members of the Liberal Party are siding with them. They object to taking on any more exiled royals. Britons have become quite vocal about having to foot the bill of yet another royal family, complaining that their taxes are already so high that they have little money left for their own food and shelter. Apparently Arthur Bigge, First Baron Stamfordham, has been grumbling to the king that, should the Romanovs be taken in by the UK, there could be an uprising similar to the Easter Rising in Ireland last year!"

Sir George covered his face with his hands and scrubbed as if he were washing. "What a debacle!" he said. "Our ambassador in Paris—do you know Lord Francis Bertie?"

Simon shook his head, not recalling the man.

"Lord Bertie says that the French government won't have the Romanovs. They're worried about unrest and the war with Germany. Perhaps if the former empress were not of German lineage, the concern might not be so great, but … well …" He gazed at Simon and shrugged, sighing deeply. "I don't know what's to be done. And now I'm the one tasked to tell Nicholas Romanov that England will not have him!"

"But … what if they were self-sustained?" Simon said.

"Self-sustained?" Buchanan said. "You mean, pay for their own keep?"

"Yes," Simon said. "I mentioned the possibility to Lord Nicholas some time ago, but he wasn't ready to listen. I think he might now."

"I don't know about him," Buchanan replied, "but I'm certainly keen to hear all options."

"I'll go with you and explain along the way," Simon said. "When are you going?"

"Tomorrow morning, first train," Sir George said. "May as well get it over with."

"Good," Simon replied. "I have a few things to take care of this afternoon." He rose from the guest chair opposite Sir George's desk. "I'll meet you at the train station tomorrow." He reached to shake the ambassador's hand and departed, his mind scrambling as he mentally organized what needed to be done.

CHAPTER 41

Simon raced home and dashed off two telegrams. The first he wrote to Lockhart, suggesting a meeting in Petrograd the following week. The second message was directed to his father, advising that he would accompany Buchanan to Tsarskoye Selo to inform the Romanovs that the offer of asylum had been withdrawn, closing with:

> *They all put on a brave face, but when alone with me, they let their guard slip. I see the worry on their faces. I plan to meet with my Moscow friend next week to discern whether we can't do more to help from this end. London is, to say the least, a great disappointment. These people are not bad, Father, just misguided. Unfortunately for them, their misguidance affects more than just themselves.*

While Simon wrote his correspondence, Zima began packing his valise.

"You must find my behaviour curious," Simon said when he noticed. "Especially my odd disguises."

"We did at first," Zima replied, "but quickly realized that everything you do is your business, not ours. It is our job to support and protect you without question. You are good to us. We have no reason to do less."

Simon set his pen down and peered at Zima, amazed at the man's declaration. "Thank you for that, Zima," he said. "You have no idea how much that means to me, especially finding myself in Russia without the immediacy of friends and family. And considering I'm rarely here."

Zima paused in his task and smiled warmly at his employer.

"No need for costumes today," Simon said when he noticed the items Zima had assembled. "I am accompanying the British Ambassador to Tsarskoye Selo. No time for my usual shenanigans!" He quirked his lips into a lopsided grin, feeling a little bashful.

"My wife and I had often wondered whether you might have a special relationship with the Romanovs," Zima said, as if Simon had answered unspoken questions. "Not that it matters to us. We're grateful to have employment that pays well and keeps us together. You treat us with respect, provide comfortable lodgings, and share your table. No Russian noble has ever done that. I assure you, sir, that you have our absolute loyalty and discretion."

Simon blushed at the man's sincerity.

"In your absences," Zima said, smiling at his wife when she appeared in the doorway of Simon's room, "we've had plenty of time to imagine what it would be like to live on our own and take care of ourselves. You often suggest that we invite friends or family to visit while you're away."

"Indeed," Mrs. Zima said, slipping her arm through her husband's as she stood next to him, "your generosity is most welcome. The truth is, we know no one in the city. Our families and a few friends are in the country. We prefer to keep to ourselves and venture out only when necessary."

"On occasion," Zima said, "we might take an evening stroll along the river, or lunch in a nearby park, but we prefer our privacy, and cherish the time we have together."

"We missed so much in the early part of our marriage," Mrs. Zima said, gazing into her husband's eyes.

"In fact, our life here would be idyllic, were it not for an incident a few days ago," Zima said, muttering as he considered what clothes to pack for Simon.

"What incident?" Simon said, jumping to his feet, fists clenched at his sides. "Tell me …"

Zima's face puckered as he conjured the event anew. He glanced at his wife, who urged him onward. "It's a bit of a story, sir," Zima said.

"Then let's sit in the salon," Simon said, leading the way.

Once they were settled, Simon invited the couple to tell their story.

"As I mentioned, sir, you were away," Zima said. "Late one afternoon, we heard a pounding on the door. When I opened it, two heavy-set men in long, black leather coats scowled at me. One gruffly announced that they were Okhrana. The second fellow pushed me aside, demanding to see you."

Simon noticed a slight shiver pass through the valet. His wife clutched his hand, and he continued.

"I blocked the entrance and told them that you weren't in." Zima's voice sounded defiant. "The gruff one insisted that you were here, that they saw you enter the building the evening before, and that they had not seen you leave."

"I came from the kitchen," Mrs. Zima said. "I told them that my husband didn't lie: that you were not here. They pushed their way in, almost knocking my dear Sokol to the floor."

"They paced throughout the flat, demanding that you show yourself," Zima said, continuing the tale. "When they finally accepted that you weren't here, they demanded that we tell them where you actually were."

"I told them that we didn't know," Mrs. Zima said, lifting her hands in a shrug. "I said you never told us your business or where you went, and that you often came in after we were in bed and left before we rose. They stomped through the flat, pushing furniture, knocking over lamps and ornaments, shoving books to the floor." Mrs. Zima's voice was indignant. "When they started throwing things about your room, I asked them what they wanted, suggesting that we might help and avoid more damage. That only increased their anger. They examined your room thoroughly. They checked behind the door and the curtains, inside the clothes cupboard ... even under the bed!"

"They were just beginning to accept the truth," Zima said, "when the gruff one thought he found something on your secretary. He picked up a sheet of notepaper and handed it to his partner. Apparently, he couldn't read English. The partner said that it was a letter to your father about the weather and a visit with a friend, but it appeared to be unfinished. Then he threw the letter on the desk."

"That made them furious," Mrs. Zima said. "They became more aggressive, tearing the linen from your bed, overturning the mattress, slicing it with their knives and pulling out the stuffing! They stomped on the floorboards and banged the walls, as if they were looking for a secret hiding place. Surely, one of us would've found a secret hiding place by now, if one existed." She dusted her hands, gazing at her husband. "Not that we've been looking!" Embarrassment stained her cheeks, and she fanned her face.

Simon raised his hand as if to dismiss her worry. "Give me a minute," he said disappearing into his room. He returned shortly, satisfied to learn that the secret cavity in the side of his secretary had not been disturbed. The Romanov treasure was safe. "Continue," he said as he resumed his seat.

Mr. and Mrs. Zima glanced at each other, shrugged and continued the recounting of their report.

"The most frustrating part about it," Zima said, "was that there was nothing we could do to stop them; we could only watch. In the end, they found nothing, of course, but left such a disarray that we spent hours restoring everything to order."

"But … why didn't you tell me?" Simon said, shocked by their story. "Did they harm you?"

"We weren't harmed," Zima said, "and while they certainly made a mess, we were able to repair and restore everything. We didn't mention this to you because whatever their mission, they were unsuccessful. You have enough to worry over without fussing about us."

He glanced at his wife, then continued. "There is one more thing, however. Before they left, they threatened that, should we tell you, we too would be investigated by the Okhrana."

"We told them that we knew of nothing questionable or suspicious about you," Mrs. Zima said, "that you are a gentleman with integrity and excellent repute."

"You should have told me sooner," Simon said, shaking his head, "especially when they threatened you."

"Oh, we weren't worried about their silly threat," Mrs. Zima replied as her husband patted her hand. "We had every intention of telling you. We've just been waiting for the right moment."

"Well … I'm sorry that you had to endure that intrusion," Simon said, "and I'm pleased that you let them have run of the flat. I wouldn't forgive myself if either of you came to any harm on my account."

He leaned toward them, clutching his knees as he spoke. "I can assure you both," he said, "that I have done nothing to justify such a visit by the Okhrana, and I would do nothing to jeopardize your safety. Should they come again, don't resist. There is nothing here to fuel their interest."

Zima and his wife appeared to relax after that

conversation, their sense of loyalty toward the young man seemingly strengthened.

CHAPTER 42

"But …why?" Nicholas Romanov said, unable to understand the withdrawal of the offer of asylum.

"As I understand," Sir George said, "it wasn't the king's decision to make; he was merely required to endorse it. The British Government expostulated on the matter for a long time. The final straw came when Arthur Bigge, First Baron Stamfordham, reminded King George of the Easter Rising in Ireland last year."

Simon listened as the ambassador reiterated concerns voiced the previous day.

"Sir," Simon said, interrupting the conversation when he intercepted an expression from Sir George that asked for help. "If I may speak frankly, I think I can elaborate upon the ambassador's concerns."

"Simon, you know you need not censor your thoughts in our presence," Lord Nicholas said, reminding Simon of their earlier arrangement.

Simon rose from the chair by the cold fireplace and paced toward the curtained windows. He returned to the presence of his hosts, clasping his hands behind his back and gazing at an unseen spot in the ceiling. Finally, he lowered his gaze directly to the former royals.

"The British people harbour a strong dislike for the things that your crown has represented," he said tentatively, pausing when Alexandra gasped.

"Continue," Nicholas said sharply.

"Since Queen Victoria's time, the United Kingdom has moved forward in industry, human rights, the abolition of poverty, world affairs, and so on. They don't see that same philosophy practised in Russia."

Nicholas jumped to his feet, clearly agitated by Simon's remarks, but Simon continued.

"In their view, Russia is a backward nation, her every success riding on the backs of impoverished and ill-fed peasants. They believe that the nobility in Russia has no regard for those who unwittingly support their wealthy status."

"Oh my!" Alexandra said. To that moment she had said nothing, resting quietly on a chaise lounge with her feet curled under her. She lowered her head and dabbed a tear pooling in the corner of her eye.

Nicholas stopped pacing and returned to Simon's side, his face red with rage. "Your words are harsh and cruel," he said with a booming voice. "I suppose I could stand here and argue, but the reality is that you're expressing the thoughts of Georgie's subjects." He tugged on his beard, his agitation obvious. "Tell me, Sir George, do you agree with Simon's interpretation?"

Sir George leaned forward in his chair, resting his elbows on his knees and wringing his hands together. "I'm afraid, sir, that I do. I may not have said it so simply, but …

yes, I agree. To rub salt in the wound, I received a message yesterday from the French Republic. The sentiment of that government was written in language harsher than Lord Simon has stated." Sir George gazed at his hands and shook his head, exhaling on a heavy sigh.

"Regardless, sir," Simon said, "Britain has opted to follow parliamentary democracy and the rule of law." He clutched his hands behind his back and paced toward the window.

When he returned, he stood behind the winged chair that he had recently vacated, hands resting on its back. "Perhaps there is one other option that might be considered," Simon said. Three pairs of eyes trained on him, supported by hopeful expressions.

"Continue," Nicholas said again, his countenance appearing calmer.

"I believe," Simon said, glancing toward the ambassador, "Britons would be more welcoming if you were self-sustaining. You'll recall that I mentioned the possibility last year."

"I recall," Nicholas said, his voice gruff. "Are you suggesting that I find employment?"

"No, not really," Simon replied softly, his arms draped casually over the back of the chair. "What I suggest is that consideration be given to what you have on hand. For example, have you any assets that could be transported to England easily, or liquidated perhaps?"

Alexandra sat quietly, clasping her throat, switching her gaze between her husband and Simon.

Simon straightened, raising his hands toward Nicholas as if to defend himself. "Please bear with me for a moment …" he said. "I have heard you mention several times, sir, that you would enjoy tending a garden. Would you consider purchasing a small estate, and running it? You could tend to the gardens, certainly, but you might also employ a few people who could help with livestock and anything else that could be sold for income, such as produce, cheese, and meat. Your neighbours would embrace you because you contribute to the local economy. You need not feel like a prisoner in some manor house, which is how many of the refugees feel because they cannot accept that they must be part of the community in order to be welcomed by the townsfolk."

Nicholas twisted an end of his moustache while he contemplated the suggestion. "That, young Simon, is an idea meriting greater thought," he said a few moments later. "Perhaps you'd help us put together a counter-proposal?"

—·—·—

The British ambassador returned to Petrograd on the last train, but Simon remained with the Romanovs for a few days longer, assisting the former monarchs with the crafting of their proposal.

He also enquired whether his students had been practising their lessons, and gave them additional drills to work on in the event his return was delayed. He took the time to speak with Gibbes and Gilliard as well.

"Have you any news for us, Temple?" Gibbes said.

"Anything you can share that might help us prepare one way or another?"

"I don't," Simon replied, feeling frustrated. "All I know is that enquiries are being made abroad for a country to step up and offer the family asylum."

An animated discussion followed as Simon explained Britain's position.

A while later, Simon rose from the table where the three men had been drinking afternoon tea. "I must go now. Hopefully I'll have more information when I return."

When Simon entered the foyer of his flat, Zima greeted him. "My Lord, a shabby-looking fellow arrived this morning. He refused to give his name and insisted that he be allowed to wait in the parlour, as if he knew you would return today … even though we've had no word from you to say so."

Simon handed his coat and hat to Zima and turned toward the parlour. "I know the man, Zima. As do you, if you think on it," Simon said, grinning. "How about a pot of tea for Mr. Lockhart and I?"

"Mr. Lockhart!" Zima replied. "Why … of course he is!" Zima scratched his head in amazement. "My wife just placed fresh tea on the table, sir. I'll bring another cup."

"I couldn't wait another day! I had to come," Lockhart said, rising to greet Simon with a handshake. "We received a message yesterday from Sir George summarizing recent events." He resumed the chair in which he had been sitting as Zima entered with a tray of extra tea things. "I'm terribly sorry if I caused any trouble Zima, my good man."

"None at all, sir," Zima said, chuckling. "You two gentlemen never cease to amaze—and amuse—me."

"Is it alright to speak candidly?" Lockhart said sotto voce.

"Absolutely!" Simon said. "Zima and his wife are fiercely protective!"

While they enjoyed the tea and biscuits prepared by Mrs. Zima, Simon brought Lockhart up to date.

"I was afraid of that," Lockhart said. "The word on the street in Moscow is that if the Romanovs don't leave soon, their safety will not be assured. If Kerensky's government is smart, they'll move the royals somewhere far away from here."

Nicholas and Alexandra considered Simon's suggestion at great length. Once they were certain of their intentions, they wrote a letter to George and Mary detailing their plan, and a second letter to Simon's father asking that he investigate the availability of suitable property.

Slowly and discreetly, with Simon's assistance, the Romanovs began liquidating larger items that were theirs to sell, while Alexandra and her daughters began removing precious gems from jewellery settings, tiaras, and even royal gowns to sew them into the hems of their travelling clothes, the bottom of valises, and their corsets.

———•—•——

Following his return to Petrograd with the ambassador, Simon resumed the wearing of disguises, making every effort to avoid detection: especially his comings and goings from the flat. Thanks to the description given to him by his employees, he was able to identify the two men claiming to be Okhrana officers. Knowing who they were made Simon's task of tailing them easier. Lockhart increased the frequency of his visits, arriving on the days when Simon returned to Petrograd. Together, they pursued every lead.

CHAPTER 43

As the sun rose to announce a warm spring day on the first morning of one of Lockhart's visits, Zima pointed through the lace curtains, careful not to cause movement. Simon was adamant that no motion be made by the windows that might draw undesired attention.

Two men hovered near the corner of a building across the street, having arrived only moments prior. They focussed on lighting cigarettes, and had yet to notice that the sun cast their shadows into the street. Simon and Zima covertly monitored them for several minutes. When one noticed their shadows on the road, he dragged the other under a shaded portico.

"That's my cue," Simon said. "I'll be back in a few minutes. Wake Mr. Lockhart." He grabbed his top hat and evening cloak and left, quietly taking the back stairs down to the street. Careful not to be seen, he circled the block, returning on the far side of his two trackers. As he neared the corner, he began whistling out of tune and staggering, as if he had enjoyed a night of heavy drinking. He used the ornamental cane that his father had given him to maintain his balance.

As he approached the trackers, he stopped and

fished in his pocket. A few seconds later, he tugged his hand free and dangled the flat keys before him. Then he resumed a staggering gait toward the entrance of the apartment building.

"Good morning, gentlemen," he said, slurring his words as he stopped mid-step. He tipped his hat to the trackers, then once again resumed his unsteady gait and off-key whistling.

While Simon fumbled his way into the building, he was able to glimpse astonishment on the faces of the Russian police officers, and gesticulations that suggested an argument. Once inside, he raced up to the flat, taking the stairs two at a time. He doffed his outwear and grabbed the disguise that he planned to wear that day. "Are they still there, Zima?"

"Yes, sir," Zima said, chuckling.

"They certainly are an angry pair of clowns!" Lockhart said.

"If you're ready, we'd better be off," Simon said to Lockhart, before ducking out the door. Lockhart followed close behind.

On the second departure, Simon and Lockhart exited the rear of the building and crossed the street, out of view of the two officers. Simon had expected them to leave soon after he had entered the front door of the building, and was amazed that they still lingered.

They remained only a few more minutes, as if to finish their cigarettes. One threw his cigarette on the pavement and ground his toe over the butt. The second fellow did the same before following the first around the corner. Simon and Lockhart jogged behind them, keeping a safe distance so as not to be seen.

The two men dressed in black did nothing to disguise their movements as they marched across the Birzhevoy Bridge. At the Trezzini Hotel, they turned left, and soon right.

"Imperial Guard?" Simon muttered. "Why there?"

He and Lockhart hid behind the thick trunk of an ancient birch tree. They watched the trackers halt at the gate and speak to a guard. The guard stepped into the gate house. Through the small window on the street side, Simon could see him use the telephone.

Ten minutes later, Major Ivan Vasiliev hobbled through the gate—a cane in one hand, the other arm in a sling—and crossed the street to where the two men appeared to be waiting for him.

"What the—" Simon's words hissed involuntarily. Knowing the next word would be an expletive, he held his breath. The objects of their attention were too close; an unexpected sound might risk their exposure.

The dominant policeman reported a lack of success in tracking Simon. Although he spoke deferentially, his demeanour did nothing to curtail the major's rising ire.

"I'm paying you two good money!" Vasiliev said, his voice raspy and angry.

"Major, please!" one of the men said, casting a furtive glance toward the guard house, then the opposite way. "Someone might hear. You could blow our cover."

"Blow your cover!" Vasiliev said, clearly agitated. "Blow your cover! Do you two imbeciles not realize that you have no cover? Everyone knows that Okhrana officers wear black leather coats. What you seem not to realize is that the Okhrana has been dissolved!"

"Not everyone knows that—" The second man, beginning to protest, was silenced by his partner's jab.

"You'll recall, Vasiliev," the first man said defensively, "that when you dictated our assignment, the Okhrana still existed."

"I don't care, Volkov, and I won't argue with you," Vasiliev said curtly. "I should think you'd have enough sense to change your disguise!" He straightened his tunic with his free hand. "I don't have time for this. Just tell me about Temple. Have you learnt anything to prove that he's a spy?"

Simon's head snapped toward Lockhart, his eyes wide. "Volkov?" Simon said soundlessly. "Spy?"

Lockhart smirked and shrugged his shoulder.

"Not yet. Perhaps tomorrow we'll—" Volkov said.

"There is no tomorrow. Your work for me is done. Crawl back to my brother-in-law before I squash you like the bugs you are." Vasiliev severed any further conversation. "I see now that I'll have to manage Temple myself."

"What about our pay?" Volkov said, whining.

"Your pay?" Vasiliev replied, turning on the cane. He looked over his shoulder at the two men, eyes glaring with rage. His mouth gaped and shut several times, as if he were struggling with a retort. Instead, he huffed loudly, then limped back toward the garrison. "Return tomorrow," he said, shouting an afterthought over his shoulder. "The guard will have payment for your sloppy work!"

Simon and Lockhart lingered behind the tree for several minutes until the two Okhrana officers disappeared around a corner. Then they retraced their steps to the bridge and boarded a tram back to the flat, reviewing the Vasiliev revelation along the way.

"I didn't recognize Volkov in that garb," Simon said mirthfully. "Have you been giving him lessons too?"

Lockhart's eyes widened, as if he were aghast at the accusation, before he laughed aloud.

When they arrived at the flat, Simon apologized to Mrs. Zima, telling her that they had unexpected business that would keep them out for dinner. Then he dashed off a note and asked Zima to arrange for its delivery.

CHAPTER 44

Later that evening, Simon and Lockhart entered the dining room of the Trezzini Hotel.

"I haven't been here since Crocker left for England with his new wife," Simon said. "My gosh! That was almost two years ago!"

In the darkest corner of the restaurant, he spotted Artyom Egorov and greeted him warmly.

"Simon," Egorov said, rising to welcome his friend. "It's been a while since last we met."

"It has indeed," Simon replied. "You remember Bruce Lockhart."

"Of course!" Egorov motioned toward empty chairs. "I was delighted to receive your invitation to dine at this fine establishment again."

"It's good to see another friendly face," Simon replied, smiling at the soldier. "So much has happened in this city—in this country."

"And in our personal lives," Egorov said with a grin. "I have two pieces of news that may surprise you."

Simon cocked his head to the right, the better to hear his friend's voice over the din of the restaurant.

"I'm to be an uncle very soon, and I've been promoted

to captain!"

Simon was delighted to hear about the child, and made a mental note to dispatch a parcel to Crocker. He also applauded Egorov's promotion. As they reflected on other activities and engagements that had kept them apart for many weeks, aromatic and tasty courses came and went.

"Now that we have shared recent events," Egorov said, "tell me the true purpose of your invitation." He leaned back in his chair and raised a glass of cognac to his lips.

"Astute as ever," Simon replied, a wide grin brightening his face. "Perhaps a walk across the bridge … in aid of digestion?"

"A most brilliant suggestion, Simon," Lockhart said, rising.

<hr>

As they walked across the Birzhevoy Bridge, away from prying ears, Simon described the episode that he and Lockhart had witnessed earlier in the day and the events that led up to it.

"I was not aware that Major Vasiliev was in Petrograd, let alone that he would have me followed. Were you?" Simon said.

"As a matter of fact," Egorov replied, "I was advised two days ago that he'd be returning, but I didn't expect him so soon. I'm not surprised he's having you followed. I should have suspected." He stopped mid-step and leaned on the railing of the bridge, peering down as if the flow of water below was of interest. "You've seen firsthand what damage comes from his wrath. He's a man who will have revenge, and, in his opinion, you have wronged him. You stole from him."

"Stole from—" Lockhart said.

"My sister," Egorov said flatly. "You can be assured that this is all about my sister and her disappearance." He glanced at Lockhart. "I presume that you know the story of Henry Crocker and my sister, Varvara."

In response to Lockhart's nod, he continued. "Vasiliev will have learnt of Simon's involvement by now. And I can also assure you that if Henry Crocker were still within the borders of this country, he would be long dead; my sister a widow for the second time. She perhaps dead too."

He turned to face Simon and Lockhart. "I'm troubled by your mention of Volkov," Egorov said. "I've only known him to be Lebedev's sidekick: quiet, unassuming. To think that Vasiliev has claws into him is deeply troubling." He paused in thought, then straightened as he continued. "I must tell you some things. First, you were truly not aware that Vasiliev had returned?"

"No, I wasn't," Simon replied. "So far as I knew, he left last winter."

"Correct," Egorov said. "He was sent to the front through the winter. During a skirmish two months ago, he was badly wounded. His injuries restricted his return until recently."

"Alright," Simon said. "That was first. Next?"

"There is a suspicion within the ranks that he has

some connection to the former Okhrana, which confirms your observations this afternoon. What you saw would confirm that either the Okhrana has not dissolved, and has merely moved underground, or that the major hired former Okhrana agents to do his dirty work while he was away, and they are merely using their former identity because it's convenient and they are hungry. Plus, Volkov is clearly fingered as Okhrana now, which suggests he may be dabbling in two pots too. Perhaps even Lebedev." He shrugged as if the possibilities were many.

Egorov returned his gaze to the river, bracing his booted toe against a pillar, as if to stretch his calf. "You've been aware of being followed almost since you arrived in Petrograd," Egorov said. "Vasiliev probably left orders with Volkov or one of his other henchmen to continue the surveillance."

"Good god!" Lockhart said.

"Third, I've had my own suspicions lately that Vasiliev has even more devious parts to him. Earlier today, I overheard him speaking German on the telephone. I don't speak German well, but what I overheard may make sense to you. The words that I understood were radio, spy, and Temple."

"Whoa!" Simon said quietly. "That's the second time I've heard that he thinks I'm a spy?"

"Well," Egorov replied, "my German is poor, but I gathered that his intention was to at least brand you as a spy, perhaps suggesting that you use a radio to broadcast confidential information about the Romanovs."

"What!" Simon said, choking on the comment as he spun toward Egorov in disbelief.

"Well," Egorov said again, eyes full of mischief, "it's no secret within the garrison that a handsome, young Englishman has been tutoring the grand duchesses and the tsesarevich. Some even say he's caught the eye of Grand Duchess Maria."

Lockhart chuckled quietly, acknowledging the reality and listening intently to the banter between Simon and Egorov.

"Guilty," Simon conceded. "Artyom, while I can't tell you my purpose, I can assure you that my duty to the royal family is as loyal as yours—presuming yours is loyal." It was Simon's turn to smirk.

"It is," Egorov said, his voice serious, "but I can't say the same for Vasiliev. I don't trust the man, and now I have reason to worry about you. If the thugs who have been following you have failed, and Vasiliev says he will take care of you himself, he will." He turned toward Simon and grasped his friend's shoulders. "Simon, you must take care! He's pure evil."

Simon gazed upward to the full, brilliant moon that lit Petrograd as if it were mid-day before landing his gaze on Lockhart.

"It's late, my friend," Simon said when he finally spoke. "None of us will function tomorrow if we don't get our beauty sleep."

Egorov accepted Simon's hand and smiled warmly.

"I'm going to follow Vasiliev for a while," Simon said,

"to see what I can find out. In the meantime, if you're able to find out anything further about Lebedev and Volkov, that would be helpful. The pieces are slowly falling into place, but I feel the key ones still evade us."

"Bruce, a pleasure to see you again," Egorov said. "Until next time."

Lockhart grinned. "Soon, I hope."

"I'll send you an invitation to dinner in a few weeks," Simon said. "I'll ask Mrs. Zima to prepare something, and we can review our findings at the same time."

"Be safe, my friend." Egorov stepped away from Simon and Lockhart, saluted smartly, then turned about-face, marching toward the hotel where they had recently supped.

Simon and Lockhart headed in the opposite direction, striding briskly toward the flat, the evening chill beginning to settle on their shoulders.

CHAPTER 45

A few days later, Simon caught Nicholas Romanov alone in his study. He reminded the tsar of his earlier concerns and recent difficulties involving Vasiliev.

"I'm not surprised, in a way," Nicholas said. "I recall that he was never a liked or likeable man. Aside from the 1902 incident, his conduct has been the topic of a few heated discussions amongst the generals. They usually ceased when I approached, but I overheard enough. Isn't there a saying about keeping your enemies close?"

Simon nodded sharply in response.

"I've heard rumours, too, that his wife turns a blind eye to his mistresses so long as he ensures that his family maintains a particular social standing and his discretions remain private," Nicholas said. "Since I stepped down, I've had plenty of time to reflect on many things, including your earlier references to Vasiliev."

"I also heard recently that he may be a police-plant," Simon said, "and a German spy. According to rumour …" Simon shrugged, abashed at repeating gossip. "Since his demotion from lieutenant colonel, the man has refused to advance beyond the rank of major. Apparently, he finds it convenient to remain at a lower rank where he has some authority, but not so much responsibility that his ability to achieve his own goals is obstructed. He possesses a ruthless drive and will stop at nothing, including murder. Yet, instead of having you assassinated in Moghilev, he managed to get himself blown up."

"Is anything to be done to stop him?" Nicholas said.

"I hope so," Simon replied. "We have an abundance of information that suggests he and Lebedev are up to no good." Simon paced before the tsar's desk. "What we really need is something that will confirm their connection and their plot."

"It would certainly be helpful to know the name of the person he spoke with on the telephone," Lord Nicholas said, stroking his beard. "Several high-ranking officers speak German."

"We are gradually eliminating individuals, sir," Simon said. "In the meantime, we're monitoring Lebedev's activities, and I wager he'll reach out to that superior again before long. If another assassination attempt is in the wind, we'll want to be ahead of the plot."

"Another—!" Nicholas said, momentarily stunned. "They must be stopped. I can't be looking over my shoulder every minute! I wish I could help, even tag along." He rubbed his hands together, as if anticipating the outcome. "It would certainly break the tedium of our miserable lives here under house arrest. Sometimes, I feel like a lion caged up at the zoo by a bunch of Bolshevik keepers. They don't want anything untoward to happen to us before they're rid of us. In an odd sort of way, I suppose that may be the only thing keeping me alive."

"This whole circumstance must be horribly frustrating for you," Simon said with empathy.

"Frustrating and worrisome. I couldn't bear for something to happen to my family."

"I understand," Simon said. "Kerensky's government is, as you say, concerned about your safety, and the growing revolution is definitely a threat. The city's in chaos. I suspect they'll try to move you to a safer place."

"Safer?" Nicholas seemed taken aback by the word. "Surely, we must be safe here. Who could reach us? Who would try?"

"The mobs," Simon said. "People have been flocking from the country into the city. Few have anywhere to go, and, as we've already discussed, they have no money and no food … and they're angry. They've been promised everything by the Kerensky government, and given nothing, simply because there's nothing to give. The one thing the Bolsheviks have managed, however, is to direct the anger of the mobs toward you. Away from themselves."

Simon tugged on an ear as he collected his thoughts. "I'll speak with Captain Egorov—my friend in the Imperial Guard. He may have heard something since last we spoke."

"Any word from England?" Nicholas said.

"Nothing yet," Simon replied. "We can only hope the old saying holds true: 'no news is good news.'" He shrugged and rose from the armchair, making his way toward the office door. "I'm off to the city shortly, but I'll return at week's end, hopefully, with more information."

He paused abruptly, bowed smartly before the man who was once tsar of all Russia, then closed the door quietly behind him.

———

A few days later, Simon had Zima deliver a note into Captain Egorov's hand, inviting him for dinner. The note was to be given to no one else, and Zima was to bring it back in the event he could not complete the task. The note contained a cautionary reminder that his apartment may be under surveillance.

An hour later, Lockhart knocked quietly on the hall door and slipped through the opening when Zima greeted him.

When Egorov, dressed in peasant clothes, arrived soon after, he advised Simon that the apartment was indeed under surveillance, by none other than Vasiliev himself.

"I walked right past him," Egorov said. "He didn't take his eyes from that window!"

"I see," Simon replied, tugging his ear. "Zima!"

Zima and his wife both appeared in the doorway of the parlour.

"Is everything alright?" Zima said. "Your voice sounded urgent."

"I have a challenge for the two of you," Simon said, chuckling, "if you're up for it."

"Another of your games, sir?" Mrs. Zima said, giggling like a young girl.

"Ah! You two know me too well!" Simon laughed, and

his employees smiled, their eyes twinkling with mischief. "The flat is still being watched. How would you feel about giving the man something to see?"

"What have you in mind, sir?" Zima said.

"Well, he's obviously hoping that I'll do something to compromise myself," Simon said. "I have an idea, but you must feel free to decline if it makes you feel uncomfortable." Simon explained his thoughts, leaving his guests and his employees slapping their knees with pleasure.

"Very well, sir," Mrs. Zima said, grinning from ear to ear. "We're happy to do our part."

In the next moments, Zima stepped toward the lace-covered window and turned off a lamp. Immediately, the interior lighting dimmed. Momentarily, he stood alone in a pool of moon glow. Then Mrs. Zima approached. She snaked her arms around his neck, rising on her toes to kiss him. As she did so, Zima raised a free hand and tugged downward on a heavy blind. They lingered in their embrace a while longer, then stepped slowly away from the window.

When Simon turned off a second lamp near him, the room fell into shadows, lit only by the flame of one candle.

Zima and his wife returned to the kitchen to finish preparing the meal. Simon, Egorov, and Lockhart spoke quietly for ten minutes, then Simon blew out the candle.

"Sir, the meal is ready," Zima said. "Will you eat in the dark?"

The three young men laughed, imagining the scene.

"Here, let me check," Egorov said. "I know where the

man was standing." He rose from his chair and peeked through the blind and the lace curtain, watching carefully for movement on the street. "How convenient that we have a clear night and a bright moon to reveal that which seeks to hide from view!"

"And how convenient that the kitchen has no window!" Lockhart said flippantly.

"I think he's gone," Egorov said, his voice serious, "but give me a few minutes to check below." He stepped quietly into the hallway and tripped silently down the stairs to the back of the building.

"The street is empty," he said, entering the kitchen a few minutes later. "However, to be on the safe side, I suggest we eat in here … by candlelight. I'd hate to dispel the mood set by Mr. and Mrs. Zima."

CHAPTER 46

The following morning, dressed in one of his disguises, Simon appeared outside the garrison. The trees on the opposite side of the street were in full foliage, making it easy to find shelter while he waited for Vasiliev to appear.

The wait was short-lived. The major approached the garrison gate on horseback and continued along the drive. *Damn! I'm going to have to run to keep up. I hope he doesn't go far!*

Conveniently for Simon, Vasiliev brought his mount to a halt outside a house on the far side of the Winter Palace. A groomsman took the reins and led the horse toward a small stable at the side of the house. Vasiliev hobbled up a short flight of stairs and rapped heavily on the door.

To Simon's surprise, Maksim Lebedev answered the door himself. Simon had not seen the statesman in months. He had, however, heard about Lebedev's exploits, including a move to the Bolshevik party when the Menshevik party had dissolved. Like Vasiliev, his reputation for brutality was becoming well-known, especially when it concerned punishment of rebels.

Vasiliev glanced over his shoulder before entering

the house. Then, the door slammed behind him.

If those two have their heads together, serious trouble is afoot. I must know more.

Abandoning his lookout, Simon strode smartly along the street, away from Lebedev's house. He jogged toward a shabby hotel several blocks away and ducked inside. When he asked to use the telephone, the desk clerk eyed him suspiciously.

When Simon placed several coins on the counter, the man pointed toward a telephone mounted on the wall. Simon dialled the garrison phone line and asked to speak to Egorov. In a low voice, with his back to the desk clerk, he explained the circumstance.

"Keep an eye on him," Egorov said. "I'll check his office for clues."

"Be quick about it," Simon replied. "I've no way of controlling his departure. Plus, he's on horseback. I'm on foot." Simon replaced the receiver and, with a brief nod of thanks, hastened out the door.

Outside the hotel, he retraced his steps to Lebedev's house, checking to see whether Vasiliev's horse remained in the stable. Satisfied that it did, he found another location from which to observe any comings and goings and waited.

More than an hour passed before Vasiliev, appearing angry, stormed down the front stairs as quick as he could hobble and snatched his horse's reins from a stable boy.

I hope it's been long enough for Artyom to conclude his search.

Once Vasiliev rounded the corner, Simon raced to the

hotel again and asked to use the telephone. The second time, Simon was greeted with a smile and a wave of the desk clerk's arm. *A few coins are always a worthwhile investment.*

"Any luck?" Simon said, speaking quietly into the receiver.

"Yes," Egorov replied, "I've found a few documents that might have merit. Some are in German, so I can't be certain."

"Great!" Simon said. "Should we meet now to discuss, or will you come for dinner? Mrs. Zima is making borscht."

"It can wait," Egorov replied. "Is Bruce Lockhart with you?"

"No, he had business at the embassy, but he'll be back at the end of the day." Simon replaced the receiver and left a few more coins on the desk for the grinning clerk.

———

That evening, the three young men dug into steaming bowls of borscht and warm rolls fresh from the oven, eating as if they had not done so for days. Mrs. Zima flapped her apron at their flattery, then returned to the kitchen so they could speak in private.

"What did you find?" Simon said without preamble.

"I found several documents written in German," Egorov said, shrugging as if to apologize for not being able to read them. "I also found some drawings of a transmitter radio and a code book. The best discovery, though, was a small, black book with notes concerning your surveillance and a note—both written in Russian." He spooned borscht into his mouth, then broke off a piece of his roll and popped it in as well.

"And …" Lockhart leaned forward, elbows on the table, waiting for Egorov to continue.

"Of course, I have no evidence other than what I read," Egorov said, "but I can confirm my earlier suspicions. Simon is to be framed as a spy, and Vasiliev intends to use the radio as evidence."

"Do you know when, where, or how?" Simon said, feeling the food in his belly curdle with his concern.

"I believe it will be tomorrow evening. He has arranged to broadcast near your flat, then he will report you as the perpetrator."

"Then I must follow him tomorrow evening and somehow thwart his efforts."

"We."

"We?"

"We … I'm coming with you," Lockhart said.

"And me, of course," Egorov chimed in, "but first we must report this to General Count Fyodor Arturovich Keller. We're going to need back-up."

"I know he's your uncle, but would he be bothered with this?" Simon said cautiously.

"Of course," Egorov replied, his chest seeming to inflate with pride. "He and my father were lifelong friends and staunch supporters of Nicholas Romanov. He is also my godfather, and has mentored me since my father died!"

Egorov smirked and cleared his throat. "General

Count Keller remains loyal to the crown, as I do. Like us, he will be happy to be rid of Vasiliev. My uncle may be counted on without question. And, if I know him well—and indeed I do—he will likely volunteer for the endeavour. He's always enjoyed a good tussle!"

By the time the last crumb had been eaten, the three men had formulated a plan for the following evening. Having cemented Vasiliev's relationship with Lebedev and the Bolshevik party, as well as with Volkov and the Okhrana, Egorov undertook to explain the situation to his godfather and win his support.

By noon the next day, the general had been briefed and had ordered that the garrison commander use his discretion and provide whatever assistance might be required.

Later that evening Simon, Lockhart, Egorov, and a handful of reliable guards observed Vasiliev carrying the portable radio into a vacant building two blocks from Simon's flat. Quietly, Simon led Lockhart, the general, and a few of his men into an adjoining room while Egorov and the remaining men guarded all exits.

Listening carefully to the Morse-code message, Simon transcribed it. He scribbled the message on a piece of paper and handed it to the general. "Do you speak German, sir?" Simon said in a whisper.

"Not well, but my aide does," Keller replied. "Unfortunately, he isn't here."

"Permit me, sir," Simon said, swallowing his anger. "Vasiliev has confirmed that the royal family is to be transferred to the town of Tobolsk before the end of the month. He will provide the exact date shortly." Simon's widened blue eyes peered at the general. "The Germans mean to kill the royals and blame it on the rebels!"

"That's proof enough for me," Keller said curtly. Speaking over his shoulder, he whispered orders to seize the radio, Vasiliev, and any evidence found with him.

———

Simon returned to the garrison with the soldiers. Once Vasiliev was behind bars and initial paperwork underway, the general invited Simon to join a celebration of the garrison's success.

"That man has been a thorn in the side of this garrison from the day he arrived. I'm glad to see the end of him," Keller said, raising a glass of vodka in salute.

"Will he be imprisoned?" Simon said.

"We have enough information to put him away for a very long time," Keller replied. "Now, we need to let the judicial process do its job."

"What about Lebedev and Volkov?' Simon said.

"Don't worry about those two," Keller said. "Vasiliev has already named Lebedev as the organizer, and confirmed that Volkov has been an accomplice. He's also agreed to name other well-placed individuals. You likely know this, Lord Simon—but for the others I will repeat: not only was he placed in the garrison as an informant for the Okhrana, but he reports to the Germans as well—a double agent!" He rose from his chair, filling empty glasses with more vodka.

"I understand that Lebedev is married to Vasiliev's sister, Galina," Keller said, continuing to share the early results of the major's interrogation, "and that the Vasiliev elders are both German-born and highly placed in German political circles. Vasiliev's sister is also involved. With Lebedev's connections, the Vasiliev family has been covertly working to overthrow the tsar, intending to hand Russia to the Kaiser on a silver platter—with Lebedev appointed puppet-master for all Russia!"

"Thanks to the *involuntary* testimony of Lebedev's aide, Aleksandr Volkov," Egorov said, his words ringing of irony as he rose to stand next to his godfather, "we are beginning to understand the intricate weaving of their evil web, and their intent to lay the blame for everything at the unassuming feet of Lord Simon!"

"To Lord Simon Nightingale-Temple!" the general said cheerily, raising his dripping glass in a toast. "He has been instrumental in uncovering a heinous crime against Mother Russia. While the people may never know it, we here tonight must recognize his heroics for what they are! To Lord Simon Nightingale-Temple, a man of many talents!"

"Hear, hear!" the group said, cheering together.

Simon jumped to his feet and raised his glass in salute to the men who helped bring down an attempt to overthrow the country. He had been in Russia for two years, and during that time he had made a few loyal friends, but it had been a long time since he had been part of such a celebration. His belly clenched with a brief and sudden nostalgia as he recalled the crew of RMS *Guardian*.

By the time Simon staggered home, the false dawn had already begun to glow. *I need to be on the first train*, he thought. *I'll sleep then*. He hastily bathed, changed, and sped out the door, his valise in one hand and a basket of food assembled by Mrs. Zima, including a can of strong tea, in the other.

CHAPTER 47

"I have news, sir," Simon said as he entered the former tsar's office. "Some good, some not so good, but hopefully delivered early enough to allow time for preparation."

"Tell me the good news," Nicholas said, tossing a pair of reading glasses on his desk and pinching the bridge of his nose. "God knows I could use some."

"It's about Maksim Lebedev and Ivan Vasiliev," Simon replied, his voice full of pride. "With the assistance of General Count Keller, Captain Egorov, and other members of the Imperial Guard, we managed to trap Ivan Vasiliev, who in turned betrayed his brother-in-law Maksim Lebedev and Lebedev's aide. All have been detained and are being interrogated. So far, we've confirmed that Vasiliev and Lebedev are both German informants. Vasiliev is a double agent, planted in the imperial garrison by the Okhrana. They planned to frame me, claiming I'm a German spy and the mastermind of a diabolical plan to overthrow your crown and the Duma."

"You ... a spy!" Nicholas surrendered to a belly-shaking laugh. "If they only knew!" Still chuckling, he added, "I'm pleased to hear that General Count Keller was involved. He's a good man! My compliments for a job well done."

His smile faded as he regarded Simon's frown. "What's wrong? What else have you discovered?" He straightened in his chair.

"The Bolshevik party intends to move your family to Tobolsk—"

"Tobolsk?"

"You're familiar with the place?"

"Yes, it's in the Urals. When?"

"Any day."

"Why?"

"They'll tell you it will be a place of refuge, a place to keep you safe from the revolution, which grows stronger every day."

"For how long?"

"Until suitable asylum is found, I suspect," Simon said, trying to soften the news. "You're to remain there for the winter. In the spring, they intend to secret you out of Siberia via Japan."

"Are we to live in some pigsty of a farm?" Nicholas' impatience seemed to overtake him. He jumped to his feet and strode thoughtfully before the grand bay window that overlooked the gardens. "Look how serene they are," he said, watching his family strolling along a pathway.

"Your daughters will be wondering about their lessons," Simon said, nearing the window.

"Say nothing to them," Nicholas said, his voice pleading. "I would speak with my wife first."

"Of course." Simon turned toward the office door.

"Simon," Nicholas said, calling the young man back. "Thank you, for all you have done for me, for my family. On many occasions, your news has been painful to hear, but you have always been honest, and I appreciate that."

"Sir," Simon said, bowing. Then, he opened the door and left Nicholas to his thoughts.

The following day, Simon responded to Nicholas' summons and listened to his proposal for a family holiday in the mountains.

"You need not pack for parties," he said, his voice sounding matter-of-fact. "We will merely enjoy our time together in the country. Long walks in the sunshine, maybe some hunting and fishing, visits with the locals, that sort of thing." He gazed upon the innocent faces of his children.

Simon stood at the back of the room, listening to the ruse, watching the former tsar. For an instant, he thought he saw heartbreak in the man's eyes.

"When do we leave?" Olga said enthusiastically.

"How long do we have for packing?" Tatiana chimed in.

"I haven't decided yet," he replied, "but since I've been relieved of duties, let's pack for cooler weather—maybe several months."

"How wonderful!" Alexei said, clapping his hands in delight.

"Off you go, then," Nicolas said. "But keep this a secret for a bit, will you. I'll inform the servants next."

Alexandra followed her children out of the office, fighting tears. When she turned away from her husband, Simon saw her back straighten, as if to summon courage. "Shush, children," she said, her voice quiet. "Let's not upset the servants. Go to your rooms and wait."

Half an hour later, Nicholas stood before his most trusted servants, tutors, and doctor.

"Where's Gibbes?" he said, his eyes searching the room.

"He had to go into Petrograd, sir," Gilliard replied. "He'll be back in a few days.

"Very well," Nicholas said solemnly, looking upon the faces of those he had trusted for many years. "I have been advised that the Bolshevik party plans to move my family to the Urals. I don't know how long we'll be gone, but I expect at least through the winter, perhaps until the spring." Soft chatter scattered amongst his audience.

"You've all been so kind to stay with us as long as you have," he said, interrupting their wondering. "The time has come, however, for you to consider your own futures. We will find no fault with you should you choose not to accompany us."

"I will accompany you, sir," Gilliard said, promptly stepping forward, his chin high.

"And I," others chimed in, including Yevgeny Botkin, court physician, Anna Demidova, lady-in-waiting for Alexandra, Alexei Trupp, head footman, Ivan Kharitonov, head cook, and Simon Nightingale-Temple, tutor and family friend.

For those who knew that a transfer was imminent, time passed slowly. When, five days later, government officials arrived with an armed guard, including Captain Artyom Egorov, they were surprised that the news was received as calmly as it was.

"The Imperial Guard will remain here to protect you," one of the officials said. "We are concerned for your safety."

A few additional servants were invited to accompany the royal family, including Alexei's sailor nurse, who had been tending Alexei when the earlier summons was issued. Because of the early warning, luggage and other personal belongings were packed quickly and loaded onto wagons.

As the footmen carried the luggage and chests from the palace, Simon went in search of Egorov. When he found his friend, they walked toward the lake to keep their conversation confidential.

"What do you know about this excursion?" Simon said.

"Not much," Egorov replied, "except what we've learnt from Vasiliev and his colleagues. As a result, we're to monitor anyone outside the immediate party who tries to communicate with them, and to keep the area around them safe. While you and others have been trying to find a home for the Romanovs, not one country has stepped forward. The government's at a loss for what to do next. Since the rebellion has begun to settle down, western allies are losing interest in the matter. And, just recently, I heard that the Germans claim that they would welcome the restoration of the monarchy—if the Bolsheviks fail! It's all just dregs that filter down by word of mouth, so who can say how much is true or reliable. My godfather says he knows nothing more as well."

"What do you think will happen, if no one grants asylum?" Simon said. "Have you heard anything more about an assassination threat?"

"I don't know," Egorov said. "I'm surprised that none of their families will help. You'd think between the crowns of Denmark, England, and Germany, someone would have a care! They may not be ideal monarchs, but the Romanovs are good people, for God's sake—and their relatives are rulers of those countries!" He kicked at a clod of dry dirt. "I've heard nothing more about an assassination threat. Perhaps that's become irrelevant because we interrupted Vasiliev's plans."

"I've come to a similar conclusion," Simon replied. "I have written father several times, literally begging him to find a solution, even with one of the colonies. He says King George wants to help, but still fears a British rebellion in retaliation. Anything they manage will have to be discreet. He continues to look for accommodation as well. I just wish they'd hurry up. I understand that it can be colder in the Urals than here in the wintertime. And here is plenty cold!"

"Indeed," Egorov said, turning his face to the sky and squinting into the sun. "We should appreciate the sun's warmth while we can."

"The footmen must have everything loaded by now,"

Simon said. "We'd better turn back; but first I want to give you this and ask that you keep it safe for me." He tossed a small pouch filled with notes and coins.

"What's this?" Egorov said, snatching it deftly.

"A while ago, Lady Alexandra asked me to liquidate some assets, which I did. She then charged me to keep the sale proceeds safe … which I've also done." Simon grinned at his friend. "Given we have no idea of our future, I am hedging my losses. I've given a quarter of the proceeds to each of two other trusted friends, and now a quarter to you. I hold the fourth quarter. My hope is to restore every note and coin to the rightful owner when this uncertainty ends. Should it not, however, she stands a better chance of recovery if it is in parts, rather than one whole."

Simon shoved his hands into his pockets and kicked at a pebble, eyeing his friend. "Will you do this for me? For her?"

Egorov stuffed the pouch into a pocket and placed his hand over his heart. "Come," he said. "We must hurry."

As they jogged back to the palace, Simon elicited Egorov's promise to inform him immediately of any whisper of assassination, and to keep an eye out for Gibbes, who had not yet returned from Petrograd.

CHAPTER 48

When the entourage arrived in Tobolsk, they were taken to the mansion of the former governor, where they were expected to reside throughout the winter. Their greatest challenge was finding fuel sufficient to keep themselves warm and with which to cook meals.

Not long after their arrival, Gibbes reached the mansion gates, fighting through the guards and insisting that he had a right to be with the Romanov family. When asked about his absence from the palace at the time the family was moved, Gibbes reported that he had been detained by a medical ailment that required immediate attention and demurred to say more.

In October, news arrived at the mansion regarding a recent change in the governing party. Neither Nicholas, nor his entourage, responded with alarm or concern for their safety. They continued to be confident that loyal supporters were organizing a rescue attempt. Each day passed in the predictable tedium of close confinement.

But for Maria, the young Romanovs preferred to pass their time with the younger imperial guards. Early in the new year, Egorov covertly cautioned Simon that, in his opinion, some of those guards—of whom he knew little—were becoming too familiar with the the young ladies. Simon shared the observation with Nicholas, and he quickly put an end to the socializing. Thereafter, loyal members of the group tightened the circle of protectiveness around the family.

Maria's preferred shadowing of Simon was deemed acceptable by her parents. On those occasions she often donned a pair of trousers and pinned up her hair, then asked him to continue her wrestling or boxing lessons. The others had lost interest when they arrived in Tobolsk, so the training became personal. Sometimes too personal for Simon, especially during the close contact of certain exercises.

On one such occasion, when he had pinned her to a makeshift mat in the barn, his chest tightened when he looked into her wide, blue eyes and caught a faint scent of lilac. *I could kiss her, and no one would notice.* Instead, he swore silently and pushed free of the hold.

Relief passed through him whenever she appeared in a skirt. On those days, they donned heavy coats, fur hats, and mittens and wandered the length and breadth of the mansion's grounds, speaking in one of the several languages that she had been taught. He described his home in Jarrow, his family, and his life at sea, and asked her more about her own life. She told him of family vacations before the war.

"It was tradition to take to the seashore or the mountains when the weather turned warm," she told him. "In those days, we lived simply, as the locals did.

No glitter, no pretense. It helped that we stayed many weeks at a time. We melded into their society. We even learnt their accents and dialects."

She laughed aloud, as if remembering. "By the end of our vacation, Papa often teased that he would send us to the kitchen if we didn't speak proper Russian or French when we returned home. Of course, we behaved whenever he was around. But, alone … we spoke as we chose."

"We had similar experiences when we vacationed in Ireland, Scotland, and Wales," Simon said. "I had a knack for picking up the rhythm of the locals, which annoyed my brother terribly. He had little talent or time for such things. He was all about playing games to win, and didn't hesitate to throw a tantrum on the rare occasion when he lost."

On other days, Maria asked him to teach her something she had little chance of knowing, given their current circumstance. It became a challenge for him to find alternative ways to quench Maria's curiosity. He found himself constantly reviewing all that he learnt in college and at sea, searching for nuggets of detail that had fascinated him, hoping she would be equally intrigued. And she was.

He told her about unusual sea animals, the rescue of a French Canadian, and Bear Island. He taught her basic principles of first aid, how to focus on surroundings during difficult situations, how to listen and examine the circumstances around her, how to fend off an attacker, and many other skills that he had learnt during his training with Lockhart: even disguise and deception.

"I wish we had horses to ride," Maria said one day. "I miss riding with you, racing across the fields, my hair flying in the wind."

"I never thought I'd hear you say that!" Simon replied. "I recall how concerned you were when the subject first came up."

"But you've made it fun!" Maria said. "Our instructors wanted us to know the technique, but they never explained the simplicity of feeling the animal's movement and becoming one with it. It's difficult when riding side-saddle. Astride, I can feel every movement, every muscle through my thighs. I can almost sense its thoughts." She gazed at Simon and sighed longingly.

Simon coughed and turned away to hide his embarrassment, chiding himself for reading more into the comment than appropriate. "Your skills have improved remarkably," he said as he reined in his emotions.

He often found himself in uncomfortable situations with Maria, forced to struggle with self-control in her presence. He was keenly aware of his feelings for her, as well as his social position. A close friendship was acceptable, but care had to be taken to avoid any overture that could compromise his presence.

Week after week of house arrest passed at a snail's pace. Simon worked tirelessly with the two tutors to keep everyone occupied with indoor and outdoor activities. Simon found these occupations much easier when others were around.

In March 1918, the royal party received notice that their rations would be reduced to those of the soldiers. Ten servants were returned to Petrograd, and butter and coffee were no longer supplied. The family groaned at the news, but accepted the hardship as a brief interlude to their departure.

On April 30th, in the early hours of the morning, a division of Red Guards arrived at the mansion. After rousing everyone from their beds and ordering them to dress for travel, the leader, Vasily Yakovlev, informed Nicholas that he and his family were to be taken to Moscow.

Amid resistance and loud protests, the family and their few remaining servants were hastily loaded into a convoy of four-wheeled carriages destined for Tyumen, where they were to board a requisitioned train. The river, they were informed, was still partially frozen, so use of a ferry was out of the question.

Sisters and servants alike huddled together, some unable to control their sobbing, others visibly shaking with fear.

The journey from Tobolsk to Tyumen was long and taxing, requiring two overnight stops, where the captives ate little and slept less. The procession also stopped frequently to change horses, providing the nervous passengers with brief opportunities to stretch their legs.

Early the second day, the armed escort halted as a second convoy approached. They wore the uniforms of the

Red Guard. Yakovlev's men advanced to intercept them.

Yakovlev's raised voice drew the attention of Simon and the Imperial Guards. What they said sent a chill down Simon's spine.

"Surround the carriages," Simon shouted to the tsar's guards. Heart pounding with adrenaline, he raced toward the carriage occupied by Nicholas and his wife. He approached from the opposite side, out of sight of the Red Guards, and knocked on the carriage door.

"What is it?" Nicholas said, sounding confused.

"Sir," Simon replied, opening the door, "another Red Guard faction is arguing with Yakovlev. They want to take you to Yekaterinburg. Yakovlev won't hear of it. His orders are to take you to Moscow."

"My children?" Alexandra said, anxiously leaning toward the door.

"Safe for the moment, ma'am," Simon said, hoping his words offered assurance. "The Imperial Guards have their carriages surrounded, and Yakovlev's guards have encircled all of the carriages and the Imperial Guards."

"For the moment, you say," Nicholas said, as if grasping for something concrete. "That sounds distressing. Surely, I must be able to help?"

"Remain inside your carriage, sir," Simon replied, his voice firm. "Let's see what comes from their discussions. Right now, their guns are trained on each other."

"Keep us informed," Nicholas said curtly, reaching for his wife's hand.

"I will," Simon said, eyeing each of them. "If you

hear gunfire, get down on the floor. Don't come out." He closed the door and crept to the opposite side to better observe the stand-off.

Seeing Egorov standing near the carriage occupied by the young women, Simon motioned that they exchange places. "I need to speak with them for a moment," Simon said urgently when they met halfway.

As before, Simon stepped cautiously to the opposite side of the carriage and cracked opened the door.

"Simon!" Maria said, sounding surprised. "What's going on?"

"We're under attack by another Red Guard faction," Simon replied calmly, managing to control his voice despite his rapidly beating heart. "They're arguing over who will host your family next."

"That's ridiculous," Olga said, her annoyance obvious. "Why would Yakovlev—"

Gunfire and yelling shattered the quiet around them.

"Down!" Simon commanded the young women. "On the floor. Now!"

Three obeyed and cowered on the floor of the carriage. On hands and knees, Maria scrambled toward Simon. "Give me your pistol," she said. "I know you have one in your pocket."

"No!" he said curtly, hefting the rifle, feeling uncomfortable with her demand. "Get back with your sisters." A pointing finger emphasized his urgency.

"Your knife, then," she said, her large, blue eyes pleading. "I need something to defend us."

"No." Simon glared back.

"But—" Maria said, beginning to protest.

"Back!" Simon said, the word sucked into oblivion by a round of bullets whizzing over the carriage. "Down! All of you!" he said, his words hissed with urgency.

"Give me the pistol," Maria said insistently, holding out her empty hand. "If I'm going to be attacked, I intend to hurt someone too."

Simon gazed at Maria, saw the defiance in her eyes, and nodded. "Very well," he said, withdrawing the pistol from his pocket, "but be careful. One careless move, and you could have us all shot."

Maria accepted the pistol, her face serious, and nodded. He watched her check the gun as she had been taught, then crouch near the opposite door. "Ready," she said quietly, as if speaking to herself.

Sporadic fire rang throughout the forest. Simon slammed the door shut and crouched behind a wheel, surveying his surroundings. Random bullets sprayed the clearing. One sliced through the left sleeve of his jacket. He gasped.

"Are you alright?" Maria's voice sounded muffled through the door. The door began to open slowly.

"Yes," Simon said, pushing the door closed again.

A tackle from behind caught Simon off-guard. He fell sideways, smacking his head on the forward wheel, dazing him. He rose slowly, shaking his head to clear his thoughts. Blinking rapidly, he saw that a dark silhouette hovered over him. He heard the snick of the pistol aimed at his chest.

Beyond the pistol, he saw the carriage door open. "Simon?" Maria's voice was clear through the gap. "Si—"

The silhouette stepped back. Keeping the pistol aimed at Simon, he yanked the door open. Gasps escaped from the carriage.

"What have we here?" the silhouette said with a sneer. "A trove of treasure?" He waved the pistol. "All of you—out, now!"

On her knees, Maria straightened to fill the entrance to the carriage, obscuring visibility of her sisters in the dark interior. "Perhaps not," she said, raising the pistol toward the silhouette's head. "Drop your pistol, or I'll shoot." Her voice was calm, determined.

The silhouette's firearm wavered between Maria and Simon.

Seeing his indecisiveness, Simon lunged, tackling him to the frozen ground. They rolled together, struggling for control. A shot fired. The forest stilled. Simon lay motionless, sprawled across the silhouette.

Egorov erupted from the trees and slid to Simon's side. "Maria?" Egorov said, looking toward the gaping carriage door.

"I'm fine," she replied, her voice shaky. "We're fine." She glanced over her shoulder. Her sister's faces slowly appeared behind her, nodding.

You alright?" Egorov said, turning his attention to Simon as his friend began to stir. He grasped Simon's arm and helped him to his feet.

"I'll do," Simon said, brushing twigs and dirt from

his clothes, using his body to obscure a view from the carriage. He spread the hole in his sleeve and examined the graze to his flesh, then turned toward the carriage.

His eyes warned Maria and her sisters back into the carriage before he once again closed the door. "But I think his might be a different story." He spoke quietly, a curt nod drawing Egorov's attention to the supine silhouette. Vacant eyes stared into the treetops.

Egorov squatted near the body and removed the pistol from the man's grip. "He's not going anywhere," Egorov said, his voice low. "The bullet had a clear path under his chin, into his brain." He shook his head as he rose. "Help me move him out of the road."

They hoisted the man by the shoulders and dragged him out of view.

"We managed to chase the others off," Egorov said. "Yakovlev wants to press on before they try again. He insists we reach our station before nightfall, and that's a few hours yet."

Simon returned to the carriage and opened the door.

"Simon!" Maria said, seemingly surprised to have her support suddenly removed. Still on her knees, she fell forward, wrapping her arms around his neck.

Simon's arms rose to encircle her, holding her securely for a moment longer than might be socially appropriate. Realizing his faux pas, he coughed to clear his throat as he set Maria on her feet. He then reached for one of her sisters.

Egorov set the last sister on a tuft of lichen growing

at the side of the muddy ruts. "If you have any business that needs tending," he said, his words devoid of deference, "you'd best do it now. We have orders to move out in ten minutes."

"I'll go," Olga said without hesitation.

"Me too," the others said, gathering their skirts to lift them clear of the mud.

"Ten minutes," Egorov said abruptly, directing them away from the site of the silhouette's body.

———

From the station, Yakovlev sent a telegram to Moscow reporting the attack. In response, he received new orders advising that, once the royal party had boarded the train in Tyumen, the train was to divert through Omsk instead of Yekaterinburg en route to Moscow. The leaders of the Omsk division of the Red Guard were less likely to harm the family, he had been told.

Soon after the train redirected toward Omsk, it was intercepted by a division of more than one thousand armed Red Guards. The division leaders accused Yakovlev of being a traitor intending to secret the family to exile.

While a heated and animated discussion ensued amongst the Yekaterinburg delegation and Yakovlev, the passengers nervously donned their winter coats and hats and disembarked to stretch their legs along the rail line. Armed guards had been stationed to ensure their wanderings remained close to the train.

"Now what's going on?" Nicholas growled as he

tromped toward Simon. "No one will tell me anything."

"Let me investigate," Simon said tersely, setting off in search of his friend.

When he spied Egorov, he jerked his head toward the rear of the cars where they could speak privately.

"Have you heard anything?" Simon said quietly, slapping his arms and stamping his feet, hoping for warmth.

"Not much," Egorov replied in hushed tones. "But I gather that the Yekaterinburg delegation is claiming entitlement for the detention of the family. Passage through the region has been denied. We're all to transfer to the local train immediately."

Simon thanked him for the information and briskly disappeared around the last car, hastily returning forward along the opposite side of the train. When he found Nicholas, he relayed a summary of their situation.

Nicholas closed his eyes and inhaled deeply, as if that alone might resolve his quandary. Simon was struck by the deep worry lines etched into Nicholas' face and the dark shadows that underscored hollow eyes above protruding cheekbones.

"Are you well, sir?" Simon said, concerned.

"Tired, young Simon … very tired," Nicholas said, sighing heavily again. "I don't suppose you've heard from your father?"

"No sir," Simon replied, hesitantly. "It was difficult to send messages from Tobolsk."

"You should find Yekaterinburg less difficult," Nicholas

said, gazing toward the nearby forest. "Historically, it's been supportive of the royal family. Hopefully someone will yet be helpful." He tightened the collar of his coat against the cold. "Please ask your father to hurry. How difficult must it be to find a small town with a house for my family? We don't need a palace. A small manor will suffice."

"I'll do my best," Simon said, clipping his word. "In the meantime, what will you tell your family?"

"I'll tell them that we are merely moving closer to the main railway line," Nicholas said with a heavy sigh, "and that we'll soon be on our way to Japan, and a new home. Pray God I speak the truth!"

While Simon tried to make sense of their circumstances, a flurry of telegraph messages were being transmitted amongst the commanding officers and headquarters in Moscow. Agreement was finally reached, and the train continued to Yekaterinburg on the understanding that the family's safety was tantamount to what they would receive in Moscow.

***

In Yekaterinburg, the Romanov family alone was instructed to disembark. Communist guards tossed luggage out of the baggage car into spring mud. The Romanovs were ordered to collect their own bags and take them into a two-storey house that Simon later learnt was owned by a military engineer.

Servants, tutors, and Imperial Guards were forced

to remain on the train. Through dirty windows, they anxiously watched the family struggle with their soiled bags, their faces etched with frustration and fear.

"My dear Anastasia!" Gilliard said anxiously, attempting to shove his way past a communist guard. "Let me by. I must help the poor girl. The mud will ruin her shoes!"

The communist guard menacingly shoved the butt of his rifle into Gilliard's shoulder. "Sit down, old man!" the guard said with a growl. "If you don't like what you see, turn away like the others."

Simon stood next to Gilliard, a hand on the man's shoulder. Together, they observed the family disappear into the house and watched the windows for confirmation that they were safe. It was only then that they realized the windows had been covered with planks of wood or painted over.

"What's going on?" Simon said gruffly as he sidled up to Egorov a while later. They stood outside the rear car, watching the house.

"Whatever it is, I don't like it," Egorov replied curtly. "Even the Imperial Guard has been banned from the house. The Romanovs have been forced inside and now they're under communist guard only. Have you noticed the windows?"

"Yes," Simon said, releasing a frosted breath of exasperation. "Why would the windows be covered?"

"To block visibility both ways," Egorov said, musing. "In my opinion, the communists can't be trusted. My colonel agrees. He's been demanding access, especially for the servants, but so far … nothing! Yurovsky says they're here for a *special purpose.*"

"'Special purpose'?" Simon said, sounding confused. "Whatever does that mean?"

"I don't know," Egorov said, shaking his head. "The commander sent word to Moscow asking for more information. As head of the local Cheka, Yurovsky is stationed there, and has no business being here." He scratched his chin in thought. "This doesn't bode well."

"It doesn't," Simon said, jamming a pointing finger toward the second floor. "Look up there. Someone's trying to scratch the window clear."

"That will end as soon as they're seen," Egorov said, kicking a clump of icy snow in resignation.

A moment later, the window scratching ceased.

"Bolsheviks aren't co-operative at the best of times," Egorov said abruptly, "and these ones are particularly resentful toward the royals."

"I can see that," Simon replied, frowning. "They won't even allow entry to Lady Alexandra's maid, the sailor nurse, or the doctor. I'm certain Lady Alexandra can manage without her maid, but Alexei needs his medical support."

"On another note," Egorov said, impatiently trampling the snow beneath his feet, "You'll recall that I sent a telegram to my godfather before we left Tobolsk."

Simon nodded.

"I sent a follow-up today, as soon as the train pulled in." He covertly scanned their surroundings, then reached into a tunic pocket. "This message was just delivered to me by a courier. Apparently, Lebedev escaped soon after we left for Tobolsk. Both jailers were found dead … inside Lebedev's cell. He was last seen heading east about a month ago."

"East?" Simon said, surprised. "Do you think he's headed here?"

"I don't know," Egorov replied, tucking the message into his tunic. "But someone with authority has initiated this detainment. We just heard that the family is being transferred to Moscow—to stand trial. But if that's the case, why divert here of all places?"

"Trial!" Simon shook his head in disbelief, feeling his heart begin to pound with fear. "Let's keep an eye out. The stink of this detention becomes fouler each minute!"

CHAPTER 49

The royals were detained in Yekaterinburg throughout the months of May and June. In time the doctor, the maid, the chef, and the footman were allowed entry, but no others. The service of the sailor nurse was deemed by Yurovsky to be unnecessary, and Simon was told to go home: that he had no business in this matter. The tutors were also told that their presence was redundant.

"They'll need us eventually," Gibbes said. "I'm staying!"

The others agreed with him and sought accommodation nearby. The Imperial Guard refused to back down and insisted on proof that the royals were alive, and that they received proper food and care. Although Yurovsky assured them that all was in order, he provided no proof.

***

Early one morning toward the middle of July, Simon awoke abruptly to an unexpected knock on the door of his rented room.

"Who is it?" he said, annoyed to have his sleep disturbed. In response to Egorov's reply, he sprang from the bed and opened the door, surprised to see Egorov standing in the hallway alert and fully dressed.

"What is it?" he said, scratching his head as he glanced at his open pocket watch resting on a night table. "Has something happened?"

"I don't know what to say," Egorov said, removing his cap and running his fingers through his hair. "Something's peculiar. I can feel it! Suddenly, the communist guards seem to have come alive. It's as if a current of anticipation runs through them."

"Something must be about to happen then," Simon said. "How can we find out more?"

"I've asked amongst them whether the Romanovs are to be moved again," Egorov replied. "The response is always the same: they smirk and say something like 'yes, yes, they will soon be removed,' or 'you shouldn't worry, we'll take care of them.' Then they chuckle. Their mirth is sinister."

"That is worrisome," Simon said. "Damnation! What if they're readying for another assassination?"

"God forbid it!" Egorov said. "Regardless, I can't tell the colonel. He and the others won't believe me without proof." He stood near the door, tapping his foot in agitation.

"Then let's get proof," Simon said, hastily pulling on his clothes. "We can take shifts keeping a close watch on the house. If we see anything suspicious, we act; and if that means involving the Imperial Guard, so be it."

"Of course, but we need to be inconspicuous. The white nights are a risk. We could easily be seen."

The conversation between Simon and Egorov continued for some time, during which they discussed a rescue plan and a back-up plan.

"I'll make arrangements for the escape," Egorov said. "You speak to the tutors."

"Certainly!" Simon replied. Now fully awake, he snatched up his coat and followed Egorov out into the street.

That night, Egorov and Gibbes stood watch through to sunrise and reported to Simon and Gilliard that it had been quiet. The next night, Simon and Gilliard took the watch.

Soon after midnight, Simon spotted light coming from a room on the main floor of the house. Several minutes later, light shone in other rooms. He nudged Gilliard, who dozed next to him. Gilliard snorted softly but awoke promptly, attentive and keen. Simon pointed toward the house. Beyond the painted glass, they could see shadows of what appeared to be people dressing.

"Odd!" Simon said. "Why are they dressing in the middle of the night? This must be what we've been waiting for. Stay here. I'll get the others."

Simon left his observation post and raced to Egorov's military tent. Once he had Egorov moving, he ran to alert Gibbes.

Within twenty minutes the four men, dressed in obscure clothing, crouched at the observation point, contemplating their next steps.

CHAPTER 50

"What was that?" Egorov said, interrupting the discussion.

"I hear screaming!" Gilliard said. "Good lord, what can be happening?"

"Listen!" Gibbes said. "Were those gunshots?"

The four men remained motionless as moments ticked by.

"There it is again!" Gibbes said. "Those bloody dogs!"

"You two stay here," Simon said. "The captain and I will move in closer."

Egorov drew his gun from its holster and looked at Simon questioningly, the twitch Simon had not seen in months now reappearing. Simon patted the pocket of his jacket, recalling the words of a marine aboard RMS *Guardian* to always keep his pistol handy in times of trouble.

Before they could move, a truck rumbled up the road and drove to the rear of the house. Simon and Egorov glanced at each other, eyes round with surprise.

"Was that Lebedev sitting next to the driver?" Simon said sotto voce.

"I think so," Egorov said. "If so, this has to be what we've been expecting."

"Let's go," Simon said, creeping away from the lookout.

He and Egorov moved with stealth toward the house, each taking a different path, following the truck. When it stopped at the back of the house, they halted side by side, crouching behind a row of ornamental bushes. They watched the driver and several guards remove fuel canisters from under the truck's canopy. Lebedev stomped up some stairs and entered through a side door.

"Given the way those canisters are being carried, they must be full," Simon said sotto voce. "I hope they don't intend to burn the house down with the Romanovs inside it."

Soon, the guards finished their work and disappeared through the basement door.

"To hell with them all!" the driver said, reappearing sometime later and stomping toward the back of the truck, a younger man in tow. "Bloody monarchists! Help me get this tarp rolled out."

As the two men struggled to secure the tarp, a third soldier appeared at the door. "We're wanted upstairs," he said. "Now. Lebedev's pissed off!"

"Why?" the driver's helper said.

"We weren't supposed to take any loot. He wants to see our empty pockets."

"*Proklyatiye!*" the driver said. "The greedy swine wants it all for himself!" He dug both hands into his pockets and pulled out small objects that reflected the light of the night. Turning, he snatched a sack from within the truck and emptied his hands. The others grinned and quickly emptied their pockets before hastening back inside.

Simon waited for a count of twenty, then moved toward the gaping door. Light from the hallway lit the entrance. Before he could step further, Egorov was by his side.

"Quick," Simon said, his voice low, "we don't have much time."

Along the hallway, pale light streamed through a doorway. Swirls of smoke wafted through it. Simon scooted to the opposite side of the frame and peered into the room. In that moment, time stood still for him.

Spirals of residual gun smoke twisted and turned above what appeared to be mangled bodies. Trying to make sense of what he saw, Simon squinted, stepping into the room like an automaton, trying to avoid the rivulets of blood and body matter that blended into large, sticky puddles. The weight of his pistol wavered in his hand as he resisted the urge to cough, and he waved his hand to clear the smoke.

The settling smoke revealed the truth of what he saw. Nicholas slumped together with his son, both shot in the forehead, eyes staring unseeing. Alexandra was splayed across a fallen chair, a bullet hole between her open eyes, her mouth gaping, her throat slit. The remaining men, including the doctor and the footman, had been shot between the eyes and stabbed through the heart.

The grand duchesses and other women had been dragged into a line and placed side by side. Each had a bullet between their eyes and a slit throat, and all were stripped naked. A pile of rent clothing sat nearby. Although the men remained clothed, their pockets had been turned out, suggesting that their clothing had been searched.

Simon gagged at the smell of blood and the horror before him. Resisting the urge to vomit, time restarted. "Oh, God!" he said mournfully, motioning Egorov into the room.

"Oh, God," Egorov echoed.

"Quick," Simon said, "check for survivors."

The two men moved efficiently from one body to the next. It was clear to them that each was dead, but they checked for a pulse anyway. When Simon reached the last person, he stood and looked to Egorov, his face sullen.

Egorov stepped to his side and spoke quietly. "They're all dead," he said flatly. "From the looks of it, shot, bayonetted, then stabbed. As if one death blow wasn't enough. They've been murdered thrice! We should cover the women," he said mournfully.

"We haven't time," Simon said, scanning the room again, mentally tallying who had been slain. "Wait! One's missing. Maria!" He turned slowly, looking for clues. "There! Smears of blood."

The two men followed small red drops to a wardrobe at the far end of the hallway.

Above them, they heard the booming voice of Lebedev chastising Yurovsky and his guards for robbing the dead of their jewels. "The jewels belong to Mother Russia!" he said adamantly. "You had no right!"

"Maria!" Simon said, hissing urgently. "Maria, it's Simon. I'm going to open the door. Don't make a sound." Simon turned the knob and carefully opened the door of an old wardrobe.

Maria crouched inside, fear and panic marring her face. "Help me, please," she said, sobbing.

"Where are you hurt?" Egorov said.

"My leg. I've been shot."

Remembering the burning pain of the bullet that pierced his leg on Bear Island, Simon slipped his pistol into his pocket and leaned into the cupboard. He scooped Maria into his arms and lifted. The scent of lilacs twisted with fear as he fought for self-control and a need to find safety.

"Hurry," Egorov said, "they'll be coming down any moment!" He found a rag to wipe up droplets of Maria's blood, closed the cupboard door, and checked to ensure that they had left no clues.

As they passed the rear of the truck, Egorov paused and reached inside. He felt for the sack they had seen earlier. When he found it, he waved it in Simon's direction. "This may come in handy," he said. He tucked it inside his jacket and followed Simon into the trees.

They found Gibbes and Gilliard waiting for them near the tool shed at the back of the garden.

"Do you have the wagon?" Egorov said.

"Yes," Gibbes said. "What happened?"

"Maria," Gilliard said urgently. "Maria, you've been injured."

"But she's alive," Simon said, "which is more than I can say for the others."

"We must be away," Egorov said impatiently. "You two, return to your rooms. I'll get Simon and Maria settled and return before moonset."

"Prepare to catch the first train out of here," Simon said, clambering aboard the wagon. "Get to the British Embassy in Petrograd. Ask for Ambassador Buchanan. He'll know what to do." He settled into the wagon, clutching Maria. His hand pressed her bloody skirt firmly against her thigh. "If you can't reach Buchanan, try Bruce Lockhart at the British Consulate in Moscow. Regardless, go with haste!"

Gilliard and Gibbes each kissed Maria's pale cheek and wished her well, then disappeared.

Egorov grabbed the horse's halter and led it toward another cluster of trees, keeping to the long grass and shadows. When he determined they were out of earshot, he hopped in the cart and urged the horse into a trot along a worn path.

PART THREE

CHAPTER 51

B efore long, Egorov reined the horse to a halt next to a small cottage built deep in a nearby forest. During their earlier surveillance of the area around Yekaterinburg, Simon and Egorov had discovered it by accident. From the look of it then, no one had lived in the dwelling for many years. They had returned the following day, hastily tidied it, and filled it with supplies in anticipation of some unknown emergency.

Egorov located a small lantern and lit a candle while Simon lifted Maria from the wagon.

"She's fainted," he said, laying her gently onto a cot. Egorov held the lantern high, casting a light by which Simon was able to examine the young woman for wounds other than the sticky red on her thigh.

"I don't know how she was able to escape with just one wound," Egorov said, "considering the state of the others."

"Let's not think about that now," Simon said, pushing skirts and undergarments out of the way to reveal a puncture in her leg seeping freely.

"Have you ever tended a gunshot wound?" Egorov said, as if sensing Simon's angst.

"No," Simon replied. "Aside from being shot once myself, I've no hands-on experience." Egorov raised a questioning brow. When Simon said no more, he lowered his gaze to Maria.

"May I?" Egorov said, motioning for Simon to step aside.

"What do you need?" Simon said, stepping out of the way as he took up the lamp to illuminate Maria's injury.

"For now, set the lamp down," Egorov replied. "I need you to apply pressure to the site while I prepare. Once I start, I'll need you to keeping mopping up any blood around the puncture." He peered closer at her injury. "I can't believe how easily she bleeds."

"I've seen it before," Simon said, reluctant to disclose a private condition before determining the information was relevant. "They all seem to bleed easily, but strong pressure usually stops it in short order." *Except for the boy, which is irrelevant now!*

The next while was spent focussed on cleaning Maria's wound and staunching the blood flow. All the while, Simon spoke reassuringly into her ear.

"She can't hear you, you know," Egorov said. "She's unconscious. With luck, she won't wake up before my work is done."

"I know," Simon said, "but, when my grandfather was dying, my mother told me to keep talking to him. She said that no matter how unresponsive the body might be, the mind remains active. A reassuring voice can go a long way to keeping a patient calm."

"She's not going to die," Egorov said impatiently.

Simon looked up from Maria's face and scowled at Egorov. "Of course she's not!" he said, his words curt.

Egorov shook his head and returned to his task. "Your love will heal her," he said.

"What?" Simon said, stunned by his friend's comment.

"I've often wondered who would turn the head of the elusive Simon Temple," he said, chuckling. "Now I know." When he looked at Simon again, his eyes sparkled with mischief.

"That obvious, huh," Simon said, conceding his affection for Maria.

"I've had my suspicions," the captain said. "You moon over her! Now you've just confirmed what I thought. Hold her thigh firm. This next bit is going to hurt, even if she's unconscious. I have nothing to numb the pain."

Simon grasped Maria's leg firmly. As Egorov dug a narrow instrument into her flesh to pinch the ball, Maria's body jerked. She hissed and moaned, tossing her head from side to side. "No! Mama, Papa! No!"

Simon looked from Maria's thigh to her face. Suddenly, her eyes shot open. She seemed to glare unseeing at the cottage ceiling.

"Hold her firm," Egorov said with a grunt, "I'm almost done."

"Maria," Simon said. "Maria. Look at me."

"Simon! Where are we—" As she spoke, she tried to sit up, but collapsed back onto the cot.

"She's fainted again," Simon said.

"That's a good thing!" Egorov replied. He reached for a rag and stood tall, stretching his back. "I've removed the ball, and stitched the hole closed. You can do the rest." Pointing toward the few medical supplies they had brought earlier, he told Simon how to clean and treat the wound, and the signs that would indicate infection. "Make sure that she drinks lots of fluids, and feed her small amounts, often."

Egorov rinsed his hands in a basin of water and rolled down his shirt sleeves. "You have enough supplies and food for now," he said. "I'll go back and investigate. I'll return as soon as I have more information."

He put an arm into the sleeve of his jacket and turned toward the door. "Try not to go out. If you must, take care. Someone could be watching." He nodded toward Simon, then closed the door quietly behind him.

Simon cleaned and tidied Maria's wound as instructed, washed her face, and covered her with one of the coarse, woollen army blankets left earlier in anticipation of a rescue.

Once he was certain that he had done all he could, he knelt on a floor mat by the bed. He brushed strands of hair from her face and kissed her brow chastely. "Sleep well, my brave little sparrow," Simon said, then lowered himself to the mat, curled into a ball, and slept.

CHAPTER 52

A burning pain jarred Simon awake a few hours later. He rubbed at it vigorously, trying to stimulate blood flow into the arm upon which he had been sleeping. When the tingling began to dissipate he sat up, trying to orient himself. He scrubbed his hands over his face, yawned, and stretched. Then he realized where he was and why, and scrambled to his feet, looking for the lantern.

Simon found it on a ledge and located a box of matches nearby. Before he lit the lantern, he peered through the small, curtained window. The sun was rising behind ominous clouds. *I don't know whether a storm would be a good thing or not. Good, if it washes away our tracks. Not so good, if the roof leaks.*

He gazed up at the roof. No shafts of light penetrated. *Phew! Hopefully it stays dry.*

He lit the candle within the lantern, sheltering the cage with his hand so as not to brighten the room too quickly. Taking a step toward the bed, the toe of his foot nudged something firm. He lowered the lamp. *The sack from last night!* He set the lantern on the floor and opened the bag quietly. Emeralds, rubies, diamonds, pearls, and gold caught the candlelight and gleamed back at him.

He released a soft whistle of awe.

Maria moaned as she shifted on the cot. Simon closed the sack, stashed it out of the way, and rose to check on his patient. As he neared the cot, he raised the lantern higher, illuminating the space.

Her eyes fluttered. "Simon," she said, moaning. "Where are we? My leg!" Her hand fell quickly to her injured thigh.

"Shush," Simon said quietly, dropping to his knees beside the cot and placing his hand over hers to cease her exploring fingers. "You're safe. Are you in pain?"

"No. A little. Yes. My leg—it's throbbing. Burning."

"I expect so," he said. "Do you remember being shot?"

"Yes," she said, beginning to sob. She raised her arm to cover her eyes. "Simon, it was all so terribly awful. Why did they do it? We were told to dress quickly and go down to the basement. That rebels were coming, and we would be safe down there."

She sobbed again before continuing. "Mama and Papa. They were shot in the forehead. Alexi too. They're dead, aren't they? I saw their heads explode and spatter my sisters." Tears ran from the corners of her eyes, disappearing into her hairline.

"Shush," Simon said again. "It must have been horrific. Here … drink some water." He reached for a cup from a small table and poured water from a canteen, then slid his arm under her shoulders and lifted her. "Drink."

Maria drank deeply, handed him the cup, and collapsed onto the cot. "What about my sisters? The others?"

"I'm sorry," Simon said, his voice woeful. "They're all

dead." He let his words sink through her foggy thoughts. "Do you recall what happened after the shooting? How you got out of the room?"

"I remember entering the room, and Mama being upset because there was only one chair. Papa was carrying Alexei. Yakov Yurovsky yelled into the hallway to bring more chairs. One came, so Papa sat Alexei on it and stood behind him and Mama. The rest of us gathered behind. We were told that we were to have a photograph taken, but I didn't see a camera or a photographer. I remember wondering why the staff had been assembled. We rarely took photographs of the staff, unless they were for family use only; we respected their privacy. I was near the back when the shooting started. I must have fainted for a moment, because when I came too, Anastasia was on top of me ..." Maria dashed the tears from her face and forced herself into a sitting position, gasping as she did so.

Simon grabbed a spare blanket to support her back. "Better?" he said.

"I feel as though I've been shot in the chest," she replied. "It hurts here too." She placed her hand over her heart, realizing that the fabric on the front of her dress was frayed. "Look! I think I was shot! Why am I alive? Do you think any of the jewels were damaged?"

"Jewels?"

"Yes, Mama had us sew jewels into our corsets and the hems of our skirts before we were moved to Tobolsk."

"Perhaps the jewels formed a sort of armour," Simon said. *And that is likely the reason the women were stripped.*

"When the bullet struck the jewels, it may have ricocheted off." He rose and paced across the small room. "That could explain how a bullet ended up in your leg."

"But … if I survived, why not the others?"

"How did you reach the wardrobe?" Simon said, searching her face for distress.

Maria closed her eyes, as if trying to recall. "May I lie down, please?"

Simon scrambled to remove the spare blanket and helped lower his patient onto the cot again.

Once prone again, Maria resumed her tale. "When I came out of the faint, the room was full of smoke. The women were moaning and grabbing their chests, but I think the men were dead. Several soldiers had entered the room behind us. They aimed their guns at us and began firing and firing. The gun smoke was blinding; the air so thick that I could barely breathe. I remember thinking how much my leg hurt. I pushed my sister off me and … and started crawling. The soldiers were shouting that they couldn't see. They were waving their arms to clear the smoke and plaster dust."

She paused, gazing at her trembling hands. "I stayed close to the wall and followed it until I reached the doorway. I suppose the smoke hid me. I was so scared. I knew I had to get away. I gave no thought to my family or anyone else. How insensitive of me."

"Not insensitive, my brave sparrow," Simon said. "Your basic instinct to survive kicked in. Continue."

"All of the soldiers seemed to be in the room, shouting

at each other and flapping their arms. I peeked into the hallway. It was empty. I scooted toward the wardrobe, expecting someone to see me and call out, but no one did. When I looked back, the hallway was still empty, so I opened the door and I crawled into it. I could hear screaming and more gunshots. It was quiet for quite some time, then that horrid man, Yurovsky, yelled down the stairwell for all the guards to report to his office. Then … you were there." She sighed deeply, as if releasing her anguish. "You saved me. I knew you would." Her eyes fluttered, as though she willed them open.

Simon knelt by the cot again and took her hand.

"Oh, Simon, are they all dead?"

Simon squeezed her hand and nodded. He watched her eyes liquefy, then spill their contents when she closed her eyelids and released her grief. "What will we do now?" she said, choking on hiccups.

Simon reached for the cup of water and slid his arm under her shoulders again. "Drink a little more," he said, "then rest. I'm going to look around. Are you hungry? Could you eat something?"

"A little bread, perhaps," his patient said.

"I think we have bread and cheese," he said, rummaging through a satchel. "And I may even manage tea if I can find everything needed. I'll be back in a few minutes." Simon blew out the candle in the lantern and slid through a crack in the door.

Outside, he skulked away from the hut to avoid being seen. Under the tall boughs of a Siberian larch, he braced his hands on his knees and vomited. Then he wiped his mouth with the back of his hand, snatched up a wooden bucket that hung on a hook at the corner of the hut, and tromped toward a small stream that he and Egorov had discovered a few days earlier.

A thunderclap boomed above him, chasing a streak of lightning. He knelt at the edge of the stream and scooped handfuls of water to rinse his mouth, then washed his face and hands. When he rose to his feet again and lifted the filled bucket, the first large plops of rain spattered thirsty trees and the top of his head.

The storm continued as he moved quietly within the hut preparing tea and slicing bread and cheese. Maria dozed fitfully, as if her burden had been lifted, but he knew her relief was only temporary. By the time she stirred again, the meagre meal was ready.

"Can you sit up?" he said loudly to be heard over the din of the heavy rain.

Maria nodded and grasped his hands so she could turn on the cot and lean against the wall, cushioned once again by the spare blanket. Neither of them conversed while he helped her eat small bites of bread and drink the hot tea. She declined the cheese, claiming the smell made her nauseous. Sorrow and loss oozed between them, thick as molasses.

CHAPTER 53

Maria drifted in and out of sleep as hours crept past. *That's a good thing,* Simon thought. *Her body is healing, and, hopefully, her mind is free of memories while she sleeps.*

Late in the afternoon, Simon heard a familiar whistle—Egorov's interpretation of a nightingale's warning chirp—followed by a light rap on the cottage door. Simon grinned, recalling how Egorov had taken pleasure in adopting that chirp as their warning call. Before he could rise from his seat near the cot, Egorov slid through a narrow gap in the doorway, shaking off raindrops.

"How is she?" he said, his voice low as he nodded toward the cot.

"I've decided that I'll live," Maria said, rolling over to face him. She winced as she moved her leg.

"That's good news, Grand Duchess," he said bowing from the waist.

"I'm no longer a grand duchess, Captain," Maria said matter-of-factly, "or should I say, *doctor.*"

"Nor am I a doctor," Egorov replied. "If I were, you'd not be left with a wound that'll leave an ugly scar."

"The scar will always remind me of your kindness

and your skill," she said. Her face changed from gratitude to sorrow. "Sadly, it'll also serve as a reminder of all that I've lost." Her lower lip quivered. "I'm alone in the world now. And homeless."

"Maria," Simon said, rising to his feet, "will you excuse us for a few minutes? The captain and I need to discuss our situation."

"What happened after we left the house?" Simon said, his voice urgent as he led Egorov away from the hut to shelter under the vast umbrella of older trees.

"I wish I didn't have to say," Egorov replied. "It was horrid enough what we'd already seen." He swallowed hard, inhaling as he did so. "It's occasions such as this that make me wish I had a drink in hand. Alas, that is not what you want to hear. Let me tell you … When I arrived back at the house, the communist guards were carrying out the bodies and throwing them onto the truck. It was disgusting. Even the men had been stripped. It makes no sense. It's not as though they are unrecognizable. Their faces have been seen everywhere. Someone will recognize the bodies."

"Maria told me that the women had sewn jewels into their corsets and the hems of their dresses. She says she was shot in the chest." Simon placed his hand over his heart as she had done. "I believe the corsets may have acted as armour. That's probably why they were shot in the head. Bayonetting them was likely for certainty."

"So Yurovsky had them stripped to recover the jewels," Egorov said, marvelling, his words full of anger. "Bastard! But that doesn't explain why the men were also stripped."

"No word on how the bodies were disposed?" Simon said.

"Nothing. They'll probably be dumped somewhere, but we don't have time to stick around. We need to move. Tonight." He glanced toward the hut. "Do you think she can travel?"

"She will if she must," Simon said flatly. "She's tougher than she looks, and she can ride. If she can't ride alone, she'll ride with me."

"Fine," Egorov said. "Most folks will be abed soon, despite the light night."

Simon quickly gathered the unused supplies and sack of jewels and stuffed them into saddlebags. He passed the satchels and his rolled bedding to Egorov, then woke Maria. Chiding himself for blushing, he helped her change into trousers, boots, a shirt, and jacket, then tied her hair up and stuffed it into a soft cap. Once on her feet, he handed her a make-shift crutch and helped her hobble to the doorway, where he handed the last bedding to Egorov.

"Grand Duchess, are you sure you can manage?" Egorov said. "We will be riding hard."

"Whether I can or cannot," Maria replied, "I will. Where are the horses?"

"This way, Grand Duchess," Egorov said, leading

them behind the hut.

"Captain, you must call me 'Maria' or 'Marushka,'" she said quietly. "I should think it too risky to make reference to any royal title, especially now."

"You're correct … *Maria*," he said, offering cupped hands to aid her mounting. "It's also risky for us to be speaking French. How is your Russian?"

"It will have to do, Captain," she said in Russian, smiling coyly at him.

Simon turned away to hide his grin, realizing that Egorov was likely unfamiliar with Maria's command of Russian or her ability to change dialects and accents as she chose. He grabbed the reins of her horse and passed them to her. "How is your leg?" Simon said. "Can you bear the pain?"

"And what other option do I have, Simon?" she said, her voice harsh, as if irritated. "It hurts. That's all there is to it." She glared at the two men impatiently. "Should we not be away?"

"Very well," Simon replied, mounting the third horse, "but you must tell us if you need to stop." His lips quirked into a half grin. "If you become uncomfortable, you can ride with him." He jerked his head toward the captain.

"Now you tell me!" she said flatly.

"Enough you two," Egorov chimed in. "Let's ride. I'll lead. Simon, will you bring up the rear with the pack horse?"

"Certainly," Simon replied, taking the reins of the pack horse and falling in behind Maria. "At least the rain has stopped."

"Ha! Ha!" Egorov said with urgency, nudging the barrel of his mount and snapping the reins.

Soon they were racing over muddied farmland, keeping to shadows and trees as much as possible. They stopped on three occasions to rest the horses and stretch themselves. On the third occasion, Simon noticed Maria's limp was more pronounced than earlier, and she had begun to shake. When asked, she admitted that the wound pained her.

"Let me have a look," Egorov said. "I'm afraid you'll have to drop your trousers." He raised an eyebrow to accentuate his question.

Maria tsked her impatience and unfastened the trousers, letting them slide down her legs as she clutched Simon's arm for support. Egorov crouched before her and inspected the wound. "It's bleeding a little, but nothing too worrisome," Egorov said calmly as he helped her refasten the trousers. "We'll keep an eye on it."

"Then she'll ride with me," Simon said firmly, mounting his horse and reaching down for her. "If you give your muscles a break, the bleeding might stop."

Egorov boosted her to a sideways seat ahead of Simon. Simon reached around her to hold her steady and secure the reins. Maria snuggled into his chest and sighed.

"Are you comfortable?" Simon said.

"Yes," she said, her voice barely audible. Before long, her head lolled against him.

"My brave, brave sparrow," he said, kissing the top

of her head when he felt the weight of her sleeping body.

At moonset, the men cast about for shelter where they could rest unseen for the balance of the day. Once they were settled, Egorov retrieved a map from his saddlebag and examined it.

"See here," he said to Simon, pointing at a small dot. "We're not far from this town. I'll leave now and see what news I can gather." He glanced over his shoulder to where Maria rested against a tree trunk. "Hopefully fresh food as well. You stand guard."

"Do you still have the pouch I gave you before we left the palace?" Simon said.

"Right here," Egorov said, patting a saddlebag. "Never out of my sight!"

"Good. Use the rubles, if you must," Simon said. "The original conditions have been released."

"I'm certain they will be useful," Egorov replied.

"By the way," Simon said, "why are you here, out of uniform? Not that I'm unhappy you are, but I need to know whether someone's going to be chasing us because you're absent without leave."

Maria, who had been following the conversation, sat straighter and stared keenly at the two men.

"Better you ask now, than two weeks from now, eh!" Egorov chuckled and slapped Simon on the shoulder companionably. "As a matter of fact, Yurovsky gave me a choice. He said that if I returned to Petrograd, I would be detained with the rest of the Imperial Guard. Alternatively, I could resign from the military, right then, and he would look away while I disappeared. I took his pen and paper and wrote out my resignation, but before I handed the page to him, I demanded to be paid. He laughed at me. I thought he'd spit in my face, but his face turned sober. He reached into a desk drawer, pulled out a pouch of coins, and tossed them to me."

Egorov spat into the dust and wiped his mouth on his sleeve. "Trust me when I say that there wasn't even enough coin to buy a loaf of bread! I threw it back at his face." He chuckled. "For an old man, he was quick to grab the pouch! Then he snatched the paper from me and told me to get lost. He said that if he ever saw my face again, he'd kill me."

"And the horses?"

"Ah, well, not all the horses could be accounted for the next day, and the house was in chaos while everyone not involved in the butchery pretended to search for the missing royals. The Bolsheviks would have everyone presume they'd escaped in the night." His glance at Maria was solemn. "I'm sorry," he said to her.

Maria acknowledged his condolence. A single tear traced along her nose and caught on her lip.

"I see," Simon replied. "What about the servants and the tutors?"

"They were all released, unharmed. Gilliard and Gibbes left on the first train in the morning. They decided to return to Tsarskoye Selo to investigate whether any remaining valuables might be gleaned for sale.

"Apparently, many items were hidden throughout

the palace," he said. "If the Bolsheviks haven't already discovered the hiding places, the tutors will retrieve them and ask Buchanan to have them shipped to your father—for Maria. I don't know where the others went. They simply disappeared. Like the horses." He grinned sheepishly and shrugged.

CHAPTER 54

Simon scrounged a pile of dried leaves, covered them with a blanket, and helped Maria recline upon them.

"I apologize that we don't have a better cot," he said.

"Simon, I'm used to sleeping rough," Maria replied. "I have only ever slept on a firm cot with a coarse blanket. Great-grandfather insisted that his family sleep as the soldiers did, and that has never changed. We weren't even allowed a pillow unless we were ill. I was allowed one several years ago, when I had my tonsils removed. I bled something awful. The surgeon almost didn't finish the procedure. He thought he'd killed me!" She giggled. "It wasn't funny at the time, of course, but when I think of the fuss he made. Oh my!"

Maria curled onto her side, careful to keep pressure off her leg, and rested her head on her arm. Simon covered her with the second blanket and stroked wisps of dark blonde hair from her face.

"This is cozy," she said dreamily.

Simon turned away from her and propped himself against the tree where Maria had been resting minutes before. Her hand closed warmly around his wrist.

With his free hand, Simon felt her forehead. It was

warm, not hot. He saw no sign of fever. He checked her pulse and found it steady. For several minutes, he watched her chest rise and fall evenly.

When he was certain she rested comfortably, he freed his tethered hand, withdrew his pistol from his pocket, checked that it was loaded and functional, and set it on the ground beside him. Then, he closed his eyes and allowed himself to doze while Egorov tended to a hasty meal for them.

As Simon's mind wandered, details and concerns of the last days played behind his eyelids like a film, except that in real life it had not been silent. He recalled the discussions that he'd had with the Zimas during the days leading up to the relocation of the Romanovs from Alexander Palace.

I'm glad that I told them to pack up everything as soon as they heard anything untoward. I can't believe they wanted to leave Russia too. But they were right: if they stayed behind, they would eventually be targeted by the Bolsheviks as being monarch sympathizers. If they find their way to Newcastle, they need only deliver the note I gave them, and father will arrange things for them.

Buchanan and Lockhart will see them safe. I'm glad I had the foresight to send them messages too. I just wish I had a way to reach them now. To let them know what's happened. Oh well; Gilliard and Gibbes will fill them in.

———

Some time later, Simon jolted from his doze when a

twig snapped several yards away. He sat erect, eyes open, hand on his pistol, listening. When the soft, clear chirp of a nightingale brought his mind awake, he spied Egorov rising from the fire with a cup of hot tea for him.

"I have a loaf of relatively fresh bread, a wedge of strong-smelling cheese," he said, handing the cup to Simon, "and …" From his pockets, he withdrew several apples, telling Simon of a small orchard that he had happened to find when he scouted their location.

"How is she?" Egorov said, indicating the still-slumbering Maria.

"Fine, I think," Simon said, resting the back of his hand on her forehead. "No fever."

"Good," he said, sipping his own cup of tea. "I've tended to the horses and set out the food. Since you've both had a chance to rest, I'll leave you to feed yourselves while I catch some shuteye."

"Of course," Simon said. "Please do."

Simon rose and stretched out his stiffened muscles, then poured some hot water from the fire into a small bowl. He quickly washed his face and hands and towelled them off with his shirt tail. As he did so, Maria began to stir.

"Hot water?" she said. "Oh, I could really use a wash."

Simon tucked his shirt in his pants as he stepped toward her.

"But first," she said, smiling demurely, "I need to relieve myself."

"Let me help you," Simon said.

Maria took the hand Simon offered and rose slowly to

her feet. She took a few tentative steps and smiled when Simon offered her the crutch that he had made at the hut.

"Let's find you a bush," he said, his arm around her waist, "then I'll give you some warm water so you can freshen up."

"Yes, you two do that," Egorov said, grumbling. "I need sleep." He lowered his head to his mount's saddle and began snoring quietly.

Simon led Maria to a secluded spot a few yards away from their camp. "It looks private enough here," he said. "Can you manage?"

"I believe so," Maria said, sizing up the area.

"I'll be over there on the other side of that pine tree. Call if you need me."

"I will," Maria replied.

While he waited for Maria, Simon contemplated what to do next. They needed to escape. In his opinion, England was the safest place to be, but Artyom and Maria were both Russian. *They may have other ideas. Artyom's sister is in Newcastle; perhaps he will consider travelling there. Maria no longer has fast ties to Russia, and she could yet be killed if she remains here. Will she travel to England?*

If they do agree to take refuge in England, how do we get there? Back the way I came, north through Archangelsk, east following the Siberian Express to Japan, or south through Persia? How are we to know which route is safe?

"I'm finished," Maria said, startling Simon from his reverie as she hobbled toward him. "What were you thinking about so deeply that you didn't hear my approach?

I could easily have the upper hand right now!" She started to laugh, then caught herself. "I shouldn't be laughing when my entire family is dead! I'm a horrible person."

"No, you're not," Simon said, his voice firm. He hopped from the log on which he had been perched and reached to lend her support. "You were being Maria. That's permitted." He withdrew a wrinkled handkerchief from his jacket pocket and handed it to her. "Dry your eyes, Grand Duchess; or should I say Grand Duke?"

"How do I look in the daylight?" she said, hobbling awkwardly in a circle.

"Every bit a peasant," Simon replied. "Just like Egorov and I."

He smiled in response to her giggle. "Let's get back then," he said. "We need to eat and get you cleaned up. We have a long ride ahead of us."

"Where will we go?" Maria said, leaning on the crutch as she limped behind Simon.

"Such a simple question, *Maria*," Egorov said as the two entered the glade. "Here, I've made more tea." He poured cups of tea for his companions and indicated the food he had set out for them.

"I thought you were going to sleep?" Simon said.

"I did," Egorov said. "A soldier learns to sleep when and wherever possible." He bent to collect boards of food and waited while Simon helped Maria lower herself to her resting place. "My hunger is greater."

He handed them each a board of food and a cup of tea, and they ate quietly for a few minutes.

"In the town, I learnt that the Bolshevik opposition, or 'White Russians' as they are being called, are marching east. They've likely reached Yekaterinburg by now. The Communists and Bolsheviks are clashing with them, trying to stop the advance. I have my doubts about the Whites," Egorov said. "They have no real structure; not enough to form a government, or other solid leadership. They have no unified idea. The Bolsheviks and Communists work better together. Yet, the Whites continue to push the Communists east."

"That's important to note," Simon said, interrupting Egorov's musings, "but I think we have a more immediate matter to discuss." He glanced first to Maria, then to Egorov. "Maria voiced it a while ago."

He retrieved the pot of tea and filled their mugs again. "Where do you want to go? What do you want to do? I know there's no place for me in Russia now. Before I leave, however, I need to know that you two are safe. So … what do you want to do?"

"I'll go with you," Egorov said easily, "to England. It's no longer safe for me to remain in Russia, and my sister is in Newcastle. I should like to see this Newcastle and get to know my brother-in-law, Henry Crocker, and their new child." His statement was firm, absolute. "What about you, *Maria*?"

"I have no home here either," Maria said. A single tear traced along her nose, and she struck it with the back of her hand. "Where can I go? Do you think it would be safe for me in Crimea? We have a house there." She sat with her back to the fire, enjoying its warmth.

"No," Egorov said, shaking his head. "Crimea would not be safe for a daughter of the tsar. If that property has not yet been seized or destroyed, it's only a matter of time."

"You can go any number of places, Maria," Simon said. "You have the jewels from your corset, remember." He scrubbed the stubble that had sprouted on his chin. "Plus, Artyom rescued some gems …" He coughed to clear his throat, glancing at Egorov. "What about Denmark or England? You have family in both countries."

"Maybe Canada or Australia?" Egorov said. "No one would know you there. You could be whomever you like."

"Yes," she replied sadly, "but I would be alone. I would have no family, no friends." She sat quietly for several minutes, watching Simon draw circles in the soft, dry soil with a twig. "Simon, do you really think I might find a home in England?"

"Yes, I do," Simon said, swallowing hard and trying not to look at Egorov.

"Then, I don't need to think about it," Maria said, her words resolute. "I will go with you and Captain Egorov to England! The land of my great-grandmother, Victoria!" She raised her chin, defiant and determined.

"Alright," Simon said, hopping to his feet and pacing across the clearing, "how do we get there?"

"I don't recommend heading east to Japan," Egorov said. "Last I heard, the Bolsheviks and the Czechs were fighting along the Trans-Siberian Railway. Plus, weather could be a factor. We're not dressed for heat or cold."

"If we head south to find the British, we could encounter the same weather concerns," Simon said. "Plus, it's a long way to the Persian Gulf. The journey could take just as long as it would to Japan."

"What about north, then?" Maria said. "Since we can't return west, and the south and east aren't appealing options. What bars us from going north?"

"To travel north—to one of the British ports—sounds reasonable enough," Simon replied, nodding in contemplation. "We'd have to head west, across the Urals, without being recognized. The more who know you're alive, Maria, the riskier it becomes for all three of us. If we can get to Vologda, we could take the train north, but we'd still have to pass through territory controlled by the Bolsheviks and a Communist stronghold."

"I don't know that we have any true options," Egorov said, "but, if we're careful, we might be able to find a way north."

Simon and Egorov discussed the last option in earnest and finally devised a rough plan.

"Nothing can be definite," Simon said. "I think our escape will be a moving target: conditional on who holds what territory at any given moment. With luck, we may find some sympathetic parties along the way."

"Good!" Maria said. "Now that we know where we're going, I'd like to wash and sleep, in that order. Suddenly, I'm very tired."

Simon brought her a bowl of warm water and a cloth, holding a blanket like a curtain to grant her privacy.

"I'm finished," she said, yawning. She handed Simon the bowl and cloth, then lowered herself to the bed of leaves. Soon, she slept.

"I guess we'd better do as we've been ordered," Simon said. "Shifts?"

"No," Artyom replied. "I think we're safe enough here. Besides …" He lowered himself to his own makeshift mattress. "I have good hearing. I'll have my pistol drawn before anyone approaches."

Simon reclined against his saddle, fingers wrapped securely around the butt of his own pistol, and dozed fitfully.

CHAPTER 55

The chill brought by the rising moon woke Simon. He stood quietly and wandered into a bushy stand to relieve himself. He then snatched up the bucket and went for water.

By the time he returned, Egorov had a small fire burning. "We'll eat quickly and be gone from here before the fire's smoke exposes us," he said.

"Oh!" Maria said, sitting up and rubbing her eyes. "I think I slept well." She stood on her own, hopping on one foot until she had her crutch under her arm. "Simon, when I come back, will you help me with my hair?"

"Of course," Simon replied.

As she disappeared into the bushes, Egorov grinned at Simon. "Dressing Maria's hair now, are you?"

"I couldn't exactly say no, could I?" Simon said sotto voce, looking over his shoulder to ensure Maria was beyond hearing range. "She has a lot of it, and I've seen her struggle to get it under the cap you gave her."

"Just make sure she'll pass as a young man."

"Yes, sir!" Simon replied with a sharp salute.

They ate hastily, then quietly saddled their mounts and rode off into the twilight.

"Let us know if you grow weary, Maria," Simon said. "You can ride with one of us, if you do."

"I will," she replied.

During the next five days, they rode west toward Perm, where they hoped to board a train bound for Vologda. They skirted small towns and homesteads, sleeping rough and taking breaks only when necessary.

They arrived in Perm late in the afternoon and found accommodation for one night. While Maria languished in a hot bath, Simon stood guard and Egorov went in search of clothing more suitable for train travel, and to purchase train tickets to Vologda.

Once the men had bathed, the three enjoyed a warm meal together in the inn's small dining room, speaking quietly amongst themselves and trying not to draw the attention of other patrons.

"What have you done with the horses?" Maria said.

"I was able to trade them with a farmer," Egorov said.

"A farmer?" Simon said. "What farmer could afford four military-trained horses?"

"A loyal monarchist, who assured me that they would be well-cared for and not overworked," Egorov said with a smirk. "He knew animals well enough, and thought he might use my stallion for breeding and use the others in local riding competitions."

"And what did you receive in exchange?" Maria said.

"A round of exquisite cheese, three loaves of bread,

six bottles of ale, and a small sack of apples," Egorov said, leaning back in his chair. "Could we ask for more?" He sat forward in his chair and spoke quietly. "I did extract one promise from him—he is never to disclose the source of his acquisition. However, just in case he encounters difficulty, I provided a receipt stating that the animals were hale and hearty and legally sold to him, by none other than Major Ivan Vasiliev himself!"

"You didn't!" Simon said, laughing at Egorov's audacity.

"I did," Egorov said confidently.

"Who's Major Vasiliev?" Maria said.

"We'll tell you later," Simon replied, chuckling softly.

"Regardless," Egorov said, "he won't bother us again. My uncle is a general in the Imperial Guard. He's detained Vasiliev on criminal charges that will see the major imprisoned for a very long time."

—⋯—

The following morning, Maria and her rescuers, who were dressed as travelling farmers, boarded the train from Perm to Vologda, a two-day journey. The men carried a carpet bag in each hand, laden with the items they would require during the two days. Maria—disguised as a younger brother—carried a small satchel, keeping her other hand free for her crutch. In a second-class car, they sought two seats together in a corner near one of the doors, and one seat near the opposite door—each man having expressed a preference for a seat that positioned their back against a wall with full view of any doors.

To Maria's delight, the car began to fill with a group of students and other academics who seemed determined to sit around a certain individual. As the train pulled away from the station, that individual began speaking. He invited his audience to suggest successive topics for discussion, on which he then spoke. Eventually, he opened the discussion to everyone, and the car erupted in enthusiastic ideals.

As if drawn by a magnet, Maria edged closer to the gathering, until they shuffled to create a space for her.

Three stops further along the line, communist guards boarded the train and wandered through each car as if looking for someone. Egorov recognized one of Yurovsky's men and signalled as much to Simon.

Simon caught Maria's eye and signalled her to remain where she was. In response, she wiggled deeper into the group of students.

Yurovsky's man scanned the car, pausing near Egorov, and turned to address his superior.

Simon saw Egorov slouch into the corner, as if making himself small and bent. Glad for the week's growth of whiskers that each sported and the ill-fitting clothes that Egorov had bought, Simon made a similar effort to disguise his shape. As he did so, he noticed Maria tuck errant curls under her cap and arrange her jacket to hide her figure.

"None of these men look familiar," Yurovsky's man said. "The soldier is tall and clean-shaven—I'd recognize him anywhere—and the girl would be obvious, wouldn't she?"

"Very well," the superior officer said with a growl, "we'll just have to keep checking every train until they show up somewhere."

The train was searched twice more before they reached Vologda, but none of the searchers were Yurovsky's men. The first time, Maria and her rescuers were overlooked. On the second occasion, the searchers carried small photographs, which they held up against anyone who resembled them.

When Simon overheard one of the men sitting across the aisle from him explain to his companions that he had seen photos being circulated in a previous car, he caught Egorov's attention and nodded toward an exit. Egorov hastily gathered their bags and slipped through the door.

Simon rose from his seat and sauntered past Maria, tapping her on her shoulder. She turned to see him jerk his head toward the exit a second time. Quietly, she thanked the group of young men and the speaker for allowing her to sit with them, then headed for the door.

Simon stood on the platform waiting for her. She jumped off the step, wincing when she landed on the platform. Simon wrapped an arm around her waist and helped her limp in the direction he had last seen Egorov.

"What now?" Simon said as he and Maria joined Egorov at the side of the station.

The train whistled a warning of departure.

"Well," Egorov said, "those men have two more cars to clear, so they'll be onboard until the next station at the rate they're moving. We could jump on the forward car and hope they don't see us, or we can find another way to reach Vologda."

"How far is it now?" Maria said, leaning on Simon.

Intuitively, his arm tightened protectively.

"Two more stops," Egorov said, twisting his mouth as he thought. "If we wait for the next train, we could encounter the same problem. Or …"

"Or?" Maria said.

"We could see about buying more horses, or a horse and wagon and make our own way," Egorov replied with a shrug. "It will likely take the rest of the day to reach Vologda. With luck, we might arrive in time for the evening meal."

"Let's see what we can find," Simon said, guiding Maria away from the train station.

———

Three nags plodded along a dusty road that seemed to end outside a rundown cottage.

"We don't want to be seen," Simon said, casting about for an alternate route. "Do you suppose this animal track leads anywhere?"

"Looks like it disappears into that forest," Egorov said, pointing off to the right. "The foliage suggests water nearby." He reined in the nag on which he rode in the direction of the animal path, and the others followed, Maria riding between the two men.

"Perhaps we might stop for a few minutes?" Maria said hopefully.

"Of course," Egorov replied, "once we're in the trees."

They stopped near the edge of a stream long enough to relieve themselves, stretch their legs, and snack on bread, cheese, and a few apples that Egorov had once again rescued from an orchard. They drank their fill of clear water, then led the horses to drink as well. Refreshed, the three remounted and plodded through the small forest.

At the far side, they were momentarily blinded as they passed from shadow into bright sunshine. Squinting against the change of light, they were caught off-guard when five young men wielding pitchforks and hatchets encircled them threateningly. Three grabbed at the halters of the startled horses stamping impatiently, while the other two held their pitchforks high.

"What do you want?" Egorov said, reining the horse out of the scoundrel's grasp. "Get away!" He kicked his booted foot at the offender.

Maria swiftly slid her crutch from where it was tied to her saddle and began swinging it at the boy who tried to clutch the halter of her animal. "Back!" she hollered angrily. "Away!"

Simon pulled hard on the reins of his horse, causing the bit to dig into its mouth. The horse reared. Simon glared at the pitchfork-wielding leaders. "What do you want?" he said, repeating Egorov's question.

"Your money, or we kill ya," one of the leaders said.

"We have no money," Simon said impatiently. "We are simple farmers on the way to visit family."

"Then we'll have the horses," the other leader said. "Give us your horses."

"They are not ours to give," Simon said, eyeing Egorov. "We borrowed them from a neighbour and must return them."

"Then," one of the leaders said, "give us the pretty boy." He leered at Maria. "We'll find a use for him."

"I think not!" Maria said, swinging her crutch again to warn them all away.

Simon and Egorov side-stepped their horses toward Maria, sandwiching her between them. At the same time, one of the thugs pulled a long-bladed knife and began waving it toward Egorov.

Egorov pulled the reins. The horse screamed angrily, rising on its haunches, and flailed its hooves at the young man. The young man dropped to the dusty grass, blood trickling from his forehead.

"You killed my brother!" one of the leaders shouted as he stooped over the injured boy. "I'll kill you!"

The four remaining young men swarmed the three anxious horses.

"Now!" Egorov said, yelling above the chaos.

Using the impetus of the scramble, Simon grabbed the halter of Maria's horse, shouting, "Ha, ha!" As one, the three horses shot across the field, clods of dirt flying off their hooves like ammunition.

They allowed the horses to race until they began to tire, then dismounted and walked alongside, looking for water.

"They'll need a bit of a rest," Egorov said, stroking his mount's muzzle, "but not long. Where there's one, there could be others."

"Maria," Simon said. "How's your leg?"

"Sore," Maria said. "Otherwise, alright." She glanced sheepishly at Simon. "I've lost my crutch, though."

"We'll buy you a proper cane when we reach Vologda," Simon replied. "Think you can manage until then?"

"I will," she said.

"I'm proud of you, Sparrow," Simon said. "You handled yourself well during that skirmish."

"Perhaps I did," Maria said, blushing, "but I'm glad they're not here to see me now." She held up her hands, seeming surprised by their shaking. "I feel like my legs won't hold me any longer." As she spoke, her knees buckled, and she fell toward Simon.

"I've got you," he said, his arms reaching to save her from a fall. He scooped her in his arms and carried her to a gnarled root.

"Why do you call me that?" Maria wiggled to settle on the root. "Sparrow," she said. "You've called me that before, usually when you think I can't hear."

Simon felt the crimson blush creep up his neck as his thoughts scrambled for an explanation. "People tend to underestimate sparrows," he said. "They are quite impressive … and very brave. I used to watch them when I was young. I'd spend hours riding on my father's estate. Sometimes, I'd sit on a log—as you are now—and just watch. While naturally they fall prey to large birds, wild cats, squirrels, and such, the alert ones survive. They're small and fast. Aside from that, they love to sing and …" He hesitated before adding the last thought. "Ancient Greek culture believed them to be a symbol of love."

Maria's eyes widened instantly as the last words penetrated her concentration.

"We should go," Egorov said, breaking the intimate moment. "Are you ready?"

"I am," Maria said, standing with determination. "I just need help with my re-mount."

An hour and a half later, the three riders entered the southern border of Vologda. They had been following the train tracks, ensuring enough distance to not be seen. Atop a small knoll, they paused to find their bearings.

"There," Egorov said, pointing. "The train station." He moved his arm to the right. "And an inn."

Near the inn, Egorov left Maria and Simon in the shadow of a mercantile and entered the inn. Not long after, he returned. "We have rooms," he announced, handing them keys to adjoining rooms. "Take the bags. I'll dispose of the horses and get supplies."

"When you return," Simon said, "I'll need to send a telegram."

Through the window of telegraph office, Simon surveyed the street, as he hastily wrote a note for his father:

Condolences to the family STOP

Two siblings and I headed north STOP
Hoping for transport late tomorrow STOP

Satisfied that he had not been followed, he paid the agent and waited for confirmation that the message had been sent.

By the time he returned to the inn, Egorov had bathed and changed.

"Best to eat in," Egorov said. "I've made arrangements. Come."

He led Simon and Maria along the corridor and down the stairs to the main floor, where a small dining room accommodated the inn's few travellers. They ate a traditional Russian meal of potatoes and fish, then retired to their rooms.

"I wish we could go for a walk to stretch our muscles," Maria said, lamenting. "I'm awfully tired of riding!"

"We've almost reached our destination," Egorov said. "Two more days—"

"Yes," Simon said, "two more days and we'll be shipboard. Then, you can walk as much as you like."

Maria smiled at her rescuers, resting her chin in her hands. "I owe you two everything," she said. "I should be dead, like the rest of my family …" Her smile turned upside down as sadness overtook her face. "But you saved me instead. I must ensure that the remainder of my life is served in their memory."

She leaned back into her chair, her hands flopping into her lap. "I think I'll retire now," she said, rising to her feet. "I'm tired, and I should pray for the souls of my family before I sleep. Good night."

CHAPTER 56

For Simon, the train ride to Arkhangelsk was markedly different from the reverse trip with Crocker. Crocker and his new wife would have enjoyed the benefits of a first-class return, whereas Simon, Maria, and Egorov had no choice but to purchase second-class tickets.

Simon and Maria shared a bench near one exit, while Egorov sat at the opposite end of the car. In between, an assortment of passengers travelling north played games, tended to caged farm animals, and otherwise entertained themselves.

As the train slowed into the Nyandoma station, Maria dozed, her head resting on Simon's shoulder. With the whistle screeching to announce their arrival and smoke billowing from the engine, vision of the platform was momentarily obscured.

As it cleared, Egorov jumped to his feet and strode toward Simon. "Lebedev," he said, the tiny scar twitching beneath his eye, "and Yurovsky—they're on the platform near the first-class cars."

"How many are with them?" Simon said, keeping his voice low.

"They seem to be alone."

Simon glanced along the platform as passengers disembarked the car.

"They've boarded in first class," Egorov said, his mind contemplating various possibilities. "Just when we need cover, the car has to empty!"

As he spoke, a door opened to admit a small family numbering a father, mother, two small children, and four grandparents.

"Maria," he said quietly, nudging her to wake up. "Maria, we have a problem."

He glanced at the family once more, then announced that he had a plan. Extracting himself from Maria's sleepy grasp, he approached the elders of the family and sought their help.

"Come," he said, returning to Maria. "I've explained to these folks that you are being pursued by an unwanted suitor, a dangerous man. "Our cousin and I—your brother—are taking you to stay with our grandparents, where you'll be safe. Your suitor refuses to accept your rejection and has followed us. They've agreed to have you sit with them, so we can be free to defend you, if necessary."

Maria and Egorov gawked at him momentarily, then she rose to her feet and stood next to Simon.

"Come, *Marushka*," Simon said, guiding her toward the family.

He introduced them and encouraged her to sit amongst the elders, who openly welcomed her and teased her about being dressed as a young man. Maria warmed to them immediately and apologized for being a nuisance, but the elders would have none of it. They claimed to understand her predicament and promised to keep her safe.

Simon and Egorov resumed their seats at opposite ends of the car and waited.

The whistle shrieked, and the train began to roll again. Time passed, and Simon dared to wonder whether Lebedev had not boarded after all. Nearing the small settlement of Shalakusha, however, the door near Egorov opened slowly. Lebedev filled the doorway with his rotund frame, eyeing Simon immediately. His sneer of recognition sent a cold chill down Simon's spine.

Between them, the small family shared bread and cheese and fussed over the two small children. Simon watched Lebedev's eyes, sensing his impatience with the placement of the family that separated him from his target.

The middle-aged statesman stepped into the car, swaying with the movement of the train. Behind him, Simon glimpsed the top of Yurovsky's sooty-grey hair.

The family followed Simon's gaze. Spying Lebedev, each parent grabbed a small child and backed toward the elders, while the elders closed ranks around Maria, men on the outside, ready to join in any fight.

Simon reclined against the back of the bench and stretched his legs, smirking at his aggressor.

Lebedev advanced angrily into the car. Yurovsky tromped in behind him, waving a pistol. The family pressed toward the side of the car.

"Where is she?" Yurovsky said, threatening Simon

with his waving pistol.

"Who?" Simon said, unmoved.

"You know damn well who!" Lebedev said, glaring. The train lurched, forcing him to dance sideways to keep his footing. "Where's the girl you stole from me!" His voice was forceful and demanding.

Simon straightened in the chair, running his fingers through his beard. He rose slowly to his full height, towering above the intruders.

"I know nothing about any girl," Simon said. "I heard how you butchered those good people in Yekaterinburg and departed. My work in Russia is finished. I'm simply returning to England." He rested his hands on his hips in defiance.

Nearby, he heard the family whispering about 'the butchering of good people.' Their eyes seemed to widen with awareness and shock.

"We've tracked you," Yurovsky said, spitting his words. "We found your horses. With a little persuasion, the farmer agreed"—he coughed, clearing his throat—"to tell us how he acquired them. Imagine our surprise to see a bill of sale signed by Ivan Vasiliev!"

"When we accused him of stealing state property and the penalties he'd face," Lebedev said, inflating his chest, laughing with arrogance, "he directed us to the inn."

"Once I snapped the innkeeper's fingers, the old hag was delighted to share what she knew about her three *gentlemen* guests." As he spoke, he turned abruptly, coming face-to-face with Egorov, whose pistol targeted his heart. In defence, Yurovsky raised his own pistol, aimed at Egorov's forehead.

A collective gasp from the small family distracted Lebedev momentarily, then he picked up the tale. "By the time we tracked you to Vologda," he said, his voice sinister, "this train had already departed. I must tell you, Mr. Temple, that it took some effort to reach Shalakusha ahead of you." His gazed narrowed on Simon's face. "I don't like being rushed."

Alarmed by a scuffle behind him, Lebedev's rant ceased as he spied Yurovsky's pistol slide past him toward Simon.

Simon trapped the gun with his foot as Egorov's pistol slid toward the family. One of the grandfathers snatched it up, skilfully aiming it toward Yurovsky, despite his unsteady hands.

Egorov and Yurovsky tussled hand-to-hand: knuckles smacked cheekbones, arms twisted, and bellies were punched, accentuated by grunts of pain and surprise.

Once Yurovsky seemed to have the upper hand, Lebedev ignored the skirmish and returned his attention to Simon, his voice confident, calm, and evil. As he spoke over the panting of wrestling men, he withdrew another pistol from his pocket and waved it at Simon. "You may think you're clever, Mr. Temple," he said shouting, "but you will not succeed. You cannot outfox me! Now … where is Maria Romanov?"

A second gasp issued from the small family as they muttered the name of a grand duchess and gazed at the young woman they sheltered. Mother and father rocked their whimpering children, shushing them to quiet. Maria's saucer-like eyes pled them to silence.

"The last I saw of that family," Simon said, jerking his head toward the scuffling men, "your partner there had them locked up in a house with painted windows." He paused, peering down his nose menacingly. "We are the ones who should be asking questions!" His voice boomed with anger.

Another collective gasp arose from the family. The elder women covered their mouths in shock. The young parents collected their sleeping children to their bosoms.

"Shut up!" Lebedev said, screaming at the family as if he had been reminded of the audience. He waved his pistol wildly.

The frightened family tightened their circle and stilled. The grandfathers tensed, as if preparing to join the fight. Simon caught the eye of one and jerked his head toward the car's door. The man nodded and whispered to his family. As one, they crept toward the door leading to the forward car.

Seeing Maria exiting the car with the family, Egorov summoned renewed strength and gut-punched Yurovsky, sending him flying into a corner behind Simon, where his crumpled form stilled.

Egorov backed toward the last grandfather, reaching behind him, palm up, waiting for the pistol. Once its weight was in his hand, he advanced toward Yurovsky.

Having regained his wits, Yurovsky lunged at Egorov's

feet, knocking him back. Egorov lost his hold on the pistol, sending it sliding toward the grandfather again. The two opponents struggled toward it.

The grandfather snatched the pistol, for a second time slowly raising it toward Yurovsky. Before the door closed behind the family, the other two men reappeared and joined their elder. Fists clenched, they seemed to be calculating an opportunity to jump into the mêlée.

Behind them, the door burst open, temporarily drawing their attention. Maria shoved through, snatching the pistol from the grandfather and aiming it at Yurovsky, her flawless face marred with determination. "Stop, Comrade Yurovsky," she said boldly, shouting to be heard, "or I'll shoot." She sneered angrily. "I caution you to heed me. I've been trained to kill by the best marksmen."

Yurovsky lunged toward Egorov, wrapping his arm around Egorov's neck. A long-bladed knife gleamed from his free hand, the tip of it pricking Egorov's overstretched neck.

Off-balanced by the shorter man's hold, Egorov raised his arms for stability, signalling Maria to wait. Maria stood motionless, the pistol trained on the small space between Yurovsky's caterpillar brows.

Simon took advantage of the distraction, bending to retrieve the pistol dropped by Yurovsky at the beginning of the fight. Calmly, he raised it toward Lebedev, whose attention had been swivelling from one threat to the next.

"Well, Comrade," Simon said, seeming to startle Lebedev, "it seems we have you outnumbered."

"Drop the knife, Yurovsky," Maria said, her voice sounding like a rabid dog, "or you will die without mercy—the way you killed my family."

Lebedev glared from Maria to Simon to Yurovsky, a look of horror on his face as if he realized the severity of their predicament. Simon stood unmoving but for the rhythm of the train, his eyes narrowed and determined.

The grandfathers and young father edged away from the door, surrounding Yurovsky, appearing ready to pounce when needed.

"Put the knife down," Maria said, slowly emphasizing each word as she positioned herself for the kill shot. "Now."

Yurovsky danced nervously from foot to foot, keeping Egorov between him and Maria's firearm. Slowly, he edged toward the door, Maria tracking his movement.

With the next lurch of the car, Yurovsky shoved Egorov toward Maria and lunged for the door. Maria sidestepped Egorov's fall and pulled the trigger.

CHAPTER 57

The engine whistled briefly, announcing the next stop. The car lurched in response to screeching brakes that began to slow the train. Lebedev shifted to maintain his balance. Simon pounced, crashing to the floor with Lebedev beneath him. Egorov snatched a sliding pistol and aimed it at the tussling men.

Simon's fist connected with Lebedev's flushed face, snapping the cartilage of his nose. Stunned, Lebedev grabbed his nose, groaning and writhing in pain. Simon regained his feet and withdrew a pistol from his pocket.

Maria stepped closer to Lebedev, ignoring Simon. "Now, how would you prefer to die?" Maria said, her voice cold as she took aim. "A shot to the head, perhaps? Like my family died?" Her eyes narrowed with focus. "Or perhaps the heart, as I was?"

Seemingly stunned by her questions, Lebedev rose cautiously to his knees, panting, his eyes wide. He swiped at blood trickling from his nose, then grabbed a bench to hoist himself to his feet. "Shot in the heart? You?" he said, his quickened breathing forming bloody bubbles. "Then you must have the jewels!" He scrambled to his feet and lunged toward her.

Maria stepped back, tripping over the family's lunch basket and releasing her grip on the pistol.

One of the grandfathers scrambled toward the pistol, snatching it up and aiming at the statesman, while the other grandfather bent to Maria's aid.

"Get up," Simon said, angrily wagging his pistol at Lebedev's torso. "You're finished. You and your scheme to deliver Russia to Germany tied up in a pretty package is over. It'll never happen."

The train's whistle pierced the second-class car, announcing its impending arrival at the next station. Locking his eyes with Simon's, Lebedev sidled defiantly toward the rear door.

"You may have beat me this time, Temple," he said, his lips curved in a snarl. "But I'm not done with you yet! Run where you will, but I will find you." His eyes narrowed with hate. "I'll find you and the little bitch, and then I'll cut the two of you down. Mark my words!"

Before Simon could respond, Lebedev whipped the door open and tripped onto the car's small landing, reaching for the handrail to break his fall. The car lurched sharply. Lebedev screamed with terror as if he realized what was to come. Unable to find his balance, he flew over the handrail.

Simon raced toward the door, his reach only able to grab the man's airborne shoe. The effort was in vain; the inertia of the statesman's weight could not be stopped. Simon felt the man's foot slip from the shoe and watched in horror as he bounced off the coupling and rolled onto the narrow track, into the path of the oncoming car's wheels. Knowing how Lebedev landed on the rail, Simon imagined a fatal injury.

The car swayed again, brakes screaming as the train slowed into the station.

Yurovsky's bloodied body lay at the foot of the forward door, his hand cradled against his chest. Slowly, he pushed himself to a sitting position and examined his injured hand. "You shot my fingers off, you bloody bitch!" he yelled at Maria.

When Simon stepped toward Maria protectively, Egorov's scraped knuckles jammed into his chest. The soldier shook his head, his expression seeming to warn Simon away from her.

"Too bad," Maria replied, growling with anger. "I'm usually a better shot. If the train hadn't lurched, the bullet would have pierced your brow. Murderer!" She stood over him, kicked his ribs twice, and spat in his face. "Perhaps it would have been too easy a death."

Egorov removed his hand from Simon's chest and slid onto a bench.

"You alright?" Simon said, casting a glance at his friend. "You look exhausted."

"I need a minute," Egorov replied wearily. "See to Maria."

Simon approached Maria and gently relieved her of the pistol. With his free hand, he circled her waist and pulled her to him. The family of men closed in on Yurovsky, manhandling him to his feet. Yurovsky put forth no resistance.

"My brave sparrow," he said, stroking her back and kissing the top of her head. "Are you alright?"

When she indicated that she was, he guided her to the bench, encouraging her to sit next to Egorov, and handed him the gun. Then he swung open the forward door, intending to locate a police officer.

His departure was momentarily delayed when the women and children of the family barged into the car, racing toward their menfolk and enquiring after their wellbeing. Assured that they were unscathed, the grandfathers instead directed the women to Egorov and Maria. Before the door closed, Simon saw the worried grandmothers already tending to Maria and dressing Egorov's injuries.

The train was delayed for less than an hour while Yurovsky was taken into custody and officials were sent along the track to recover Lebedev's remains. When the settlement doctor reported that Yurovsky injuries were not life-threatening, Simon reasoned with the officials that he should be permitted to deliver Yurovsky to port authorities in Arkhangelsk.

Happy to be rid of the messy incident, the officials agreed, and undertook to ship Lebedev's remains to his wife in Petrograd.

Egorov's injuries were minor: being the taller and stronger of the two opponents, he sustained a cut above his eye, a bloody nose, skinned knuckles, and a fat lip. The doctor examined him, treated his injuries, and declared him safe to continue to Arkhangelsk.

While Simon and Egorov settled the paperwork, Maria waited on the platform with the family. The family expressed relief to be off the train and hoped that the ensuing nuptials of a cousin's daughter would help erase memories of the altercation they had witnessed on the train. They promised Maria that they would never speak of the attack and wished the young woman a safe journey, but not before coercing her to admit that she was a daughter of the executed tsar.

"Please," she said, grasping the hands of the grandfathers and appealing to their sense of understanding, "I am no longer a grand duchess. I'm merely an orphan without a home. I must leave our beautiful country and start a new life. Although it's no longer safe for me, I sincerely hope that Russia remains a safe and happy place for each of you." She looked over her shoulder to locate the men. "Wait a moment longer, please."

"Simon," she said quietly as she approached his side. "Have we any rubles left?"

"Yes, why?" Simon said. "Do you need something?"

"No," she replied, "but I'd like to give something to those good people. They have been most loyal."

Simon reached into his pocket and pulled out a pouch of Alexandra's money. "This is the last I have of your mother's rubles," he said handing it to her. "I think you'll find around a hundred thousand in it."

"Is that very much?" she said, her naïveté surprising Simon.

"More than they're likely to see in a lifetime, I'm sad to say," Simon replied, turning toward Egorov. "Artyom, do you have the leather pouch from the truck handy?"

"In here," Egorov replied, hoisting one of the travel bags, pointing to a spot inside.

Simon opened the bag and retrieved eight small stones, which he turned into Alexandra's pouch and gave to Maria.

"Thank you," she said, and ran toward the family, who waited patiently on the platform.

She gave the pouch to the father of the children, expressing again her thanks and gratitude for their support, then raced back to the train as the last boarding whistle sounded. She clambered into the car and found an open window, through which she waved vigorously.

The family waved back as the young father opened the pouch. She smiled broadly when she saw his reaction.

"I haven't felt this happy in a long time," she said, sighing deeply as she turned around and wriggled between the men. "You know, suddenly I'm very hungry. Do we have any apples left, Artyom?"

PART FOUR

CHAPTER 58

Several hours later, the train screeched into the Arkhangelsk terminal station. A mass of British and Russian security swarmed the platform.

"British security seems to be questioning folks exiting the first-class cars," Simon said, peering through a window, "likely asking for documents. "Russian security personnel seem to be stopping folks exiting the second-class cars."

Cautiously, Egorov stepped onto the platform, scanning for danger. Spying none, he signalled to Simon and Maria. Yurovsky, hands bound behind him and mouth gagged, allowed Simon to assist him from the car.

As Maria stepped onto the platform, a Russian security officer approached. Seeing the gagged man, he waved an arm for another to help.

"Officer," Simon said, before the man could speak, "we wired ahead asking that we be met by British Military Police. This man and his companion attacked us at the last station, and we want him charged for attempted murder."

Yurovsky attempted to wrench himself from Simon's hold, protesting through the gag.

The officer eyed the small party before turning to his colleague. "Find one of the senior British MPs immediately," he said.

The man turned on his heel and raced along the platform.

"In the meantime," the security officer said, "I'd like to see your papers."

"Of course," Simon said, acknowledging the request. "They're in our bags. Do you mind if we step over to that bench?"

Simon gently pushed Yurovsky toward the bench, pressing firmly on his shoulder for him to sit. Yurovsky did not resist.

Egorov sat a bag on the bench and began to rifle through it. "I found two," he said, "but I can't find my cousin's, and we don't have anything for him." He jerked his head toward Yurovsky. "I can search him, if you like."

"That won't be necessary," a British officer said, halting next to Simon. "Lord Temple?"

"That's me," Simon said. "I sent a telegram—"

"Yes, sir," the officer replied. "We received it. My men will take custody of the prisoner." He stood aside and two officers stepped toward Yurovsky, each taking him by an arm and guiding him into the terminal.

The senior officer thanked the Russian security guards and led Simon and his party into a hut on the far side of the train station. For the next thirty minutes, they provided the officer with an overview of the incident on the train.

"I suspect there's more to the story, sir," the officer said, taking notes as the three companions took turns speaking, "but I have orders to release you immediately to the captain of RMS *Guardian*. His shuttle boat is waiting on the pier." Simon followed his pointing finger and easily identified the ship's insignia.

"The prisoner will be taken into custody and held until we have your full, written reports, following which a judicial inquiry will be carried out." He handed Simon three forms. "Naval post or embassy packet will suffice."

Simon thanked the officer and escorted his friends outside.

"I can take over from here, sir," a Russian seaman said, reaching for Simon's bags.

Simon looked up, scanning his memory as he tried to place the familiar face. "Do I know you?" he said, puzzled.

"Yes, sir," the seaman said, grinning, "you do. You and another tall, lanky fellow saved me from Okhrana thugs in a dark alley."

"Of course!" Simon said, recalling the incident.

"Allow me to carry your bags, sir," the seaman said, glancing at Simon's companions. "You two look familiar too, but I'm afraid I can't place you just now. Him"—he thumbed over his shoulder at Simon—"well, he saved my life. I'm more likely to remember someone who does that."

His grin widened into a somewhat toothy smile as he hefted Simon's bags and started across the docks. "Follow me," he said, cheerily. "I'll get you through this mob quickly. Where are you headed?"

"Actually," Simon said, taking Maria's bag, "that insignia over there."

"RMS *Guardian*?" the seaman said. In response

to Simon's nod, he squared his shoulders and marched straight into the crowd. "Make way!"

Seeing a familiar face loitering beneath the *Guardian's* ensign, Simon raised an arm in acknowledgement and smiled broadly when it was returned. "Thank you very much for the escort, Petty Officer," Simon said.

"My pleasure, sir," the sailor replied. "I reckon we're even now." A moment later, he disappeared into the chaos.

Simon noted the gold stripes on the cuffs of his friend's sleeves. "Lieutenant Commander Jordy Montrose," Simon said, happy to see his friend. "You must have stories to tell."

When Montrose returned his salute, Simon introduced everyone using first names only.

"Many stories, indeed," Montrose said, raising an eyebrow questioningly. "This way. Captain's waiting." Montrose waved his hand toward a small naval vessel.

"Ah! Lieutenant Temple," Captain Hartford said from his position near the bow of the boat. "I'm pleased to see you again, son. Welcome back. Better late than never, I suppose."

"Captain!" Simon replied, saluting. He stepped easily aboard, turning to offer his hand to Maria, while Montrose gave orders to return to RMS *Guardian.*

A few minutes later, the small vessel hovered alongside the armed merchant cruise ship while the shore party scurried aboard.

"My quarters, second dog watch, all three of you," Hartford said, eyeing Simon with a raised brow. "You'll have to excuse me now. We sail in thirty minutes."

"Yes, sir," Simon and Montrose replied, respectfully stiffening as the captain departed.

"You've been assigned to the cabins that you and Henry Crocker had on the way up, plus one." Montrose said matter-of-factly, relieving Maria of her bag as he led them toward a ladder. "I met him on his return, by the way. Nice chap." He turned slightly, his lips quirked. "We didn't see too much of him and his wife once they boarded, though."

"Hey!" Egorov said, chuckling. "That's my sister and brother-in-law you're joking about."

"Here we are," Montrose said, grinning unabashedly at Egorov as he opened a cabin door and invited Maria to precede him. "I'm expected on the bridge in a few minutes, so I'll leave you. Maybe we can catch up in the next few days, Simon?

"I'd like that," Simon replied, saluting Montrose.

"Lieutenant?" Egorov said when the three were alone and checking out the accommodation in each cabin. "You never told me you were navy."

"We always had more important things in mind," Simon replied. "It wouldn't have impacted our objectives."

"True enough," Egorov replied, swinging open the door to his cabin.

"They're all similar," Simon said. "Maria, do you have a preference?"

"Perhaps this one in the middle," she said, hobbling toward the entrance of the centre cabin, "then I'll have a hero on either side." She smiled fondly at the men, grabbing a hand from each and squeezing them affectionately.

"Done," Simon said, tugging his pocket watch from his vest. "We're to dine with the captain at six o'clock. We have thirty-five minutes to freshen up. I'll knock on your doors at ten minutes to."

He waited in the corridor while Maria entered her cabin. "By the way, Maria," Simon said, his eye catching something notable, "that door there"—he pointed, drawing her eye—"is an adjoining door. I'll unlock my side. If you feel threatened at any time, you need only open it."

Maria blushed, thanked him, and closed the door behind her.

⸻

At ten minutes before six, Simon rapped lightly on the doors, both of which opened promptly.

"I feel terrible that the only clothing I have are the ones Artyom purchased in Perm," Maria said. "I should think evening dress would be in order when dining with the captain."

"Right you are," Simon replied, leading the way, "but Captain Hartford won't mind, considering we're basically fugitives."

"I managed to wipe mine down," Egorov said, eyeing his polished boots, "but not enough in my opinion. You're certain he won't mind?"

"Yes," Simon replied. "He may be firm with his crew, but he is also fair-minded. I served under him for a year before heading to Russia. I also have his absolute confidence. He's a friend of my father; you may speak freely."

He stopped at the captain's outer door and rapped lightly.

"Enter!" Hartford said loud enough to be heard.

"Ah, Lieutenant Temple," Hartford said as Simon swung the door open. "Do come in!"

Simon entered, nodding respect to the captain as his friends followed.

"I didn't expect you'd have full mess kit with you, so I haven't changed," the captain said.

"Thank you, sir," Egorov said. "We were limited to what we could carry. Food seemed more important."

"I've arranged for a change of clothing to be delivered to your cabins during the next watch," Hartford said. "A drink perhaps?" He turned toward the liquor trolley.

"Uh, sir," Simon said. "Earlier, I thought it best to limit introductions."

The captain turned to face his guests.

"May I introduce Captain Artyom Egorov, recently of the tsar's Imperial Guard, and Grand Duchess Maria Nikolaevea, third daughter of the former tsar of Russia."

Captain Hartford responded to Egorov's salute and bowed from the waist when introduced to Maria.

"Please, Captain," Maria said. "I am no longer a grand duchess. Simply an orphan whose surname happens to be Romanov."

"I'm sorry for your loss," Hartford said with compassion. "Let's have a toast to welcome you aboard RMS *Guardian*, and another in honour of your family." He returned his attention to the trolley. "Scotch, brandy?" Hartford said, scanning his collection of bottles. "Perhaps a good Russian vodka, Captain?"

"Vodka, please," Egorov and Maria said as one, then chuckled.

"Scotch for me," Simon said. "It's hard to find a good scotch in Petrograd, unless one is familiar with the British Ambassador."

"Dinner will be along in a minute or two," Hartford said, handing glasses of preferred beverages to his guests. "For the next two hours, my ears are yours."

Simon began the tale of their travels from Tsarskoye Selo to Yekaterinburg. Maria and Egorov interjected to clarify or elaborate. Simon felt an easing of the tension between his shoulder blades, appreciating how therapeutic it was to finally speak of their experiences. They glossed over the night of the execution, allowing Maria time to tell the story. When she did not, Egorov picked up the thread of their escape.

But for a brief interruption when their meal was delivered, the conversation flowed. When the under cook departed, Hartford excused himself and followed, bidding the under cook wait. When he returned a moment later, he continued with a question he had been asking before their meal arrived, one of many that were to follow.

As Simon had observed during previous meals with the captain, he recognized a certain stiffness in the man and listened. "Watch change," he said. "I presume you're on the bridge, sir?"

"I am," he said. "My last watch for two days. I've enjoyed our conversation, and hope we'll have time for another meal together before we reach Newcastle. In the meantime, you must excuse me."

The three guests said their goodbyes and returned to their cabins.

"If you two aren't terribly tired," Simon said, "would you like to join me in my cabin? I think we have some plans to make."

"Could I have a few minutes?" Maria said. "I'd prefer to wait until the clothing arrives and change into something less itchy."

"Certainly," Simon replied. "Artyom?"

"Good idea, Maria," Egorov replied. "I'll come along as soon as I've changed."

CHAPTER 59

A few minutes later, Egorov knocked on the door and let himself into Simon's cabin.

"Montrose left a bottle of vodka on ice and a note for us to enjoy," Simon said, pouring out two glasses and handing one to his friend.

"Then, here's to Jordy Montrose," Egorov said, raising his glass in toast before sitting in one of the armchairs. "I think I'm going to like this Jordy Montrose." He grinned and sampled the vodka appreciatively.

"I'm glad to hear it," Simon said. "He's a good man." He lifted his own glass in salute. "I've been meaning to ask you, and my curiosity has just got the better of me: what's the story behind the scar under your left eye?"

"Ah!" Egorov said, his hand creeping toward his eye and tapping the small spot. "A souvenir from a skirmish years ago."

"And a tell-tale of your deepest anger," Simon said, quirking his brows.

"I'll have to address that," Egorov said, looking mortified. "But enough of my scar. He rested his elbows on his knees and hung the glass from his fingertips. His words were hushed. "Before Maria comes, I want to ask you a question."

"About what?" Simon said, sitting in a second armchair.

"Maria, of course," Egorov said. "She's a woman with no home, no family, no land. Have you given any thought to proposing?"

"Wha—" Simon replied, choking on the word.

"Look. You love her," Egorov said. "Besides, you must've noticed how she lights up whenever she's near you. I've seen my sister in love—twice—and I'd say that Maria is no different."

Simon nodded, thrusting fingers through his auburn curls. "I've sensed an interest, but because of my position within the family, and my mission, I dared not act on it."

"Perhaps it's time?" Egorov said, raising an eyebrow of encouragement. "Your love has given Maria the strength to reach this point. It's helped heal her wounds. She is a remarkable young woman. Others wouldn't have survived what she's been through. She is courageous, determined, beautiful, and kind. If you propose, I guarantee … she won't deny you."

"But … protocol!" Simon said, protesting.

"Protocol be damned! She's an orphan!" Egorov jumped to his feet. "Who is to stand in her way? Family? Even if her relatives were here, who would have the authority to deny the Russian tsarina?"

"When you put it that way … I suppose you're right," Simon replied, stunned by the course of the conversation. "What am I to do about it?" He snatched the bottle of vodka and refilled their glasses.

"Ask her!"

"To marry me?"

"Yes!"

———————

Simon knocked lightly on the door of Maria's cabin. As he did so, he cast a furtive glance at Egorov, hoping to dismiss his friend.

"No way," Egorov said. "She'll need a witness. So you can't change your mind."

Maria cracked open the adjoining door. Seeing Simon and Egorov, she opened it wider.

"I was just going to knock on your door," she said, giggling. "What do you think of my sailor suit?" She twirled, her unbound hair flowing behind her. "Will you come in, or should I come there?"

Simon stood back and allowed Maria entry, complimenting her attire while delivering a piercing glare to Egorov behind her back.

Maria turned and gazed from one man to the other, a small grin playing on her lips. "What are you two up to now?" she said.

"We're not," Simon replied, running a finger around the inside of his shirt collar, as if to loosen it. "I mean ..." He cast his eyes to Egorov.

Egorov's brow rose with encouragement.

"Please have a seat," Simon said. "Vodka?" In response to Maria's nod, he poured a glass for her, and topped up

Egorov's glass and his own.

"Well, you see," Simon said, trying to find the necessary words. He swigged the shot of vodka and set the glass on a dresser. "Artyom and I ..." He swallowed hard, praying for divine intervention.

Egorov smirked and waited as quiet settled in the cabin. When Simon failed to speak further, Egorov stood up impatiently. "For God's sake!" he said, tugging Maria to her feet and placing her slender hand in Simon's. "He's trying to propose!"

Maria glared at Egorov, snatching her hand from Simon. "Are you serious?" she said, sounding annoyed. She turned her large, blue eyes toward Simon, a small frown between her brows. When Simon failed to speak, she glanced at Egorov.

Egorov shrugged a deferral to Simon.

"He is," Simon said his words croaky. "Er ... I am." He snatched her hands, drawing her to face him. "My responsibilities in Russia and court protocol dictate that I have no right to ask ..."

Maria plopped into a vacant chair and folded her hands neatly in her lap. She bowed her head as if in prayer and sighed. Several heartbeats passed before she spoke.

"I was raised to believe that my parents would arrange my marriage," she said, her voice low, as if she confided in her folded hands. "I never dared to think that I would marry otherwise."

She raised her face to Egorov, who now occupied the other chair, then glanced at Simon and began to laugh.

Her laughter was so hysterical that she grabbed her middle and leaned forward, tears trickling down her face. "Oh, goodness," she said, hiccupping as she brushed the tears aside.

"Dear Artyom," she said, leaning toward him. She clutched his hand and smiled warmly. "Dear Artyom, my ever-devoted and loyal guard, I believe that you have just assumed the role of surrogate parent."

She giggled, releasing his hand, and turned to Simon. "Simon, can this be true?" she said. "Do you truly want to marry me? A poor, country-less grand duchess with no name and no status?"

As if waking from a dream, Simon reached for Maria's hands, raising her knuckles to his lips. His eyes found hers, pools of tears collecting on her lower lids. Her lips parted slightly, expectant, hopeful.

"Yes," he said, dropping to his knees. "Yes, Maria. I'm asking you to marry me."

Maria glanced at Artyom, whose eyes shone with amusement.

"You may not believe this," she said gazing at the man kneeling before her, her voice sober, "but I have prayed for this moment for a very long time. I dared not hope. I expected my parents to marry me off to another country." Her eyes filled with sadness, and a moment passed before she straightened and spoke again.

"But my parents are not here to tell me what to do, and I have no kingdom to command." She rose from her chair, standing tall, squaring her shoulders. "I must therefore decide for myself … and I decide 'yes'!"

She swiped tears from her eyes and reached for his freed hand. "Yes, Simon! I will marry you." She turned her gaze to Egorov. "With Artyom's blessing, I presume?"

"Of course!" Egorov said, returning to his feet and reaching for the vodka bottle. "A toast."

Simon grinned in disbelief, then took a step backward as Maria flung her arms around his neck with impetus.

"Kiss her, fool," Egorov said, laughing, "before she changes her mind!"

Early the next morning, Simon met with the captain to inform him of the engagement.

"Given Maria's tenuous citizenship," Simon said, "I think the sooner we're married, the better. I don't suppose a chaplain is aboard?"

"I'm afraid not, son," Hartford said, "but don't let that stop you. I have the authority to marry you!" He retrieved a notebook from his pocket and scanned through pages of script. "As I mentioned earlier, I have the next two days off. How about tomorrow evening? My cabin."

"Thank you, sir," Simon said, snapping a salute of gratitude.

While one of the other officers loaned Simon a lieutenant's mess kit—and a captain's mess kit was found for Egorov—finding something appropriate on a warship

for a woman, let alone a bride, to wear was a challenge …
until Captain Hartford recalled several bolts of a cream-
coloured silk that he had purchased as a gift for his wife.

"Mrs. Hartford won't mind," the captain said.
"Although she'll receive several gifts when I return home,
I'm certain the most outstanding gift will be the story of
the gift that dressed a princess."

Simon and Egorov tried on the uniforms the next
morning, pleased with the fit.

"I can't wait to see you put a ring on that slender
finger," Egorov said as he adjusted his tie.

"Ring!" Simon said, mortified. "I don't have a ring!"

"Maybe we do," Egorov said, his voice calm. "Let's
check the jewel bags."

They each took a bag and began sorting through them.

"Look!" Egorov said, holding up a pair of matching
pearl earrings. "I forgot that some of the jewels were still
in their settings."

They continued rummaging.

"I found a string of pearls," Simon said, pleased to
think Maria would have something pretty to wear. "Now,
all I need is a ring …"

Suddenly, his finger snagged on a loop, and he drew
it out. It was a simple gold band, inset with a pearl and
two diamonds. He held it up for Egorov to see.

"That will do nicely," Egorov said. "I'll take the
earrings and necklace to Maria as soon as I hang up this
uniform."

Just as Simon disappeared into his own cabin, a crewman knocked on Egorov's door and handed him a box. "From the captain," he said, and turned on his heel.

CHAPTER 60

That evening, *Guardian* ambled slowly along the Norwegian coastline as an orange sunset sizzled on the horizon. Jordy Montrose and the captain waited with Simon in Hartford's quarters.

"Drink, gentlemen?" Hartford said, hoisting a decanter. In response to their urging, he poured each a glass of whiskey. They congratulated Simon and toasted his pending marriage as they awaited Maria and Egorov.

"We haven't had a wedding at sea since before the war," Hartford said, reminiscing. "Neither of you have had that experience. You haven't been at sea long enough, and it's certainly not a common experience on a warship."

Montrose opened the outside door in response to a light rap. The setting sun lit two silhouettes from behind: one man, one woman. Egorov waited while Maria preceded him through the doorway and smiled proudly at the collective gasp from within.

Simon stood next to the captain, awed by Maria's beauty and his love for her, realizing for the first time that he no longer had to restrain his emotions.

"Shall we begin?" Hartford said, setting his empty glass on a table. He took up his Book of Common Prayer and opened it to a marked page.

Egorov led Maria to stand at Simon's side, then stepped behind to stand with Montrose.

"I've never seen you look more beautiful," Simon said quietly in her ear, "and that's saying a lot, considering I've never seen you any other way."

Maria gazed at him with bright blue eyes, her smile dazzling him. The lustrous gown, sewn in haste by a ship's crewman who called tailoring his former profession, draped simply from her shoulders, caressing each curve as it fell to the floor. It concealed a pair of worn, button-topped boots, saved by Simon when they had departed the hut in Yekaterinburg. Unadorned but for the pearls at ears and neck, hair falling freely down her back, she radiated with joy.

"Does it trouble you that I will be leading a simple Unitarian service?" Hartford said, cutting into Maria's musings.

"No, Captain," she replied, peeling her eyes from Simon's, her cheeks reddening. "So long as the service binds me to this man in marriage, I have no concerns at all."

"Then, shall we begin?" Hartford said.

"There is one matter that must be acknowledged before we're wed, Captain," Maria said, dropping her hand from Simon's arm to find security in his hand. She squeezed it for courage, then released it.

Moving away from Simon, she solemnly addressed the men. "From this moment forward, I will no longer be known as Grand Duchess Maria Nikolaevna, daughter of the tsar of Russia," she said with certainty. "I wish to be known as Mary Romanov, soon to be known as Mary Nightingale-Temple, loving wife of Lord Simon Nightingale-Temple." Her eyes momentarily held Simon's. "This is my first and last royal decree as empress of Russia! Does anyone dispute my words?" Although her expression appeared serious, her eyes twinkled.

"Not I," the men replied in unison.

"Then let us begin!" she said, eagerly returning to Simon's side.

As the witnesses looked on, Hartford guided Maria and Simon through an exchange of vows. A short time later, Mary Nightingale-Temple snuggled into the embrace of her new husband and received her first kiss as his wife.

From a nearby table, the captain removed a serving dome to reveal champagne glasses. With a flourish, he opened a cupboard and extracted a bucket of ice that had been chilling a bottle of French champagne. He popped the cork, filled the glasses, and handed one to each of his guests. "To the bride and groom," he said, raising his glass.

"Hear, hear!" the others said in unison.

"I'm afraid I can't provide a meal fit for an earl and his wife," Captain Hartford said in confidence, "but I've asked the chef to do his best. In the meantime, let's enjoy the bubbly!"

Unknown to Simon and Mary, the captain had arranged for the installation of a second bed in Simon's cabin. The newlyweds were pleased to discover a double bed—created by tying the legs of the two single beds together—when they returned to Simon's room.

"Remind me to thank the captain tomorrow," Simon said, drawing his bride into his arms and placing a lingering kiss on her expectant lips.

Alone in Simon's cabin several hours later, the groom drew his wife into his arms and kissed her well until she pushed him away gently.

"You're taking my breath away," she said, smiling sweetly. "I need a minute to recover."

"While you do that," he said, his voice husky, "perhaps this will pass the time." He reached into a night table drawer and withdrew a small leather pouch. "I thought I'd left this for Zima to take to England and was surprised to find it this morning when I was flipping through papers."

"What is it?" Mary said accepting the feather-light pouch.

"Open it," Simon said, his eyes full of adoration.

Mary gently teased the drawstring open and removed a crumpled piece of blue tissue, feeling a slight weight within it. She handed the empty pouch to Simon and spread the crinkled tissue to reveal a miniature crown, encrusted with tiny diamonds, seed pearls, and a red spinel.

"Mother's crown!" she said sounding reverent. "Where did you get it?"

"Not long after I began teaching you and your sisters, your mother gave me the Rosebud Egg. She asked me to sell it, and to use the money to keep you and your siblings safe in the event anything happened to your parents. She anticipated harm would come to them, but she was certain that her children would be safe. She gave me several other items of value too. I sold some of the smaller things that were easy to move discreetly, including the egg's ruby necklace, but I couldn't bring myself to part with this."

His finger nudged the miniature crown in her palm, setting it upright. Light set fire to the diamonds. "You've left so much behind, and I know that you'll always have pain and longing when you think of the past," he said. "My family will do everything possible to ensure that you always feel welcome and loved. Sometimes, that might not be enough. Hopefully, the crown will remind you of your family, your history, and your right to the throne."

His fingers closed around hers, wrapping the tiny crown within her hand.

Mary threw her arms around Simon's neck and held him fast. Simon snaked his arms around her, holding her tightly.

Sighing, she pushed away from him, creating a gap within which she opened her hand. "This small thing is so important to me," she said, her voice breathy. "It means more than a right to a throne; it's a symbol of my mother's love. The Rosebud Egg was her most prized possession. Father gave it to her as a symbol of his love and devotion. This is my keepsake of her love and devotion to her children."

She released a long sigh, as if she had forgotten to breathe. "Thank you, Simon."

Simon drew her to him, encircling her trembling body with his steady calm as the ship swayed gently. In her ear, he whispered a promise of his eternal love and devotion.

NOTE TO READER

Thank you for reading *Tsarina's Crown*, the first book in *The Nightingale and The Sparrow Chronicles*. I hope you enjoyed the adventure. Coming soon: *Tsarina's Jewels* and *Tsarina's Secrets*.

Other readers find reviews helpful for locating books they prefer to read. All reviews are appreciated.

Don't forget to visit my website: jerenatobiasen.ca, to read about my other works and inspirations, and join my Readers Club.

ABOUT THE AUTHOR

Jerena Tobiasen—award-winning author of *The Prophecy*, a 3-volume, historical fiction saga including *The Crest*, *The Emerald*, and *The Destiny*—lives in Vancouver, Canada. If she's not home, she's likely travelling.

Jerena embellishes her writing by travelling to foreign lands, visiting museums and libraries, conducting interviews, and travelling in the footsteps of her characters. Her experiences and discoveries enrich the authenticity of the historical fiction she crafts.

In 2019, Jerena travelled extensively throughout southern Europe, northern Africa and the Arctic collecting data for her new series, which she wrote during the Covid 'shut-down'. In June 2022 she and her assistant travelled throughout England to complete some last-minute research.

Jerena also writes short stories and poetry. Several of her short stories, travel commentaries and an assortment of other writings can be found on her website *jerenatobiasen.ca*, where you'll also find an invitation to join her newsletter.